SPARKS

A POST-APOCALYPTIC
FAIRY TALE

J. R. DEVOE

Dark Tide Publishing

First Edition: November 2024

Cover by MiblArt

ISBN 978-1-0690223-2-5 (paperback)
ISBN 978-1-7771231-9-2 (eBook)

www.jrdevoe.com

For my Mother,
My Gateway to the World

CHAPTER 1

NYA

This is going to sound crazy, and maybe it's my destructive nature corrupting my moral sense, but watching two armies march to annihilate each other is an inspiring sight. If only my dear Deka could live up to the moment.

It takes him an embarrassingly long time to mount his horse for the first time. It's even worse learning to ride her. Over the manicured grass before Lex's fortress walls, he makes a real spectacle of himself, hanging sideways and falling off at least a dozen times.

Eventually he asks for another saddle. Not another horse. Just a different saddle. For some reason I may never understand, it actually works. On that curved leather seat he sits straight and noble, almost lord-like. His swift mastery earns him applause from Lex's warriors as he trots to take his place behind her at the descending trailhead.

I'm less convinced of his sudden skill. So, with a hundreds' foot plummet waiting to our right, I sit behind him on the saddle to catch him should he fall.

The trail down from Lex's fort is long and narrow, and quiet too. No one in the dual column of marching soldiers whispers a word. Even the horses bearing their commanders seem loath to cause a stir.

The measured pounding of six thousand feet from Lex's three thousand house guards—hand-picked warriors bearing her elite star shields—stomp in perfect rhythm behind us. At the head of each unit of one hundred troops, which I've heard Lex call a *Century*, rides the Century's commander on horseback. These Centurions hail from the elite exiled houses who'd lost their status during the crown's rise in Polaria, and they are eager to reclaim their family's honor.

Lex leads them all from high upon a white stallion, crossed katanas over her back and a lengthened spear in one hand, from which a purple banner streams overhead.

I'd be lying if I said Deka's uniform doesn't make him look bad in a good sort of way. The all-black material, with its rigid vest and violet long coat, makes him look like a force to be reckoned with. Our horse I know for sure is such a force. 'Svenia' is her name, and she's got a bad attitude.

Lex glances over her shoulder at Deka. "I'm impressed. I thought you'd have fallen off by now."

A rearward glance reveals we are halfway down the track carved precariously into the cliff face.

Deka strokes the strip of our mare's pale gray mane. "Svenia is smart. She knows I'll drag her down to whatever fate awaits me."

"Svenia?" Lex says, turning more in her saddle to show us her puzzled look. "That's a curious name. Where'd you come up with it?"

I sit up straighter at this too. How did he come to learn her name? I know it because my folk converse naturally with all sentient lifeforms. But I'd not told Deka her name, I'm sure of it. Or maybe I did. Exposure to the nuclear bomb Lex calls 'Little Boy' has left me with some nasty side effects, delirium chief among them.

Deka fails to produce an explanation. He doesn't mention me as the source of his information, and Lex quickly loses interest and returns her attention forward.

Her warriors know the trail well. Lex had bragged of their training as we watched them form up before her fortress. Every summer day saw them march way down to the river, where they'd row boats against the current for two hours before jogging back up. In the winter this happens every three days, so that by now they know each rut and stone, every twist and turn. No doubt some could do it blindfolded. This would be just a leisure stroll if not for our current destination.

The trail dips between mountain peaks and levels into a valley floor. To our right, high up on a hill across the river, the heads of wooden dragons oversee our arrival into their domain. They belong to the giant long boats her warriors had trained with on the river, the same I'd noticed on my first flight in. As if the grueling regime wasn't hard enough, they'd also been forced to carry their boats up that high steep hill, and then swim back across the river.

Lex stops to the side of the trail bottom to watch her house guard march past. Added to the rhythmic stomping is now the squeaking wheels of five dozen supply wagons rolling behind.

"Well done," she says to Deka. "The others were betting how long you'd last before she dumped you over."

I join Deka in looking back up the trail and the sheer rock face below it. Nearly three thousand warriors slink down behind us, among them a few too many disappointed faces.

Lex hands him the lengthened spear with its long purple banner. "Feeling confident enough to ride with one hand?"

He fumbles the banner pole, resting it over Svenia's neck so its long narrow fabric almost brushes the ground. Lex gasps and hisses, reminding me of her attendant's warning. *Allowing a family banner to touch the ground is a supreme disrespect.*

I grab the pole from behind and guide it into the holder protruding from Deka's right stirrup. This does the trick, satisfying Lex, who thankfully shifts her attention away from us.

The beaten trail forks just ahead. Right veers toward the river in the direction Deka and I had taken from the sea; left curves into a valley that slopes down toward Polaria like a giant half-pipe, where there now flows a great stream of bobbing fireballs.

I rub my eyes to make certain they're not deceiving me, because those distant torches illuminate the grandest assembly of humans I've ever seen.

"A good many Ortarians have answered my call to arms," boasts Lex. "When word of our march spreads, the rest will rush to join us as well. Too much glory awaits beyond our horizon. No Ortarian would dare miss this chapter in our history."

My head spins and my belly roils with nausea. I hug Deka from behind and rest my head on his shoulder.

"This is good," he assures me. "More warriors to fight the Watchers."

"It's not that. I'm just sick is all."

He probably thinks I'm lying, that I'm feigning weakness or something. Less than an hour ago I was hauling a ten thousand pound bomb across soggy ground. And now...

"What happened to that wild boost Little Boy gave you?" he asks.

"It was dirty energy. Like when you celebrate by drinking fermented berries, but then you—"

"Pay for it the next day," he says.

My belly grumbles. Deka hunches his shoulders in anticipation of what may come up.

A lone rider gallops from the flowing army toward us. Where Lex's house guard uniforms present them as fierce and able, hers screams magnificence. A thick band of red and black eye paint matches her long hair, starkly contrasting her olive skin, and her slick black attire clings to her torso so tight it gives her body an unnatural and yet flattering shape. A curved sword rattles from her left hip while a round shield bounces off her horse's right hind. And instead of the silver octagram that adorns Lex's house guard shields, hers displays a cartoonish red demon face with its tongue stuck out to the side as if chewing it. If another face bore such an expression it would appear silly, but this beast is fierce with insanity.

"Raven," Deka says over his shoulder. He proceeds to tell me how she dazzled everyone with a display of blind swordsmanship during Lex's recruitment trials, which he called the Blood Ballet, subduing her opponent without a fight and earning Lex's private company.

Lex's force continues to stream through the trail base,

congealing at the forked junction, where they form into neat blocks of fighting units.

We follow Lex to meet the rider, slightly back and to her right, her purple pennant streaming overhead from the pole in Deka's hand. Lex stops and allows Raven to close the remaining distance. Deka edges Svenia up alongside while I ensure the Arcturus standard is flying freely in the breeze above.

Raven slows to a trot, but her beast is restless and circles us instead of stopping. The way she looks at Lex is the same way Deka looks at me right before he kisses me, the hard facade of a stoic shattered by the threat of never seeing their beloved again.

"Twenty and a half thousand now march down the valley," declares Raven, "but word is still spreading to the outer reaches. You can bet we'll double our numbers before we reach the border, with plenty of reinforcements coming down behind them."

"Good," Lex says. "Pursue your course and we'll follow the river."

Raven nods in understanding. She gives me and Deka a wary look, then inches her horse close to Lex for a private discussion. Curiosity begs me forward to listen, but Deka turns his head to speak to me under his breath. "You have to escape the first chance you get."

"I can't. I won't leave you."

"You can and you will." Sizing up the endless flow of warriors moving down the valley, he says, "We don't need your kind in this fight. We're strong enough on our own."

His cold words plunge like an icy dagger into my heart. "But Lex will hurt you if I leave."

"Not if she thinks you were killed or captured. I'm serious, Nya, our journey together ends here. The sooner you accept that, the better off we'll both be."

I squeeze him tight. He squirms in my hold, which gets my heart drumming a song of despair up his spine.

Raven accompanies Lex back to her lines, where she uses a flowered branch to flick blood onto the ranks of Lex's warriors. Those who receive droplets on their face smile with relief.

My belly groans in disgust. "Who is she, anyway?" I ask.

"Warlord Supreme of all Ortaria," says a man's voice from behind us. His name is Argyle, commander of the First Century. His pock-marked face bears many scars, and his head of gray hair could as easily be more from stress than age, given the life I imagine he's lived. "She is the reason for Lord Arcturus's influence here. When the lord first built her fortress on the mountain, she had arms and uniforms enough for three hundred guards. But thanks to Raven, word of her exploits have spread far and wide. Ortarians come from all over with hopes of serving her.

"Now, that fortress bears a new name among the wild folk—*Valhalla*. There, you die the animal you were, and are reborn the immortal warrior you were destined to be. Here you see them as just faces standing in neat ranks, indistinguishable from each other. But in their home villages, they are legends honored among the gods."

Raven finishes her grotesque ceremony, then wheels her horse around and gallops back toward the flood of bobbing torches.

"Forward march!" shouts Lex as she trots down the rightward path.

Despite the trail being narrow beside the river, she insists that I ride at her side, our legs almost touching.

"You're attacking the border to distract for Little Boy's crossing," Deka says.

Lex smirks, keeping her gaze ahead.

I look to the sky, but clouds prevent me from seeing the balloon. We see well enough to navigate the riverside, so I assume Raven's use of torches is to distract from our mission here.

Lex looks over her shoulder to speak to me. "There's a narrow pass that chokes the river ahead. Go check it out. If it's clear, then sweep the nearby mountains for outposts."

I give Deka a hard squeeze. He pries my hands from around him to break my embrace.

Tears burn my eyes, and it takes everything in me to keep them from spilling over. So that's it. He really does want me gone.

"Remember what I told you," he says. "Watch for ambushes."

It takes all my strength to resist giving Deka a kiss goodbye. Instead, I throw back my robe and rise into flight. A southern gale quickly claims me and hurls me along, far from this place and all its miseries.

My heart grows heavier with each beat and drags me down. Where will I go? What will I do? Who can I turn to if not Deka?

The answer comes swift and clear—*Regulus*.

He'll take me in. He knows my worth. Although I've known him only briefly, I know he'd never be so cold to me. He is a master of his world and need not bend to the will of others. People swear oaths to fulfill his desires, not the other way around. A man such as him need not appease anyone.

Tears blur my vision and burn down my cheeks.

Screw you, Deka! Screw you and your sapless heart!

CHAPTER 2

DEKA

When Nya peels from my back, I immediately miss her warmth. She doesn't say a word, just flies on ahead over the narrow river. When she disappears through the green wisps of aurora seeping down from the clouds, part of me knows she really won't come back. The fight is out of her. In my mind's eye I see Lex's war journey shine with the golden light of victory. Nya's path here leads only to darkness. But still...

My heart beats with sorrow. This rhythm is opposite to when she'd hugged me from behind, when her hands over my chest made my heart flutter. How such a powerful being could be so gentle and delicate must be a miracle of nature. Already she haunts me, the phantom beat of her heart against my back sending a broken tune reverberating up my spine to fill my head with her woes.

I swallow the lump in my throat and sit up straight on my horse. It has to be this way. She's worn out her welcome with Lex, and once her purpose is served, the Wolf will see her for the threat she is.

"Why not travel by river?" I say, remembering the beautiful longboats near her fortress. There must be enough there to carry her entire house guard.

"In an ideal world we would. Unfortunately, Polarians have some nasty surprises waiting downstream for just such an incursion. Not to mention all the shallow spots and shortage of safe places to land. We'd lose too many to the rocks and riverbank."

This is a great shame. I'd much prefer an adventure by water than upon horseback, no offense to Svenia.

We carry on for a long while, so long my inner thighs burn and chafe, until we come upon a bottleneck. When Lex gives the order to halt, I'm quick to dismount and stretch my legs. I know she may scorn me for it, but at this point I'd sooner ask for forgiveness than for permission.

She watches where the rock faces of two mountains loom over the river like two sides of a gateway. The matching height of these opposing walls suggests they were once connected, but something catastrophic had cut the slope in two. Steep rocky mountains stretch far to our left and right, making a bypass too grand a task for this army and its horses. A narrow path between the leftward rock face and river is the only passing point. It's also the perfect place for a trap.

The horses whinny and shuffle restlessly. Svenia bounces on her forward hooves, so I stroke her neck to calm her.

"You think she bailed on us?" asks Lex.

"No," I say, but I pray I am wrong. I hope Nya is well away from this place. "Something must have happened to her. We should go check it out."

"Why? So she can ambush us? For all I know she has

Polarian Rangers waiting up ahead. Maybe she hopes you'll slip away when their guns start tearing us apart."

"She'd never do that. She's too good-hearted."

Lex's face twists in revolt. "You have no idea what's in someone's heart. Do not overestimate the power of love, young Deka. It will only disappoint you."

Someone must have stomped out Lex's tenderness pretty hard at some point in her past. I'm guessing that someone is the man she called 'Toris' on the radio, the man who many others call the Lord of the Sea.

Despite her suspicions, Lex is too impatient to wait. She orders six mounted scouts to ride ahead. They're to string out so that the first stops within view of us. The next will stop in view of the first stopped rider, and so on so there's a relayed line of sight back to Lex.

We watch in silence as the scouts follow the narrow path along the riverbank. One stops before the choke of sheer rock wall, while his five companions carry on down through. He orders his horse into the shallow water to keep himself visible to his companions riding ahead.

Lex squeezes her reigns and watches me through the corner of her eye.

Will she really punish me for Nya's desertion? I suppose I'll have my answer soon enough.

My grip on my cracked leather reins tightens. A skilled rider rode this saddle before me, right up to his death. And it was not his horsemanship that killed him. This I know for certain, for my gift of touch extends beyond weapons-handling and combat, and grows stronger each time I use it.

The nearest scout stands high on his stirrups and peers

through a spyglass downriver. He swiftly spots something that sends him reaching back for his crossbow.

A shadowy figure zooms overhead and dives straight for us. This arrival spooks every horse around. They whine and reel, and the Centurions on the slope struggle to steady them.

My heart sinks when I see Nya's brown hair waving between her outstretched wings.

She lands before Lex and falls to her knees, breathless, obviously unsettled by something. When she lifts her head, though, she does so with a smile.

Lex looks down her nose at Nya. "Where were you?"

Nya stands and wobbles on her feet, then points back through the river choke and says, "The border—it's deserted!"

Lex's nostrils flare. "You take me for a fool?"

"It's true! There's a bunch of soldiers squeezing into a steel snake, and another snake just left with a whole bunch more. They're all going to Mount Tuck!"

I know Nya well enough to see her excitement is sincere. Crazy as Regulus abandoning the border sounds, I know Nya either believes that's what she saw, or it's actually true. And I suspect the 'steel snakes' she speaks of are passenger trains.

Lex spins her horse around and summons her Centurions. Their horse heads lean in close for their riders to have a huddled discussion. The talk is quick and agreeable, and ends with the dispersal of pathfinders to scout for traps.

"It will take our scouts some time to survey the border," Lex says. "We'll make camp here."

"I'll provide air cover," Nya says, then she springs into flight.

A whip snaps up to catch her by the ankle. Lex hauls on the

other end with her right hand while her left uncoils a second whip from her saddle, which she flings at a surprised Nya. The leather lash wraps her torso like a snake, binding her arms to her sides and her wings to her back, dropping her to the ground.

It all happens so fast. Before I know it, two warriors are clapping a steel collar around her neck. Karl and Karla, I've heard them called, twins from Ortaria's farthest reaches. Karl wears his brown hair in a long braid that touches his waistline, his temples shaved to the skin to display swirling blue tattoos. His sister boasts similar markings on her left side, but her straight hair hangs halfway down her neck on the right, concealing whatever art lies beneath.

I whack Karl aside with Lex's standard pole and then press the tip to Karla's throat. Steel sings from a blade leaving its scabbard, then the sharp cold edge of Centurion Argyle's sword presses against my throat. A trickle of warm blood slides down to my collarbone.

Lex pushes the blade aside and throws an arm around my neck to usher me away. "It's just a precaution," she says, "until we can verify her claim. If what Nya says is true, then she'll be released at once."

All I can do is watch as they clip a chain leash to Nya's collar and haul her away. She gives me a troubled look, but I try not to fret. She's been through worse. And I suddenly see how perfect this is, for now she has seen her place is no longer with us. She'll wait until the right moment to dust that collar and be on her way, and I'll be ready to provide her a distraction.

"Keep a close eye on him," I hear Lex tell her warriors as she marches off through the chaos of them preparing camp. "I want eyes on him at all times."

CHAPTER 3

DEKA

Grey tents spring up all around me, their pointed tops wavering until stakes peg their flared-out bases to the frosty ground. Lex's warriors are eager to get into shelter and off their feet, though none dare remove a shred of their uniform in sight of her. Instead they retreat into their tents, from where I hear whispers and mutterings compare their paced distances. The consensus is that we've been on the move for twenty-four hours and have put forty good miles behind us.

It's little wonder my saddle had caused me such discomfort, though I dare not complain around the thousands who've traveled the whole way on foot.

Green light dances and swirls over gray tent roofs. The entire camp glows with aurora light from above. It weaves defiantly through dark clouds, a limelight serpentine shining down from the heavens. The majesty is lost on all but me. Everyone else goes about their business, including Lex's steward.

"This way," he says.

He guides me to a great black tent half blossomed at waist height. Here he instructs me to fix the Arcturus pennant to the pointed top before they raise the grand assembly. Warriors pound two wooden posts into the ground nearby, with a crossbeam between them, to which they hobble the horses. Mine included.

So, whatever assistance I offer Nya must not involve Svenia.

I scan the surrounding terrain and note where the lookouts are taking position. In doing so, I feel I'm being watched, though it's not from those up high.

Lex's steward stands behind me, studying my behavior. Hector is his name, and he's becoming a problem. I've seen how he glares at me when I hold the Arcturus standard. He believes the honor should be his. Instead he rides at the back of the baggage train.

I keep my back to him and feel the knife handle protruding from my waistband. This blade may get its first taste of blood soon.

"Come," Hector says, "we need to unload the Commander's gear."

I follow him back toward the supply caravan of covered wagons, sixty of them in total.

Somewhere through the commotion of sprouting tents comes the retchings of a girl. I trace the source of this noise to the base of a steel pole, where a figure kneels and vomits. The edges of her four oblong wings glow radiantly with green aurora light, which illuminates their inner supports like emerald tree branches.

She's really making a show of it. Her performance works so well they've posted only two guards to watch her. Wait until she blows that chain apart and beats them with their own steel pole. But there's too much activity around, too many other eyes watching her. Strong as Nya is, she can't take on an army alone. She'll need some help.

I join Hector at the commander's cart. First off is her council table, which together we carry easily enough, but he recruits others to deliver her bed pieces.

As we pass Nya, he watches her closely and speaks to me over his shoulder. "Better hope she's right. If our scouts catch even a single Polarian Ranger, well..."

I clench my teeth to restrain a threatening backlash. Hector better keep his taunts in check, or he'll be feeling my blade sooner than he'd like.

Once we unload all the bigger furniture, it's just piecemeal work—lanterns, blankets, ornamental weaponry and the like. I lose pace with Hector to ensure I'm at the baggage cart when he's organizing Lex's tent. In a hasty rummage through what's left I discover a crate with 'Lamp Oil' stamped on the side. A warning label on top lists ingredients of canola oil and methanol, among others.

My heart thumps against my ribs.

I pull two bottles from the box and set them aside, then pop the corks from the remaining ten and place them on their sides. Fuel spills onto the wooden cart deck and drips to the ground below.

I make my way to the tent nearest Nya with the other two bottles in hand. One I've uncorked and carry upside down, pouring a trail from the wagon toward the flared-out tent flaps on the ground. It takes the second bottle to get me all the way there. Murmuring comes from inside the octagonal tent, so I stick my head in through the doorway.

The troop of ten notice me and sit up straight on their cots.

"Lord Lex needs you to fetch some water."

Their exchange of confused looks tells me this is not among their expected duties.

"We're too busy unloading her gear," I add. "Shall I tell her you require a written order?"

This gets them on their feet and flinging on their long coats. They groan and grumble as they amble out, with no idea I just saved them from a fiery death.

I keep myself busy around Lex's tent, setting up banners and smoothing the ground to lay out her rugs. It's only a matter of time before someone returns to the cart carrying a torch.

"You smell that?" asks Hector from the doorway.

"Smell what?"

I'm centering Lex's council table when I hear a *WHOOSH*. It comes with a flash of orange, pulsating light.

Shouts of panic rise in alarm. "Fire!"

Warriors race to scoop water from the river. Others use shovels to fling dirt onto the outlying flames.

Nya's guards remain steadfast at their post. There are plenty others to fight the baggage train blaze. That is... until a line of fire races from the cart to the tent nearest them. It goes up fast, forcing both to drop their spears and take up shovels to fight the flames.

I stand between two tents and watch Nya pull feebly on her collar. She's still faking. Why? Is she being watched by someone I can't see? There's no time for this.

I rush over to her. "Come on, Nya, dust that chain and get out of here."

She looks up to me with desperate, panicked eyes.

"I can't!" she says as she pulls futilely on the chrome collar.

The ambient orange glow dims, inviting shadows to creep in around us. They're getting the fire under control.

I search the area for something to break open the collar.

Nya bursts into a coughing fit, almost choking, drawing me back to her side. I fling my coat over her shoulders and kneel to rub her back.

"You should've kept going like I told you," I tell her.

She shivers and hugs my coat around her body to guard against the chill, yet her hair drips with sweat. In this moment she is the most pitiful thing I've ever seen.

"Why don't humans ever trust me?"

"They'll soon see their error."

She sits straight and gives me a surprised look through her sunken eyes. "You believe me?"

Guilt and shame overcome me as I see how my behavior has affected her. "Of course."

Her green eyes brighten with enough warmth to heat me for a whole winter night. Then she winces in pain, curls over, and retches fiercely.

This escape plan isn't going to work. Even if I break her free she'll not make it far on her own. I'll have to wait and figure out another way.

BOOSH!

"Whoa!"

Shouts of panic rise loud into the night as the fire flashes back.

"All hands to cart four!" shouts Lex. "Remove that canvas and haul it clear. Hurry!"

Her panicked tone draws my attention to the baggage train, where fire engulfs two wagons behind the charred remains of the first. Warriors race to haul off the cover of the fourth, where embers eat at the canvas. As they pull it away to reveal what's inside, cold sweat slicks my skin.

Little Boy sits heavy on the deck, far from the sky where it's supposed to be. If I'd looked more closely before, I'd have noticed the reinforced wheels and heavy-duty axles.

"Get it away from here!" screams Lex. She paces frantically, surveying the fiery carnage. "Move it! Now!"

Flames roar from the third cart, illuminating the sideways balloon-shaped bomb, from its rounded head to its finned tail.

Centurion Lantz, commander of a low-ranking century, leads a dozen warriors to the cart handles. Their efforts to spin the wagon yield not a smidgen of give. Centurion Argyle finishes dousing the tent blaze near us and directs his troops to help tow Little Boy from the caravan.

As the flames grow larger, panic rises.

"It's gonna blow!" someone shouts.

This sends a few running for the hills.

"It won't detonate!" Lex yells. "Stand your ground. Fight the fire. You there, help move the cart!"

Lex's assurances reach some, who do their duty by joining the wagon-moving effort or fighting the fire, but panic deafens the ears of a few. Nearly one hundred flee to the hills.

Fools. Through the planetary memory bank inside the Great Pyramid, I have witnessed the devastation of a nuclear explosion with my own eyes. They won't make it beyond the blast range on foot.

I kiss Nya on her forehead and say, "I'll be right back."

I bolt toward Lex's tent, weaving through the chaos of warriors fetching water and sand. Centurion Argyle grabs a shovel from a frantic soldier and locks eyes on me.

"You, banner boy, get over here."

I have no choice but to obey. Not even by duty. His tone alone is enough to break the will of any man. Saying no is not an option with him. When he offers me the shovel, I can't help but marvel at the size of his arm. It's like a hairy oak branch. Lex must have to feed this Centurion a king's share or more.

As I accept the shovel he pushes me toward the blaze. "Fling as much dirt as you can to smother it."

Sure, I could do that. Or I could make a wide detour instead. Like maybe around the flaming carts, then past the hundreds of warriors desperately towing and pushing Little Boy away from the flames and heat, all the way back to Nya.

She sits with her back to the steel post, knees pulled to her chest and her head rested on them, trembling from either illness or fear.

"Hang in there, Nya. I'll get you free."

I start digging around the post. The dirt is loose and comes up easy. I make great headway fast, so I lean my weight into the pole and rejoice to feel it move. Another two feet of digging should do it.

"Almost there, Nya."

The speed at which I fling out the next two feet could challenge records. When I push the pole this time it topples and hits the ground with a thunk.

"Hey!" comes a man's voice.

Nya's guards approach me from behind. Black smoke

billows where there'd just burned wood and canvas, the tent fire snuffed out and buried under a mound of dirt.

The nearest points his spear at me. "Hands up."

I drop my shovel, and they're on me before I can do anything. One guard seizes my wrist and sniffs my hand. A devious grin brightens his face. "Looks like we found our arsonist."

"Nice work, troops," says Hector. He marches up from the side with a gloating stare. "I'll take him to Lord Arcturus."

"The hell you will," says one guard. He whistles for two replacements to come take over their watch of Nya. "It's time we got a little recognition."

He grabs me above the elbow and hauls me toward Lex's tent. His partner leads the way, taking us into Lex's strategy room. Only a smoky breeze makes a stir in here.

"She's still out fighting the fire," says the guard at my side. He sends his partner to go retrieve her.

Without thinking, I draw my knife and drive it into his flank. He growls and seizes my wrist, holding the blade in place as he drops to a knee. I lean into him and knock him onto his back. His grip on my arm remains firm, dragging me down with him, where we wrestle at his side. I'm vaguely aware of Hector snatching up his spear and circling around us. Then comes the sudden urge to move.

It's as if my muscles know exactly what to do. My free hand seizes the wrist gripping mine, while my left leg springs to roll me over top of my opponent, all the way to the other side of him. He rolls with me, presenting his back where I'd just been struggling a second before.

The spear plunges between his shoulder blades. Though I can't see it from this angle, I'd not mistake the sound for anything. And his eyes flaring wide in surprise, along with his mouth gaped in agony, leave little to doubt.

Hector's face bears a similar expression as he releases the spear shaft and steps back in shock.

I push the guard aside and stand to join Hector in watching his victim wheeze his final breath.

Hector laughs madly in shock and disbelief. He's lost it. I should thank him before Lex takes his head.

He composes himself remarkably fast. Darkness grows in his stare.

"You have twenty seconds," he tells me.

I give him a befuddled look.

"One... Two... Three..."

My mind connects some dots: the two relief guards who know I tried to free Nya... the smell of fuel on my hands linking me to the fire... the blood now on my hands, but not on Hector's...

"... Six... Seven..."

I'm not shirking this kill.

"Eight... Nine..."

I have to get out of here.

I'm hardly out the door when he yells, "Murder! The Bannerman killed a guard. He's headed for the choke!"

I have no time to think, only react. My frantic dash through tent rows is all a blur as I weave my way downriver.

Alarm horns rattle me deeply. Each blast feels like it's closing in on me as my hearing sharpens, as if the blowers are on my heels, which spurs my feet faster in frenzied escape.

An arrow whistles past my head and clacks off a rock. I duck and stumble through low brush to the choke. A few more smack the rock wall by my head or bury into dirt around my feet, but soon I escape their range.

A thunder of hooves freezes my feet beyond the narrow pass. Arrows are one thing, limited by their archers' ability to keep up. Cavalry are a much different story.

The only weapon I managed to grab in my escape was one of Lex's whips from her saddle, its worn leather now soft in my grip. Of course I'd choose the most non-lethal, hardest to master weapon of all.

I stare at the rushing water. I've suffered its chill before, and the memory freezes me like a statue on the riverbank. I stay like this until the riders slip through the choke, horse hooves splashing through a shallow rise.

A desperate scan all around reveals a straight path on which the horses will catch me, or slopes too steep to climb, leaving only one option.

My whole body shivers at what's to come, but it's not enough to stop me from leaping into the frigid winter current.

CHAPTER 4

DEKA

The river engulfs me with icy regret. Bone-shattering cold numbs my brain, but my mind remains alive with excruciating awareness.

Had I considered my other options well enough? How did it come to this?

Love. That's how.

See where your heart led you? wails my tortured mind. *You were the envy of many, Anterra's next rising star, and you gambled it all on a lost cause.*

I'd try to silence this nagging part of me, but it's the only thing keeping me lucid right now.

I try swimming to the bank on the right side, but my arms are heavy as lead. All I can do is submit to the current and endure my scolding thoughts. Although they come through different words, they all follow a similar pattern, with the focus on berating me for my stupidity.

Fool. Stupid boy. Foolish stupid boy.

Until there comes a warning...

It's time to get out. You need to get out. GET OUT!

My frost-crusted eyes flutter open to an unexpected sight. A stone archway curves over the river between two turrets standing high upon each bank, with steel bars in between, spaced just wide enough to allow water through. When a dead tree floats into this river gate, the bars spin to reveal serrated sides that mince the great wood into splinters.

The gut-wrenching shriek gets my arms flailing and pumping, but my efforts are in vain. The current is too strong and I am too weak. In about ten seconds that gate is going to chew me to pieces and no one will ever know what happened to me.

I'm about a stone's throw from the bars when I hit something that jars me to a stop. My arms curl instinctively around it, and here I see my lifeline comes in the form of a steel chain stretched tight across the river. With this current, the frosty links would have no problem smashing a boat to pieces and sacrificing her crew to the river, where there waits the saw-toothed gate to hell.

Seeing the meat grinder so close drives my arms to haul me to the right bank. Here I curl on my side in the night shadow of the rightward turret, wheezing, waiting for the gate's defenders to come seize me. I pray for it. If they have any humanity at all, they'll at least dry me. In this state, I'd even consider a bullet a mercy.

Frigid water gushes through the river gate bars. A tree branch screeches through the roller blades, its demise accompanied by a high-pitched squeal.

A shiver rattles me to my soul. That could have been my bones.

Then a tree trunk rams the gate. It's long and wide and hits the bars head on, and the whole length takes a terribly long time grinding through. The course grating gives a better impression of a bone grinder and is enough to get me on my feet.

I don't know if it's due to the contrast between the chill water, but the night air feels warmer now. My shivering seems to have come mostly from expectation. But this may change and may do so quickly. Perhaps I find myself between phases of shock or some strange physiological phenomenon, so I proceed like I don't have much time.

Horizontal slits in the turret above provide the gate guards sweeping coverage of the area. A spiral stairway of stone curves up around the back to their nest, where at the top I find a rusted steel door. When I push it with both hands I'm surprised it actually moves.

Although the unlocked door had come as a surprise, the empty machine gun nest beyond does not. Nya's claim of an abandoned border had raised suspicion in all but me. Their failure to see her sincerity has become a costly tragedy.

A doorway across the room opens onto the arched bridge. Beyond the conical roof of the opposite turret, high up on a hill, stands a steel tower with a dish similar to Lex's radio antenna.

A log hits the grinder as I cross the river. The faint tremor that shakes the stone walkway sends a quiver up through my heart.

The left bank turret offers me creatures of comfort, most notably a brown bear rug sprawled over the stone floor. In no time I peel off my drenched clothes and fling the bear fur over me. The soft dry embrace of the makeshift cloak on my cold wet skin is the greatest feeling ever. I could curl up here right now, but I'd never get moving again, so I continue down a far stairway below ground.

I'm no stranger to subterranean living — I'd spent most of my life with cavern walls for a sky, yet the ambiance of this brutal defense installation manages to exceed that of my home colony. Faint blue light glows from every corner, a form of emergency backup system that casts warm coziness, leaving only scarce corners for shadows to hide.

The first underground level hosts a neat arrangement of stone tables and wooden benches. Plates and cutlery sit in a mess, as if the occupants had left in a hurry, though a quick search reveals not a crumb to tell of what they ate. Something tells me Anterrans aren't in the habit of wasting food, especially in the dead of winter. Another validation of Nya's claim.

A brick chimney in the far wall hints to a fireplace or cookery below, so I continue down the spiral stairway to the next level. Here I find a broad steel oven. Its polished door displays a reflection I hardly recognize. With the fur cloak around my shoulders and the bear's head drooped over mine, I no doubt embody the barbarian image that had kept this fort's inhabitants restless on their watch.

I play with the oven dials until one introduces a steady hiss of gas. A push of a red button ignites a pale blue flame inside.

I hug the cold steel door until it becomes too hot to touch. I'll need more than just heat to recover, so I crank the dial to summon a greater flame before making my way down to the storage level.

Empty munitions boxes litter the floor, further confirmation of this fortification's swift abandonment. Across the room, a blast door with a padlock displays a sign that reads: "Warning - Liquid Hydrogen. See Chief Cook for access."

So that's what's fueling the stove above. Lucky for me it was not considered an essential resource to bring with them.

I find what I'm looking for in an adjoining chamber. Given the circumstances, I could have fared worse. For the most part the shelves have been picked bare, but I find a stack of wool blankets and hug them to my chest with one arm. With my free hand I pile the remaining canned food into a wooden ammo crate, then place a jug of mead on top.

Back in the cookery, the sweltering air slicks my brow with sweat. I retrieve my uniform from up in the turret and hang it over the stove, then settle into a nest of blankets on the floor, where I peel open tin cans to devour their mushy contents.

This dining experience differs greatly from Lex's hospitality in considerable ways. Most obvious is the clumped brown meat contained in each can. It tastes of dirt and flavored ash. I'd been spoiled at Lex's fortress, but memories of my home are near to remind me of harsher times.

The mead is a different story. I wash my meal down with this liquid gold, which thickens my eyelids and soothes me into a blissful slumber.

Sleep must take me for quite some time, because when I wake my purple long coat is dried to near cracking, with the whole right side burnt black.

I have no time to waste, so I squander not a second. I gather what cans remain into a canvas rucksack and dump out the ale jug to make room for drinking water. An axe and

Lex's whip stuff neatly into side pouches, where a strap secures the upside-down axe handle. Lastly, I set a portable tank of liquid hydrogen on top of the main compartment and pad it with a blanket. I'd used the axe to bust open the lock, and the foot-long cylinder was by far the smallest of its kind in that cold storage.

That takes care of provisions, but then there's the matter of fashion. I can't go wandering dressed in an Arcturus long coat, nor can I garb myself in Polarian camouflage, which leaves only the bear fur. Yes, I'd do better to wander the forest dressed in this.

When I leave the river gate battlements I don't look back. Nya doesn't have time for me to laze about in comfort. She needs a rescue party, and I know exactly who's going to help me.

CHAPTER 5
DEKA

I crouch at the edge of the chasm where I'd fallen from Nya's makeshift tree bridge. It happened nearly two weeks ago, before I'd come to know Lex, back when Nya was still by my side. It wasn't hard to find. The wind carries many secrets to those willing to listen. From nearly every direction had come the creaking of trees and the rattle of bare branches or rushing water, except from one direction, where there came the unusual rustle of leaves.

I follow skeletons of dead winter trees toward lush summer sentinels, whose rustling leaves make a raucous in the polar breeze. I've seen enough of Anterra to know they are out of season, enchanted by a force unnatural to this land —that of an invasive species.

Back when I'd attempted my crossing, with Nya flying to my left for support, something had drawn my attention above and startled me into my fall. Evidence of the culprit appears on a tree near the chasm, where a pine branch holds a powder-blue feather on display. The feather is long and soft as silk and comes not from a bird.

I plow deep into the forest and gather dry brushwood, piling it high. From my pack I pull an igniter and strike sparks onto the tinder. Small flames hiss as they grow, spreading and smoking until the heap is a bright orange beacon of crackling wood.

I scour the forest floor for more, building a fire so grand that when I'm forced to wander a good distance away in search of more combustibles, it still warms me.

Until it doesn't.

An all-around look catches not even a flicker of orange. Only dense smoke hints at the direction where my blaze had been burning.

I return to the spot to find a smoldering pile of ash.

I sling my bag and race to do the same in a new area, gathering up all the dry kindling and setting it ablaze, traveling wide in search of more timber to build it up, only to have it go out on me.

I do this twice more, like a pyromaniac hell-bent on destruction, until I'm certain it's no ill luck or act of nature undoing my efforts.

For the grand finale I produce the can of fuel from my bag. I splash liquid hydrogen between a tight cluster of trees and up their trunks, leaving just enough to sprinkle a trail to a safe distance, where I lie in wait. It takes only a spark over the nearest pool to ignite my masterpiece.

An explosive flash near blinds me.

Flames scorch the dozen trunks and the ground between them with violent majesty. The fire rages upward, swirling like an upside down tornado, incinerating bark and splitting trunks, torching long branches and burning their leaves to a crisp.

Sparks shoot into the sky. Some soar high, others drift down upon unscathed trees a good distance away, violent spores spreading far and wide. Something should be done quickly to minimize the damage.

Glowing heat roasts my face. I never thought I'd shun a source of warmth in this dark cold realm, but that was before I discovered the magic of liquid hydrogen. Fire sprawls from the burnt trail between me and the ravaged cluster of trees. I'll have to relocate if they don't make their move soon.

They must know I'm here, but they can't hold back any longer. Two winged figures swoop down from the treetops and dump dirt onto the blaze... to little effect.

Four more arrive carrying a great hammock of weaved leaves, upon which a massive raindrop jiggles. They dump it into the heart of the blaze.

A balloon of black smoke swells out to swallow me. I use it for cover to stalk closer, so that I'm within range for their next dive.

My reflexes are sharp in the cloud of billowing smoke. When I snap Lex's whip up at four wings breaking through the plume, I catch a fire diver by the ankle. She writhes like a kite in a hurricane, jerking my arms this way and that. I haul on the whip and loop the handle around a branch as my prize flails overhead.

I grab the thong of the whip with both hands five feet from the handle and sit down. My wriggling catch sinks about a foot. Maintaining my hold with one hand, I scoot ahead and grab higher on the lash with the other to haul another section down. The struggling Fori drops another two feet.

I keep doing this until she's thrashing off the ground like a fish out of water. Here I stomp on the whip near the end to pin her lashed foot to the ground, then grab her anchored leg. I really wish I'd thought this part through.

She kicks my face with her free foot and knocks me onto my back. In my brief daze she manages to unwrap her ankle and spring up into the tree.

I rub my nose and smile. They got some fight in them. Good.

"Come down here," I say. "I need to talk to you. I'm a friend of Nya's."

The forest becomes unnaturally still. That massive water bubble they'd dropped had doused the fire good, leaving only small patches burning on the fringe.

"She's in trouble. She needs your help."

Stillness is again their response. It seems they're in need of a little persuasion.

I unstrap the axe from my pack and hold the blade to an unburnt oak, then take a mighty swing to bury it into the wood. Chipped bark flies off in every direction.

"Stop that!" demands a girl's voice from above.

"Are you going to help me?"

More silence. Infuriating, cowardly silence.

I swing again, driving the wedge deeper. As I take another swing, I swear I can feel the burn of their raging stares on the back of my neck. Another swing embeds my axe blade so deep it gets stuck. I'm wrenching it free when a weight crashes onto me and throws me to the ground.

Two hideous faces lean close to mine. Their rippled skin encroaches on jagged hairlines, scars from a good many fire. If not for their white eyes I'd think them Watchers, but only Nya's Fori cousins would risk their lives to save a few trees.

They pin my arms down while a third drops in to steal my axe. Their breath smells of moss and soil.

I don't fight them. I'm not here for that. "Nya needs your help. Take me to your Elder at once."

They exchange puzzled looks.

"Who's your elder in these parts?" I'll call her out by name if I must.

"What's it to you?" says the Fori pacing behind with my axe. Unlike her sisters, her skin is unblemished. Slicked-back hair with streaks of rainbow-colored locks covers her head, not a single strand singed.

I can't help but stare. She is one of the most radiant creatures I have ever set my eyes on. And it's not the first time I've seen her.

I have no idea where I've encountered this Fori before, but this is definitely not our first contact. Perhaps she was a random face on the Great Pyramid during the battle. Many Fori and Ori had scrambled madly alongside me toward the summit, though it's unlikely any who'd not jumped through the portal with us would have survived and escaped to this place.

"There's a great battle brewing nearby," I say. "One of the human armies captured Nya. They'll kill her if we don't do something."

"We don't get ourselves tangled in human affairs," says the Fori gripping my right wrist.

"Nothin' but trouble is what they are," says her sister on my left.

"Besides," says the rainbow-haired Fori, "what has that scamp ever done for us? We'll do better without her."

The Fori pinning my right hand shoots her a scolding look while her counterpart offers one of surprise.

"We should at least bring him to the Ko," says the scolding one. "See what she says. If the Evening Star gets free and hears we didn't help her, at least we'll be able to pass the blame."

Her sister turns and stares off, tapping a finger over the edge of my axe blade, thinking deeply. Apparently the threat of Nya's retribution is enough to break her resolve. She shoves my two captors aside and offers a hand to help me to my feet.

"They call me Sekarra," she says. "It means *Black Rainbow*."

"I'm Deka."

"I know who you are. Come, this way."

A sharpened stick jabs my back. "No funny stuff, hear me?"

"Got it," I say to the blackened fire diver.

The trio escorts me to the bottom of a cliff, where gray granite walls stretch far to my left and right, with a towering height of about three hundred feet. A dead end.

Sekarra points skyward. "Her nest is halfway up."

The rock face doesn't offer much for holds. Even at the bottom I struggle to find a good place to start my climb.

Sekarra huffs with irritation and nods to her two sisters. Each hooks an arm under mine to lift me. They grunt and fuss in our rise, and for a moment I sense at least one consider giving up until Sekarra joins us.

"Almost there," she assures them, which is all the help she offers.

They set me on a ledge before a cave. A hunched figure

in the nearby darkness stirs, turning its back to me. Faint green light glows from an unseen source, giving her powder-blue wings a turquoise hue. This Aeri is shorter than those I'd fought at the Battle of Giza. And a woven scar up her spine distinguishes her from The Ripper's companion. But this Aeri does keep some dark company of her own.

The restless shifting of a thousand bats echoes out from deep recesses and reminds me of rustling leaves. I can't even guess how many of them hang upside down from the rock ceiling.

"Who disturbs my peace?" says the Aeri in a low grumble.

"I'm a friend of Nya's. I've come to tell you she's in grave danger."

"Her peril concerns me how?"

"She once told me Ko Tora was a mighty warrior. Someone she could rely on."

The Aeri straightens. "There is no Ko Elder here. Just a weary servant whose glory days are past."

"Then you must not have heard... There's plenty more glory to be had for a great leader like yourself."

A sardonic laugh echoes off the rock walls. "Perhaps such flattery would have worked on me before, back when my ego held more sway over me."

"What about honor? Does that no longer matter to you either? She'd come to your aid without question and you know it."

"She is young and foolish, and a dust maiden at that." Tora lowers her head. "I'm too old to be fighting hopeless wars, young human. Klora's rebellion was our last true hope, and she turned me away. And you know what? I don't blame her. Look at what I did to Nya's army. I fell for a trap, led us from the high ground and divided our forces."

Nya never spoke much about the war, but Mora had told me the story many times.

"Yes, you did err grievously," I say. "Now it's time to make up for it."

Tora scoffs meekly and shakes her head. Her self-pity is almost cringe-worthy.

"Even in chains she still manages to nag me," says Tora with a shake of her head. "Birds of a feather..."

I wait for her to finish her sentence. She doesn't. "What?"

Tora hangs her head. "Just quit your pestering, *friend* of Nya. Allow me these final hours of peace."

"Sure, I'll go," I say, feeling a surge of Nya's sass build in me. "But I'll leave you with some words of warning. You know those demons that haunt your dreams? If there's one thing they hate more than the light, it's a coward."

The back of Tora's neck burns red—with anger or shame, I do not know.

I survey the army of bats dangling from the rock ceiling. "Your friends here won't save you in the darkness of your afterlife. Only your deeds shall follow you there."

Tora's wings arch over her head, shelling her. A choice made.

I step out of the cave, where a group of Fori have gathered on surrounding ledges. "Look, Vera, it's him," says one. "Nya's..."

The elder called Vera smacks her upside the head. "I know who it is." To my fire diver escort, she says, "Get him out of here."

The journey down is much faster, a controlled descent.

"I'll take it from here," Sekarra tells my handlers when we reach the ground.

Each gives her a look of caution, but neither protests.

Sekarra jabs me with my axe head, prodding me toward the direction we'd come from. "Move it."

I want to scream in frustration. Instead I walk.

Well that didn't go over well. I guess my only option now is to drag a jumbo cylinder of hydrogen here and hold every tree in this forest hostage.

Sekarra leaps from branch to branch overhead, watching me closely. When we put a good distance between us and their hideout, she drops behind me and follows on foot.

"Tora lost her fire," she says.

"Hanging out with the likes of you, what do you expect?"

Sekarra leaps in front of me and pokes my chest. "Listen here, *homo sapien.* Yeah, we douse fires, but sometimes we light 'em, too."

"Oh I'm sure you do. Only when it's safe and you have a clean escape, right? Nya told me fire divers were the bravest of her kind. All I see is a bunch of cowards hiding under rocks."

Sekarra grits her teeth and presses the axe head under my chin. "I fought with Nya at the pyramids. I lost half my family on them bloody steps, so don't you lecture me about bravery. My kind sacrificed more than enough to stop your extinction. If you were smart, you'd do them right by finding a place to hide away too."

"I will once I free Nya," I say. And it's true. I've made up my mind on that. The coming battle will be so colossal that Nya and I won't make a difference anyway. "You're just gonna let her waste away?"

"Not a chance."

Her words take me by surprise.

Sekarra gives me a taunting smile. "I knew the second you said she was in trouble I was going to help her. I just had to be sure you got enough iron in you to take the heat of what's to come."

My heart skips into a hopeful dance at this welcome turn in the conversation.

"You humans have a lot of bad qualities," Sekarra says, "but your hearts carry fire hotter than any inferno I've ever seen. It's what makes you so dangerous. But it's why we envy you."

I give her a curious look. Nothing Mora ever told me indicated anything more than pity for us.

Sekarra's upper lip curls into a sly smile. "I've seen you two together."

My face burns. "What?"

She gives me a bright smile and nods, and that's when it hits me. She was there when I was injured in the forest, after Nya left me to find help. It was she who brought me my compass and guided me in my daze toward Lex's rescue party.

"Don't worry, Deka. We don't normally trust your kind, but I know you're different. I saw how you cared for her. You'd have died right by her side before leaving her. If something happens to Nya now, the fire in your heart will tear this whole world apart. That much I know."

I throw my arms around Sekarra and sob uncontrollably. She tenses in my embrace, but I need this. I've never felt so lost or alone in my life.

Eventually she gives me an awkward pat on the back and pushes me away.

"I assume you have some sort of plan."

I nod.

"Well, too bad," she says. "Whatever it is, my idea is better. Here's what we're gonna do..."

CHAPTER 6

DEKA

The Wolf is up to something. Whatever it is, it's important enough to stall her invasion, because I find her camp exactly where I'd left it. Surely her scouts have returned from the border by now. They should be proceeding with great haste and they are not.

Sekarra and I watch the stagnant camp from a grove across the river. Well... *I* watch while she dances on one foot behind me, chanting non-sense in what I assume to be a pre-action ritual. I certainly hope it is, anyway. I'm having doubts about this cousin of Nya's.

"How many fires have you started?" I ask.

"Are those words of doubt I hear?"

I turn as she digs into a pouch dangling from her belt.

"Don't let my flawless physique fool you," she says. "I've bathed in the flames of so many fires they should start calling me the Fire Falcon. Which do you think sounds better? Fire Falcon, or *The Falcon of Fire?* I'm going for a fierce yet elegant vibe."

I never thought I'd say it, but I'm starting to see Nya is fairly mature compared to the rest of her race.

Sekarra withdraws a leafy wad and unfolds it to reveal a shimmering ball of liquid, much like a fist-size rain drop. She claps it between both hands and smears the gel up her arms and across her chest. Her skin gleams wherever it touches. As she lathers it through her rainbow hair, slicking it back tight to her scalp, I realize this salve is what has kept her in such prime condition.

"You have any more of those?"

"It won't do you much good," she says, rubbing the gel into the creases of her ears. Sensing my incredulous stare, she says, "I crafted these specially to match my body's chemical makeup. Your skin is different. It may even work as an accelerant and burn you faster."

I shiver and hug myself.

"Just sit back and let me work my magic. You ever see a whole mountain range burn up?"

I shake my head, trying to imagine those rocky peaks with crowns of fire. "What special concoction do you have for that?"

She holds her foot to her belly to rub salve between her toes. "That's easy. It's just four parts hydrogen... with a dash of carbon. Plenty of that around."

Methane gas, says my mother's voice from the recesses of my memory. She'd taught me this chemistry in my childhood, to educate me on the dangers of our subterranean habitat. If memory serves me well, Sekarra's plan might work better than expected.

She saves her eyes for last. This requires a dab of blue

mixture from a small pouch, which she applies delicately with her pinkie finger.

"Let's run through this again," I say. "You scoot across the river to those mountains..."

"Uh-huh."

"... and light a big fire..."

"*Huge* fire, yeah."

"...which should draw their attention..."

"Sure."

"... so I can slip in behind them..."

"Of course."

She's hardly paying attention.

"What if the distraction doesn't work?" I say. "The Wolf is sharp-witted. She'll suspect a ploy."

I'll admit the plan lacks creativity—it's essentially what I did before, only with a partner and on a grander scale—but nothing incites panic in humans more than a surprise inferno.

"Well, then, I'll just have to fireball those dwellings there."

"But Nya—"

"Okay, ready?" Sekarra says, her eyes narrowed on the mountains with razor-sharp focus. "Keep your head down, y'hear? It's about to get real hot up in this atmosphere. Oh! That's good. Try to remember that one."

She springs into flight.

"*Wait!*"

She ignores me and speeds upriver, south toward Lex's fortress, and when she crosses to the opposite bank I could mistake the small black shadow for a crow. There's no way Lex's sentries have detected her.

I nestle low amongst frozen ferns and peer through their

frosted leaves to spy on the camp. A sudden bustle of warriors emerging from their tents suggests some source of excitement. Lex's soldiers move with enthusiasm, some bouncing on the fringe of a crowd congealing at the center of camp. Around where Nya's steel anchor post had been planted.

A brick of angst sags deep inside my gut. It grows heavier when silence suddenly grips the crowd. It follows a collective gasp, as if all the air had been sucked from their lungs.

Only one thing could hush a mob with such a thirst for violence, a distraction from all other desire. My Nya could stop the whole world if she wanted to.

My heart sears inside my chest. Whatever is happening... I can't just sit back and wait. Besides, I have to see her face. If it comes to Sekarra fire-balling the camp and the flames scorch Nya like the other fire divers... It's not the most noble motivation, I know. But I'll admit right here that I'm far from perfect.

Frosted ferns graze my cheeks and neck as I slither from their cover, a mild nuisance compared to what awaits me nearby.

I dip my toe into the river and bite my bottom lip to keep from crying out. My head nearly explodes from the cold of it. It's the worst feeling imaginable.

It's too soon to endure such glacial temperatures again. I just can't do it. Instead, I retreat to my hiding spot.

A look to the looming mountains reassures me of my move. High slopes waver like desert dunes in the midday heat, while the peaks above them wobble and wave behind a curtain of rising gas.

My muscles loosen in relief. That's one quarter of the target area already primed. Soon those highlands shall burn bright with flame, and the heat cast will be enough to get me jumping into the river. Then adrenaline will help me tear across the current to the opposite bank.

Stick to the plan. It won't be much longer.

I'm settling down onto my elbows when a voice echoes across the river. It carries words that freeze me worse than any winter-water embrace ever could.

"Nya - one called Evening Star!" says Lex. "Intruder upon our affairs, dark shadow in our night, deceiver who stains us all with her soot tongue... You have been found guilty of meddling and mischief. Your sentence for these crimes is death."

All I can hope when I charge into The Artery is that Sekarra is about to strike her flint. The water could be a hundred degrees colder this time and it would not slow me.

I conquer the river in what could be record time and collapse on the opposite bank. From the ground, I'm able to see between neatly-spaced tents to a crowd gathered before a stage, where Nya kneels with her back to the Wolf. She struggles on all fours, arms shaking under her weight with hardly enough strength to keep herself upright.

My thighs tighten as rage and fear pump life back into my numb muscles, enough to get me on my feet. At this angle I see Lex's sword is still sheathed. I won't do Nya any good kneeling beside her, nor will I be of much use without a weapon, so I sneak into the nearest dwelling.

This tent shelters two rows of sleeping pads, with not a weapon between them. Seriously, not even a fork. It's the same with the next tent, and then the next.

A horse snorts nearby. I turn to see a ring of them hobbled to a hitching post near Lex's tent. The only one looking at me I know too well, and the daring look in Svenia's eyes tells me she's game for some mischief of our own.

Her hot breath blasts my shaking hands as I rush to untie her. Once she's free she jerks back on her reins, and this worries me deeply. Did I misread the nature of her mischief? Is her plan to escape this place on her own?

As if sensing my doubt, she presses her long face into mine. I stand firm and stroke her neck, and her steadfast posture comforts me. She's not going anywhere without Nya and me.

Yes, this could actually work. A horse plowing through the crowd will be chaos enough. Add to that a wildfire ravaging the hills, and we have ourselves a getaway.

Svenia and I watch Lex draw out the sentencing. But such a thing can only go on for so long, until finally she draws her sword.

A balloon swells inside my throat, choking me. I really wish Sekarra and I had established a panic signal. Now would be a splendid time for such a thing.

I watch the hills for a spark. Or a moving shadow. A crow or a raven, anything that could be mistaken for a fire diver at work.

Nothing.

The rock weighing inside my gut becomes a boulder. Did she back out? Or did she ever intend to go through with it? Perhaps this was her way of ridding their hive of me for good.

Svenia folds her front legs under her chest and lowers her head, inviting me to mount.

All right, I say to myself. *A charging horse alone will have to do.* I'll just have to make sure Nya doesn't get trampled in the mayhem.

I balance naturally on Svenia as she rises, her bare back sagging as if to conform to me. She stamps her hooves onto the frozen ground, preparing to charge. As Lex raises her sword with both hands, I grip the reins until my knuckles crack and lean forward.

"Wait!" shouts a man's voice.

Lex freezes her swing as her eye flares wide with rage.

I praise and yet pity the intruder.

Lex spins to face him with her blade cranked back with both arms, fixing to lop off *his* head instead of Nya's.

From high on Svenia's back I spot four warriors shuffle through the crowd. They drag something on the ground, something that compels the mob to part before them.

They stop at the foot of the platform stairway and present to Lex a net with Sekarra thrashing inside.

"We caught her casting spells in the hills," says a scout. "She looks just like that Nya one there, same wings and everything."

Lex bristles, their superstition clearly rubbing her wrong. She points her sword at Sekarra and says to Nya, "A friend of yours?"

Nya hardly takes notice. The spark in her eyes is faded beyond care, swallowed into two sunken pits of death. At this point I'd say she considers Lex's sentence a blessing.

Tears of rage and despair warm my eyes.

Lex gives Sekarra a kick. "Got some fight in this one, eh? We can make a good show of her. That gives me an idea..." She raises her sword with one hand and says, "I present this gift to my warriors. Do with her as you please."

Morale in this stagnant camp must have suffered in recent hours, because they embrace this entertainment with fevered zest. Cheers explode into the polar night as warriors haul the netted Sekarra into a tent behind the crowd.

I slide absently from Svenia's back and steady myself against the hitching post. Our plan to charge and snatch had involved only a single target. Even with the element of surprise, I'll now only manage to rescue one.

Could I ever forgive myself for leaving Sekarra here, after she'd come to help me in my greatest hour of need?

Sacrifices are required to keep what we most desire, advises the wise voice inside my head. I welcome its blessed words, for it grants me permission to do the otherwise unforgivable.

About two dozen warriors cram into the tent to begin their fun with Sekarra, but most of Lex's legion remains to watch Nya lose her head.

Sekarra screams.

I squeeze Svenia's reins and resist the urge to unleash her upon the tent. Despite the assurances of my conscience, I cannot leave her. But I have no time to devise a plan... No time to breathe... What I need right now is a miracle.

A gentle *swooshing* noise draws my attention to Lex's strategy tent, where a torch flame spars against a draft. The way the fire dances, bending but unyielding...

I rush to the steward's tent and fling aside stacks of boxes in search of oil. Nothing. As expected, I'd burned most of it during my first breakout attempt.

Desperation drives me to Lex's sleeping quarters, where the only bottle I find contains wine. The content of this fruity beverage won't ignite the fire I need, but...

I double back to the warriors' tents and discover a stash of clear bottles amongst their cookware, each containing transparent liquid. I pop the top from one and take a whiff, and the smell nearly gags me. Just what I need.

My hands move instinctively, tearing a rag into strips and stuffing them into two bottle necks, almost as if I've done this before. I fling a torch outside onto the ground, then hold both bottles over the upright flame until their rags light up. I toss one at Sekarra's captivity tent, and then the other immediately behind it.

The dwelling lights up like a colossal torch head. Furious flames ravage the canvas and hurl black smoke into the night sky, with screams of agony joining soon after. The tent sides bulge where warriors try stabbing their way out to safety.

This was supposed to serve as a distraction for my rush to save Nya. Instead, I watch the fiery carnage escalate. It's the most horrific thing I've ever witnessed, worse even than the murders of my mother and my dear friend Mali, because this atrocity is entirely of my making.

What made me think this was a good idea? How is Nya's withering life worth two dozen of my own kinsfolk?

Their screams rattle me to my soul and shall haunt me until my own final breaths.

I stand frozen in place, trembling in terror as I watch warriors fling shovels of sand and splash buckets of water onto the blaze. These attempts are no match for the flames, which consume the tent until only the steel center pole remains. It stands perfectly upright despite the loss of its supports.

A blackened lump stirs around its base. The curled figure rises, sending onlookers stepping backward in surprise, for nothing natural could survive such a blaze.

The survivor stands nearly five feet tall with its head lowered, all five feet of flesh charred to a crisp. Only...

She lifts her head and opens her eyelids to reveal a mischievous stare. It's matched by a wicked grin, and it's now that I realize it's not scroched skin that has blackened her body, but the cinder of the tent and its dead. This is confirmed when she slides a hand down her arm to slough off a black sleeve, soot and ash caked to her skin by a protective salve, then hurls it at Centurion Argyle's face.

It's all chaos from there. She swings the tent pole with both hands and cracks the nearest bystander in the head. Those around him can't get away fast enough, desperate to retrieve their shields as she swipes and wallops anyone in reach with the eight-foot pole.

Sekarra's rampage wreaks havoc upon the execution ceremony, shaking even the fearless Wolf herself, which actually works against me.

Lex holds Nya close like a shield, a sword to her neck. As the Black Rainbow takes to the sky and whizzes overhead, Lex shouts, "Shield dome!"

Two dozen warriors rally to form a circle around Lex, locking their shields overhead to shelter her and Nya under a half shell.

I weave through the calamity toward the dome of locked shields. "Alexandra!"

"Deka..." The shield wall facing me loosens and cracks, then opens to reveal Lex. But I see only Nya in this moment. Her desperate, sunken eyes watch me through black pits of death.

"Let her go, Lex."

"You left me!" growls the Wolf, her grip on Nya

tightening. Her clenched teeth show me anger, but her eyes swirl with grief.

"We're not your enemy," I say. "This is just retribution for taking Nya prisoner. They'll back off when you release her."

"I see only *one* of them." Her eye narrows on the distant sky, and the calm order falling over the camp tells me they've chased Sekarra away. This is confirmed when all the guards lower their shields and break apart the dome.

"More are on their way," I say, a desperate lie. "If you don't let Nya go, they'll attack in force."

Lex presses her blade hard against Nya's throat. "Then perhaps I should be quick about it."

I step forward with both hands raised. "Lex, please, I'm begging you. I'll do anything you want. I'll serve you until my dying breath."

"Hah! You already made that oath, and then you broke it. I can't trust you. You're nothing but a traitor to me now. Grab him!"

Ten sets of hands glom onto me and throw me to the ground, where they pin me down.

Others size up the smoldering black heap that had been a tent and their fellow warriors. All lost because of me.

Lex hands Nya off to Karl and Karla, who let her fall to the ground.

"Archers, watch the sky. I want every crossbow loaded and ready." She crouches before me. "You have no idea how lucky you are, Deka. The death I offer is a kinder fate than you deserve."

A circle of warriors forms around us, blocking my view of

Nya. Their scathing stares bear down upon me, eyes eager for blood.

Lex twists her lips, hesitating. She can't do it. We've formed a bond, her and I. We're more akin than no two others on this continent.

Or so I think.

"Rip him apart," she says.

This round sees a thousand hands grab hold of me. They tug on my limbs and claw at my skin like a pack of hyenas, jerking my arms and legs in all different directions.

"Stop!" I shout. Something strikes my face. "Lex, tell them to..."

My words fade to faint mutterings.

"What's that?" asks a muffled voice.

Does he actually care what I have to say?

"What *is* that?" says a girl.

The accosting hands release me as my assailants stand straight and turn their attention skyward. Peace befalls me as I find myself in the eye of a storm, but I do not relax. Something tells me the worst is yet to come.

Through gaps between shifting warriors, I spot a black cloud rush toward us. It surges and swells like a dark aurora, squeaking and clicking louder in its approach from downriver.

"Cover!"

Round steel plates interlock over and around Lex to form a dome. Warriors caught outside throw up their shields to form shelters of their own, haphazard clusters sprouting everywhere to repel the screeching cloud of a hundred thousand bats.

Shield domes break apart as the swarm of beating wings overruns the camp.

I roll onto my belly and bury my face into my arms. A steady rattle nearby tempts me to tilt my head slightly to watch a gust of bats pummel Lex's dome in a concerted effort. The shields hold tight and the dome remains solid, better than any other. Streams of bats try to break them from all angles. This works on other domes who'd remained intact against the initial wave. All it takes is a single bat to slip under a shield edge.

Lex's dome sits firm against the blitz until two massive feathered wings swoop through the cloud at a low angle and rams them at their base.

The shields bust apart in spectacular fashion. Lex and her warriors fly off into the swarm in every direction, arms flailing and legs kicking, leaving only Nya in place of the dome.

The nearest warrior recovers swiftly and scrambles to pounce on her. He's mid-jump when Tora dives in and scoops him up. Together they disappear into the cloud of leather wings, where his screams quickly fade.

"Valkyrie!" shouts Hector from somewhere unseen.

Most warriors crouch or curl on their sides and shrivel under their shields, which makes my scramble to Nya so much easier.

As I cradle her onto my lap, it strikes me how light she is.

Warriors swat and tug at bats entangled in their hair, but the creatures avoid Nya's. Aside from her, only those without hair remain unscathed. Like me.

And Lex.

She stands before us, a vile look in her eye and a fierce

grip on her sword. I can see she wants to dice me up real good, so when she steps toward me I lift Nya and turn to run.

I immediately slam into a solid mass that knocks me to the ground. It speaks to the level of chaos that a rowdy beast like Svenia could sneak up on me. She looms over us, frantic eyes rattled by the relentless storm of bats. She screams and rears up on her hind legs.

I roll over Nya to protect her for when the two front hooves pound back to the ground. Instead, Svenia drops onto her forelegs beside us. I'm not sure what spell or enchantment inspires her to do this, but I quickly accept her invite, placing Nya on her back before climbing up behind.

I look over my shoulder as Lex attacks. Svenia kicks her in the chest with her hind legs and drives her back through the ring of swirling bats.

And then we're off, charging through hell on Earth.

CHAPTER 7
DEKA

Svenia barrels through the whirlwind of bats, trampling any warrior who gets in our way. Shields crunch under hooves, bones snap with sickening sharpness, and wails of despair add to the nightmare I've unleashed.

Somehow Nya remains oblivious to it all. She slouches between my arms before me, wobbling side to side with Svenia's jouncing. The swarm parts ahead of our approach, swirling in a vortex as if we're the hurtling eye of a hurricane. There seems no end to the bats. It's as if they're moving with us to conceal our escape. I'm almost sure of it until we break out under wide-open sky, where the dazzling green aurora greets us.

I almost scream in relief.

Svenia carries us up a slope, challenging steep goat trails that only a horse driven to madness would dare risk. I'm tempted to slide off and guide her up before she hurts herself or dumps us, but there's no stopping her. All I can do is lean forward into Nya and hold the reins for dear life.

We crest onto a plateau that overlooks a valley that

stretches between Lex's fortress pathway to the grand Ardis Valley. Here she slows and wanders aimlessly, unsure where to go.

Shouts echo from behind. I shouldn't look back, but I can't help it.

The cloud of bats at the river enshrouds Lex's camp completely, breaking only to make way for Tora's expansive wings as she dives in and out.

Nya whimpers in front of me. Her head droops deeper, her whole body limp and sagging forward.

"Tell me where to go," I say. Right now I'd ride to any horizon with her.

She slouches farther forward. I try pulling her back, but she resists. Then I hear her words. At first they sound like gibberish: *"Ess ben da-dee, noin nine dee-dah."*

Svenia wheels hard right, almost flinging us sideways from her back. Nya clings to her neck, pressing against the back of her head, where she continues to whisper exotic words. *"Ess ben da-dee, noin nine dee-dah. Aeir for..."*

Wind whistles past my ears as Svenia gallops full tilt across the transverse valley. She rides with such purpose that her head lurches forward with each fall of her hooves.

I stoop over Nya and see our destination through the space between Svenia's ears—a cluster of trees that spills down from between two mountain peaks. Under the wispy curtains of the meandering aurora, the forested pass resembles a colossal patch of emeralds.

Nya nestles back into me and wraps her arms around mine, then pulls my elbows tight to her sides. Svenia takes this for a command to ride harder.

Harsh polar air thrashes my face. Tears trickle over my

eyelids and freeze halfway down my cheeks. Our race across the open is a blur, until sentinels of trees take form through my blurred vision, their ranks tight and forbidding, a wall that threatens an abrupt and fatal end to our current haste.

I pull back on the reins to slow us. Svenia responds with a defiant forward jerk of her head to cover the remaining open ground and charge through the treeline.

A wide branch appears across our path. I duck forward into Nya to narrowly avoid it.

She whispers more words I do not understand. *"Aeir foer nein, noin nine dee-dah."*

Svenia weaves around trees so closely their bark scrapes my knees. Bare branches and pine bows claw at my face, but there's no breaking her from Nya's spell. All I can do is submit to her course, which I soon regret when she plows into a wall of pines.

I growl in anger as a mob of wooden fingers rake my face. Somehow I still have both eyes when we break through, and here my outrage evaporates like the rising wall of steam before us.

Even from a few feet away, the hot spring soothes my skin with a gentle, caressing warmth. A rock ledge beneath the waterline circles the pool like a bench, and a surrounding wall of pines provides absolute privacy.

Nya slumps over my right arm. I lean over her left shoulder to notice her eyes closed and a string of drool dangling from her mouth.

My reaction is counterintuitive, yet I do it without second thought, tossing her from horseback into the spring.

Scalding water splashes me and gives Svenia a fright. She

rears and dumps me onto my back, where my head hits something hard and knocks me senseless.

It takes me some time to sit up. The world spins like a cyclone around me, so I close my eyes for a minute to steady myself. When I open them again, the round enclosure of trees continues to whirl, but at a slower rate, so I focus on the pale haze that is Svenia. As my vision steadies and sharpens, I see she's laid down with her eyes closed in rest.

I'm on my feet in a second. How long have I been lying here? Did that hit to the head knock me out? And Nya...

I rush to the pool edge and see her through the still water. She floats at the bottom, her slack arms floating to the side and her head drooped forward.

Still water... Not even a ripple. How long has she been down there?

Too long.

I stick my foot in and immediately regret it. The rising steam does not lie. Science rarely does. After the frigid Artery, I never thought I'd deem any heat too hot to bear, but this continent of extremes holds many surprises.

Some might judge me for my hesitation—that not even boiling water should stop me from diving to her rescue—but scalding myself to death won't help either of us. That's a fact. Instead, I shove a branch down into the water and prod her shoulder.

She jolts and thrashes in fright. I scoot along the pool edge to reposition the stick in front of her to grab so I can pull her out.

A bubble balloons from her open mouth and rises. At surface it explodes and blasts my face with scalding water.

I release the stick and turn away to wipe my face. A few

seconds later brings an eruption that sends me diving onto my belly with my head buried under my arms.

Nya coughs and sputters as she thrashes through the waterline, her mouth wide in hysteria as she gasps for air and rubs her eyes.

I scramble to recover the branch I'd just dropped. "Hold on!"

"Are you kidding?" Her struggle turns to laughter. "This is amazing!"

I freeze and watch to see if the water has boiled her brain. What I see instead is life blooming back into her green eyes and a smile stretching from ear to ear. If this is a side effect of some sort of neural scalding, I'll happily take it over what she's suffered in recent weeks.

She blinks to focus her eyes on me, and when she does it's as if she's seeing me for the first time in ages.

"You're shivering," she says with great concern.

She's right. I stand at the pool edge hugging myself, my teeth chattering loudly.

When she waves me in I hug myself tighter and back away.

Her brow creases with a look of disappointment. "You think I'd ever beckon you into danger?"

Yes, I know you would, is what I almost say. She'd not do so knowingly, of course. But still, all the same...

Nya's lips tighten and quiver. Her eyes twinge with hurt. "You don't trust me."

It's less a matter of trust and more to do with miscalculation.

I ease forward and stare at the steaming water. At the pool edge I rock back and forth on my feet, contemplating.

Finally I stick my foot over the water to feel the steam.

"I'd ease into it if I were you," Nya says suddenly, almost urgently. Her concerned expression justifies my hesitation.

I dip my toe into the water, and immediately the temperature forces me into retreat.

Nya, on the other hand, is in the midst of a miraculous recovery. This thermal pool infuses her with energy straight from Earth's core. I see it in her eyes, where the spark of life shines brighter by the second.

An icy gale blows down into our sanctuary and is enough to drive me in for a more determined attempt. It takes me a good while, easing my foot down to my knee, but I do it. I'd never known water to be so hot until now, so I withdraw my leg to check for blisters. A sheen over smooth brown skin assures me I'm safe to proceed.

This time my foot touches the rock ledge lining the inner pool.

Nya bites her lip and watches my gradual submersion with growing satisfaction.

I sit down on the rock ledge, where the waterline caresses my neck. My body adjusts to the heat remarkably well. The more I acclimatize, the more I dread the idea of leaving this hot embrace for the endless and unforgiving cold.

"What do you think?" Nya says. Frost hardens her hair into thick white strands as she treads water at the center of the pool.

Strange. I didn't think my fair dust maiden could swim.

As the hot water soothes my skin and relaxes my muscles, I feel as if this place was crafted especially for us.

"I saw it on my way back from the border," Nya tells me.

"Is it really deserted?"

"Yes. Regulus is moving his whole army to Mount Tuck."

Envy sears my heart and wrings my stomach. *Yes, he moved them there because of you.* I wouldn't be surprised if Regulus did it simply to impress her. And why should I even care? A few days ago I was trying to rid myself of Nya.

But that was then, before I'd witnessed her mortality. Back before I almost lost her for good. Now, though...

Regulus is a king who commands the greatest army of humans on Earth. What could I possibly offer this mighty dust maiden that could rival a fortune like that? I couldn't even blame her if she'd been seduced by such power.

"His soldiers will come back if Lex crosses," I say.

"Hopefully they'll think she's coming to help. That's what I told Regulus when I last saw him. Besides, it's a long way to Amyria on foot. The battle on Mount Tuck will be fought by then."

Nya's cheeks glow red as white puffs of breath wisp from her soft pink lips. Below water, the graceful sway of her arms and the smooth rhythmic kicking of her legs mesmerize me.

She gives me a curious frown. "What is it?"

I shake my head. "Nothing."

"You didn't duck all the way yet."

I rub a hand over my head to wet my short, fuzzy hair. "There. Happy?"

Nya lowers her chin and gulps water into her mouth, then squirts it at my face.

My retaliation comes swift and in the form of a handful of water flung at her head, which she promptly returns with a splash of her own. I'm winding back for another when Nya smacks her hand onto the surface to send a wave crashing over me. I cough and sputter, breathless.

As she winds back for another blast, I spring off my ledge and into her embrace.

She wraps her legs around my waist and locks her ankles behind my back. Hooking her hands under my shoulders, she pulls our chests together and presses her nose to mine. Her sweet breath heats my lips more than any thermal spring ever could.

My feet dangle in watery weightlessness, but my chin remains above the surface. Growing up along the sea has taught me that I'm not at all buoyant, and with another body clinging to me we should sink. I attribute our buoyancy to some grace of Nya's.

Here in the weightlessness of this Antarctic hot spring, I soar. Wrapped in the embrace of this intergalactic pixie, I am the luckiest human to have ever lived. Her lips beckon me in for a kiss, and I gladly obey.

Nya jerks her head back. The bliss in her eyes darkens to concern.

"What is it?" I say.

"We could do it, you know... Just run off and leave it all behind."

I press my forehead to hers. "Just tell me where."

"Anywhere." Her skin melts into mine, so that I can't tell where she ends and where I begin. "We'll spend our winters in a mountain cave for all I care, cozying by a fire, and spend the summers raising all sorts of mischief. You watch over me through the long night, and I'll protect you during the six-month summer."

"And if the Watchers open the gate before we see another sunrise?"

She squeezes me tight. "Then we shall face that end

together. Lex doesn't need you to win this war. If you're all the difference she needs, then her cause is already lost."

"Okay." I'm sold, fully. Until now I'd always mistook Nya's wisdom for foolishness. Why is that? Is it so unreasonable to think a being who's lived four hundred and thirty-six years couldn't have learned a thing or two about life? Is it possible she knows I could never say no to her again?

Nya grabs the back of my head and pulls our lips together. In this steaming water, her body bound to mine, we are one.

Her heartbeat taps on my navel. A tingle prickles my spine, stirring parts of my soul that have cowered in darkness for longer than my mind dare surmise. This electric charge spreads to the water around us, upending my hairs from toes to scalp.

"Well," says a woman's voice from nearby, "isn't this a romantic little respite."

Nya pushes me away to confront Lex. Only, the intruder is not Lex.

The Ripper stands at the pool edge, flaunting the trophies of two vanquished dust maidens—a long golden hammer in her hands, and a black antler crown upon her slick white hair —both symbols of mighty heroes defeated in recent weeks. Ko Skadia's hammerhead rests on the ground between her feet, both hands resting atop the handle bottom before her waist. Aurora limelight slides over the black diamond points of Klora's Krown upon her head.

"Oh, don't stop because of me," she says. "Please, go on. You really deserve it. You've done so well setting up the battle to come. Quite the puppetmaster you are, Evening Star."

Nya floats in front of me and holds out both arms to shield me.

Drusilla ambles around the spring, swinging her hammer casually. "I had a nice little chat with the Watchers when I returned to Giza. They told me an interesting story. Rumor has it I slipped free of my natural timeline. That I'd be dead if I stayed there. But, I'm just wondering how that comes to pass. I'm not yet in my prime when I meet my end. So, tell me, Nya, why do our people believe me dead? What gives them this crazy idea?"

It's now that I see the Ripper's black eyes. She's gone Berserk. Blind rage skillfully triggered by the Watchers, her malice directed toward Klora and her kin.

"When a maniac Watcher starts messing with space-time," Nya says, "all sorts of strange things happen. Don't forget who our enemy is. It was Jexa who ordered your death."

"And it was Jexa who brought me back to life."

"That makes you friends now?"

I feel the exact second when Nya's fright flashes to anger. The water bubbles and the steam thickens around us, forcing me to float away to avoid being boiled alive. This confrontation is about to turn physical, so I scan our surroundings for a weapon.

"The Ripper has no friends," says Drusilla, "only enemies, some she considers worse than others."

"You think killing me here will go unnoticed?" Nya says. "The others want nothing to do with this war, but if you make a martyr of me—"

"Fear not, dear granddaughter, The Evening Star does not set on this night."

Granddaughter? I look to Nya, who gives me a look over her shoulder that tells me she'd been meaning to tell me this.

"I've made an arrangement with Jexa," says the Ripper, mother of Klora and grandmother to Nya.

"She's back?" says Nya.

"Yes, and she wants to make things right. She has Klora's spark. All she needs is the gateway to manifest her physical form on this plane. Then we'll have our fight. It shall be fair and for all to see."

"Jexa doesn't give gifts. What does she want in return?"

"A duel. Against you. Consider this an invitation. If you're inclined to skip out like they say, you'll condemn *his* people to death."

Drusilla doesn't spare me a look, but she's clearly referring to my human kin. I sit up on the pool edge, retreating from her attention. Nya glances over her shoulder at me.

"The friends you left at the pyramid are in Watcher hands," Drusilla says. "If you're not at the southern gateway when Jexa opens it, she'll slay them all. Wouldn't that be a pity? I've heard you've grown quite fond of them."

"You're pretty confident in Jexa's odds," Nya says.

"With me fighting on her side, these humans won't stand a chance. You know this."

I snatch a nearby stone and hurl it at the Ripper's face. She raises a hand to catch it, but the rock shatters against an air burst before reaching her. It's all the distraction Nya needs.

She thrusts both hands in an uppercut motion to blast a wall of water at the Ripper. I bolt around the pool to tackle her in the confusion and reach The Ripper's position just as the wave splashes onto the ground. But she is nowhere in sight. Only Ko Skadia's hammer remains standing on its head, handle up.

Nya stands at the bottom of an empty spring, ankle deep in water. She looks up at me with worried eyes, but her concern is mixed with something else. Exhaustion.

Her wet wings fail to lift her from the pit floor, so I lower a tree branch to pull her out. Her feet slip on the wet rock face and arms shake in her struggle to maintain their grip. She climbs over top and wobbles in her stance, so I grab her shoulders to steady her.

"You need a trip to Lex's underground gardens," I say. "Those lights will fix you right up."

Nya eyes up the hammer nearby. "How'd she know where to find me?"

I have a better question. "How did you forget to tell me she's your grandmother?"

"Why does it matter?"

She's deceiving you.

"What else are you hiding from me?"

"Nothing."

"What did you do when Lex sent you to scout the border?"

"I scouted the border. That's all."

"Liar! Tell me the truth. You went to see Regulus, didn't you."

Nya frowns and steps back. "Deka, what's gotten into you?"

A fire of black flame consumes my heart. "I've had enough of your lies and deceit. You're always up to something, aren't you. Why can't you ever be honest with me?"

"I am."

"Lies! Lies! All lies!"

The ferocity of my tone stops me. Nya has a point—something *has* gotten into me. I hardly recognize my own voice.

I look to Nya to apologize, but she gasps long and hard as her eyes flare wide with fright. Something about my appearance has her so startled that she claps a hand over her mouth in horror.

I turn to the pool to look upon my reflection in the shallow water, and the image staring back at me almost drops me dead. The face is my own, but the yellow reptilian eyes—each with a vertical slit—are those of a Watcher. And that voice inside my head...

Suddenly I recognize it.

I turn to Nya as her four white knuckles connect with my face. It's the last thing I remember of our brief romantic getaway.

CHAPTER 8
NYA

S venia's hooves thunder over the frosted ground. She weaves around trees without slowing, bearing Deka and me perilously close to trunks and branches. I don't like this horse-riding business one bit, but I have no choice.

Deka groans. Blindfolded and bent over Svenia's back before me, he remains oblivious to our harrowed flight.

I sink low over him to narrowly avoid a branch. When we break into the open, I breathe a sigh of relief as Svenia rides like the breeze toward Lex's camp.

A horn blows to announce our approach. The Wolf's lookouts in the hills do nothing other than watch me ride by. As I crest a ridge overlooking the river, a rabble of warriors scramble into neat lines before their camp to greet me.

"Shields!" yells the Wolf from out in front.

A row of white stars over black backgrounds lock before the front rank, several hundred across, covering each forward warrior from knee to chest. A second row drops on top, overlapping the bottom row, protecting from chest to head. Then rises a third row overhead, forming a half shell. The same happens in reverse order behind, from top to bottom, as the rear ranks complete the dome.

Lex stands alone in front, feet shoulder-width apart and the Arcturus standard in one hand, the other hand planted on her hip.

I dismount and lead Svenia by her reigns down a goat trail to meet with the Wolf.

Lex's gashed face twists with revolt at our brazen return. "You must have a death wish coming back here."

"Deka's had an accident," I say. *He's been compromised,* is what I should be telling her. How long has that Watcher possessed him? Did she see everything we've been up to? Was she there through all of our intimate moments?

My belly twists into knots. I'm so sickened I could retch.

"Deka's about to have more than a bad accident," Lex says. "All three of you, actually, in about three seconds."

Svenia doesn't understand human words, but she senses the vibe of hostility toward us. I can tell she wants to go trample that shield dome in a rampage of stomping hooves, so I stroke her neck to calm her.

"There's a dangerous enemy about," I say, the memory of the Ripper still rattling me. "I need to leave Deka with you while I go deal with her."

Lex smirks. "Oh, sure, just hand him over. I'll show him the greatest of care."

I leap away from Svenia and land behind Lex. She whirls about to face me, but I sidestep around toward Svenia, bringing Lex in a full circle back to me. Her nostrils flare in anger.

"If something happens to Deka," I say, my hands throbbing with anger, "I'll rip the face right off you."

Lex grips her standard with both hands. I flick it with a finger and turn the pole to dust, releasing its long purple banner to the wind. The fright in Lex's eye is priceless.

"Don't try me," I say, and I see I've earned her respect. "Hunker down here until I return."

"You're certainly audacious, I'll give you that. Right now I have one hundred crossbows aimed at your heart, yet you presume to belittle me with orders and threats."

Behind her, between evenly-spaced gaps in the shield wall, small glints of pointed steel back her claim.

I swallow hard. They'd certainly put a swift end to me.

"I'm your only chance against The Ripper," I say. Then I grab Ko Skadia's hammer from a lash strapped to Svenia's back.

My weapon draws whispers from behind the shield wall. The dome cracks and loosens in a few places, then crumbles as warriors jostle for a better view. I'll admit it's a beautiful design, but I sense there's something more behind their wonder. From all the whisperings arises a common word: *Mjölnir*. Even Lex cannot deny its splendor, her mesmerized eye appraising the handle's marvelous design—yellow gold interwoven through platinum white.

She shakes her head, as if breaking from a trance. "We weathered the last attack with only a few scratches."

I scoff. *Yeah, a couple of cowards doing a flyby is some attack.* "You'll not be so lucky against The Ripper."

"You'd do well to not underestimate me."

I squeeze my hammer handle. "You'd do well to—"

A nearby horn cuts me off.

"Enemy scout!" shouts a man. "Four o'clock!"

I'm unsure where four o'clock is until Lex spins and locks

her stare upslope, to a cliff where a silhouette shifts uneasily from the sudden attention.

A flurry of arrows arch up from the shield dome. The highest smacks the stone cliff face twenty feet below the observer.

She dives from her perch and swoops over the camp. Green aurora light outlines her four wings, and the lime glow over silver hair leaves little to my imagination as to the identity of our spy.

My heart thunders inside my chest as I survey the tent city so close to the river. "Get your people to high ground," I tell Lex. "*Now!*"

Lex frowns at me. "What—"

"Ripper!"

Lex spreads her arms and takes a few steps back, as if in invitation. Her one eye flares wide with urgency when she says, "Well then, Nya, go after her."

I find myself instinctively stepping backward. *Go after ... The Ripper?* I was just trying to get Lex to hold ground here to buy Regulus some time. I'd have to be mad to actually give chase to the mightiest Entropath to have ever lived.

Lex sneers at me. "If I had wings like yours, I'd rule the world."

Thunder rumbles from the south, upriver. The shaking earth, however, warns that it's no weather phenomenon.

"Get to high ground!" I shout. Then I spring sideways into flight, Svenia's reins in hand to guide her uphill.

A few of Lex's warriors heed my warning and scramble up along with us, but most join their commander in staring curiously upriver, where white fog emerges from the southern darkness. It approaches swiftly and thickens as it rolls downriver at frightening speed. But this is unlike any fog I've ever heard before, and *heard is* the correct word for it, because this white wall rushes toward us with a thunderous roar.

Everyone now scrambles uphill to escape the torrent crashing down the valley. The flood scrapes distant slopes, bringing trees and boulders and who-knows-what-else with it. No doubt we'll find chunks of Lex's dam in the mix as well.

The flood sweeps Lex's camp away in a blink, along with a hundred stragglers who'd not made it to high enough ground in time.

The torrent swells and rises to fill both sides of the valley with brown water. Its width spans the range of a hundred crossbow bolts and surges up the slope toward us, so close that cold mist sprays my face and whips back my hair.

Lex jumps back to avoid a branch from a passing tree. I shake my head as she scrambles up to join us.

She watches the mighty deluge in shock. Truly, she cannot hide it. Her bottom lip quivers and her one eye blinks in disbelief.

"See what we're dealing with?" I shout into the deafening rush.

"She is only one," Lex mutters. Her words would be too low to hear at the best of times, but I read her lips well enough. She meets my stare.

"You see me now?" I say. "You know I'm real. You've seen the Ripper is real, too. Look at what she just did. She's just playing around here. When she decides to get serious..." I give her an ominous shake of my head.

The gushing water is enough to split this continent into another two halves. Lex watches the great deluge and nods her head in acceptance. After some time, when the river has tamed enough for me to hear her, she shifts her attention fully to me.

"When you scouted the border, did you come across a gate over the river?"

She's testing me, to see if I actually checked. "Yes. A stone bridge with steel bars underneath."

"And?"

"Two towers with cone roofs overlooking each side."

Lex offers me a satisfied nod. "I need you to make sure those defenses are gone."

"You'll enter Polaria by boat?"

"The Artery empties into the sea near Mount Tuck. It's the fastest way to get there."

Lex's words tug on my heartstrings. But I am wary.

"Do you even have boats?"

"We have riverboats a plenty."

Of course. Somehow I'd forgotten about the dragon ships near Lex's fort. They sat high up the bank, almost on display, which might have saved them from the exploding dam.

"Raiding parties used them to slip into Polaria many years ago," Lex says. "When the Defense Force caught on, they started watching the river. If we cross the border by boat now, Regulus will assume we're invading."

"Not if I tell him otherwise. Only, how do I know that's not what you're doing?"

Lex folds her arms and raises her chin. "You don't. But I'm sending Deka downriver in the first boat. Black flag or white, that fort will chew us to pieces. Unless you want to see him ground down to fish food, I suggest you do as I ask."

My belly twists into knots. This wolf always goes straight

for the heart. At least she's made it an easy decision by offering me no other choice. And whatever Lex's intentions, at least she's moving in the right direction. Plus, she has something I need.

"I must pay a visit to your underground farm first."

Lex responds with a sardonic laugh. "You can go live there for all I care. It won't do you much good."

My cheeks burn red hot. I grit my teeth and say, "Why not?"

"What do you think the dam was for? It powered the lights."

This hits me like a punch to the gut, but I don't let it get me down for long. The Ripper just struck close to home for Lex, hopefully close enough to convince her of the threat and show her our true enemy. She does seem to have had a change of heart. Evidence of this comes in her choice of words a few moments ago. She'd said she was *asking* me to scout the river gate, not ordering. Such language sounds unnatural coming from the Wolf's tongue, yet her tone seemed sincere enough. Perhaps the Ripper's stunt has put the fear of their almighty Mother in her.

Lex gives me a solemn nod, not a slightest hint of mischief in her eye. "I'll do my best to keep Deka safe."

"Just watch yourself around him," I warn. "Assume anything he sees, the Watchers see."

"That explains the blindfold. And whatever he hears..."

"We can use to our advantage." If the Wolf's cunning had duped me into trying to assassinate the good King Regulus, I believe she'll find a creative means to exploit Deka's condition.

"Okay, Nya. I'll play your game."

"How quickly can you make it to Mount Tuck?"

"In a matter of days. A week at most."

"Good." As an added bonus, Lex's activities should keep Jexa's attention away from Mount Tuck.

She gives my shoulder a squeeze. "Shine bright, Evening Star. And good luck."

I turn and kiss Deka on the forehead above his blindfold, then I spring into flight.

CHAPTER 9

NYA

I don't trust that Wolf for a single second. But what choice do I have? I tried wishing her away, keeping her at bay, and slipping away, all with disastrous results. She's a player in this game whether I like it or not. That's why I must be quick about my task, so I can return to keep an eye on her.

Gusty air currents work against me no matter how high or low I try. It takes considerable effort to make any sort of headway. If I had to contend with this even for a small stretch of my journey from Africa, I'd be a corpse at the bottom of the ocean right now. At this point, even a gentle headwind would be most welcome, because ole *Mjölnir* here is becoming quite the burden.

I reach what remains of the river gate in pitiful time. On my first pass there'd been two cylindrical towers with a stone archway connecting them. Logs and tree branches would hit the gate and emerge as pulp on the other side. There's no trace of them here now, but a steel communication tower on a mountain above the flood line to my left assures me this is the spot. The timber that floats beneath me now will reach Mount Tuck before long.

As I carry on downriver, a cold hand squeezes my heart. Every beat that takes me away from Deka fills me with enough despair to drag me lower. We were so close to leaving together. He was all in with me! And yet...

I'd have found no peace on the run with him. Even in the depths of the deepest far-off cavern, Jexa would have found me and murdered me in my sleep with my sweet Deka's hands. Well, I'd thought he was sweet until an hour ago. He's been bewitched, and I suspect only those impure of heart can be possessed in such a way. Which means he's corrupt to his core. Not like Regulus. Jexa had to infiltrate him through his adviser.

It all makes sense now, why Deka and Lex have such an affinity toward each other. They're both rotten to their core, their hearts consumed by shadow. Sheffa had warned me about humans back on the beach in our sanctuary, when Marlok pursued Ko Skadia and Huxley made advances on me. They're masters of showing you what you want to see, disguising their lustful intentions with lies and kind gestures. In that, they are no better than the Watchers.

My heavy heart drags me toward the rushing flood. Or maybe it's fatigue. All this travel is so tiring, and running on adrenaline isn't sustainable. With each second my hammer becomes ever more the burden. If I don't find an energy source soon, there's a good chance some lucky farmer will find himself a fancy treasure in his field come Spring. He'll discover it next to my frozen corpse. Unfortunately for him, I still have one thing I can turn to.

I think of Lex, how she murdered Sheffa to deceive us, then turned Deka against me.

Anger simmers my blood enough to elevate me back up to my cruising altitude.

When my flight starts to drop again, my muse becomes Drusilla, who ruined my bliss in the thermal pool with Deka. We'd still be there if not for her. She'd gone there to issue me a challenge. *How dare she!*

My wings buzz so fast they shoot me up higher than before. In my fury I rise... rise... rise...

A bad idea.

From this high altitude, Amyria's lights are a mere flicker in the lowland fog. Mount Tuck is about the same distance to my right, and the vastness between us crushes what spirit I have left.

I now wish I'd asked Lex for some alone time with Little Boy before rushing off on my mission. I'd gone in search of the nuke when scouting the border, desperate for an energy boost. I'd also hoped to ground the balloon before it reached Amyria, but Lex had moved it to a wagon in the supply caravan, probably back at her fortress when Deka and I went to the quartermaster to get his uniform. I guess she'd had second thoughts about bombing the capital when her rage over my failure to kill Regulus had settled.

In a stroke of luck, assistance offers itself here in a different form.

A look over my shoulder reveals a silver snake slipping through the hills to my left. I'd noticed similar machines shuttle soldiers away from the border a few days ago.

I bank left and swoop down to intercept the railed

transport. Hard gusts blow me back and off my course, so I must use precious energy to correct myself. Still, the train slips away.

I call upon dark memories to surface, and in my mind I confront what Deka had done to me back at Lex's fortress. How he'd lied to get away from me so he could swear himself to Lex. The image of him kneeling to take her blood oath gets me huffing steam.

Dark energy pumps from my chest, infusing my wings and driving them to unnatural speed. My jaw clenches so tight I crack a molar.

When I land on the train and cling to its metal roof, it takes godlike restraint to keep myself from punching through its smooth steel.

Relax, I tell myself. *Release this anger, or it will consume you.*

Relaxing is easy enough, but the letting go will take some time.

The train slides overland with impressive speed, but the wind whipping back my hair is little bother after what I'd endured in the upper air currents. And funny enough, sitting cross-legged on this rear section grants me a farther view than from up high. Here I can see all the way to Mount Tuck! I also see the blur of Amyria's light had come not from fog, but from my teary-eyed vision. But it's the lights of Mount Tuck that now command my attention.

The flickering dots strung all the way up the dark mountainside burn away the shadows shrouding my heart. They're really there, the king's warriors, preparing to fight the Watchers.

I smile and break into relieved laughter. In the great King Regulus, we have found our champion. Under his banner, we will orchestrate our victory over the Watchers. I can only hope Alexandra will step up and do her part as well, or at least stay out of our way while we smash Jexa's army.

CHAPTER 10
DEKA

I wake with a splitting headache and my hands in chains.

From the elevated bank of a surging river, I watch the approach of at least two dozen wooden war ships. If not for the distinct violet coats of Lex's warriors lining the riverbank, I'd assume I've slipped into an old Norse saga. What river is this?

The same one you left.

I smack my head. "Shut up, you!"

You shouldn't be so hard on yourself, responds the seductive voice inside my head. She no longer disguises it as my own. It's soft and gentle, yet no more soothing than a serpent's slither.

I squirm. My skin crawls knowing what's inside me. Nya should have killed me. Instead, she turned me over to imprisonment. She left me. Again. *She left me. Again!*

I pull on my manacles. *How could she?*

She doesn't respect you.

'You're not welcome here.'

Hey now... Who saved you from that meat grinder on the

river? Or from taking a spear to the back in Lex's tent? How many times have I guided your hands in your most dire moments? I've been quite busy keeping you alive. Show a little gratitude. You'd be feeding fish right now if not for me.

"Why would you help me?"

So we can be friends. I've longed for a companion like you.

A cold wind forces me into a huddle. At least Nya had the decency to leave me with my cloak. I do my best to pull the bear fur around me.

Lex marches upriver behind the line, toward the fleet's approach. Two crossed swords hang on a harness from her back, their handles sticking diagonally over her shoulders. It had been my father's dream to get his hands on a katana—the sword of the samurai—and he would have sold me for a chance just to hold one.

I stand and wobble on my feet. "Lex!"

She marches on by without breaking step.

"You need something?" says Karla. She stands watch over me with her brother.

"I need to talk to Lex."

"Oh, yeah, she did leave you a message," says Karl. "Didn't she?"

"She did," Karla says, then she nods for her brother to backhand me.

It's a pitiful hit, but I feign pain by coughing and spitting. I wait a minute before speaking again. "What waterway is this?"

"The Artery," says Karl. "Next answer will cost you a couple of teeth."

"It's the sound of his voice, isn't it," says Karla.

"Yeah. Can't stand it."

"We should slap him with a talking tax."

"Talking tax, yeah. I love it."

"Every word will cost you a tooth. Hear?"

I frown and survey the river. There's no way this is the Artery, unless I'm hallucinating. Or perhaps we've traveled onward to a point where the Artery joined with another river. Though, that doesn't explain the familiar arrangement of mountain peaks surrounding us. And where is the baggage train? The supply wagons are nowhere in sight. Perhaps she'd loaded them onto the approaching ships.

I spot something nearby that doesn't belong.

A pile of spears lies next to a mound of shields under heavy guard. As my vision sharpens, I notice a heap of coats between them.

My gut wrenches. Was that the price to rescue Nya and Sekarra? Aside from those burned up with the tent, it seems a hundred more had met their end between then and now. Did Tora become unhinged and break into a murderous rampage? Perhaps her bats carry lethal toxins or had spread a rampant fever.

I shift my gaze to avoid drawing attention to the memorial of what I'd done.

The remainder of Lex's army watches the fleet approach from the river's edge. It's an impressive sight, each vessel a true work of art. Their curved bowsprits stand high to mirror the raised sterns at their back, and their long wooden hulls could comfortably hold two dozen warriors with enough provisions for a month-long journey. Suddenly my scattered memory reminds me I'd seen them overlooking the river near Lex's fort.

Oars work from the flanks like crawling centipede legs,

clawing against the wild current to cross over to this side of the river. Their keels are sturdy and built for ramming, as seen when they swing their course head on with the riverbank without slowing. The first of the fifty-odd boats grinds up onto the bank to the sound of applause. The others follow one at a time, landing to our right, on the upriver side.

Thousands of spear shafts bang on shields from the riverbank. My heart beats to their rhythm in anticipation.

Varnished wood crunches over rocks as more boats slide to a stop.

"Minimum fifty per ship," orders Lex. "No more than sixty."

She dispatches a rider toward Raven's coalition, probably to inform her of our new crossing time. If any Polarian soldiers remain at the border, the approach of twenty thousand riders will provide a nice distraction for us on the river.

Karl and Karla haul me down to the first dragon boat. The rowers stand and stretch their arms, shaking out their hands.

"You did us a favor," Karla says, smirking at the oarsman. "Trimmed the fat with that stunt of yours. We have no room for cravens in our ranks."

I recognize some of the faces on board, a sullen bunch, but they no longer wear their coveted long coats.

I look back to the heap near the piles of discarded shields and spears. Then I recall about as many had fled the fire that threatened to detonate Lex's bomb.

By the taunts hurled from shore, I gather Argyle had ceremoniously stripped the cowards of their coats and taken their weapons. Then Lex sent them packing.

"Why the long faces?" says Centurion Lantz, who'd shown steadfast bravery moving the bomb from the blaze, to the disgraced oarsmen. "You should be happy to still have your heads."

Nods and shouts of agreement from the riverside tell me the sentiment is shared wide.

I breathe easier in their presence, for their cowardice tempers the disdain against me and my actions. And it all comes from a misunderstanding. What they don't know is that a warhead like that could bathe in fire and it would never blow. Either a timer needs to be armed, or a detonator must be triggered. And Lex carries the only detonator around her neck at all times.

Fortunately for all, they'd not wandered far after their dismissal. So when the dam broke, which is apparently what happened, Lex's riders had an easy time rounding them up to retrieve the boats. I'm guessing a promise of redemption is what persuaded them.

Karl and Karla escort me to Lex at the first boat.

"It's unfortunate about the chains," she says, sizing up the mast rigging, "but you burned twenty of my warriors to death."

"Then why am I still alive?" I say, and I choke on my words, knowing full well I'll dislike the answer.

Lex's expression darkens. Then she forces a smile and says, "I've found a new purpose for you, Deka." She turns square with me and grabs my shoulders. "One of great importance." To my guards, she says, "Put him on the first boat."

Cold sweat slicks my brow as the memory of the river

gate grinder springs to mind. I grab Lex's wrist with my chained hands. "How far upriver are we?"

Lex jerks her arm free and gives me a look of caution. "If it's the wood chipper you so fear, it's probably gone."

"Probably?"

"The first boat will find out for certain."

My heart slams against my ribs. "So that's my purpose."

"Don't worry, Deka, I'd not ask my followers to do something I've not done first. I'll be right there beside you."

Her mouth twitches with a smile. Then she wades out into waist-deep water and climbs a net hanging from her flagship's starboard side.

I get shoved along by her fifty honor guard in their rush to join her climb up the rope. They spill over onto the open deck, then hang their shields over the side to preserve precious space within.

As I assess the wooden frame, I find cause for concern. My journeys on the Mediterranean had been in plastic vessels crafted from scavenged sea junk. It's my understanding that wood has a much shorter longevity and rots without dutiful care.

"When was the last time these boats traveled the river?" I ask.

Lex slides her banner from its pole and hooks it to a rope, then hoists it up the mast pole. The purple flag darkens to a black streamer against the night sky.

"I won't lie, Deka, this will be a perilous journey. The river can be merciless at the best of times, but in the midst of night and with this current... well, we shall face many challenges on this watery road. But rest assured, this is our surest way to defeat Regulus without dropping the bomb."

I won't argue with that. "Where's Nya?"

"It seems she tired of your company. My scouts spotted her flying north into Polaria. Lucky for you, your noble steed remembered how to find us."

My belly clenches at our last memory together. Of course she'd get as far away from me as possible. I squirm in my own skin, wishing I could rip myself from this body. Instead, I puke onto the deck.

"Do that over the side," shouts the helmsman from the tiller.

"No manners," adds Karl. He jerks me along by my chain to a stern bench on the starboard side, next to where the boat master leans against the tiller. "Here. A seat worthy of a prince."

He leaves me with the helmsman and goes about helping rig the lines.

At midship, Lex's warriors swing a hoist arm over the port side. Pulleys wail as all fifty fighters haul *Little Boy* aboard. The boat lists hard to port during the lift, then squats when the bomb swings to center. They pry up the deck planks and lower it down upon a steel cradle inside the hold. The boat master directs them to shimmy *Little Boy* aft, toward us, to better balance the boat. My sailing master from home called this *trimming*.

They load a few more items below and then replace the centerboards to cover the hole. While everyone hurries about, I distract myself by admiring the woodwork. Intricate carvings tell stories of encounters with sea dragons and terrors of ages past. I rub a hand along the starboard rail, admiring its smooth finish. Someone must have devoted a lot of effort to its care.

"You're the oathbreaker," says the helmsman nearby. Or helms*woman*, I should say. She looks like she's been at sea her entire life — her weathered face blistered from radiation, and sun-bleached locs halfway down her back. Her violet coat is too small to button, revealing a sweat-stained tunic underneath. Her coat likely came from a cowardly warrior who'd fled from the fire. Lex affords no room for the gutless on her ship, so she sends them down to board whatever dragon boat will take them. Every inch of the flagship is reserved for a warrior. Or those with special purpose.

"Trust me, oathbreaker, it's a kind name for ya," assures the helmswoman. "You'll hear a lot worse from this lot."

I ignore her and slide my finger through the recesses of a curled dragon claw carved into the wooden gunwale.

"These boats is old," she says, "but they'll get us where we need to be. Wood ages better in fresh water, y'know."

Lex jumps up onto the prow to inspect the other boats' readiness down the line. "We're all set. Jorda, take us to Polaria."

"Port side - push off!"

The rowers to my right shove their oars against the ground to push us clear of the bank. The hull rumbles and shudders as we scrape our way out into deeper water. Once our keel slips free of the shore, the current sweeps us along. The rush tries to spin us side-on, but boatmaster Jorda orders the port side to row backwards while we push our oars forward. Both sides rowing in opposite directions manages to set us straight.

More boats slide from the bank to challenge the current behind us. My rear-facing position at the back of Lex's boat gives me a front row seat to the calamity taking shape beyond our stern.

Two boats spin into each other from the launch. One is unevenly loaded and immediately capsizes from the collision. The wails of drowning men and women sends a shiver through me, because there's nothing we can do. Those coming up behind them struggle to keep their own boats upright, each crew desperately working their oars to center their bow downstream. If not for the vast width of the waterway, this would be a crippling disaster. Here we have room for mistakes. But this is only the beginning.

The front of my boat drops and throws me back as the wooden tail of our stern reaches for the sky. I hook my legs under the bench to keep myself from flying backward. Freezing water sprays the back of my head as our dragonhead prow carves through vicious rapids, making the downward slide seem extra long before we level out.

"Starboard - row!" shouts Jorda from the tiller.

I pull with all my might and watch our tail swing leftward. We straighten out just as the next two boats crest the rapids. The first takes it well enough, but the boat behind slides over broadside. The rapids swallow the crew in three gulps. Any who may have survived are plowed over by the fleet of wooden hulls that follow.

"Port side - pull!"

The opposing oarsmen to my right row for about a minute to bring us around a bend. Before losing sight of the rapids, I witness two more crews dumped from their dragons. Lex doesn't notice. She has an eye only for ahead, her foot up on the prow and her right arm wrapped around the carved dragon neck of her flagship.

"Starboard - row!"

It's like this for an insufferably long time. We're tireless in our efforts to keep straight and center, bracing occasionally for the terrible rapids, after which we row more to keep facing forward. With the strong current pushing us, our rudder offers little help. Jorda's voice commanding our oars does all the work to keep us alive.

"Starboard - pull! Port side - push!"

Lex chose her boat master well. She's swift with her orders, and eager to give the rowers a taste of her whip if they falter, which is rarely necessary, because Lex had chosen her crew well too. None are the craven who'd fled the fire. Our boat sets the pace and shows the others how it's done.

Somehow I manage to avoid a smack from Jorda all the way to the border. A few of Lex's warriors have become well acquainted with the sting, much to my surprise and their disdain. I actually don't mind rowing. It keeps me warm, so I'm always ready for the next order to push or pull.

Soon we pass a familiar sight, one that almost lends credibility to the claim of this being The Artery.

The radio tower protruding from a high hilltop off our port side resembles the same one that had stood over the river gate I'd taken refuge in not long ago. Yet the tower fortifications are nowhere in sight.

I stand from my bench to survey the banks.

"I blew the dam," Lex tells me. She stands on the center plank to my right.

I stare at her in disbelief. That feat of engineering had been her pride and joy.

"To get where we need to be," she says, "we must make great sacrifices."

No one speaks a word as we cross from Ortaria into Polaria.

In this silence, an odd sensation stirs deep inside me. With the river wind blowing on my face, not even the chains around my wrists can restrain the smile tugging at the corner of my mouth. There's little in this world that can rival a good sea adventure.

Lex returns to the bow and faces her crew with her sword raised high. "Next stop: Amyria!"

From her fifty warriors comes fifty raised fists, along with a unified, *"Hoo-rah!"*

CHAPTER II
DEKA

Monuments to nature's violence welcome us into Polaria. They stand high among mountain peaks, carved into gray cliffs since the days of the colossal melt that relieved this continent of its ice crown. The floods dredged gorges into canyons, meadows to valleys, and cut slopes in half in their savage descent toward the sea. I note where icebergs had cut gashes across mountain-sides, sculpted lesser peaks into lopsided cones, and wore down the range of rock teeth that have kept both Anterran nations separated for four hundred years. Ice tracks tell stories of power only nature can produce. And through it all now cruises its most violent rival: a Little Boy and his scorned mother, off to wreak havoc in the name of justice.

The high peaks that dominated my surroundings for weeks shrink over our wooden dragon tail as mountains flatten to slopes. Jorda shouts the occasional paddle order to keep us off the rocks, however, the more torrents we slide down, the lesser the current we find awaiting us at the bottom, and the more I notice her steer with the tiller as the easing current offers her more control.

As the danger wanes, threats of a different kind rise in the mutters of Lex's warriors. They taunt me whenever she leaves earshot.

"*Traitor*," they call me.

"*Murderer.*"

"*Murderous traitor.*"

"You'll get yours," threatens Karla in my ear. She and her brother occupy the bench behind me, ever on watch.

"Yes," says Karl, "all will be made well at the Tree of Life."

"*Yggdrasil*," says Karla in a tone that sounds as if she's correcting him.

I sense everyone behind me shift excitedly. Their whispers reveal many see Lex's cause for a pilgrimage. Yet their armaments speak more of a crusade.

"*Yggdrasil*," they say.

"You'll hang from its branches," says another girl from farther back.

"For nine whole days," adds her male partner.

"Only *then* shall your soul be redeemed," says Karla.

I row harder, desperate to suppress a shiver. Though, excitement stirs deep within me as an unwelcome presence reveals itself.

'You hijacked me during the gate jump, back in Giza, didn't you.'

You made it too easy.

I squirm, recalling the urge to kill Hadria, but not to turn myself in to the nearest Watcher patrol. The intruder in my mind hoped I'd lead her to the caverns of my home. She'd have used me to finish off the last of my people.

I admire your creativity, trying to figure out what was happening to you. "The pyramid as the planet's memory bank..." It's a clever idea, I'll give you that.

I search the sky in all directions for signs of Nya. For a flicker of light to give me hope in this darkness. But my heart knows she is nowhere near. She abandoned me. Again.

'I'm glad you're here,' I tell the intruder in my mind. 'Through my eyes you shall witness your defeat.'

These eyes shall witness much defeat, you are right.

"Raise the colors," orders Lex.

Jorda whistles sharply through her metal teeth. Behind us, crews race to raise their purple Arcturus banners. Lex stands on the bench to my right, smiling at the forty-four purple pennants waving high from their mast poles.

"Pull in your shields," she says.

Warriors exchange puzzled looks as they unhook their protection from the outer rails.

"Wouldn't want to give the wrong impression," Lex tells Jorda. "Most of our supplies got swept away in the flood. We need to stop at the first settlement to replenish our food. I'll reward them well, show them we're friendly. Word will spread."

Her warriors set their shields inside, out of sight, then stand up onto the centerboard to stretch their legs. They gather at the front of the ship, some seeing their homeland for the first time in over a decade.

"Are you going to kill me?" I ask Lex.

She narrows her eye on the river ahead. "Many will find death upon this path."

"What about *Eeeeg... Eeeeg-d...*" I struggle to recall the name.

Lex tenses. *"Yggdrasil."*

The way she shoots a glare at her warriors, as if they've let out a vile secret, is cause for concern.

A lump swells in my throat. "Is that my purpose? A sacrifice?"

Lex grips her sword hilt and lifts her chin. "I'm giving you a chance to atone for your felonies. You drank from my well, and then you deceived me. You must be cleansed. It's for your own good. You'll hate me when the time comes, it's true. But in the end, when the ravens bring news of your passing to the All-Father, you shall rejoice with him in the halls of the slain. And, when *my* time comes, we shall be reunited in his company. Together we'll drink ale from curved horns until the end of time."

"You don't really believe in all that." I'd seen a book on Norse mythology open on a table in Lex's library, as well as her disdain for superstition. She indulges them in exchange for their loyalty.

"Careful, now. It would be a shame if you lost your tongue. You should be grateful for this chance to repent."

"Dress it up however you like, it's an execution."

She glares down at me, her lip curled in disgust. "And yet it's a better end than what you gave my warriors."

With that, she stomps forward toward the gaggle. "Back to your oars," she tells the others. "This isn't a sightseeing tour."

All fifty warriors return swiftly to their benches.

The clunk of Lex's boots pounding up and down the centerboard have become a steady, predictable rhythm. She paces constantly, fore and aft, aft then fore, over and over.

"Anything?" she asks the lookout. She does this at each bend in the river, and I start to feel bad for him. He peers through a brass spyglass in constant surveillance of either bank, removing it only to switch eyes. Lex nearly pounces on him whenever he clears his throat. If he doesn't report something soon, I suspect she will take her impatience out on him.

My pity doesn't last long. I'm cold and tired, starved and under constant threat from outside and within, and from further within from there. It's exhausting.

I lean against the bulkhead for a moment's rest. I'm starting to fade when the lookout finally speaks.

"Smoke spotted," he says. "Two points off the starboard bow."

Lex snatches his spyglass and leans so far forward she almost falls overboard. Something quickly catches her eye that sends her stepping back in awe. She collapses the eye piece and marches toward us with a bounce in her step. It's the first time I've seen her with a genuine smile.

"It's Owidaya," she says. "Should see salmon farms when we round that bend."

She checks her tunic buttons and fastens her collar, then smooths the wrinkles from her overcoat. When she looks down at me, I swear for a moment she's about to ask how she looks.

Bells chime in the distance.

Lex sprints forward and jumps onto the bow. She holds

the dragon head and hangs sideways in an effort to appear magnificent. The display reminds me of the parade floats in mother's books, only on water.

"Can you smell that?" she says. "They're preparing a feast of salmon for us. Their long-awaited liberators have finally come."

The bells ring louder, more excited as we near the riverbend. Jorda's row orders fade. As we round the corner, Lex is already waving to those on shore.

Cheers erupt from the town as red fireworks hurl up into the sky and explode. Their sizzling sparks fall over a hill, where a circular building of stone overlooks the river. Warriors dressed in camouflage sprint up toward the fort, six of them fumbling with firearms. Townsfolk scramble up an overgrown path with them and slip through a narrow opening in its base.

Another fireball streaks up high overhead, and I see now it's no celebratory gesture. That flare is a call to arms. And suddenly the frantic chiming of bells sounds more like an alarm.

Lex slumps down from the prow. She looks up at her banner to ensure it flies freely, and indeed it does.

Under the red light of falling distress flares, the silhouettes of a half-dozen shooters position themselves on the stone ramparts.

"Children and old folk," says Karla, squirming in her seat. "Easy pickings."

"Let's bag us a fortress," says Karl, shifting excitedly beside her.

"Maybe that creature was right," Jorda says, referring to Nya. "Might be that Regulus sent all his troops to Mount

Tuck. Half of them there look like retired militia, th'other half junior cadets. They'll take off runnin' if we land in force."

Lex storms toward us and jumps down to sit on the bench beside me. "Steady as she goes," she says, pulling on my oar as if she can't get away from this place fast enough. Her eye glistens with crimson light cast up off the water.

Jorda leans over and speaks under her breath. "Would be a mighty fine prize to steal."

"We didn't come here to conquer rat nests. We came for the crown jewels."

Yes, you've come to kill a king.

Our boat cruises past the town, where water flows high over the window sills of the shore-front buildings. Walls of green sandbags surround the upper dwellings, results of a desperate attempt to save whatever they could from the flood.

"Would be good to establish a foothold along the river," Jorda presses.

"Why?" snaps Lex. "We'll not be returning to this swamp of a town."

"I'm just thinkin'—"

"I'm not paying you to think. Keep us steady on our course, or I'll have you switch places with Deka here. The next time my feet touch land will be outside Amyria. Got it?"

Jorda gives her a grave look, then pulls on the tiller to swing us out to mid-river.

Pop... Pop-pop... Pop-pop-pop... If I hadn't experienced a gunfight before, I'd mistake the noise for a nearby avalanche or distant thunder. However, flashes of yellow light from the stone walls overlooking us confirm my assumption. So do the splinters exploding from Lex's mast.

Everyone on the starboard side raises their shields.

TING—the impact of lead striking steel rings loudly. *TING-TING... TING!*

I slide down as far as I can as bullets smack the wooden hull and ring off steel shields overhead.

"Row!" Lex shouts.

"Row-row-row!" echoes Jorda.

It's hard pulling an oar while trying to keep your head down. Our efforts under fire are uncoordinated and keep Jorda busy on the tiller. I'm expecting to feel the sting of her whip any second, which I'd take over a bullet to the face any day.

Then comes the sickening sound I've been dreading, of a bullet punching through flesh and bone.

I don't have to look far to see who ate it. Jorda lumbers forward, and the clink of her metal teeth hitting the deck is almost worse than the smack of the bullet's punch.

Lex stares in shock as blood blossoms through the white locs of her fallen boat master.

Ting! Ting-ting-ting! Ting-ting! The constant ring of steel and whiz of bullets block out the noise of splintering wood.

Lex springs up to take the tiller, swinging us away from land. She doesn't need to utter a word. Both sides row hard and steady to escape the range of their bullets. Instead, she leans onto the tiller, watching a stream of blood run across the centerboard from Jorda's head and onto Karl's lap.

I row hard enough for two as Lex watches muzzle flashes crackle steadily from the fort. The look in her eye is something I've never seen before. Not in any human, anyway. It's hurt and hate, confusion and dismay, all wrapped up in a terrifying hurricane inside one lonesome eye. This reception has wounded her deeply.

All I can do in this moment is row like my life depends on it, because indeed it does. But to what further perils are we approaching, not even our wise leader knows.

CHAPTER 12
NYA

I probably deserve a smack for this, but there's something to be said in praise of human ingenuity. Sure, their innovations destroyed this world and almost every living thing on it, but I can't knock them for that now. Not while I hitch a free ride across the vast planes of Polaria, making great haste toward Amyria with no effort required on my part.

Cold wind whips my face as I sit cross-legged on the curved steel roof, where I watch Amyria's golden glow rise higher and brighter over the horizon by the hour. I'll be in Regulus's company soon, and my heart races at the promise of our reunion.

My only concern arises during the occasional stop to load passengers. Regulus has called his county militias to arms, with many already at Mount Tuck, but word was slow to reach some settlements. Stragglers gather at what seem to be random pick-up points along the tracks. Normally I just have to lay low as they squeeze into the cars, until we happen across one particularly large group.

The gaggle of three hundred, huddled together for warmth on the windswept plain, rejoice at our arrival. Their cheers smother the squeal of the brakes as we slow to a stop. When the train doors slide open, they're met with resistance as they try to cram inside.

"We're all full!" shouts a man from within.

"Next car!" orders an officer from the unit outside.

The mob moves up the line.

"Full!"

It's the same story for the next three cars. The soldiers, desperate to escape the cold, make their way back down toward the back. Toward me.

I lie low on the roof as the mob grows frantic in their search for shelter. They shove against this last car so hard it rocks on its tracks.

A whistle blows from the front, warning the train is about to leave.

Shouts rise in panic.

"Onto the roof!" orders an officer.

My heart slams against my navel. He can't be serious!

Regulus's well-disciplined troops don't even question it. The clamber of hands and boots on steel warn of soldiers scaling the ladders on each end of my car.

I roll over the side as the first head of orange hair rises over the back.

Clinging to the undercarriage, I watch hundreds of black boots stampede toward the ladders of the forward cars. Although they'd not questioned their officer to his face, their mutters spare no reservations at their displeasure. They acquaint me with words I've not heard in this language before. Words I'd dare never repeat.

My arms shake in my struggle to hold onto the under-structure. The hammer resting on my chest and belly isn't helping. It weighs a ton. My wings wrap from behind to hold it in place, sealing tight over its handle and head.

The humans take forever boarding the roof. During this time, I sense an occasional glance cast underneath the train. There's concern about the tracks. *Sabotage* gets mentioned a few times. I'd not even thought of that, but if the Watchers wanted to remove a slew of enemy pieces from the battle board, they could do so easily with a busted rail. These humans are sharp. It seems the Watchers have met a worthy match in these southern folk, who are lords of war in their own right. Even the lowly-type who must ride on the tops of trains.

Failure to respond to a summons must incur a severe penalty, because three blasts from a whistle inspires manic shoving at the ladders. Feet bounce with urgency along the fringe. When a clink indicates the brakes releasing, a fight breaks out at the back.

A young lad gets tossed to the ground, where he spots me and points in fright. Fortunately, a boot to his face shuts his eyes for the moment.

Steel screeches as the train lurches forward. With our increasing speed comes a swell of relief in me, completely opposite to the human response. Those remaining alongside struggle to grab hold of a ladder. Five fall behind and give chase down the tracks, falling farther behind with each step.

I clamber upside down to the back and then over the rear lip, where I cling to the ladder. The stragglers down the tracks spot me and point me out. "Hey!"

Their alert is met with boos from above. I chuckle and

stick my tongue out at them, but we accelerate away too swiftly for me to see their reactions.

I hook one arm around a ladder rung and try to make myself comfortable on the ledge. It's funny how things work out sometimes. Sheltered from the wind, it's actually better back here. I could almost fall asleep until a retched noise gets me sitting on edge.

The fallout comes before I can look up—chunks of half-digested meat hurled over the back of the train, with a rogue drip spattering on my nose.

I gag and wipe it off, making more of a fuss than intended. When I look up, I see no sign of the motion-sick roof-rider, so I sit back with my arm hooped through the ladder.

In the silence, I notice all chatter has stopped. Aside from the clickety-clackety roll of the wheelset over the tracks, only the wind whispers secrets to me now.

"We know you're down there!" comes a man's voice. "If you knew where this train was headed, you'd jump off right now."

He thinks I'm a citizen in search of adventure or hitching a ride to the nearest town. I should take his advice. With the train's forward speed I'll be a shadow in seconds if I fly straight rearward, leaving their imaginations to guess at what I was.

Palms pad on steel overhead, and the sound of boots scuffing behind warn of someone crawling to investigate.

My heart races. Will he shoot me? Maybe he'd not even think I'm a citizen. He might take me for a spy without question.

I hug Ko Skadia's hammerhead over my heart. I don't think I can handle another bullet blasting through me.

I hear him sprawl out on his belly, his uniform brushing over the steel rooftop as he inches closer to the edge. Then comes the scrape of steel—a gun sliding across a metal roof.

Suddenly I realize how meek I must appear, cowering down here, clutching my only belonging as if afraid someone may steal it from me. This won't do. It's best I give these soldiers a taste of what they're in for.

I set my hammer aside and leap high over the roof, then zip ahead to the forward end of their car, where I land near the opposite ladder.

"It's okay!" I shout. "I'm a friend of King Regulus."

I hold up both hands to shield my face.

The only thing shot my way are stricken stares. Stunned silence grips the twenty-five soldiers huddled at center, a good many paralyzed from fright.

Yes, this was a wise move on my part. Better they acclimatize to the sight of me than a swarm of Watchers in a murder frenzy.

A young girl with black hair is kneeling by where I've landed. Her green shirt fits her like a parachute, blowing wildly in the wind, the wide sleeves flapping back from her thin arms like the patagium of a flying squirrel. She appears too frail to hold a weapon, let alone kill a Watcher.

She smiles at me, but it's a twitchy reflex of shock. Her eyes roll back as she slumps sideways and falls over the side.

"*Sasha!*" wails an elder woman.

I dive over after her.

Everything happens so fast, yet somehow I manage to

grab her and seize the rear ladder while keeping hold of her. The force nearly rips my arm from its socket, yet by some miracle I manage to hang on. I set Sasha on the ledge and collapse beside her.

Pain in my shoulder cripples me. I'm aware of a commotion above, of warriors making their way down to retrieve their comrade. They pull her to safety, and that's when the real miracle happens.

A green strap falls beside me, blowing like crazy in the wind. "Wrap that around you," says a man from above.

I obey, and they hoist me up onto the roof.

An elderly warrior coddles Sasha at center, stroking her hair. "There, there. Just breathe. You're all right."

Whispers from the others carry all sorts of speculation about me.

"From where do you hail, girl?" asks the elder warrior. Her gray hair tied back tight suggests she's the oldest of this group by far.

"You wouldn't know it," I say.

"Humor us," she presses, insisting on an answer.

I point straight up.

Everyone looks to the sky, where an infinite number of stars stretches toward eternity.

"Somewhere out there," I say.

The only human who doesn't look up is the elder. She gives me a deep look of appraisal, though her neutral expression conceals her impression of me.

A middle-aged boy braves an approach. "You hurt your shoulder? I'm a medic. I can help."

I'm suddenly aware I've been cradling my arm. He

reaches out to touch me but I recoil and almost fall overboard, so he backs off and raises his hands to calm me.

"So it's true," says a soldier. "We're being invaded by some supernatural enemy."

I shake my head. "Supernatural, no. This enemy is very real."

He gives me a confused look, like we have different understandings of the word 'supernatural'.

"Which one is yours?" says another soldier. He lies on his back and hasn't taken his eyes off the sky since I'd pointed upward.

"None. I'm from another galaxy, the same as our enemy."

This opens me up to a barrage of questions...

"What's your home planet called?"

"What's it like there?"

"Do they all fly like you?"

"I heard they're demons. Is that true? You know, demons. Spirits of the underworld?"

I'm reluctant to call the Watchers by what we know them: the Fae. I've seen how this branch of Deka's race views those entities. That tender image won't suffice. This army needs the fear of Darkness put in them to adequately prepare, so I hold nothing back.

"They're a swarm of genocidal maniacs. Killing off races is what they do, and they do it very well."

The faces before me blanch, even those with darker complexions.

"But fear not," I say. "Mount Tuck is their weak spot. Most of their abilities will be rendered useless there. Hold the high ground, and we'll defeat them, sure as the flowers will bloom come Spring."

Their dismayed faces tell me they've seen many a Spring without bloom. A few curl up onto their sides to block out any further words I may speak. I really need to brush up on my inspirational talk.

"You're not alone," I tell them. "Help is coming. Powerful allies are on their way, and together we'll smash the Watchers on the slopes of Mount Tuck."

"How old are you?" asks the medic, sizing me up with great curiosity.

"In Earth years? Four hundred and thirty-six, give or take."

His mouth gapes. Of all the news I just dropped on them, this seems hardest to grasp.

"You must have seen so much."

"I'm sure I have, but I've forgotten most of it. Only my time on Earth remains fresh in my mind, so... less than year."

We must have been traveling through a subtle valley, because, after a gentle rise, we crest a hill to see Amryia's glowing domes standing high between us and the horizon. I lose my audience as they shift their gazes around toward the city. Their awe-stricken faces tell me I've seen their capital more times than they have.

I sit in silence and let them savor the moment. To really instill in them what they're fighting for.

"May I?" The healer kneels before me, intent on fixing me up. I reluctantly release my arm and watch him take it in a firm yet gentle hold.

"On three," he says. "One—" *Pop!*

Only shock keeps me from screaming. I'd been expecting a tingly feeling to rise from my deep tissues to reverse my injury, so when he jerks my arm, the surprise cranks the air from my lungs. It takes every morsel of restraint to not fling him overboard. Instead, I allow him to lean me forward, where my lungs beg for air with shuddering inhalations. He remains at my side, a gentle hand between my wings as he coaches my breathing.

"That's it, you're okay."

I'm about to call him out for his lie when I realize he's right. Lifting my arm, I feel no pain at all. It's as if the injury never happened.

My heart beams with hope. Having skilled healers such as this boy in Regulus's army assures me of their capacity to sustain a prolonged clash against rivals.

A sharp bend in our trajectory tells me we're near my departure point.

I stand and spread my wings. "This is my stop. I'm off to see your King. I'll tell him of your loyalty, how each of you answered his call with great courage. Especially Sasha, the bravest Polarian of all."

Young Sasha curls timidly into her elder's side, but when I wink at her she cracks a smile.

My heart aches for them, each and every one. How cruel their fates must be to force them to huddle on the roof of a speeding train at midwinter. And yet it's only a mild introduction to the miseries to come. It'll be worse at Mount Tuck, where food will be scarce and hungry bellies abundant. Where full-time troops exploit the system like a criminal enterprise. They'll have to prepare for the Watchers while fighting to keep each other fed. To survive, this new group of fresh blood will require a respectable reputation.

"I have something for you," I tell them. "Wait here."

I slide down the rear ladder, to the ledge. From behind

the rungs I pull my hammer. In my trauma I'd hid it there to keep it safe from what could have turned out to be hostile hands. The last thing I'd expected was for them to treat my wound.

I set the hammer down in the middle of the group, in front of Sasha.

"This belonged to my elder. She could bring down entire mountains with a single swing of it. It's yours now. Tell the others that you caught me spying and killed me, then threw me from the train."

Sasha inches forward and strokes the handle in awe.

Truth is, that thing is too damn heavy. By off-loading it on them, I relieve myself of an anchor to have delivered to my ultimate destination. We'll deal with the awkwardness of me asking for it back when the time comes.

"It'll be waiting for you at the battle lines," says the gray-haired senior, "should you need it."

I give her a nod of appreciation.

A short distance before Amyria, where an elbow in The Artery twists the river toward Mount Tuck, the railway bends sharply to track the river to the sea. I use this sharp turn to slingshot myself from the train. An updraft from the river provides me a gentle boost, and soon I'm soaring toward Amyria's nearby domes.

A flutter ruffles my entire body at the promise of seeing Regulus so soon. I find myself wondering about where he sleeps, what his bedchamber looks like, if there's a bath in there...

I shake my head and smack my face. What's gotten into me? I'm like a... like a... A what?

I don't even want to know. It doesn't matter. I'm a

messenger now, an envoy on a mission to assure the mighty king of the movements down his central waterway. Together we'll watch Lex's fleet sail around the elbow toward Mount Tuck. In that moment, high up on his balcony atop his great tower, we'll witness the first of many victories together.

I smile, looking forward to the moment.

CHAPTER 13

NYA

My approach to Amyria differs greatly from the last time. Unlike then, when I'd come as a conniving assassin, I arrive now as a royal consul. An adviser to the King. A welcome emissary to his court. A...

I smack myself. *Not again, Nya!* How many smitten tirades is that now? If this is how I'm behaving on my journey to see him, I'll certainly have to watch myself in his presence.

His choice of lights tonight is a fine one. The white spotlights give his skyscraping spire a defiant appearance. His seat of power gleams like an enormous lighthouse, a beacon to all the militias coming in from the countryside, like those on the train I'd just left. I saw first-hand the wonders it worked on their spirit. I bet the Watchers hate it. They prefer their prey to cower in the shadow of their approach.

I avoid the stairs this time, instead flying straight to the pointed top. I land on his balcony and practically skip into his tremendous throne room. Whatever doubts I harbor about Lex's intentions, I can't let him see them.

There's no moonlight to illuminate his throne on this night, so I continue my trot, only to find his seat... empty.

Of course. He'd be mighty bored sitting there all day. He has better things to do.

Soft blue light glows behind the throne, defining its perfect silhouette. I walk behind to investigate its source and see it emanates from a tall doorway. The soft inviting glow lures me through, and each step down the passage is another step taken into a different world. Well, it's still this world, just to be clear. Only, it's in miniature form.

The model of Anterra that occupies most of the round gallery looks much like Lex's map, only three dimensional. The detail is exquisite. On the Polarian side it is, anyway. I can trace every bend in The Artery, see every town for its comparative size, and follow the railway that runs from the mountains toward Amyria before curving hard toward Mount Tuck, where it empties into the sea.

Across the border is a different story. Ortaria is full of shadows and blank spaces, chunks of wood not yet carved into mountains or valleys, streams or canyons. They placed Lex's dam true enough, and her stronghold, too, but everything else is a haze.

I make my way around the table, admiring this work of art, until an even more magnificent installment catches my eye.

The model of a pyramid mountain across the room sucks my breath away. It boasts strings of horizontal lights that wrap the slope in straight, evenly-spaced lines, each a different color, rising from its base to the apex in a rainbow pattern. A *rainbow mountain.* There are blue lines at the bottom, violet above those—which are slightly narrower due to the slanted slopes—then green in the middle, and orange above that, then a narrow red band below the peak.

A closer inspection reveals slices cut between each color. Trenches. Barbed strings zigzag across each colored zone, which I take for obstacles, and it's clear I'm looking at Mount Tuck's defense plan. And overlooking it all is the crown jewel, a fortified nest where the Capstone must sit to open the gate.

My wings instinctively flutter in sync with my heart. I can hardly contain myself. Regulus, that *rascal*... He's really gone all out! All because I told him to.

I blush.

A gasp draws my attention to my left, where a girl in a powder-blue service uniform stands with a cleaning brush in one hand, her other covering her mouth.

"So it's true," she says in awe, sizing me up, giving particular attention to my wings.

"Where's the King?" I say, and I cringe at the eagerness in my tone.

The girl points beside me, to the Rainbow Mountain.

This claim almost drives me to my knees. "He's there?"

"He went to lead the defense himself. Called the whole country to arms. Well, anyone who can fight, I mean. They're to rally at their county armories for orders."

I stare at the map model and shake my head in disbelief. The girl creeps closer.

"You're the only thing he's talked about all week," she says. "Aside from the battle plans, obviously. But you got mentioned more than a few times during those, too. That's what they tell me, anyway. Those who heard. They think he's gone mad. I wouldn't be surprised if his generals are plotting to overthrow him. So much talk about killer faeries and pixies... It all sounded like madness. But here you are."

The girl reaches out to touch me.

I smack her hand away. "Where does he sleep when he's here?"

She shakes her head, awareness returning to a dazed stare, as if she'd been enchanted by my presence. Instinctively, she looks over her shoulder to the door through which she'd come through.

I shove past her and walk toward it.

"It's a restricted area," she tells me. "Only servants and guests are allowed."

I stop. "Guests?"

The girl shrugs awkwardly. My cheeks and neck burn.

Beyond the door, a spiral stairway takes me down to a level below the strategy room. Red carpet runs the length of the circular corridor, with matching banners of satin strung at even intervals along the curved walls. Between each banner hangs a framed image. The first displays a parade in Amyria, with glass buildings surrounding endless ranks of troops. The next few depict soldiers on watch in bunkers and trenches. One is a close-up of a warrior's face peering over the sight of a machine gun, his face painted green and black.

As I walk the curved corridor, I notice a common thread in each image: Regulus. It doesn't matter if it's at the head of a parade through urban lanes, or hunched over a machine gun on watch at the border, he's there. Like in the photo of wounded warriors. Dozens of them rest in a muddy trench, with blood-soaked bandages wrapped around their heads and limbs. Regulus kneels in the background with a comforting hand on a wounded girl's shoulder. Bandages cover her eyes, and her pained smile suggests his presence is of supreme importance to her. That he's acknowledged her sacrifice is enough, but his touch would make her happy to do it all again.

Of course he'd accompany his troops to Mount Tuck. Those ornaments on his coat—the bits of metal dangling from ribbons, the braided ropes, the pins and patches—are more than just decorations. He earned each of them from kneeling in the mud with his servants, for standing watch at the border while they slept, and for comforting them when they were hurt or afraid.

My heart swells. Polaria is lucky to have him for their king.

Halfway around the curved corridor that rings the entire level, paintings give way to preserved memories of a different sort.

Statues sporting steel armor stand with stiff postures in the glow of red orbs at their feet. A few wear nothing at all. For some strange reason, their exposed anatomy makes me blush.

The only break in the inner wall is a doorway to his bedchamber. If not for its grand space and sheltered position at the spire center, I'd assume this to be his servants' quarters. The room boasts only a small mattress against the far wall, and a few stacks of books teetering near the foot of his bed. A pitiful rival to Lex's library.

I blame Lex for my disappointment. The guest rooms of her hideout boast mountain views from grand beds dressed in silk sheets, each with their own bath beneath a skylight. I expected Regulus to top those luxuries in ways I couldn't imagine.

I pick up a few books and flip through them. Their brittle pages tell me they are ages old, perhaps older than me—original copies to Lex's replicas. In this at least he has bested her.

Only a rare page shows a picture, so my interest quickly fades.

I lay on the great king's bed and stare at the ceiling. What sort of troubles kept him staring at those cracks in the concrete for hours on end? Was my arrival a relief to him? Could a friend not subject to his rule, nor that of his enemy's, bring a priceless comfort to him? Someone to share his heavy burdens, perhaps? An equal he can trust?

My jaw stretches wide into a yawn. I roll onto my side to face the wall and close my eyes, trying to imagine what it's like to be born a king. It feels... lonely. Isolated. Maybe it's what drives him to his outlands. Perhaps to have a suite of comfort waiting would be a distraction during the nights when he's watching over his border.

Despite my fatigue, restlessness taunts me. It's this room. How can anyone sleep in such a cold enclosed space with no sky? I don't get it. Why does the most powerful human alive choose to live this way? He could have the most magnificent bed in the whole world. Besides, that girl servant has been watching me since his strategy room. Even now she waits outside his door.

I return to the balcony at the far end of the throne room. It was here where Regulus and I had watched the fireworks together, back when we first formed our alliance. Much has changed in the city since then. The lanes below are empty, save for the last few companies responding to the summons. They cross open ground around the tower base between domes. Their banter, however, suggests they've defied orders by donning their uniforms. They'd been ordered to stay back. Unfit for service or something like that. They disagree with that assessment. The subject of their conversation is speculation around the sentence they'll be handed for disobeying. Could they be branded outlaws for unlawful service? Shot or hanged for their noble disobedience?

Their discord fades as they enter a dome.

Stillness sits heavy in the air, almost suffocating. This must be what the Watchers strive for when they arrive on a new planet. How many cities like this have they exterminated? Whatever the number, that's where it shall stay. Their intergalactic campaign of terror ends out there, on a rainbow mountain called Tuck.

A swishing noise invades the stillness. At first it's a whisper—a faint fizzing in the air. The more I focus on it, the louder it becomes, directed my way as if calling to me.

I dive from the balcony and swoop down through a hole in the nearest dome. Sure, it may be a Watcher lure, but it's a call I cannot resist. Something about it... I can't explain.

It's nighttime under this dome. The artificial skylights hang from the rafters in darkness, the only light emanating from lanes and pathways below—street lights casting just enough soft blue glow for citizens to navigate safely.

The dome amplifies the noise, which now sounds like rustling. It's so loud, almost everywhere, that I struggle to tell exactly where it's coming from. I hover in place and close my eyes until my intuition tugs me toward the center, to a smaller dome within this one. It's like a shrunken version of the city domes, except at its base, where no wall bars entry. It's wide open save for evenly-spaced supports.

I swoop under, and the sight within stops me mid-flight. Hovering in place, I sink slowly to the ground as I take in this wonder.

The beauty reminds me of the Heart Spire of Ko Mirah's Hive, the tree Jexa scorched to ash. Such trees are the best source of energy, so I flutter up to sit amongst its branches midway up.

I shudder. This is no Heart Spire. The energy radiating from within is different. Rather than uplifting and bright, it's dark and damning. A Heart Spire taps into a planet's core and spreads that energy for lifeforms to thrive. This tree draws only from the ground around her roots, soil nurtured by blood and sacrifice. A tree of survival.

I find a Y-branch and nestle in to sleep. It's as good a place as any, and with Regulus at Mount Tuck, I have no need to assure him of Lex's approach. But as my awareness of this world fades, those of the nether-realms slip into my mind. Images of twisted faces watch me, human eyes bulged out and swollen tongues sticking from their mouths as they sway from branches overhead. One looks too much like Deka.

I roll from my perch and glide out from under the dome. In a nearby park, I find better accommodation in a maple tree. She is young and innocent, has known only the singing of birds and the laughter of children. Her branches have not felt the harsh cry of a winter storm and never will. I'll have no trouble sleeping here, and once I'm rested up, I'll go dust that murder tree into a bad memory.

CHAPTER 14

DEKA

"We need food," says Karla. She squints at the boats behind us, interpreting their lookouts' hand signals.

"Amyria has plenty," Lex says from the tiller. "We'll be there in a day at this rate."

Karla shifts uneasily, her fingers twisting with reluctance to send Lex's response to the amphibious army behind us. She sees what I see. Boats drifting close together, their occupants exchanging whispers while sending impatient glares our way. The dam flood had swept away all of our food, a sloppy move on her part, an oversight I have a difficult time comprehending. Lex may soon have a mutiny born of hunger to deal with.

But Lex is no fool. She squeezes the tiller, deliberating.

"That should be Corpisaul up ahead," she says, nodding to a column of faint gray smoke rising from beyond a bend. "My father's hometown. Mostly First Class Citizens live there—politicians and diplomats. No fort sits this far downriver, so there'll be little resistance. They'll give us what we need, and we'll be on our way."

"Beg pardon, my lord," says a warrior from a port side bench, "but there's no more class system here, remember?"

Lex's eye twitches. The land around us is the same as she'd left it, but the Polaria she once called home is no more. She raises her chin and says, "Even better. The serfs will be more easily swayed by Freya's Tears."

Freya's Tears? I'm not sure I like the sound of that.

She nods to the deck at the bow. Two warriors flip up the boards, and four more join them to haul out a wooden chest. Karla flips open the lid to reveal a heap of gold coins. *Freya's Tears.* She scoops out a handful and starts counting them. "How much?"

"All of it."

Karla stops and gives Lex a questioning look.

To me it's obvious what she's doing. A generous trade will generate excitement. Word of Lex's charity will spread, opinions will shift, and loyalty to Regulus will waver.

"Tell the others to hang back," Lex says.

Karla signs the message with her hands. The masters of the forty-some boats trailing us order their rowers to reverse stroke, reducing their speed until they hold fast in the current, moving neither forward nor back.

From under the stern seat, Lex pulls a white flag with a purple diagonal stripe slashed through it.

"Take the helm," she tells Karla, then she marches to the bow and raises the treaty flag from a pole.

Up ahead, a mess of planed wood litters the bank—remnants of docks destroyed by the flood. Shifting shrubs betray observers, but not a single bell stroke warns of our approach. A favorable sign. Perhaps her father's hometown honors his legacy.

"My name is Alexandra Arcturus," calls Lex from the bow.

"We know who you are," responds a man's voice from the bushes. "What is it you want?"

"Just a bit of food and safe passage. We'll pay you handsomely."

The only noise for a long while comes when our oars dip gently into the river in reverse paddle against the current.

"Give us a minute," comes the voice of another man. "We need to wake the Reeve."

Lex hunches her shoulders and tightens her fists. Then she loosens them and says, "Of course! *Take your time.*"

She paces impatiently down the centerboard. "When we land," she tells Karla, "I'll handle the payment while you lead a party to inspect the food. If all looks well, I'll sit down with the Reeve while you load the ships. It's time to start making alliances on this side of the border."

"Smoke!" shouts Karl from the bow.

Lex shakes her head with irritation. "Yes, there was smoke..."

Karla stands on her tiptoes to see over Lex. Lex follows her gaze to a plume of black smoke and jolts. Moments ago it had been gray and hardly visible; now it billows black, growing darker by the blink.

Lex draws her sword and kicks the chest of gold in rage. "Raise the black! Five ships on me - we're going ashore. The rest, carry on downriver."

Karl blows a horn, long and loud, as Lex's warriors race to lower the Arcturus banner. They replace it with a tattered black flag. Several horns respond from the ships to our rear as they raise their black banners following suit.

"Row!" shouts Karla. She pushes the tiller to swing our dragon head toward the wall of bushes.

Ten of us remain seated on the benches while the rest grab their shields and spears. They gather to either side, each with one boot up on a gunwale, all of them banging their spear shafts on their shields.

Lex drops a loaded crossbow onto my lap. "Watch the boat. If anyone escapes down this river, it'll cost you both your eyes."

Then she marches forward and shoves through the crowd to climb onto the prow.

I like her, says Jexa.

"You must be enjoying yourself," I mutter.

It's what I live for.

To deny Jexa the entertainment, I remain facing astern.

I row until we slide into the muddy bank. Lex's warriors howl with excitement as momentum launches them onto shore. Two more ships land to either side of me to unload their screaming warriors, everyone eager to wet their blades and salvage whatever food has not yet burned.

Screams of terror rise into the night. Not long after the first steel rings does the wind bring the coppery stench of blood. Strange that I can even smell it at this distance. Stranger is that I feel myself becoming aroused by it.

Shame consumes me, until I realize it's not me getting off on this.

I flip up the helm bench at the tiller and dig inside until I find a strip of black fabric—Lex's backup raiding flag. I tie it tight around my eyes, then lower my head to my knees and stick my fingers in my ears. Hunched over like this, I breathe only through my mouth to deny Jexa even the smells of the raid.

Oh, you think you're so clever, trying to block me out. But I have eyes everywhere. Unlike you.

'Shut up.'

Well someone has to look out for you, Deka. Nya abandoned you, and Lex is about to carve out your eyes.

My heart stops cold. I can't stop myself from thinking of four fateful words, compliments of my ever-curious nature: 'What do you see?'

I'd love to show you, but your mind doesn't work like mine. You can't tune into my frequency. You're just going to have to open your eyes and see for yourself.

I keep my eyes covered and closed.

Would you like to see what I've been up to?

I don't, but she shows me anyway.

Grim scenes play out on the back of my eyelids. Cities of crumbled buildings host skirmishes under gray skies, where humans in tattered clothes swing their final blows against a relentless Watcher assault. She shows me every death. I smell them, too, all the vile scents of a slaughter.

Then we're over a barren wasteland, where Watchers circle humans dressed in dusty long coats. They fire at their enemy circling overhead. The Watchers wait until they run out of ammunition, then swoop in. They take their time with this lot, toying with them. The terror of my foreign kinsfolk rattles me to my soul.

Too harsh for you? Perhaps a little romance will cheer you up.

The next scene gets my heart racing.

Nya walks the halls of a great tower, where an even greater king rules. Something on the walls has her transfixed. I've never seen her so enthralled. The image sharpens to reveal portraits of... Regulus.

My heart squeezes.

He poses in the still image with a group of soldiers on a field exercise, judging by the yellow caps on their rifle muzzles. If the host whose eyes through which I now witness this did not reveal to me from her memories which of the young men was her king, I'd have no idea which was him. The informal group stand with their arms over each other's shoulders, with Regulus at center. Their smiles and jovial stances seem genuine, as if there's a real connection there. In his heart he is one of them.

My own heart balls tight like a fist. The way Nya looks at him... She's never looked at me like that. With curiosity, sure. But she *reveres* this young king. And why not? He commands legions of fanatic followers. He shapes the world to his desire, and can offer Nya things I could hardly dream of. The way she lies on in his bed, longing for his comfort, makes me nauseous.

Seen enough?

I have.

I remove my blindfold and scan the shoreline, where blue timber smoke hangs heavy in the air. Rustling in the reeds draws my attention to a boat slipping out into the river. A boy and girl push the wooden vessel into waist-deep water, where the boy helps the girl climb in.

Karla races from the town and sloshes into the water. She pulls an axe from her belt and flings it at the boy as he jumps in.

The girl pulls him low so that the axe finds only wood.

Karla looks straight at me and points to them. "Quick! They're getting away!"

I raise the crossbow and aim at the couple now fumbling with the oars. They remind me so much of Mali and me, on the day we fled our caves for the forest. That beautiful forest that devoured my dearest friend. I can't even remember what she looks like. That's the worst part. Will it be the same for Nya after so little time passes after my death? What will it be like to never see her face again?

My finger feathers the trigger. It's them or me, for what am I without my sight? This world would rip a foreign blind man to pieces.

"Hurry! What are you waiting for? They're getting away!"

She's wrong. They've *already gotten* away, drifted beyond range of my crossbow. But I can still save my eyesight from Lex's wrath.

I swing my aim to line the iron sight with Karla's chest. One pull of the trigger, and no one will ever know those two escaped. With a single bolt I can keep both of my eyes.

I'm starting to squeeze the trigger when her brother Karl rushes down to join her. By the time he looks my way, I've already lowered the weapon, but he has other concerns. He drags Karla back to town, where an urgent matter beckons.

I curl onto the floor before my bench and await Lex's punishment. I should take in the sky to savor my last moments with sight, but the horrors of a village raid are not the last images I wish to remember. Instead, I keep the memory of that boy and girl fresh. Maybe they'll find safe haven in the capital and grow up to live normal lives. This day would forever haunt them, sure, but they'd honor their village by living every day like it's a gift. They'll grow old and have children without ever knowing how close I was to ending their bloodlines. That their future had cost another frightened boy his sight.

Or, just as likely, Lex's boats downriver will catch the pair and string them up.

I'm not sure how long the raid lasts. An hour? A day? Time has lost all meaning for me in this land of the comatose sun. It's like living in a cave, only there's no exit to visit for a dose of daylight.

Loud swishing of the reeds and splashing water announces Lex's return. She climbs aboard, grabs my crossbow, and before I can stutter an excuse, she cracks me behind the ear with the butt. It's the last thing I remember of the Wolf's welcome home party.

CHAPTER 15

NYA

An unusual noise stirs me from my slumber.

I wipe my eyes and blink to focus. Sunlight shines from artificial lamps in the blue sky above, bathing the deserted glass buildings in daylight. The false sun blesses us with a magnificent afternoon, but there's not a person to be seen. So what woke me? Did I imagine the strange noise?

A shriek jolts me to my feet. To my left, where a wall of high glass buildings borders the field, races a young girl from a grassy lane. She carries a round object under her arm in a dash across the open field. When a mob emerges from the lane behind her in pursuit, she squeals and runs harder toward me.

"Where you got to run to?" shouts a boy.

"There's nowhere to hide, runt!" adds a girl accomplice.

Their prey must have had a good head start on them, because in the open field the bigger children quickly gain on her. At this rate they'll catch her before she reaches me in the tree line.

I reach overhead and grab two branches. A gentle

vibration rattles out through my palms, one strong enough to shake the entire tree. Her leaves swish and branches creak as I unleash a loud growl.

The girl slides to a stop and stares at the shuddering tree in fright. Her pursuers halt short of her and gawk at the vibrating branches that growl louder in its aggravation.

"Who dares disturb my slumber?" I say in a low grumble.

Two children turn and bolt back the way they came.

"*Answer me!*"

"We're sorry!" shouts a boy from the pack of pursuers. His grander size and confidence suggests he is their leader. "We were just playing."

"It's true!" says the girl in front. She holds up a bundle from under her arm to show me it's a wicker ball.

The boy falls in beside her and places a hand on her shoulder. It seems to provide her a measure of comfort.

"You, girl," I say, "step closer."

The pair exchange wary looks. Finally, they advance together.

"*Alone,*" I add.

They both pause. The boy gives the girl a look of caution, which she returns with an assuring nod. She continues solo to the tree line. From my branch, hidden behind a wall of leaves, I say in a softer voice, "Is it true? Were you really just playing?"

"Yes."

She holds up the wicker ball in offering, though she can't see me.

I slink across the branch overhead for a better look, careful not to rustle any leaves. Inside the wicker ball hangs a suspended egg.

"How does it work?" I ask. "The game?"

The girl hugs the ball close and looks around warily. "Who are you?"

Right. I suppose it's not polite to remain hidden.

I drop from the tree and snatch the ball from her, then flutter out over the group in the field. I land behind them to examine the contraption.

A symphony of gasps rise from them, along with a delayed squeal from the startled girl. Hushed mutterings speculate what I am, what they should do, and how they should feel.

Pixie. Faery. Sprite. Wood nymph.

Mischievous. Evil. Spirit.

"Can't be none of them," whispers a boy. "She's way too big."

"And just how many *pixies* have you seen before?" I say, with a wink to the girl who'd made that guess.

The girl smiles and elbows the boy. "See, Max, told ya."

"Where are your parents?" I ask.

A few children hug themselves and look to the ground.

"King called them to service," Max says. "All of them. That'll be me next year, when I come of age."

"Do you know where they went?"

They all shake their heads.

"Sometimes they get called for a weekend drill or something, but never all at once like this."

"Probably lots of trouble at the border. That Wolf is always up to no good."

Many nod and mutter in agreement. Little do they know, Alexandra Arcturus is the lesser of far greater threats. But I'll not worry their young minds with that. If their parents standing watch at the distant border is a better image than a Watcher invasion on Mount Tuck, then I'll gladly leave them with that.

"Will you play with us?" asks the girl.

My heart flutters. I hold up the wicker ball and stare at the egg suspended inside. No one ever asked me to play a game before, not even Jinny.

"What are the rules?"

"Don't get caught. Don't break the egg. You get two points for stealing it off someone, and one for passing it off to a teammate. If the egg breaks during a steal, the stealer loses the game."

Seems easy enough.

The hardest part, I quickly learn, is keeping my feet on the ground. My instinct to escape or cover distance by leaping into flight gets me labeled a cheater. I hate that name, so they only have to call me out three times before I learn.

The first few matches I don't touch the wicker ball at all. I'm content just running in zigzag patterns over soft green grass, laughing with the other children as we bump into each other. One match ends with all fifteen of us piling into a big heap. Max somehow saves the ball and its egg from our crushing weight, so we carry on with another match.

My moment comes when a boy from the other team looks over his shoulder and slams into me. He fumbles the ball, and I'm swift to snatch it.

"Run!" shout my teammates.

Adrenaline pumps through me. One second the ball sits firmly between both hands, the next—*POOF*—it explodes into a cloud of atomic particles.

A strange sense of shame overcomes me, rooted in letting

down my team. Sure, I'd been famous for my slack work efforts during my servitude, but here I actually care about our success. "I'll make you a new one."

"How did you do that?" Max says in astonishment. He searches my hands and the ground around my feet. "There's not even a drop of yolk."

"It's what I do. I make things disappear."

Bright smiles and giddy chatter livens the mood as a new game takes shape.

Children race in every direction in search of objects for me to dust. First up is a park bench. They watch in amazement as I blast it to splinters with a flick of my finger. My next victim is a fallen tree branch, which I hurl skyward as a cloud of dust.

A new game emerges from these demonstrations, the goal of which is to bring me something I cannot dust. I win every round with ease, so they expand their efforts, scavenging an exotic collection of items from nearby buildings. I don't know what most of it is, but they seem to be of value to someone, judging by the mischievous grins watching me. I suppose I'll be lucky to have to explain myself to their owners, as their return would only follow our victory at Mount Tuck.

Then comes a challenge. Although it's a mere wrist watch, I'm hesitant to try my luck against diamond-studded gold. Depending on the quality, it may knock me unconscious or throw me into a seizure.

I'm mustering the courage to try when Taryn, the first girl I'd met here, comes to the rescue with a newly-fashioned wicker ball. Her companions eagerly split back into two teams. They've already seen me dust a lamp post. Obviously this piece of junk is no match for a destroyer of worlds.

The game resumes from right where we'd left off. They take their scores very seriously.

We play on for hours more, laughing and yelling. The constant laughter nourishes a part inside me that no sunlight could ever reach. This joy provides me the purest energy, infusing me with hope and enthusiasm, the fire of the divine. I could do this all day. And I will. I'll wait here and watch over these children until Lex's fleet rounds the elbow.

We play until fake dusk turns the dome sky pink.

I blow up the gate at the spire base and lead my new friends up to Regulus's throne hall. The high climb is easy, even after a second run down and up to retrieve a straggler. Another day or two of this play, and I'll be better than ever. These children harbor so much life, their spirit still full of innocence—the purest energy in the whole universe. It stirs memories of my early days, brief flickers of ages past, back when I was a spawn and everything was so new and waiting to be explored.

Sitting on the balcony, watching the pink dome roofs fade to indigo twilight beneath us, and the endless night all around, I have found a purpose greater than any other. I'll continue my watch over these children even after Lex's force has passed en route to Mount Tuck. The absence of fire along the river assures me she has so far held true to her word.

I breathe a sigh of relief and satisfaction. They don't need me to win this fight. And if the worst scenario plays out, it would be cruel to leave these young ones to face it alone.

Yes, that's what I'll do. It's the greatest gift I can offer in these dark hours.

CHAPTER 16
DEKA

I'm blind!

My hands reach instinctively for my eyes but stop short at my hips. A rattling chain tells me I'm bolted to the floor between my feet, seated upon a bench.

I look around and blink, and it's in the blinking that I feel the fabric of a blindfold. Or maybe it's a phantom sensation. I've heard that can happen with lost limbs.

"The Commander is running out of uses for you," says Centurion Lantz's voice.

"But do not despair," says a second unknown man, "*Yggdrasil* is near."

"Can you hear her leaves rustling in the breeze?"

I can.

Background chatter from the rest of the crew suggests I've been moved to a different boat. The absence of Karl and Karla's taunts alone are evidence enough of this. Lex's flagship spares no room for disappointments.

You really put yourself in a bind, haven't you.

"Shut up."

"What did you say?" says a girl nearby. Then she smacks me upside the head.

I sense Jexa's satisfaction swell inside me. Such a strange feeling, hosting this parasite.

I tilt my head back in an attempt to see under the bottom of my blindfold.

Don't worry about your sight, Deka. I have plenty more to show you.

My belly clenches.

What's that? Can't stomach it? Well then, you should reconsider your desires. Nya's future is no place for the faint of heart.

'Show me,' I tell her in my mind. I know I'm playing into her game, but I can't pass up an opportunity to see Nya. To know she has a future beyond the coming weeks will bring me peace when I arrive at my own end.

An image takes shape behind my eyelids, of a dark queen who rules from a throne of diamond upon a disk of cosmic dust. Her black antler crown gleams with the light of a hundred million races, souls crammed like compressed gas, each of the twelve points sizzling from the pressure — the sparks of all who once loved her and all who failed her.

She raises her hammer, and the Universe trembles. And somewhere beyond the reaches of light, the dragons rejoice to the song of their new champion.

I know what Jexa is doing. She's taken Nya's image and placed it upon her own. 'Your trickery won't fool me. Nya doesn't have it in her. She fights for freedom.'

Isn't that how we all start? Fighting for ourselves and those we love.

'What do you know about love?'

I've known passion hotter than Dedrudius' Bane, young human. Nothing like that tame little affair you two had.

Through Jexa I know Dedrudius was the brightest star to have ever gone supernova. It blew apart half a galaxy and destroyed a million sentient races with it.

Your weakness will become her strength.

The image of Nya, seated upon her throne with an antler crown sparkling upon her head, meets my stare with two black holes where her eyes should be.

Your death will destroy her... For a time. She'll seek out comfort only darkness can offer, and in this she will discover her limitless capacity. Left unchecked, she will destroy the universe and all its creations. It's in every dust maiden, a nuclear rage that, once unleashed, cannot be tamed. Klora had it. So too did her grandmother. The greatest of their kind, both fallen in their prime. But not Nya. She has something they never did — the love of a human boy, a fragile little creature who she could not save.

I see Nya's face through a bubble of curved glass. Its uneven surface suggests molten beginnings, perhaps from a disaster of whatever has her in tears now. She cries from her normal green eyes, swollen red with heartache. In the glisten of her tears I see a reflected image, of me swaying by a rope from a hanging tree.

Darkness falls around her. The sorrow behind her pained stare becomes shadowed by a rage so fierce that her clenched teeth crack. Black veins branch up from her neck to her face, creeping up to her eyes, where a single black tear drips over and down her cheek. She closes her eyes, and when they open again, she is no longer my sweet dust maiden. She has become a goddess of misery and retribution.

The Dark Monarch.

'So she'll defeat you,' I say, trying to poke a hole in Jexa's claim, where she'll have to admit that her own downfall lies near and at the hands of a servant.

I will be the first of many, Jexa admits. *Her eyes will see only enemies. Her heart will know only distrust. She'll wander the galaxies, desperate to fill the void expanding inside her.*

A pyramid gateway blasts open under the purple sky of a distant planet. From an entry in the base emerges a black shadow with four wings and antlers. The humanoids there fall to their knees to welcome her.

She'll seek out the finest warrior scholars of every race from here to the particle horizon, the farthest edge of the universe, and bring them to her court in the heavens. All will fear her, and all shall fail her. Because, you see, Deka, you cannot be replaced. And the entire universe shall suffer for it.

'How do I stop it?'

Everything in me warns that to ask a Watcher for advice is asking for trouble, but I can't help it.

Pray to your gods that death takes her before it finds you. That's your only reasonable option. If she perishes before your demise, she'll still be the beloved dust maiden you knew. Of course, you could stop yourself from dying, but that's not realistic, is it? This world devours the weak. Just look at you now. You'd be celebrated for skewering those boat-folk. Instead, you let them get away. The Nya of the future would not approve of such impotence. Better you both perish in the coming days, wouldn't you say? I can help you with that, if you'd like.

Jexa's attempts to fill my head with lies presents me with an opportunity. If the Watcher Marshall has opened a gateway to my mind, and gateways work both ways, that means...

I take a deep breath and think only of Jexa.

Is that you knocking at my door, Deka? Trust me, you don't want to see what's inside. It's for your own good.

'Now you're concerned about my well-being? No, that can't be it. I know. You're afraid of what I'll find.'

I have no problem opening the door. But you won't be able to see what lies beyond.

She proceeds to show me how the radio systems of my ancestors worked. How they needed to tune to a certain frequency to hear its message, or else you just get static. I know about this already, from the Capstone and its Alignment. So Jexa is saying...

That you'll never align with me, son of man. Bad as your race is, we are nowhere near the same. You think you know suffering. Your misery shall one day end, briefly. In that, you can harbor peace inside your gentle heart. Only the eternal may drink from my well.

'You aligned with me.'

Hah! I know what it is to be human, with all your carnal desires. I too was seduced by the offerings of another, and offer he did. Now he lives through me, and now on through you. And you too will go on to bless others with your service to our Lord Master.

'I serve only one.'

How? By hanging from a tree? You think she's so perfect, don't you. Would you like to know a secret about your fearsome wolf mother? Something not even her most loyal servant knows?

I find myself back on Lex's ship, watching her through

the eyes of another warrior. Lex sits with her legs stretched across my bench—well, the bench of my host through which I now watch—her back to the bulkhead, one eye closed and her hands folded on her belly.

Listen, Jexa says. *Do you hear it?*

She conveniently blocks out all other noise—the swish of water, the clunk of oars, the mutterings of warriors—all but a faint crackle. It rises with each fall of Lex's chest.

A memory flashes in my mind, of Svenia booting Lex in our escape from her camp, the force sends her flying back through a cloud of swirling bats.

How long do you think she has? I think you should be worried for her.

Concerning as this is, I wasn't referring to Lex as the one I serve.

And what can you offer her? *Why would Nya choose you over, say... anyone? The strong attract the strong. Why do you think Ko Skadia chose your war chief? Yes, I've seen your memories. Every last one of them.*

This hits a nerve. An image of Marlok and Ko Skadia's romance returns to me, each a chieftain of their kind. What could I offer Nya that Regulus does not already possess? He has a powerful army and vast lands, resources beyond my comprehension. I am nobody with nothing. Except...

Opportunity. I could claim some of that for myself, if I regain favor with Lex.

You're quite the dreamer. Assuming she doesn't die before reaching her objective, the best you can expect is a swift death from her. And if she drowns in her own blood before then, what happens to her army? What do you think they'll do with you?

Things I'd rather not think about.

'Are we coming to the part where you offer to help me?'

You humans... you just take, take, take. What do you ever give in return?

'Have you not been entertained?'

By my own skills? Which you've used for your own gain?

'You want a duel with Nya. You needed me to save her.' I'm suddenly aware that the knowledge of plant medicine I used after our fall in the river, and then the competence of my antics when causing havoc in the camp, and then my escape, had all come from Jexa.

So we helped each other out. I'll admit, I was a big admirer of your cause back then. But now I can't help but question your commitment. You could have shot those villagers—I'd have made sure your aim was true—but you failed to do what needed to be done. Spending time with you is a significant investment on my part. Why should I invest any more energy than I already have?

'Because if I die, you'll seal your fate. Nya will become the Dark Monarch and destroy you.'

You've been paying attention. Good. So, are you now willing to do whatever it takes?

'I won't sacrifice my humanity for you.'

Oh, don't worry, I won't have you butcher babies or the like. But I will require payment first.

'What do you want?'

A sacrifice, made in my name. One done by your own will —a death you must bear yourself. If you're to be of any use to me, I'll need you in an esteemed position. That means never letting a hit go unanswered again. It starts with the girl who just struck you.

I pull on the chain bolting my wrists to the floor. 'If only I could.'

There's a knife under your seat.

I lean over and feel underneath, and sure enough, my fingers touch a grooved handle. The blade is still in its scabbard, secured to a belt stored under my bench by the oarsman behind me. He's up taking a walk down the centerboard now, stretching his legs.

Lure her close with a tale. Some juicy information that, if passed on, might earn her good grace with her commander. Something that may earn her a seat on the flagship.

'And when I kill her? What then? Just sit here while fifty of her boat-mates bury their blades in me?'

I'm not like the cruel gods who ignore your cries for help. I answer every prayer made in my name swiftly, especially those paid for in blood.

My whole body tenses. Jexa can be exceptionally persuasive, so much that it requires constant effort to keep myself reminded of that. But if I'm to rise through Lex's ranks, it won't be through more wolves' blood. I've already sacrificed enough of them to my struggles. It's time I give something back. Something personal.

That should be easy. Just sit back and relax, and soon you'll sway from the Tree of Life. A bit ironic, isn't it?

Irony, yes. There's plenty of that going around. By infiltrating my mind, Jexa has exposed her nature to me. Only a few elements of it, sure, because I'd been so focused on myself. That's where a sacrifice comes in. To outwit Jexa, I must first understand her, to see existence through her eyes. To do that, I must align with her. Fortunately for me...

There's another well I can drink from.

I grip the knife handle with both hands between my knees, point facing up. I laugh madly as I work up the nerve to do the unthinkable.

"Hey, Commander," shouts the girl who'd hit me in amusement, "I think he's losing it."

Footsteps approach over the centerboard and stop abruptly nearby. "He's got a knife!"

I swing my head down... down until sharp pain explodes in my face, sending waves of agony through my body. The sensation is overwhelming, making me feel like I could break these chains if I tried. But I don't. Instead, I growl in frustration, but it's only for a split second, because I quickly find myself in another world, one devoid of all noise.

The Artery of this realm flows with green mist, much like the aurora that dazzles the sky above Anterra. Bare tree branches hang over narrow sections of the river, where two ravens watch my approach with great interest.

The current pushes me toward the rightward bank. When I instinctively reach for the tiller, I realize I'm not in a boat. I'm just... here.

The river disappears over a drop-off. A rock ledge to my right beckons me to safety, where my course takes me to overlook a waterfall. It spills down through a hole in the world, a puncture in the cosmos through which the aether of this realm feeds that of another.

The falling green mist spirals into a black void. As my mind adjusts to this new experience, my human perceptions fade away. Illusions crumble. This is no river nor aurora, nor am I upon a bank. What I'm looking at is the greatest undertaking in the Universe: the forced feeding of a black hole one trillion times the size of our Sun.

I witness a Universe expand faster and faster toward a cold dark eternity, devoid of light and even time. Galaxies will decay, planets will crumble, and when the last star burns out, that will be it. An infinity of particles ever drifting away, specks of dust floating in a silent nothing. A universe dissolved. There are some races who have accepted this fate —religions whose peace arises in silence. But they are rare.

Only a master manipulator can stop this Great Entropy, a divine orchestrator of energy. There does exist such a being, entities so distraught over the expanding universe, obsessed by the great looming darkness, they'll do anything to reverse it. Cold-blooded creatures with even colder hearts. Beings of fire and scale that will stop at nothing to prevent the inevitable 'heat death' of our Universe, who pump cosmic amounts of gas and light into a swelling black hole, hoping to create a gravitational force significant enough to trigger the great Omega—the point where expansion slows to a stop and then reverses.

I see the universe as a giant spider web, a delicate balance kept in its form by two opposing forces. Dark energy pulls at the edges, threatening to tear it apart, while light energy, like that from stars, keeps everything in place. When too much light energy is fed into The Dark, it upsets the balance. The web starts to wobble and tear.

Their mighty effort has already cleared an area of one billion light years across, a massive void in space where the Omega drain has siphoned every particle within range. A Darkness Divine. And yet, still... the Universe expands. What they require is something far heavier than stars: *Sparks* cast out from the divine fire that gave birth to the Universe itself. Each conscious fragment, rich with their egos and karma from countless lifetimes, their essences tethered to dimensions beyond what our eyes can see, each worth the weight of a million suns within the dynamics of a crushing black void.

When this powerful soul energy is added, the hole swells and grows stronger. This creates an enormous imbalance, like adding too much weight to one spot in the web. The Dark's pull becomes stronger... the fabric of space begins to tear... and everything starts to collapse inward...

A burden besets me. It is one I never thought could be a curse: *knowledge*. I share this charge with a rare few—warriors of neither light nor dark. We have walked the same path, through ages and eons past. Made divine sacrifices in the pursuit of wisdom. Many have quit early or failed late, with only a few of us making it so far. Yes, *Us*. And it's clear now where I stand.

I look back up the celestial river, into the aethers of my homeworld. With a gentle wish, the current reverses, dragging me back with it, back to the final hours of my people.

CHAPTER 17
DEKA

The howls of wolves call me back to reality. This world is a blur, but the swerving aurora above and the swish of water washing a riverbank assure me it is Polaria.

The wooden bench creaks beside me. A calloused hand grabs mine and squeezes it, and in this I feel I am unchained.

"Let no man ever speak ill of your name again," Lex says.

I tilt my head to see the blur of her face. I blink a few times to focus my eyes, and the first thing I notice is the reduced span of my vision. Instinctively I reach for my left eye and touch velvet fabric, and a blast of sharp pain scolds me for doing so.

"Between the two of us," Lex says, "we form one virtuous vision." Her tone is lighter, as if some great burden has been lifted. Or... a void has been filled.

The shrill cries of starving wolves echo over the river.

Goosebumps ripple my skin as a shiver rolls through me.

Lex helps me sit up so I can survey my surroundings.

"We didn't find much food during the raid," she says, "but it did wonders for morale."

A look around shows me warriors with hands cupped over their mouths, casting out their ominous cries. They are eager, uplifted.

Lex snaps her fingers. Footsteps pound the deck boards behind and stop beside us. Lex accepts a shield from a warrior and offers it to me.

"I should have never doubted you. By keeping you so close, I smothered you with distrust. But now..." She sets the shield on my lap. "You'll lead Century Thirty. That's two ships at fifty oars a piece. They're good fighters, eager to prove themselves."

I pull the shield close, my heart racing with excitement. My own command?

"We lost a Centurion during the raid," Lex explains. "Damn fool tried to set fire to an orphanry, so he lost his head to my sword. I'll not have such disgrace stain my name. Show his fighters how a real leader behaves. Serve me with honor, and you'll see yourself a general before the end."

I hold the shield out to admire the eight-point star over black background. *General. Warlord.* Yes, it is in my blood. It is what shall bring me back to Nya, all while Lex does me the honor of eliminating Regulus from my path. When she regains control of Polaria, I'll be one of the most powerful men on Earth. The strongest of the strong.

If I serve her well in these next few hours.

I stand and wobble, catching myself on the wet gunwale. I pound my fist against my chest and say, "My blood is yours."

Lex responds with a faint, satisfied nod. My vision has sharpened enough to see a twinkle in her eye.

"We'll be coming up to Kaladia soon. It's a proper city with a sizable militia base. No doubt they heard what happened in Corpisaul. Even if Regulus summoned all his troops to Mount Tuck, he'll have left a force to defend his greatest inland port. Most of the country's crops pass through there on their way to Amyria. If he loses that hub, his capital won't last another winter."

I slide my arm into a sleeve strapped to the backside of my shield. It wraps me from elbow to wrist, where through the far opening I find a rubber hand grip. Spiderweb strap-work fastens the sleeve to the shield, a shock absorption system in the concave backside. It'll cushion well against a hammer swing, provided it's not from Nya, but how about a bullet?

I think I'll soon find out.

The fleet lands on the rightward bank, where Lex convenes a summit of her twenty-some Centurions. We drink ale from curved horns around a map sketched into the dirt. One of the raiding parties had found barrels of the liquid gold and gifted the largest to their chief commander, the one-eyed god reborn.

In the background, warriors trade scraps of food scavenged from the raid. Heated exchanges rise loud as hunger becomes a spirited force.

"They'll be expecting an attack from the river," says Lex, "so that's what we'll give them. I'll lead half the force to make up the forward assault while the other half lands behind us, upriver and out of sight. We'll keep their attention while Centuries Sixteen to Thirty flank them."

They'll expect the land attack, Jexa whispers.

"Keep only three boats back," I say.

This draws many curious looks from the Centurions, and a scornful glare from Lex. These gatherings aren't for discussing strategy, I see. They're to get everyone on the same page. The Wolf speaks and the pack obeys.

Until today.

"If word did reach them," I say, "they'll know how many boats we have. If only half show up, they'll wonder where the rest are."

"Three boats is too small of an attack force," says Argyle. "One machine gun could stop a shield wall that size dead. We need more for the rush."

"He's right," Lex says. "A high-caliber bullet will punch right through a single shield. But several interlocked will absorb the impact. We need a sizable wall to advance against a sustained battering. The bigger, the better. We've learned these lessons in blood."

"We need to land without them seeing us," I say. "The fewer, the better."

"Of course," says Argyle. He's the only one without a horn in his hand. Instead he grips the hilt of his sword. "I'm sure this makes perfect sense to the boy who just gouged out his own eye."

"Sensible acts are predictable," I say, standing firm at center. "Have the main force hit the town while the other half carries on downriver. They'll think it's going down just like Corpisaul. Once we've hit them and moved on, they'll send most of the garrison to protect the settlements downriver. They didn't burn all their food back in Corpisaul. You just couldn't find it. If someone breaks into your home, what's the first thing you do after they leave? Check to make sure they didn't find your valuables. You said by mid-winter food is the highest commodity? Do a quick pillage, and after we've moved on, the villagers will head straight to their food vault to take stock."

Lex nods faintly, her eye narrow, suspicious of my direction.

"That's when the follow-up will hit," I say, "two boats driving in hard and fast to catch them with their pants down."

Lex folds her arms and strokes her chin, staring intensely at the map.

"It's bold and risky." She snaps her fingers. "I like it. Centuries One to Fifteen will hit the town with me, Sixteen to Twenty-Eight will carry on downriver. Deka, you'll lead the secondary strike. But you'll have the Twenty-Ninth backing you up. That's four boats instead of two."

This hits me with unexpected force. I'd been expecting a warm-up to test my performance commanding a single century. Leading an entire prong of the assault is a whole other level.

Centurion Lantz, commander of the Twenty-Ninth and my subordinate in this attack, squeezes his horn until it cracks.

This is how it starts, says Jexa. *You'll be warlord before you know it, a mighty ruler of men. Then all the dust maidens will swoon over you.*

I nod and bang my fist on my shield. *Let's do this.*

Lex gives me a satisfied smirk, one that tells me she's a fan of my rising stardom.

CHAPTER 18

DEKA

I don't have many memories of my father. Aside from his frequent scoldings, our conversations mainly involved tales of epic Viking conquests from ages past. I guess he was trying to inspire a sense of warrior adventure in me, because he gave up after I traded in my spear for a fishing rod. If only he could see me now.

Horns blow from three dozen longboats rounding the riverbend ahead. My ship trails a good distance behind, the middle right of four whose oars work in reverse to slow our advance. My wooden dragon head floats through green mist, fog dyed by the aurora above. I stand at the helm, arm propped on the tiller, feeling like myself for the first time since Mali died.

A winged figure glides overhead, spying what her master misses through my remaining eye. Another flies close behind. Renowned Watcher strategists have come to place bets on how this will unfold, staking their reputations on the outcome. All while learning how we fight. Their foul spirits bewitch my brethren, who howl into the night.

Gunfire ripples from beyond the bend. Steel rattles and shouts rise as Lex makes her run at the town.

"Slow," I tell my oarsmen. We must give Lex time to do her business, to make a show of force before fleeing to rejoin her advancing raiders downriver. She'll not wish to divide her army for long when so deep in enemy territory. That's what any Polarian defense commander worth his bars will assume.

My oarsmen slow us to a stop at center river. Our three support boats fall in beside us, their rowers working in reverse to oppose the current. Lantz crouches in his boat, stewing. He doesn't like backing up the new Centurion. Judging by the glares around me, my warriors aren't pleased by my new appointment either. I can't say I blame them. I've killed more wolves than any Polarian during this campaign so far.

We all sit in silence. Those with any humanity left prepare to part with it. The tolls of war. The time to do what's right are for better days, and it's clear there is no moral guardian keeping measure of our deeds.

Gunfire intensifies to a climax. Then it's mostly ringing steel and shouts as a tidal wave of a shielded warriors spill from their ships onto shore. Gunfire becomes sporadic. The action occurs beyond my sight, yet I picture a shield wall forcing its way up a lane, driving back the defenders with bold moves and uncomfortable speed.

They don't seem to push far inland, as the attack ends sooner than I'd been expecting. Within a few, minutes three horn blasts tell me they've moved on. It's the most nerve-racking sound I've ever heard.

I start my countdown of ten minutes under my breath. *Six hundred seconds.* That's how long I have left as the boy named Deka of Westerly. That's when I become everything or nothing.

Six hundred seconds goes by pretty fast when your heart is pounding two hundred beats a minute against your ribs.

I whistle three faint chirps through my teeth.

The oars to either side of me work in unison to propel us forward with the current. We round the bend in no time, where a row of white-washed buildings pump out black smoke.

I sprint forward and jump onto the prow. Half my rowers climb up from their benches, their shields and spears in hand as they line up to either side of me. A commotion from the boats behind suggests they are following suit.

My sword hilt becomes slick in my clammy grip. Four boats against a settlement that size, a *city*, suddenly feels like a reckless endeavor. What was I thinking? Were the others right? Had I pushed too hard for madness? Am I leading us into a disaster?

My keel scrapes over a submerged stone dock, past a plundered warehouse, then grinds to a halt at the bottom of a steep cobble lane. A cloud of black smoke covers our intrusion, allowing us to slip in unseen.

My boots splat into Polarian muck with dozens more behind me, and together we march between stacks of salvaged wharf planks.

We follow an alley across to the main boulevard, where a rotunda stands tall at the upper end. The white building boasts columns in front and a dome over top, and judging by the crowd gathered in the square before its steps, they believe we've moved on and are tallying their losses—lives taken and food plundered.

A scream from the fringe heralds our approach. The crowd disperses to reveal a hole in the flagstone ground, over which a soldier crouches to take inventory of something below. He stands and draws his pistol, then opens fire.

I raise my shield with reflex speed—*DING*. The bullet smacks the upper edge and ricochets skyward. Then my arm jerks instinctively, left then right—*ting-ding*—to deflect two more shots. One ricochet hits a building, another finds the belly of a shield mate of my century. She keels over and falls onto her face.

The few who manage to block a bullet remain unscathed. A man drops his weapon to nurse a broken arm, while another eats her shield. Literally. An impact to the top busts open her mouth and sends her stumbling backward in a daze.

The shooter stops to reload his pistol. I'm about to rush at him when twenty Polarian soldiers spill over the town hall steps behind. Unlike their lone comrade, they bring rifles with fixed bayonets to the fight.

I step my right foot back and raise my shield to chest height. "Shield wall!"

Steel plates fall in all around me. They lock into both sides of my shield and rock side to side to test our cohesion. The warrior to my left loops her arm through mine and kneels to pull me down with her. A warrior behind me reaches over with his shield and links it to the top of mine. It's the same all the way down the line, until a whole new row is formed. It all happens before a single shot is fired, a reflex developed by Lex's rigorous training.

Thunder claps as if coming from inside my head, then the clatter of bullets against steel plates rattles my teeth. My muscles lock tight as my shield takes shot after shot, each feeling like a horse kick to the chest.

As the hammering eases, the shield over my head rises enough to open a small window, through which I see half of the Polarian soldiers reloading.

"Advance," hisses the girl to my left through clenched teeth. A friendly suggestion from my subordinate.

Ditch these losers, chimes Jexa. *They're slowing you down.*

"Advance!" I shout.

My line stands as the rank behind us raises their shields to keep our heads covered, and together we take measured steps toward the enemy. When the next volley clatters off our half-dome with full force, shields wobble and a few separate.

Shouts scold me for shuffling out of step. The warriors grunt in unison to get me in sync—*hoo-hoo-hoo*—but it only trips me up. My missteps send ripples through the shield wall, ripples that form cracks for bullets to slip between, like the one that punches through the cheek of the girl next to me. She falls onto her back, taking her shield with her, leaving a gap to my left. A few more of my warriors fall backwards or onto their faces. The wall breaks further, creating a rift for more bullets to whiz through.

"Consolidate!" shouts Centurion Lantz. So far he's remained silent, giving me undisputed command. But it's not a courtesy. He's been waiting for me to blunder.

Everyone shuffles to tighten our ranks, tripping over our fallen in a sloppy scramble.

"Spears!" barks Lantz.

Ten warriors who'd been crouched behind the shield wall launch their spears at the gunmen. Half hit their mark. But it doesn't diminish the rate of fire enough to provide relief, and no one else had brought a spear with them.

A look over my shoulder reveals two dozen of ours dead. We've only gained a few feet, and the raucous thunder and rattling steel aren't letting up.

Now would be a good time to prove yourself.

Without thinking, I yank an axe from a nearby warrior's belt and charge at the shooters in a one-man rush. I hurl the axe into the forward shooter's chest and then draw my sword as his partner watches him crumple to the ground. I ram him with my shield, shoving him aside as I plunge my sword into the soldier behind. A back-swing brings my shield into the throat of another.

The rest is a blur, until I find myself standing alone in a square littered with bodies. Onlookers include only my raiding party, their stricken stares sizing me up.

Lantz approaches, giving the bodies around me a wary appraisal, and stops at a hole in the ground nearby. It's where the pistol shooter had been crouched upon our arrival, taking stock of the food below.

A ruckus of clunking shields announces the arrival of another party. I look up to see Lex leading her crew from the river, her eye surveying the carnage around me. She joins Lantz at the opening to the food vault.

"Congratulations," she says. "I'd call this a success."

"With twenty percent casualties?" Lantz says. "I'd call it a slaughter."

"In times like this, we must give more weight to our gains than to our losses. I see enough food here to feed us for a week."

Spears bang on shields. They're all from Lex's crew.

Those who'd fought beside me to secure the vault stare solemnly, conducting a tally of their own, weighing the lives of the dead against the needs of the living.

"Load the boats," Lex says. "Leave nothing."

"Burn the rest," I add. Actually, that part came from Jexa, but Lex's smirk tells me she approves. In that, I've turned my curse into a blessing.

Yes, together we'll do incredible things.

I imagine Jexa and I have different ideas of what 'incredible things' are, but I feel her truth. With her, I can rise to unimaginable heights, all while studying her psyche for weaknesses. For every hole she sees in me, I'll find two more from her. And the more time she spends with me, the less attention she can spare to other matters. Yes, if I'm stuck with her, I'll use her to my advantage.

You learn fast.

I return to my boat as warriors hurl torches into buildings.

'I need some time alone,' I tell Jexa, my hands shaking so fiercely I struggle to sheath my sword.

Sure, I'll leave, but you won't find yourself alone for long.

She's right. Already I see them—the faces twisted in agony, their terror-stricken eyes to be forever etched in my mind.

CHAPTER 19

NYA

The children of Amyria sure do love their murder tree. Frankly, I'm a bit concerned.

"She's over six hundred years old," Taryn tells me. She pulls a fistful of ragweed from around the roots and drops it into a basket. "The Sage Amyria planted her. This place was all rock back then. She used science to sway nature, then taught others her ways before sending them out to the far reaches. Some call her the grandmother of trees."

I keep my ridicule to myself. But, seriously? Life would have found its way here regardless of their savage saint's blood magic. I know the truth behind this tree, a giant hanging post born of sacrifice. Still, I help the young capital folk pull weeds. It's a group effort, everyone taking a section of roots, and I'd feel sorely left out just standing around watching.

"Tell me about your King," I say.

Taryn's face lights up. "Oh, he's the best. Mother says when I turn thirteen she'll let me cut my hair and dye it to look just like his."

I've witnessed this curious custom, most notably in soldiers, how they style their hair to Regulus's likeness. "Why would you do that?"

"Because we love him. But not everyone does."

Max shakes his head with a regretful look. "He's got many enemies who wish him dead."

"If an assassin was to come on the hunt for him," Taryn explains, "or the Wolf's horde invaded, at least he'd have a chance to blend in."

"What if the killers thought you were the King?" I ask, anxiety swelling inside me. This is a dangerous game they play. "They might kill you instead."

"Exactly!"

Goosebumps ripple my skin. Not only do they volunteer to be his body double, but they do so eagerly.

My cheeks and neck burn red hot as I bite my bottom lip.

Max gasps and points at me. "Oh, great Mother, you like him!"

I clutch my chest. "I—"

"Who *doesn't?*" says Taryn. "He's the greatest person alive."

"That's not the kinda likin' I'm talking about, Tar."

Taryn frowns. She shakes her head and continues picking weeds. I encourage her by helping, anything to change the subject. We work our way around the trunk in two groups, clearing her roots until we meet on the other side. They consider this to have been a grand task, one that has taken a long time. They'd been expecting word from their parents by now.

"Do you know where all the grown-ups went?" Taryn asks.

"There's trouble in the outlands," I say. "King Regulus needs to show his enemy how many loyal followers he has behind him."

"Is it the Wolf? Did she finally attack the border?"

"You don't need to worry about her. She's been tamed. She's actually coming to help us because..."

A young girl's scream cuts me off. My words are enough to send her bolting out of the dome. Taryn hugs her weed basket and shakes her head in denial, eyes watering in terror. "No, no, no..."

Max puts a comforting arm around her and pulls her close. "Shhh, it's okay. Remember the King's Promise? No wolf will ever walk the streets of Amyria. Whatever he's doing, it's to keep the fight far, far away from here."

I snatch the wicker basket from Taryn's grasp. She instinctively reaches for it, but I spring up into flight, then hover out of reach. I unravel the strands and rework them into a crude game ball, with a pigeon egg I'd scrounged earlier at center.

She breaks free of Max's embrace, the fear in her eyes hardened to determination. Her mouth twitches with a smile. She bends her knees to lunge, and is about to do so when something behind me stops her dead.

I whirl around to see a crowd crossing the field toward us. It's almost an army.

"Do you know them?" I ask. "Who are they?"

"East-enders."

"I see a few Southy's, too," says Max. "Seems almost every adult got called to service. Never heard of anything like it before—no school, no civil work, no one telling us what to do."

"No one keeping order," I say, noting the aggressive expressions on the sea of adolescent faces approaching us. Miscreants who see a brief window to rule a kingdom.

Taryn shrinks behind me. Max, too.

"Where's the Omniguard?" Taryn asks Max. "Papa said they'd be everywhere."

"Yea, they're supposed to be patrolling, but they're holed up in their stations. They only respond to reports."

If I get into a fight with a mob of kids, I'll end up killing one for sure. Lucky for them, an epic idea has been brewing in my mind.

I approach the mob.

"So it's true," says the leader. "We have an alien in our midst. The King told my father about you, and my father thought he'd lost his mind."

I don't need to see the golden flicker in his eyes, nor the slit pupils, to know what has inspired this boy's campaign of mischief. His cavalier approach toward me tells me the force driving him is all too familiar with my kind. But I can use this to my advantage.

"Are you here for the tournament?"

The leader cocks his head and gives me a puzzled look. "Tournament?"

"Sure." I hold up the wicker ball. "King Regulus summoned me to host it. He has a great banquet planned for the winners."

"Prizes, too," says Taryn, stepping out from behind me.

"Yea," says Max. "The best prizes."

"What kinda prizes?"

"You get to tour the King's villa," I tell them, thinking of the exquisite armored displays. "Anything you see that you like, you can have. Anything."

This gets their attention. The young mobsters exchange surprised looks, their intrigue too strong to disguise. Those in front turn to huddle for discussion. The way the remaining crowd gathers around to listen tells me they're the core members.

If it's a Watcher who possesses the boy, this will provide a nice distraction. The less eyes on the battle board, the better. Besides, who better to show them the innocence of this race than these civilized children at play? Perhaps it might inspire some hesitation in their campaign to exterminate them.

Some time passes, then their leader turns back to face me.

"We only play Southy rules."

"Of course," I say. "Everyone knows Southy rules rule. Now, let's make us some teams."

Everything falls into place remarkably well. Life in Regulus's capital involves plenty of community activities that require lots of organization, even at the lowly levels of ten-year-olds.

Thirty teams of twenty form with impressive coordination. Each kid seems in the habit of carrying a colored sash in their tunic, which they use to identify their team. There's red, purple, orange, green, and everything in between.

"This field is big enough to play two games at once," I say, sizing up the park boundaries. It could actually host four smaller games, but this is a big deal. Can't have games interfering with each other.

"I'll draft up a schedule," says an older girl, whipping out a notepad.

"I'll get some prizes from papa's shop," offers Taryn.

Her father's shop must boast some fine wares, because the excitement in the crowd becomes electrified.

"We'll need jugs of water to stay hydrated," adds Max. This receives less fanfare, but he gets a few volunteers to go with him.

The scheduler holds up her notepad. "This whole affair will take about a week, if we're to do it right."

"Perfect," I say, feeling my own excitement grow. A week of high energy games will get me amped up real good.

When Taryn returns, I notice she's not wearing an armband.

"I never got picked," she tells me solemnly.

I place a hand on her shoulder. "Good, because no one knows the rules better than you. I'll need you officiating one of the matches."

She straightens up, her eyes flaring wide in disbelief. "Really?"

I offer her a whistle. "First game starts in ten minutes."

The organized mob plays fair and well. All they needed was someone of good faith in charge. Without authority, these types of societies tend to crumble.

Once the more timid children get used to the fact that I'm an alien, which requires demonstrations of flight and destruction, I hover over the action, caught up in every pass. It's hard not to cheer, which draws criticism from the players. A referee must be impartial.

Taryn has less fun with her role. She wheezes, her cheeks glowing red from exertion as she tries to keep pace with back-to-back matches. This physical activity has the opposite effect on her than me. I'll have to recruit another official to spell her off.

"I wish I could fly," she says with a pout.

"You can."

She gives me a curious look.

"Close your eyes and spread your arms."

Taryn obeys, a nervous smile spreading across her face.

I hook my arms under her armpits and set my wings to work, and together our feet rise from the ground. She shrieks and pulls her arms in to hug herself, so I squeeze her tight from behind. Her panicked breathing flexes inside my hold, so I take care not to suffocate her.

"Lucky you," I tell her. "This is one thing you get to do before your King does."

This claim takes her breath away for a moment. When she resumes, her heart flutters with excitement where'd there just been fear. We're above the residential buildings when she says, "Higher."

My wings obey, buzzing faster to lift us into the artificial blue sky. She stares at the Central Spire in awe, until a geodesic grid reveals itself. Here, blue sky gives way to night, as if we've risen into Earth's upper atmosphere, up to the edge of outer space.

I'm unsure how Taryn is taking this without seeing her expression. Has she ever seen the construct of her sky? Do I now break the illusion of her reality?

She reaches out as if to touch the dome roof, speechless.

"Higher?"

She nods, so upward we go. She bursts into laughter, hysterical giggling, then screams like an Aeri diving down to scare an unsuspecting Fori. She waves her arms in my embrace, thrashing and kicking in exhilaration. I lock my hands over her chest to ensure I don't drop her.

"Higher, Nya! Take me higher!"

It's a glorious feeling, being part of someone else's greatest moment. We rise closer to the curved dome roof, where the support rafters reflect an orange glow.

Strange.

"When is next sunrise?" I ask.

"Two months, four days, and twenty-two hours."

Her answer is oddly specific. How can she be so sure? I soon see it doesn't matter, because the orange glow comes not from a rising sun.

We exit the dome from a hole in the roof and collapse onto its curved surface, where a cool night breeze carries smoke and ash from distant fields.

Tears blur my eyes, through which flickering orange patches mark a trail of destruction along The Artery. Black smoke swallows the slithering aurora above the fiery patches. And in the distance beyond... A great swath of wildfire lights up the foothills of the mountains.

My heart drops like a meteor. Raven's army has crossed the border.

I force myself to look upon Mount Tuck and become nauseous with shame. Can Regulus see what's coming? Why does Lex have to make such a grand display of her deceit? Hopefully this is part of some radical plan to deceive Deka's spy. That's kind of what I was hinting at before we parted ways.

Yes, that must be what she's doing. This is actually a good thing. With Deka hosting a Watcher, reports of disarray amongst the humans will build Jexa's confidence. Two nations at each other's throats, one setting the other's world on fire. Division at its deepest. But Regulus doesn't need Alexandra's Army to hold the gateway. If the model of Mount Tuck in his strategy room is even half completed in real life, and with all his citizens called to arms on those slopes, he'll hold them off without any help from Ortaria. I just need to keep them out of his way.

My heart clenches tight inside my gut. It's the King's response I should be most worried about. Will he abandon Mount Tuck to head off the 'invaders'?

Yes. Any reasonable leader would.

"Go hide away with the others," I tell Taryn, then I leap into flight.

"Wait!"

I turn to see Taryn sprawled on her belly, desperate to stay as close to the dome roof as possible.

Oh, Magister forgive me! I almost left her here.

I scoop her up and drop through the hole to bring her back to the playing field.

"Tournament is on hold," I say. "Go to your homes and stay there until I return."

Max shoves to the front of the crowd. "What's going on?"

"The Wolf!" shouts Taryn. "She's almost here!"

That does the trick. Everyone scatters, with some banging into each other as they bolt in crisscrossing retreat. All but one flees to safety. The adolescent mob leader stands alone in the field, staring at me with a wicked smile.

"What's your name?" I ask.

He frowns. He has to think about it for a minute, then he replies: "Kane."

"Go home, Kane. Your work here is done."

He considers my command, defiance beginning to fortify in his eyes. But then he nods and gives me a wink, then turns around to follow the crowd.

Max drags Taryn through the calamity beyond. Good. One less person for me to worry about while I go stop a civil war.

CHAPTER 20

DEKA

A haze of black smoke hangs heavy in the air. The smell of burning plastic from a melted greenhouse dome is enough to gag me, yet it's nothing to the smell of scorched skin and hair.

"Commander, are you all right?"

I realize I've been wincing hard while pinching the bridge of my nose. One of my senior warriors stands before me under the bare branches of a willow tree, watching me curiously. Anxiously. I've seen how they all look at me after my first foray, where I slayed a heavily-armed enemy in reckless fashion, all while getting a few of my own killed.

"I'm fine. Back to the boats."

The shuffle of feet and clamor of weapons tells me my century obeys. They're getting good at this raiding business. A look around reveals not a structure unscathed by fire, the whole village ablaze or already scorched, yet we only just landed.

Soon you'll have a whole army of faces to haunt you.

I glance at two Polarian soldiers laid out over the tree

roots, half-dressed in their camouflage, their rifles flung into the river.

'They shouldn't have shot at us.'

Lex had planned to cruise by every settlement between here and Amyria, until a few villagers decided it was a nice day to become heroes.

Would your sweet little Mali have done any different? Can you picture her and her brother just sitting back while a blood-soaked enemy cruises unchecked into their heartland?

'They were soldiers,' I tell Jexa, eying the pair of dead Polarians at my feet. 'Dying for their country is what they do.'

When he woke today, he was a father. And she was a mother. They were brothers and sisters, sons and daughters.

My gut wrenches. 'All of this is on you.'

Keep telling yourself that. Eventually you'll have to face the truth: I'm just along for the ride. But I'll carry your guilt while I'm here.

'Care to put that to the test? Go ahead and leave, then see how many times my blade runs foul.'

Why would I do that, when we make such a fine team?

'I made it across the world without your help. I'll make it the rest of the way.'

Our partnership is in your best interest, trust me. If I leave now, you'll see what you really are.

'No longer blinded by your cloud of lies, I believe it.'

You have much you'd do well to keep hidden away. Even from yourself.

'How about you just tell me so I can face it now.'

You're not as pure as you think you are.

'That's it? I've been told I'm too soft.'

We'll see soon enough.

'Leave.'

You're a curious creature, Deka. By living vicariously through you, I've felt such terrible pleasures. The guilt your deeds bring you is unlike anything I could ever imagine. All this betrayal and killing, even when you know it will poison you for the rest of your life. It's such a dirty pleasure for me. There must be something I can offer in return.

'I don't need you anymore. I have Lex figured out.'

You don't even have yourself figured out. But... fine. If you wish me gone, say the words and I'll leave.

'Be gone.'

I wait a good while.

'Jexa?'

I wait some more.

'Are you there?'

Only the crackle of fire and nearby sobs answer me. I breathe a sigh of relief. She's really gone.

"Commander Deka."

I turn to see a young warrior at a trailhead that leads inland. Soot blackens his face, giving his frightened eyes even more urgency. He leans on his spear to catch his breath.

"What is it?"

"It's Centurion Argyle... He captured forty villagers hiding in a field. He's about to put them all to the sword."

My pulse pounds. Butcher innocent civilians? Yes, Argyle certainly would. Most who follow Lex have it in them, with few exceptions. This lad must be of Polarian birth, returned to reclaim his homeland. Atrocities like this don't sit well with his type.

"Lead the way," I tell him.

As I follow the young warrior through a winding row of

wilted corn stalks, my heart beats with hope. Down this path lies an opportunity to prove Jexa wrong. The very fact that this boy sought me out above all others is a testament to that. He sees me as a beacon of light in this army of darkness. My deeds are not so heinous as Jexa would have me believe. She has poisoned my mind. It's time to purify. And the absence of screams tells me I'm not too late.

A decorated battle banner appears first over the wilted stalks. Two dozen warriors gather in a field around its base, the red cresta of their centurion moving among them. It's a magnificent headpiece, the envy of any warrior, the scarlet hair standing high and straight like a mohawk on his helmet. To return home wearing one would be a glorious moment not just for myself, but for all my people. I'll have to remind Lex to secure me one.

Argyle's warriors stand with their backs to me, swords in hand. He paces before them, addressing detainees I cannot see.

"Commander Argyle," I say.

He halts his pacing and shoves through the line. "Ah, if it isn't the young Centurion. Come to watch the show?"

"Release the prisoners. Lex's orders."

He frowns and spreads his arms, looking around in a mock search. "Prisoners?"

His soldiers about-face to stare me down, and it's now I see they'd been looking at rolls of hay. Their line splits at the center as one half marches to my right, while the other half moves left to encircle me. A quick search for the young messenger who'd led me here turns up empty.

A lump balloons in my throat.

One of Argyle's men draws a dagger. "My brother was in that tent you burned."

Beads of cold sweat slide down my face and neck. It takes everything in me to not shout out for Lex. Instead, I keep my face hard as I pull my sword slowly from its scabbard. The faint *schwing* when the tip clears the metal throat brings a smile to Argyle's face.

A branch cracks behind me.

I spin and swing my sword high and then downward. The blade whacks a shield as a blow from someone else strikes my left flank. It's the first of many.

Blunt objects batter me—sword hilts and spear butts, clubs and bloody fists. They force me to my knees and then down onto my side. I gasp for air, but the blitz of kicking boots allows for none. My vision narrows as my mind shuts down.

The beating goes on forever. Pain grows ever sharper, my tender muscles and broken ribs feeling each strike with more intensity. A slow death for each life taken to save Sekarra. Warm blood drains from my ears, muffling their taunts, yet I hear Argyle order they leave my head unharmed. I'm to remain coherent for all of it. He wants me to feel every thump for all its worth.

It becomes unbearable. I want to cry out pleas to stop, but I can't. It must be a pitiful sight, because Argyle orders they back off.

He crouches before me. His face spirals and his words echo when he says, "Had enough?"

I try to nod, but my neck spasms from the trauma. He smiles and stands, then steps back and nods for his warriors to continue.

It's hell.

"Had enough?"

I want to scream out an emphatic *YES*, as if that helped me last time, but the relentless assault leaves me breathless.

"Had enough?"

It's a special kind of torture. This Argyle knows what he's doing too well.

"Had enough?"

Damn you, Argyle! Only...

"Had enough?"

It's not Argyle's voice asking the question.

Had enough?

Anger sears my heart. *Jexa...* She's been here the whole time. I should have known.

I won't ask you again, she says.

'Yes. I've had enough.'

Shame rises inside me, but it's only brief. Then I feel nothing. No pain. No fear. Only rage mixed with budding joy for what I'm about to do.

I find myself standing upright on my feet, though I don't recall how I got up from the ground. My two dozen assailants back away, their faces a mix of fear and surprise, shock and distress. Their gazes fix at my feet, where one foot presses down onto Argyle's neck. A lapse in consciousness must have occurred when Jexa took over, long enough to subdue Argyle and slay two of his finest.

She sends an impulse to my right thigh, forcing my knee to straighten and driving my foot down to crush the Centurion's neck.

"He made us do it," says the nearest warrior with both hands raised.

I kick up a spear and snatch it from the air, then twirl it with grace, shooting it forward and then behind, piercing flesh with each thrust, ahead and then back, my feet moving with finesse in a violent dance.

I submit to Jexa's blood ballet, the vengeful blows of my victims a fresh and yet distant memory. How much time the dance takes I do not know. It goes until I find myself standing alone and breathless, a blood-soaked spear gripped in my hands.

All around me, diced-up bodies litter the clearing. Their twisted faces stir nothing inside me, no shame nor guilt, until I sight one—the lad who lured me here. I never blamed him, not even during the worst of the beating. He had no choice. Argyle's commands are not to be refused, and for that I'd wished him no harm. Yet there he lies.

See, Deka. Incredible *things.*

I should be retching right now. The gruesome scene would force even my fierce friend Mali to spill her last meal. My war chief Marlok wouldn't even recognize me.

What will I become if I allow Jexa to continue her reign over me?

Unstoppable.

She's right. Anger and violence gives Jexa greater control over me. This dark alignment is the key to forging a strong use of her skills, but it comes at the cost of my autonomy.

I had a chance to make you beg there, when you were receiving the beating of a lifetime. And I didn't. I wonder why that is. Perhaps I've grown excessively fond of you. I find it disturbing how little pleasure your pain brings me. I'll have to watch myself around you. Or... could it be, Deka, that you're the one who can brighten my darkened heart? If your charm worked on a destructive dust maiden, then why not me?

Jexa is manipulating me. She'd have me believe I can change her. To see reason for her continued tenure.

'Yes, I'll show you the way.'

I sit cross-legged and close my eyes. I think of the last time Nya and I were together, floating in that hot spring, our bodies entwined, two hearts beating as one.

My belly twists with revolt, but it is not my own.

I think of our first kiss, on a beach under the stars of a distant planet, a hologram universe inside the Great Pyramid.

Don't you dare for a second think I don't know what you're doing, Jexa says. *If you think you can—*

I relive our kiss atop Lex's ramparts. This time I feel her warm lips melt into mine, smell that fresh spring scent of her hair, feel the silky softness of her skin.

My jaw quivers with the illness of another.

Deka, you little rat. You think you can drive me away like a cockroach in the light?

Yes. If violence and hate bring us into alignment, then love will force her out. An exorcism by the possessed host is the highest skill of the shaman warrior. This is my test of initiation.

Nya's powerful fingers skim my side under my shirt, so delicate. Almost real. My whole body tingles.

This isn't over, you disgusting little weasel. You think you can outwit me? Huh? I've seen what's in your heart. I know the workings of your mind. We'll see each other again, soon, in the flesh. Then I'll show you how...

I pull Nya close, closer than I've ever held anyone before. Passion floods me with a warmth I've not felt since our hot spring. It is that of a lover, one that holds no space for darkness or hate. A light that shines away the shadows from every corner of my heart and the darkest reaches of my mind.

And then... I'm alone. This time I'm sure of it, because the void Jexa leaves invites a torrent of all the terrible things she's been shielding me from.

First comes fear. My heart races and muscles tense as all the horrendous memories of when I should have been scared witless race back to me. A storm of angst swirls inside my chest, energy built up during Jexa's occupancy and kept at bay by her... grace? No, that's not the right word. Nothing about Jexa's nature is graceful.

Then comes the pain. It floods my body with the force of a busted dam, stabbing my chest with each breath, cleaving at my side and driving me to my knees. And my eye... it throbs with each heartbeat. My vision narrows, and the loss hits me for the first time.

My body trembles from agony, and yet I laugh. That's it. She is gone. Truly. My human emotions run freely now. I acknowledge each of them, the pain and the jealousy, the love and ambition. And when I look around...

I see what I've done without the protective filter of a Watcher guarding my psyche, and it makes me vomit.

"Traitor!" cries a man's voice.

In my distraction, I hadn't noticed the arrival of Lantz's century. They surround me completely, two ranks deep, eighty spear tips pointed my way. And this time there's no Jexa to save me.

CHAPTER 21

DEKA

I find myself in a painfully familiar position.

A committee of Centurions gather around me on the riverbank, where I kneel in chains. Their assembly has attracted Lex, who stands behind me, her sword drawn.

"You're telling me that one man, this *boy*, took out half our First Century? Among them Centurion Argyle, one of my finest fighters?"

"We have a witness."

Two warriors pull one of their own through the crowd. He sees me and tries to shirk back, whimpering as they force him forward. He falls to his knees and trembles, unable to look my way. Lex crouches before him.

"Did this boy kill fifty of my warriors?"

The witness vibrates and looks to the ground, speechless.

"Well," Lantz says on his behalf, "we don't know *exactly* how many there were. They're still sorting through the mess. But need I remind you that this isn't the first time he's done something like this?"

Lex clasps her hands behind her back and paces along

the river. She stares up at the sky, pondering. "Fifty great warriors, my *finest* warriors... gone."

"Plus the twenty-five he burned alive," adds Karla.

"When I seize control of Polaria," Lex muses, "I'll be a new queen ruling a foreign hive. Enemies will await me at every turn. Some in the shadows, some in plain sight. I'll need hardy hands and a sharp eye watching my back at all times—a *Primus Pillus*. I can think of none better suited for the task."

"*Him,*" says Lantz, "*Primus Pillus?* You're going to make the butcher of your own people your personal bodyguard?"

Lex spreads her arms wide. "If anyone feels more qualified, by all means, step forward and prove it."

My belly flips, and it takes everything in me to keep my jaw from quivering. Without Jexa's help, I'd not last long against any of Lex's warriors, let alone her Centurions.

A few grip their sword hilts, sizing me up. One leans close to the Second Century commander to whisper in his ear. He nods and whispers back. His words must confirm a claim the first man made, for his companion steps back and releases his hilt.

Lex gives them a good long while to mull it over. Too long, if you ask me.

I muster my fiercest stare, like a caged tiger, but on the inside I whimper like a kitten.

"Back to your boats," Lex says at last. "Next stop: Amyria."

The prospect of kicking in Regulus's front door so soon gets everyone moving, though some are reluctant to let me off so easily. They cast me wicked stares or devious grins. I commit each of them to memory.

"Follow me, *Primus Pillus*," says Lex. "I have something for you."

I follow her upriver along the bank, past ships where centuries regroup and prepare to sail our last leg.

"I knew they'd come for you eventually," Lex tells me.

"There's a lot you don't understand about what happened back there."

"Did you kill Argyle and his men?"

I swallow hard and nod.

"That's all I need to know."

She stops at the last ship in the flotilla, weighed down by crates and barrels of Lex's personal possessions. She reaches over the gunwale and flips open a wooden chest.

"I won't be able to do it again," I tell her.

"Are you growing a conscience all of a sudden? Will this newfound sense of morality allow me to die on your watch?"

She completely missed my meaning. Though, how would she ever guess the force behind my abilities?

Her rummaging produces two crossed scabbards, each with a long sword hilt extending from the top. Both katanas hang from a harness, which she holds up for me in offering. "This is where I'd normally get you to swear a vow to defend my life with yours, but we've all seen what oaths mean to you."

I hesitate. This is all so strange, so different than how I'd ever imagined my life to play out. None of this seems real.

Lex shakes the harness impatiently, a look of doubt rising in her.

I oblige her by slipping my arms through the crossed straps.

"When I'm seated upon my throne, and after I've blessed

both nations with harmony, I'll grant you your every desire. You may rule over all of Anterra if it makes you happy. So long as I wear the crown, it makes no difference to me. You just get me safely into Amyria, and all our debts shall be reversed."

A flurry of possibilities swirl in my mind and warm my heart. Why live Nya's dream of hiding away in mountain caves, when I could own the mountains? Nya and I would rule our territory with strength and justice. Lex will see me for a threat, of course, but what could she do? Stories of my paradise will spread. Polarians and Ortarians will flock to the borderlands in droves to live in peace, a place where two nations merge into one. Lex will hold onto what citizens remain with an iron fist, but it will only stoke their reverence for the promised land. And after a few decades of this, both cultures will unite through forces more powerful than war. I'll instill in my loyalists a passion for pushing tyrants like Lex and Regulus to obscurity. This world is done with their kind. The offspring of Nya and I will rule this great land with love and strength until the Earth itself dies. Our descendants will spread far and wide, repopulating places long forgotten. They'll bring the priceless gift of human love to those hiding in caves, lost and abandoned, haunted by vague ancestral memories of better days. It will be in those times when I atone for my sins here.

"I'll place that crown upon your head," I say, pulling the shoulder straps tight, then I draw one sword over my shoulder and hold it before me. I'm immediately enamored by the blade's mirror polish, how the purple fabric over my eye gives me a fierce, forbidding look. "And I'll kill whoever needs to die to make it happen."

Lex's smile breaks like sunlight through black clouds after a years-long storm, exposing a part of her long forgotten.

She grips the sword hilt at her hip and raises her chin, almost playfully. Almost child-like. "Fetch your shield, Primus Pillus. Amyria awaits us."

I find my shield leaned against the willow tree, beside the dead Polarian couple. I hadn't expected to need it when I went to confront Argyle. And I didn't. Not with Jexa lurking within. I'll not have that luxury in the quarrels to come.

My shield is a crinkled mess. Wrinkles in the deformed edges mark numerous close calls, where a flurry of bullets had challenged Jexa's reflexes. I'll need to beat out the dents to straighten the rippled star on the pockmarked face, though perhaps I should leave it, to warn future enemies that they weren't the first to try to stop me.

I sling the battered plate over my shoulder, and I'm headed back to the river when voices stop me.

"*Three* raids," comes a harsh whisper, "and she hasn't wet her sword yet. Not a single drop of Polarian blood."

"What are you getting at?" Karla responds in a hushed voice.

I crouch low and listen to the siblings huddled behind a tree.

"I'm starting to wonder how committed she is," says Karl. "I'm not the only one. See them Nunatak clansmen jump ship back there?"

I'd noticed this myself, boat crews swapping members at each stop or even while underway on the river. I didn't understand it at the time, but it all makes sense now. Two Polarians had deserted during the Corpisaul raid, at their first opportunity. Those who remain are feeling safe and secure for the first time in eleven years. And they mustn't like the Ortarian fervor for their kinsman's blood during the raids since Corpisaul. Deep in the Polarian heartland, their Ortarian companions feel more alone by the mile. Division grows deeper, to the point many abandon their century for the safety of more friendly faces, in case things take a sour turn. Lex's behavior since crossing the border hasn't helped matters.

"The Commander hasn't killed a single Polarian," Karl goes on, "yet she didn't hesitate to execute one of her own Centurions. An *Ortarian* Centurion, in case you've forgotten. Then she makes that foreign trickster her bodyguard?"

"Yeah..." Karla says, clearly burned over my appointment. Many aboard Lex's boat had hopes of attaining the honor for themselves.

The thumping pulse of my frightened heart wails on my eardrums. It seems I'll soon have my hands full. I think I'll be needing a second shield, and another set of hands.

CHAPTER 22

NYA

Croplands and pastures sprawl out from Amyria, all the way to the pyramid-shaped mountain called Tuck, where a forest rings the square base.

The Polarian turnout there does not disappoint. Each of the mountain's four sides boasts horizontal lines of red light that stretch from corner to corner. Whether these are tactical markers or flares, from here I cannot tell.

I glide low to continue my approach under the canopy. I do this not only to avoid spooking the defenders, but also to keep from crashing into the gateway's Anomaly. As with the pyramids of Giza, the gravitational vortex produced by this colossal energy transducer denies me the use of my wings. It's the same for the Watchers though, which is a tremendous advantage for these *sapien* defenders. Only the feather wings of my Aeri cousins may roam the skies over a gate, but they are scarce and mostly cowards.

As I approach the slope that rises beyond the trees ahead, I find myself drifting lower toward the ground. My wings buzz faster to compensate, but to little effect.

I smash through a rotten log and tumble over fallen branches that crack under my rolling weight. It's loud, but my swearing is louder until I hit a pillar of bark that stops me dead. My collision with the tree trunk puts an abrupt end to my cussing and leaves me in a daze.

Goosebumps ripple my skin and snap me from my stupor. I'm being watched.

A quick scan of my surroundings reveals a silhouette crouched on a nearby tree branch. She leaps into flight just as my attention falls onto her, two ragged wings gliding away.

Beams of light cut through the darkness around me.

"Who's there?" shouts a boy.

Footsteps swish through nearby ferns. The light beams bounce and grow brighter in their approach. They sweep side to side, criss-crossing in their search.

I wobble to my feet and steady myself on the maple trunk.

"That you, Shuby?" comes a girl's voice.

I step out from behind the tree with both hands raised. "I'm a messenger. I bring news for the King."

Eight white orbs hover in an extended line and accost me with their blinding light. Two guys and a girl scream in fright, and I should have expected what comes next, but I don't have time to tip-toe around.

BANG!

A punch through my shoulder sends me spinning to the ground. I end up on my back with eight shaking lights hovering directly overhead. My ears ring sharply as hot pain spreads from my chest to my fingertips. Rather than the usual piercing, it's more a dull, deep ache that's somehow worse. Like it'll never leave.

"Don't move!" orders a man.

The shot has left me breathless and unable to sit up or roll over despite my efforts.

I reach up into the nearest light and grasp a narrow steel tube.

My heart races, because I know what comes next.

CRACK!

This bullet rips through my palm and explodes out my elbow. It packs more punch than the first, and the searing pain makes me forget all about the ache in my shoulder. I hardly recognize my own screams. It's like yelling into a box, all muffled yet close and intense.

I can do nothing as the warriors load me onto a stretcher. They carry me up the slope while a girl to my right keeps a handgun aimed at my face.

"Are you one of them?" she asks.

"I'm a friend."

"Don't talk to her," says the boy carrying the head of my stretcher. "She might cast a spell on us."

Word of my arrival spreads quickly up the mountain.

"Nya!"

My heart misses a beat.

"Put her down," commands the King.

My captors lower me to the ground.

I can hardly roll my head to the side. This is bad. Right now I'd be in pitiful shape for even a small skirmish, but to square off with Jexa... It would be a disappointing show, that I can guarantee.

Regulus's pale face hovers over mine.

"Get a physician here," he tells those gathered around. "Now!"

He brushes my hair back from my forehead. "I did like you said. I ordered my whole army here. Do you bring me news?"

"I..." My head spins. The pain in both my arms cripples me so fiercely that I can't string together the right words.

Regulus strokes my hair softly. "Hang in there, Nya. We're going to give you something for the pain, and then something to give you a boost."

A gray-haired man appears over me, opposite Regulus.

"Give her a *dazy*," Regulus tells him. "Then some epi. Can't have her dozing off on us. Nya, stay with me."

I feel a pinch in my thigh, then pressure. A flood of golden light warms my body and fills me with such peace that I could fall asleep forever and not even care.

"We're losing her," says Regulus, his voice a distant echo. "Give her the epi."

"One round of epinephrine, coming right up."

I'm vaguely aware of my hand reaching up to brush Regulus's cheek.

Another pinch pricks my thigh. This one has the opposite effect, injecting a tornado of energy that starts in my heart and electrifies me from my fingers to my toes.

My wings spring me from my stretcher. I almost smash heads with Regulus, who falls onto his back as I land on my feet. Metal rattles as hundreds of soldiers aim their guns at me.

I gulp down the lump swelling in my throat. This is going to hurt. A lot.

Regulus jumps to his feet and throws out both arms. "Stand down. She's a friend."

All weapons lower at once.

Regulus directs his healer to wrap my arm in a sling, then addresses his troops. "Who put those bullets in her?"

A girl raises a shaky hand. A boy steps forward to join her, but I don't know who shot me where.

"Stay here," Regulus tells the pair. "Everyone else, back to your posts."

The throng of soldiers disperses, but many eyes drift my way to size me up with either suspicion or wonder, or suspicious wonder. My two assailants remain with their heads lowered.

Regulus leans close to me. "Who's burning my fields."

"It's Lex—"

The King jolts, but I'm quick to grab his arm to steady him.

"It's to distract the Watchers," I say. "She's on her way here. Have faith. She's just causing havoc to throw off our enemy."

"A ploy of division?"

"Exactly!" The Watchers can't resist carnage, so it'll also serve to keep them distracted as well. But I dare not mention words like *carnage* when trying to assure him.

Regulus's mossy green eyes stare deep into mine. It's a hard, questioning look, heavy with distrust. Then he nods, faintly. Ever so faintly.

"I'll admit, I've had my doubts since we last spoke. My generals thought I'd lost my mind. I almost had to resort to the old ways, by lopping off heads to remind them who calls the shots. But when I saw The Artery swell a few days ago, I knew right then... Nya had managed to talk some sense into the Wolf. See, Alexandra dammed off that river five years ago, to choke our fresh water supply. She was trying to lure me into Ortaria with an invasion force. Into a trap. But when she opened it up, that sealed it for me. My commanders, too. You managed to fix that which could not be fixed. You're a gift from the stars, Nya. You'll always have a place in my kingdom."

My heart flutters inside my belly. I don't tell him it was the Ripper who blew the dam. He seems well pleased thinking it was Lex, well pleased enough to hold all his forces here on Mount Tuck.

He looks to the boy and girl standing nearby. "Got a little trigger happy, did we? Well, now she's your burden to bear. Make sure to take good care of her and show her all the sights."

The medic finishes my sling. It helps with the pain greatly, but my legs tremble under my weight. Regulus sits me onto the stretcher and motions to the shooters.

They bend to grab the handles at each end, and together they lift me, wobbling as they struggle to keep their footing on the slope. I sit with my feet dangling over the side, facing up the mountain as my stretcher bearers walk diagonally upslope toward the first line of red lights.

The bustling activity on the mountain reminds me of an ant hill. Heads bob along the lowest horizontal line that stretches across the base, some dipping and rising as they fling dirt from their deepening trenches. Others scoop this discarded dirt into green bags and stack them onto a low wall on the downslope side of the trench.

It's the same at the flickering line of lights three hundred paces behind—soldiers digging trenches and building small walls before them. As it is with the next one up, and the next one after that, so on and so forth, all the way to the peak.

Shouts from around the far corners suggest it's much the same on all sides.

A violet flag flaps before the nearest trench, yet every warrior here wears a blue armband.

"My troops will prepare the first defense line for our allies," Regulus explains. "I recall purple was the Arcturus color?"

I stifle a smile. How considerate of him. "It still is."

"My officers thought it best to post them where we can all keep an eye on them."

It's sound logic, though I'm not sure Lex will approve. Then again, at that point, she won't have much of a choice.

"Captain, have the Blue Line move their machine guns to the far corners," says Regulus to a nearby soldier. "They'll have a wider overlap of fire from there."

"Straight away, Your Highness."

My throbbing arm reminds me of the damage these bullets inflict here. Normally such wounds might have healed already, but the absence of a nurturing light keeps them raw.

Fatigue sets deep into my bones. It weighs heavy in my muscles, yet my heart beats lightly with hope. Sizing up six sandbag terraces between here and the summit, it's clear the Watchers will have a hell of a climb on their horizon.

Regulus walks beside my stretcher on the uphill side. "Six defense lines stand between here and the top. Each will be rigged with explosive charges." He points to an empty wooden box with *TNT* stamped in red on the side.

An officer strings a wire from the Purple Line up to the Blue trench behind it.

"The company occupying the trench at their back will hold the detonator. That way, if the enemy overruns the forward position, they won't be able to use our own fortifications against us."

My heart races with excitement. It's brilliant. Not only will it deny the Watchers cover, but each blast up the mountain will damage the gateway. The effect on its function will only be minor at the bottom, but as the explosions rise toward the narrow summit, the impacts on the structure will degrade the gate's conductivity. It may even make it inoperable.

I relax on my litter. Until recently, a plan that involved destroying the gateway would have stressed me to no end. But the fear of never seeing home again has since become a thing of the past. Recent days have taught me a good many lessons, the most important of which is that home is not a physical place. It's an alignment of the heart. Destiny has denied me the desires of my past for a reason. My home and everyone there are a part of who I am, but they are not my future. Deka and I have a lot to work out, but things will be different after the battle. Anterra's humans will recognize their true hero here. After hearing the tales from Mount Tuck, no *sapien* will deny Regulus's right to rule. Then Deka and I will be free to wander. I'll remind him of who he was, even if it requires a trip back to his home caverns.

This is all assuming we both survive the battle, of course. Chances aren't looking good for either of us.

But no, that's not the way to think. Deka and I *will* survive the battle, and once we defeat the Watchers, we'll round up all my remaining cousins and find a nice piece of land beyond the reach of human dramas. We'll live out our days in eternal summer, in a paradise designed just for us by my Fori and Ori cousins. It will be the best they ever built, the one made for ourselves.

Thwacking steel comes from warriors pounding stakes into the slope. Their companions stretch strands of steel thorns at mid-shin height to create obstacles between trenches, with narrow lanes providing passage for friendly warriors. A machine gun points down each of these lanes to welcome our enemy.

These barbarous measures fill me with joy. Much like the Watchers, the *sapiens* are masters of war in their own right.

Regulus plants his hands on his hips and nods approvingly at his rising layers of trench lines. "No way are they getting through this."

His confidence hits me like a punch to the gut. "Please do not underestimate this enemy. They've conquered a thousand races and driven countless species into extinction. They'll study your defenses from afar and attack with a clear plan." I'd spotted one scout upon my arrival. No doubt there are others scattered near and far.

Regulus's lips tighten. "When will they come?"

The whacking of posts and tossing of dirt tapers off as nearby warriors listen for my response.

"They get their energy from the sun," I say. "It also powers their swift healing, so it would be unwise for them to attack during extended darkness. Your six-month night has kept you safe all these years, but now that you're at open war with them, they have an extreme tactic they can use."

Regulus raises his chin and gives me a curious look.

"It's called an Amplifier," I say, "an artificial sun designed to grow vegetation in rugged conditions. But it may not be enough to fuel a war machine. They'd have to string a network of Amplifiers from the north to relay the sunlight, so any energy that reaches here will be too weak to sustain them."

"Swift healing..." Regulus says, stroking his chin. "And if they attack after sunrise with an Amplifier? What's the best way to stop them?"

"Cut off their heads. That's one thing they can't grow back. Second-best way is to ram something into their heart and make sure it stays there. The heart will heal around it, but it won't function properly."

Regulus nods. "I'll tell my officers." To my escort, he says, "Bring her to the Eagle's Nest."

CHAPTER 23

DEKA

Amyria rises from the river like a long-awaited sunrise. First comes the golden glow of her lights, then the crest of the nearest dome. It rises with each mile until the city takes up half the sky before us. A twisted spire stands at center, over the cluster of domes, casting white light like a beacon, beckoning Lex and her entourage home.

I stare in wonder from the helm of her flagship, occasionally working the tiller to keep us at front and center of our flotilla. The glow burns and blurs my eyes, yet I stare on. Only...

I brush a finger over my cheek. It slides across a trail of tears. I don't care. This city is a testament to the brilliance of my people. A beacon that asserts our worth. *You see us, Watchers?* it says. *We are worthy.* No wonder Lex has missed this place so dearly.

She stands to my right, staring astern, her back to the golden glow of her desire. "Are we two boats short?" she says. "Did you do a double count last check?"

"All forty-four were accounted for," says Karl, almost struggling to contain his exasperation.

"You're sure?"

"The boat that went rogue a few days back rejoined us after the last raid, so we're actually up one. Broken rudder had them washed into a mudbank near Kaladia."

"That boat to the right there," says Lex with a frown, "is that Sixth Century? They're listing pretty hard to starboard. And they're down by their head, too. We should go ashore to balance their ballast."

"Their trim is fine," I say. I don't need to look over my shoulder to know this. "Steady as she goes."

Lex glares at me in disbelief. She opens her mouth to speak, but Karla's voice from the bow stops her: "I think that's the Elbow comin' up."

Lex's eye flares wide. She straightens, hunching her shoulders, and remains facing her trailing flotilla. She hasn't looked at Amyria once since the first dome rose before us.

"We should stop and do a count," she says. "We'll need every warrior when we—"

"Row!" I shout.

Lex gives me a bewildered look. I don't care. We need speed for what awaits us ahead.

"Row!"

Our warriors pull their oars in unison. Wood groans, grunts rise, and water sloshes as we make one last run for the capital.

The river turns sharply rightward at the aptly-named Elbow. Our momentum carries us halfway across to the far bank, but the current sweeps us sidelong, so I pull the tiller to keep our dragon head facing the far bank. Lex grabs my arm and leans close to steady herself.

"Row!"

Ten strong pulls drives our keel into soft mud. I yell for them to row harder than ever, motivating them with threats I dare not repeat beyond this moment. We slide through mud until we can slide no more. Our landing would be easier on a solid riverbank, but the flood has washed them all away.

Karla sticks an oar over the bow and jabs straight down through the mud until it stops. "About knee-high here."

Lex watches her dozens of dragon ships crawl through the mudflats to join us. A few that got swept downriver are rowing their way back up. Without the drag of a ten thousand pound bomb weighing them down, the other boats could easily surpass us if they wished, but none dare steal this moment from Lex.

"This is it," I tell her. "Give the order."

"Over the sides!" Lex yells. "Muster on the high ground!"

We carry only weapons and shields when we splash down into the mud. Karla was wrong. Our well-fed bodies are heavier than a shoved oar, and we sink to our waists.

Lex sloshes her way to the front and leads the advance. I struggle to keep up. Luckily the ground underfoot hardens after a hundred paces, and soon we rise to our knees, then to our ankles, and finally we strut across dead grass.

Lex stands where the flood-wash meets the field, watching her army struggle through the mud toward us.

"Form up in battle order," she tells her new First Century commander—Argyle's replacement—Centurion Lantz. "I want a head count."

I stand by Lex's side, silent, grateful I don't have to command a century through this mess.

The army takes nearly an hour to wade through the muck and fall in on dry land.

It's not hard to pick out the Polarians falling into line. They stare at the domes in wonder, seeing the city not as a place of conquest, but something to be protected. When they glance at Lex, their torn stares are cause for concern.

Paranoia swells inside me with every Polarian to join us from exile. How many lurk now in our ranks? Will they give their Ortarian counterparts a fight if they decide to turn on us? If they were to assassinate Lex, no doubt Regulus would issue pardons and raise them to high grace.

I pull one sword from its sheath and a whetstone from my pocket. I slide the sharpening stone along the edge of the blade, producing a slow grating sound to remind them who now watches the Wolf's back. The boy who sent nearly a century of their finest to their afterlives, all on his own. The boy who'd not beat a single one of them now if his own life depended on it.

When all have mustered on dry land, Centurion Lantz gives Lex the final number: "Two thousand, two hundred, and twenty-one present and ready to fight."

"How many ships?"

Lantz glances uneasily toward the river. "Forty-two made it ashore."

Lex's eye twitches. "So we did lose two."

"They won't make a difference," I tell her. "Not while we have the element of surprise."

Lex glares at the river, grinding her jaw. Then she

narrows her eye on her ranks of warriors, half purple and half brown from the waist down with mud.

"We can't march into Amyria looking like a pack of wild dogs. Set up camp here and wait for the stragglers to catch up. Fetch clean water from the river. Have the men shave and the women tie back their hair. Then get some rest. Final inspection is in eight hours."

Lex doesn't notice when the Ortarians plant their shields at their feet. She's too fixated on Mount Tuck. Even Centurion Lantz remains firm, failing to rush off to fulfill his master's orders in his usual manner. I see the resolve in his eyes. He's not making camp. When I gage the stares of his followers, I see mutiny staring back at me. They didn't come all this way for a holiday, and they don't need Lex to ransack the capital.

I tuck the whetstone into my pocket and pick up my shield. Lex needs to start marching forward, or there's going to be a battle on this riverbank. Luckily, I know it's not soiled uniforms and missing ships holding her back.

She stares at the mountain glittering in the distance. "It's less than an hour paddle with this current. We should go see what's happening there. At least get a measure of his forces. What if it's a diversion? He might have his whole army hiding in the capital, waiting to ambush us. We're probably walking straight into a trap."

"They're not in Amyria," I say. The innumerable lights on the mountainside move steadily. Even to set them up would require a substantial effort. And if Regulus wanted to ambush us, he'd have done so on the river, and with great success. It wouldn't take more than a dozen machine guns to turn our fleet into driftwood.

"Then Nya must have shown him some pretty convincing evidence of the invasion for him to deploy his whole army there. We should at least send scouts to see what's happening. What's the hurry to see the capital, anyway?"

I drop my shield and grab Lex's arm. She gives me a wide, almost panicked stare. I step between her and the river, where I take hold of her shoulders and spin her to face Amyria. Her shoulders hunch, muscles hard with tension.

"Your destiny is within reach," I say. "You just have to reach out and take it."

Lex stares at Amyria's domes, her neck craning back to take in their golden glory for the first time in fifteen years.

"It's better than I remembered."

"It will look even better from up in that tower, wouldn't you say?"

Lex's shoulders relax and lower. She turns to face me with a soft glowing eye and a warm smile. Then she grits her teeth, her top lip curling into a wicked grin.

"Fall in!" she yells. "Marching order! No more messing about. Tonight, we feast in Amyria!"

CHAPTER 24

NYA

The punishment for shooting a guest is to carry them up the entire rainbow mountain. It's a grueling task that sees its share of tripping, and, even at their best, the pair wobble and jar my stretcher around, which aggravates my wounds fiercely. I'd walk if Regulus hadn't threatened to have them both shot for allowing it, so I resign myself to the awful climb.

Instead I admire the wonders of the Rainbow Mountain. It's just like Regulus's model—the four thousand feet of slope on each side broken neatly into colored lines. Blue flags mark the lowest and longest of the occupied trenches, with their soldiers sporting matching blue armbands. An empty violet trench sits below them, awaiting the arrival of Lex's army. The next tier soldiers, above the Blue Line, wear green bands to match the flags flying at each end of their trench. Then it's yellow for the Yellow Line, and after that orange. Seven hundred feet separate each trench, where mazes of wired thorns force my escort to zigzag up narrow lanes toward machine gun nests.

"You're not even that heavy," the girl assures me, as if being well-fed is something to be ashamed about. "It's the shale and all these obstacles."

As we gain elevation and close distance toward the peak, the number of soldiers wearing matching armbands becomes more scarce with the narrowing trenches. Overlooking the Yellow lines, the soldiers who wear orange bands amount to a fraction of the Blue Line defenders down below, by many times.

By the time we weave through the Red Line I feel bad for my carriers. Yes, the pair who'd shot me receive my pity. Their pain by now must exceed my own, but they soldier on without making me feel the least bit a burden.

This final stretch sees many soldiers race up ahead of us. They carry pads lashed into mattresses and spring up a tent over the summit, where I am to rest.

A crown of sandbag walls box in the flattened peak, where shooters keep watch in all directions through the telescopes atop each of their long guns.

Observers also keep watch from the basket of a hot air balloon floating directly overhead. Down the mountain's back side, dozens more balloons sit on the ground in a makeshift landing field. I've heard many militia fighters live too far from the railway, so they must use this alternative transport. Depending on the wind, I'd say it's probably faster. But that train was pretty fast too, so maybe not.

Right here, this patch upon which the soldiers set my stretcher in the middle of the Eagle's Nest, is where the final battle will be fought. The four sandbag walls around us occupy the edges of the flat summit, where the Capstone must sit neatly to unlock the mighty gate below. Before long, this patch of dirt may be crowded with humans desperately fighting for their lives with nowhere to go. The Watchers will have to evict every one of them with godly force, all while dragging the Capstone uphill, and then perform an alignment ceremony.

Listing off their perils allows me to breathe easier. And if the Watchers manage to open this gate, at least none of us will be alive to see whatever comes through.

To the north, the half moon rises above the ocean horizon. If I had to guess, I'd say the Watchers will come from the long peninsula that reaches far into the sea.

Although the soldiers have fashioned me a bed under canopy, I sit on the outside of a sandbag wall with my back to it, facing the moon. I close my eyes and beckon its soft light to infuse me with reflected solar particles. But even at this high elevation she offers me little.

The Wolf Moon hardly rises over the horizon. She just skims across distant mountains, teasing me with a slight trickle of light. Starving me to death with cold indifference. Hopefully the Watchers hold off their attack until after she's grown full and gone, so I can at least heal my wounds. A few nights up here with a full moon should set me straight good enough. With this view and all the protection of man's greatest army around me, I can spend the next week in deep recovery mode.

I'm already nodding off when laughter shatters the tense stillness. It's as jarring to me as gunfire, and I immediately suspect the Aeri.

I jump to my feet and scan the sky. But it's the wrong direction.

Cheers and shouts of encouragement rise from down the

mountain, where two shirtless males compete in a digging contest. From what I gather, whoever can dig to their waist first wins.

The joy of the cheering soldiers reminds me of a similar moment with my own people. Fortifying the Giza pyramids had been exhausting work, and playful competitions like this had done wonders for our spirit. Many of those contests ended in a wrestling match. But I don't expect that will happen here, as a closer look between both contestants reveals Regulus's red hair and pale skin.

Well, that's it. I've officially seen it all. Imagine, a *king*, of all people, getting his hands dirty.

I gush with admiration for this royal boy. Would Lex ever do the same? I have no doubt, but there'd be no laughter about it.

This place, with all its menacing contraptions of war lying in wait, provides me with all the warm comfort of a Hive. The males here don't look at me the same way Lex's did, either. Polarians have a code of behavior they follow naturally, one rooted in respect and decency. Their enemies across the border might live closer to nature, but there's something to be gained from Polaria's level of civilization. At least as far as humans are concerned, anyway. In the end it all comes down to balance I suppose.

It would be mighty rude to see the hard work of those who prepared my bed go unnoticed, so I climb inside and pull the covers up over my head. Latticed branches would suit me better, but if I pretend the mattresses are stuffed with Aeri feathers, I find myself slipping into a ridiculously relaxing sleep.

If there ever was a holiday haven for an Entropath, this would be it.

Candlelight dances over camouflage netting overhead, shaping the illusion of a tree canopy. Slivers of green-and-black polymer rustle in the breeze, which I hardly hear over the cacophony of weapons clicking and slapping as soldiers test their functions—machine guns and rifles brought to readiness.

Wood creaks from a nearby chair, upon which Regulus sits smoking a pipe, his feet up on the sandbag wall. Draped over the back of his chair is his long gray coat. An armband around the upper sleeve displays the color of not one trench, but all. From purple at the bottom, to red at the top, his spirit stands in the trenches beside each of his warriors. When the fighting starts, he'll not be hiding away up here.

But for the moment, all is calm, enough so that I could almost forget we're atop a colossal fortress. I must have woken during the assigned hours of sleep for his troops.

I stretch out in the comfort of my bed, which feels like lounging on a cloud, something these humans have mastered. They take their sleep very seriously. I could get used to this. After the war, I'll persuade Regulus to turn this place into a vacation villa. He could do it. On this land, his word moves mountains.

He shuts his book and turns in his seat to face me. "You're awake."

I hold up my hands to study my arms, where my wounds have already begun to heal. It's amazing what a little rest can do. In fact, the relaxation in my muscles tells me I've just had the best sleep in over four hundred years.

I spread my fingers wide, and between them I notice Regulus watching me intensely.

"Do you like what I've done with the place?" he asks.

I survey the Eagle's Nest with a grin. Never could anyone ever impress me so thoroughly as Regulus has here.

He did it all for you, says Deka's voice in my head.

My cheeks burn. But it can't be true.

I sit up on my good elbow. "Why did you order them all here? Tell me the truth."

His face flushes red as he looks away. Then he looks back to me. His eyes... I allow them to look upon me in ways I'd never allow another. Perhaps Deka, sure, back when I thought he was a better man.

Regulus realizes he's been staring at me for a good long minute. He looks away and clears his throat awkwardly.

I slide from my bed and stand behind him. It takes me a moment to work up the courage, until finally I wrap my arms around his chest and lower my chin onto his shoulder. His thumping heart shakes us both. Or maybe it's mine. I've longed for this moment more than I'd realized.

At this hour, the rainbow trenches below are only dark lines etched across the four mountain slopes. A twangy instrument casts a solemn ballad from somewhere down the lower terraces.

"It must get so lonely at the top," I say.

He rises abruptly from his seat. When he turns to face me, I take his hand, but his other goes to his coat, where he slides the rainbow armband from its sleeve. He holds it in both hands and stares at it intensely.

"Do you know what it's like to live your whole life by the expectations of others?"

I do. Too well, actually.

"Everyone has this idea of what a king should be. An image no reasonable man could ever live up to. I could never be myself. Never pursue my desires. A king needs a queen, after all. And heirs."

My heart flutters. Could *I* be a fae queen to a human king? Monarch of two great species? Our union the forging of an unbreakable race? I'd honestly not considered it until now.

Has he?

When I seek his eyes for an answer, I find his gaze has strayed from mine, to where a Red Line officer inspects a machine gun nest downslope. He senses King Regulus watching, and when their eyes meet, I see the truth in Regulus's glowing cheeks and awkward smile.

I step back, my whole body itching with embarrassment.

"It's nothing against you, Nya. Trust me. If I could see you like that it would make my life so much easier. But I am who I am."

I find myself drifting back to his side. I wrap his left arm in mine and lean my head against his shoulder. "It's okay. We can't help who we love."

He chuckles. "So the rogue heart curse is not unique to humans?"

"Well, come to think of it... I never really loved anyone like I loved a human before."

"I'm sorry to disappoint you."

I laugh, and the sniffle that comes with it alerts me to my sobbing. "Don't be. Someone else ravaged my heart long before you ever had a chance to."

"Men are good at that. Do you still love him?"

This question rocks my belly like a motion sickness. I don't even know how to answer it, and suddenly my bed beckons me. Suddenly I need to hide away from this world and its terrible complications.

Footsteps crunch over rocks outside. They approach quickly until someone clambers over the sandbag wall to infiltrate our draped canopy. I've seen this short, black-haired girl before, not long ago. When she spots me, she freezes and looks to the ground, her face glowing.

"Hello, Sasha," I say. "It's nice to see you."

"You two know each other?" asks Regulus, accepting a handful of *dazies* from her.

"We met on the train," I say.

Regulus frowns at this, surely wondering how I'd been on one of his transports without him knowing.

He puts an arm around his young recruit and pulls her close. "Well, Sasha here has become quite the helper. She's my go-to messenger—a *Royal Runner*, you could say. But didn't I just see you down the Blue Line? How did you get up here so fast?"

More footsteps crunch over loose rocks outside, then another familiar face bursts through the draped net.

"Cheater," says an elder, the same from the train roof, to Sasha, her cheeks red from exertion. Then she takes full notice of the king and bows her head, her hand on her belly. "Your Majesty, forgive me."

Regulus steps back from Sasha and gives her a curious look. "Sasha, did you just beat Lady Dash in a race?" To me, he says, "Lady Dash here holds the world record for long-distance sprinting."

"How do you know?"

"Know what?" asks Regulus.

"That it's a world record."

He frowns, then smirks. "I suppose I don't. But I can speak for Polaria. Let's see it, Dash."

She digs into her pocket and withdraws a gold medal. A platinum eight-point star occupies the center, exactly like the emblem on Lex's shields.

"It's the only of its kind, held by our swiftest soldier. It's been in Lady Dash's grace for... how long now? Forty years?"

"Forty-four, sire."

"What do you think, Sasha? Will she make forty-five? Or did someone just give her a run for her gold?"

The way Lady Dash raises her chin and clutches the medal to her chest tells me she doesn't appreciate the joke.

"So," says the King, "what are we looking at?"

The accomplished sprinter checks a watch hung from her neck. "From Purple Line to here: eighteen minutes, thirty-two seconds."

"That's down from six minutes without obstacles. But I see you're weighed down this time."

Lady Dash unslings a heavy sack from her back and drops it to the ground with a *thunk.* "I heard of your arrival. Figured you could use this more than any of us."

My belly twists. I don't need to see inside the black wrap to know what it holds: a reminder of the clash to come. I dare not pick up the golden hammer that once belonged to my mighty elder, not even before such a small audience, for word of my weakness will spread. Instead, I nod to Lady Dash's watch necklace.

"You shouldn't be doing that," I say. "You're showing the Watchers the quickest ways to the summit."

"Indeed," Regulus says. "But unlike Lady Dash, our enemy will have a blizzard of machine gun fire to suffer through. And yet... it seems Sasha here may have found a quicker way."

"I took a shortcut," she admits. "Green Line found tunnels inside the mountain." Sasha's reservation gives way to wonder as she says, "A whole network of 'em."

"*Your Majesty,*" adds Lady Dash on Sasha's behalf.

Sasha's eyes flare wide. It seems she is unschooled in the rules outside whatever village they dragged her from. "I used a tunnel under the mountain, *Your Majesty.*"

"Well, you shouldn't go wandering down there. It's not safe."

"They're made of stone. A mason from my village told me so. He went down with an engineer to inspect them."

"Well, if an engineer says they're safe, then I think we should use them, don't you?" He pulls a blue chip from his coat and hands it to her. "Go see Doc Enderby. Tell him to load you up with as many *dazies* as you can carry. When the fighting starts, you can use the tunnels to reach the wounded."

Sasha nods enthusiastically, and, with Lady Dash, she ducks out of the canopy and races downhill.

This King Regulus keeps impressing me at every turn. He cares so much for his wounded that he devotes resources to treating them. I doubt Lex spares such a role to her wolf pack, and for good reason.

"Your wounded will only hinder you in the fight."

"Do you know why these people call me *King?*"

"Because you're a king."

"My grandmother was a queen, but few people addressed her as such. My strength comes from the love my people bear for me. Without that, I wield little more than a heavy crown." He pulls a cap from a *dazy*. "How's the pain?"

"I'm fine. I'll need my wits in tact when I check out those tunnels."

"Who do you think made them?"

"Whoever built this gateway. I'll make sure to seal them off above the Green Line. Can't have the Watchers using them to slip behind us."

"I'll send a few engineers with you."

I shake my head and flex my fingers. It seems Regulus has forgotten the nature of my work.

He nods in remembrance. "I'm glad you're on our side."

I could say the same. Without Regulus, we'd have no chance at stopping the Watchers. He must be the greatest human to have ever lived. *Regulus the Great.* That's what I'll call him after this is all over. I'll make sure everyone else does, too.

"You need more rest," he tells me, and to this I do not protest. As I crawl into bed, he sets off down to an unfinished trench on the inland slope. A few soldiers rise from the shadows to join him with shovels.

I'm about to doze off when a ripping noise shreds my nerves.

I jump onto the sandbag wall before I can even open my eyes.

A white light rockets from the forest at the mountain base and stops before the Blue Line. A parachute blooms, from which the sizzling light dangles in its descent back toward the forest. It casts a flickering glow that awakens shadows everywhere I look, giving life to the trees below, and illuminates something that moves against the leaning silhouettes.

"Halt!" shouts a machine gunner from the Blue Line.

"Don't shoot!" comes the intruder's response.

"Twenty!" calls a gunner.

"Twenty-four!"

This response satisfies the Blue Line watchman, who waves him up.

The intruder scrambles madly through the obstacles. "Where's the King?"

Regulus climbs from his trench and tucks his shirt into his trousers. One of his companions raises a golden banner high for Lady Dash, who receives the message at the Blue Line and relays it up the mountain. She weaves through razor-wire lanes up past Green Line, on through Yellow, then up to Orange and across toward Regulus.

"Urgent news from the river," she says, her voice echoing across the mountainside. She glances down at the tree line, where four patrolmen carry a loaded stretcher.

"Who is it? What happened?"

"A boy from Kaladia. The river watch pulled him from a skiff. Said him and his sister were floating down the river for days now. Poor girl just died of exposure, only hours ago. He's barely alive. They're bringing him up to speak his account directly to His Grace."

"Account of what?"

"The Wolf... she attacked his village. Butchered his family and torched their homes."

If looks could kill, the glare Regulus shoots my way would strike me dead.

"To the city!" he shouts. "Defend your capital! Defend your home!"

Soldiers spill over their trenches and wash down the mountain like a landslide, funneling through barbwire lanes like mud streams.

My whole body goes numb with panic. "Stop! It's all part of the plan! You have to trust me!"

The streams of frantic soldiers wash out at the base and flood toward the field of balloons. They've abandoned every line: from Red to Orange, to Yellow and Green, and on down to Blue.

"Wait!" I shout from the empty Red Line. They need to hear that their city is just a symbol of Regulus's power. That it's only empty buildings. "Please, don't leave! You have to stay!"

My desperate cries fail to reach the bottom, so I begin my descent to try to catch up with them. The going isn't easy. At each trench line I must leap across a wide gap, which is mighty hard on my legs. Worse are the wire obstacles that lay between the lines. Staggered lanes offer the only safe passage, where one misstep in the dark threatens to slice open my leg. Too bad it's not the only time I must do this.

I slide to a stop, the memory of my hammer beckoning me back to the summit. I'll need it in the confrontation to come, when I smash in the Wolf's shield wall and rip her guts out through her mouth.

"Damn you, Lex," I mutter in my arduous climb back uphill to retrieve my hammer. Damn you and the cave all your heathen shield bangers crawled out from!

CHAPTER 25
NYA

Most of the balloons have already lifted off by the time I reach the Green Line. They rise high into the night sky in search of an inland air current, which they find at about three thousand feet.

At least Regulus hasn't taken all of his troops to Amyria. A company of one hundred and fifty soldiers remains on each of the four mountain sides. They occupy the Blue Line, where they are spread woefully thin.

"Move up to the Red Line," I tell them. "Tighten up!"

They watch me with great distrust.

"Our orders are to hold the Blue," says a captain, "so that's what we'll do."

There's no time to convince them, so I continue my race down through the forest toward level ground.

My heavy legs lighten with each step away from the mountain. The pull of the gate's gravitational vortex weakens until my feet bounce with each stride. When I finally escape the Anomaly and take flight, the balloons have spread far and are making great haste toward the capital.

I rise high to match their altitude. Flying with one arm in a sling is awkward enough, but with the shoulder-bag that totes my hammer hauling me down like an anchor... It's a miracle I manage to stay aloft. I attribute this to the air stream that propels Regulus's balloon fleet toward his capital's domes. It provides me the same nice push it does for them, but I am lighter and have wings to drive me faster.

Silver moonlight sparkles off the winding Artery to my left, a glittery snake running from the distant border mountains toward the city, where it curves hard toward me and empties into the sea behind Mount Tuck. A fleet of wooden boats have run aground at the Elbow, from where a stream of warriors now trickles toward Amyria's golden domes.

As I reach the nearest balloon, I see how sluggish Regulus's counter-offensive is. We're still a fair distance away, yet Lex's forward party has just reached the nearest dome.

I'm so exhausted from my mountain descent and flight that I cling to the first basket I reach. In a stroke of luck, it happens to carry the King. Though, he's not so happy to see me.

He draws a handgun and aims it at my face.

"Did you know?!" he says, his voice tight with the pain of betrayal.

"No—Well, I didn't think they'd get here so quick!"

POP!

A hissing bullet tousles my hair.

I drop under the basket and come up on the other side, behind him. "Please, listen to me. Your capital won't mean anything if—"

Regulus whirls around and shoots again—*CRACK!*

The bullet blows through my upper right wing and drops me. I grab hold of the basket bottom and cling to the underside with my one good arm. Two steel loops dangle from the basket's belly. I unwrap my sling and use the swath to fasten myself to the underbelly between both hoops.

"We know you're down there," says a soldier. "We'll shoot through this floor!"

A shiver rattles me. I struggle to unfasten my lashing when a loud bang shakes the deck above.

"You idiot!" shouts a girl. "Fancy hitting a few of us with a ricochet, do ya?"

"Hold your fire," says a new voice. "I think I saw that creature fall to the ground, anyway."

"Forget her," says the King. "Save your bullets for the wolves."

I spin myself to face the capital, where thousands of shield-bearing warriors race toward the main city entrance. Urban light gleams across the bouncing string of silver stars upon their black shields.

Dangling from the bottom of this basket, all shot up with weeks-old wounds and in desperate need of sunlight, I'm really not looking forward to this showdown.

CHAPTER 26

DEKA

When I was a child, my mother told me stories of our ancestors' radiant cities of light. They covered the globe and shined brighter than the stars themselves, so that not even the clearest night could show us our place in the cosmos. I never understood how that could be until this moment. Each of the capital's domes sits like a half-risen sun between here and the horizon. To us coming from the deep darkness of the river, it is blinding.

Lex sets a swift pace from the head of her trotting army. I trail behind, to her left, wielding the Arcturus banner proudly. In this hour of glory I must be more than a bodyguard lurking in the shadows. I must be a symbol of her victory.

At times I need to remind myself to not overstep her. It's a conscious effort, for curiosity consumes me, those domes beckoning me close like a moth to a flame. What wonders do those artificial bubbles behold? I imagine great gardens teeming with rainbow fruit and chirping wildlife, a modern-day Eden. Though, from what I've heard, it's quite the metropolis in there, with towering buildings in fine repair. Picturing *that* is where my imagination fails me.

Weapons bang on shields from the warriors strung out behind us. They grunt in unison as we approach the nearest dome, where an arch doorway offers me glimpses of grassy lanes lined with slender palm trees.

Lex slows her pace as wonder seizes her. "My home... It's been so long since I last set eyes on it."

"Eyes?" I say.

She breaks step and gives me a harsh look. Behind us, over two thousand pairs of feet shuffle to a stop to watch our staredown. Her return home must have her in good humor, because she cracks a smile and then laughs it off. This giddy laughter sounds unnatural coming from the Wolf, sounding more like that of a hyena.

Lex turns and continues in haste. A clamor rises from behind.

"Valkyrie!" someone shouts.

Hysteria rattles our ranks. When the Aeri antagonist lands before us, Lex cuts her stride to a halt.

Ko Tora flares her feathered wings high and wide, stretching fifteen feet across, sending even Lex stepping back with caution. I suspect this display is of Nya's doing, and it's a nice try. But I know this Aeri has had her day.

Although I have no shortage of fine weapons to choose from, I crouch to pick up a stone. This will make a better display than steel.

I march toward the Aeri elder and haul back on my rock, and the threat alone is enough to send her into flight.

Lex continues her march with a satisfied grin. "I chose my Primus Pillus well."

We reach the city well before the Polarian sky fleet. Against the suggestions of her centurions, Lex orders everyone to form into neat ranks before the grand arched entryway, facing outward to greet the crown soldiers.

"We should take the city while it's unguarded," says Lantz.

"We still have the element of surprise," adds the Third Century commander.

"Everyone knows we're here," Lex says, her mouth twitching with a smile. "May as well make a show of it."

The armada of balloons lands two miles off, in a depression, where only the tops of the nearest remain visible.

I stand shoulder-to-shoulder in the forward row, directly behind Lex. Our line stretches as far as I can see to either side, but I have no idea how many ranks stand behind us. I've learned during drills that looking back in battle is forbidden. There is only forward.

Lex's banner flaps noisily overhead, ruffled by the same wind that carries ash from the flames that ravage distant fields. Smoke burns my lungs, but I dare not cough. No one mutters a word. Only the wind speaks here, and it whispers prayers of darkness.

A short time passes when, over the hillcrest ahead, an extended line of heads rises in an uneven bouncing motion toward us. These heads rise to reveal necks, then shoulders, and then arms cradling rifles. They aim their guns at us in their forward march.

"Shields!" shouts Lex.

Each warrior around me slides their right foot back to stand side-on while raising their shield. They lock in with that to either side, then rock them back and forth to test their cohesion.

The only gap in this wall is where I stand, front and center. Lex had directed me to this spot and for her army to form up around me. The warrior to my left flicks his eyes toward Lex, urging me to join her.

When I step out of line, a warrior slides up from behind me to fill in the gap. Her shield clunks into place, and the forward wall shifts side to side to test her connection.

The crown army marches toward us in an extended line of width to match ours, but with many more deep. They outnumber us greatly. So, so greatly. The question is: how many bullets can our shield wall withstand?

Regulus's troops stop at double bowshot range away. The front line drops to a knee, while the second aims their rifles from standing.

One lone figure continues on toward us. Lex marches forward to meet him. I hustle to fall in beside her, feeling terribly exposed with the speaking ends of so many rifles aimed our way.

As the distance between us and the advancing lone figure diminishes, a crown of red hair reveals itself to me. A disruption in the forward line behind him causes a commotion. When a figure breaks through, Regulus turns to see who's rushing out to join him.

My heart nearly bursts with joy. *Nya!* Suddenly I don't feel so exposed out here. With her on the opposing side, I am safe.

Regulus picks up his pace, almost as if to lose her. "You've got some nerve coming out here," he says, and to my surprise, his rearward shoulder-check implies he's talking to Nya instead of Lex.

She slows and trails some distance behind. To walk at such a pace seems unnatural for her, each bouncing step her body's way of resisting the urge to spring into flight.

A smile cracks the stiffness in my cheeks. It lasts until I notice Nya has acquired at least one more gunshot wound and what appears to be a broken arm. She hefts a heavy bag over her good shoulder, its weight forcing her to walk with a limp.

It takes everything in me to not drop Lex's standard and run out to hug that ragged pixie. Instead, I stop where Lex stops, which is within spitting distance to where Regulus comes to a halt.

The great King who looks no older than myself forces a smile, but his lips are tight with indignation. "Lady Alexandra, you'll have to forgive me. If I'd known you were coming, I'd have thrown you a welcome party."

"You had fifteen years to prepare for my return."

"And to what do we owe the pleasure of your visit now? Have you come to assist us in our hour of need?"

"Yes," Lex says.

My heart flutters with surprise and hope. Did I just hear what I think I heard?

Nya's surprised smile confirms that yes, I most certainly did.

"Kneel before me," Lex says, "and be pardoned for all your treasons. Have your soldiers tear off their crown patches so that they may serve proudly in my army. Under my rule, I promise you and your people prosperity until time's end. I swear this to you upon whatever gods you praise. Let it be known, far and wide, that so long as the Arcturus banner flies over Amyria, no enemy shall ever defeat us."

Regulus smirks. "It seems your time in exile has robbed you of your better sense."

"Do you reject my offer?"

"You offer me insults. Nothing more."

Lex raises her right hand high. Unified clunking rises from behind as shields stack over shields to form a curved dome.

"Then let us make this hour famous," she says to Regulus, whose eyes cannot deny the impressive display of military might barring him from his city. "March against my lines, and witness the futility of your resistance. Show your people the fate of those who dare challenge the Wolf in the dark of night."

My heart slams against my ribs. How many times has Lex rehearsed this scene in front of her mirror and in her dreams? What trick does she now hide up her sleeve?

Regulus folds his arms and raises his chin. "Yes, we could do that. And when we decimate both our armies, who will defend the people of Anterra? It seems the Wolf has a mind only for itself. Your father was a great man, that I'll never deny. What would he say of the beast who burned his childhood home two days back?"

Lex squeezes her hands into fists. Her leather gloves groan, and I can hear her teeth grind from a few feet away. Agonizing silence settles between them. The only sound comes from her banner flapping above me.

Then she pulls off her gloves, one finger at a time. "Then let us settle this the old way..."

She flings her left glove at Regulus's chest. "That's a

challenge. Duel with me, and the winner takes Polaria. That means if you lose, your soldiers will tear off their crown patches and fight for me. If I fall, my army will disband and return to Ortaria."

Regulus's nostrils flare. "I accept."

He turns with a face full of hate and marches back to his army.

Nya remains in place, bouncing on her toes, torn between coming to me or returning with Regulus. She reluctantly retreats with him.

Lex unslings her crossed katanas and flings them aside, then shrugs off her long coat and offers it to me in exchange for her standard. In the balled-up fabric of her coat, I feel a hard shape that reminds me of a handgun.

Across the field, Regulus returns to us wielding a scimitar. Its thick blade of curved steel could chop through Lex's wooden staff with a single swing.

"That's all you're using?" I say to her.

"Do you fear for my life, dear Deka?"

I survey the distance between us and our shield dome.

Lex pulls a device from from around her neck and offers it to me. A trigger with a red lock through it protrudes from the rectangular box. "If by some miracle Regulus wins, do me one last favor and shoot him in the head, then click that switch."

I suddenly remember Little Boy stowed under the deck of Lex's long boat.

I resist the urge to smash the detonator into pieces. She's mad if she thinks I'll blow us all into oblivion. Though, I suspect she knows that will never happen—her losing, that is. She's testing me.

I flick the lock out and curl my finger over the trigger.

She gives me a sly grin and then marches out to meet Regulus, who approaches shirtless while test-swinging his sword. The pink stripes that scar his skin tell of a king who sits not in lofty towers while others fight his battles.

Lex drapes the banner pole over her shoulder and saunters forward. Her casual approach and poor choice in weaponry fill me with dread. Added to this is Nya's assured demeanor as both combatants near swinging distance, which validates my concern about Lex's careless strategy.

She steps into a backward spin and swings the pole wide with both hands. Regulus raises his sword to block it, but the pole's momentum whacks his weapon aside and crashes into his shoulder, knocking him to the ground.

Lex steadies the pole and stabs down at his belly. He rolls aside, and instead of finding warm flesh, the point plunges into frosty ground. Regulus rolls back and kicks the pole midshaft to break it in two. Lex responds with a smack to his face with the splintered end of the bottom half.

Regulus crawls toward his sword a few feet away, wincing in pain, a string of blood dangling from his mouth.

Lex yanks the pointed end of her standard from the ground and stomps onto his back. He struggles to push himself up, so she puts all her weight down to flatten him onto his belly. Then she presses the point to the back of his neck.

Regulus freezes. His eyes flare wide with panic and despair. Then comes a frown of defiance.

"Now everyone has seen you for what you are, *Wolf.* You burn their homes, butcher their children, then demand they grovel at your feet. See how many kneel when you show them my head." He looks me dead in the eyes. "My blood will be the first of millions. You'll rule over a kingdom of ash and bone, misery and suffering. May the price of your victory ever haunt you and your descendants to come."

Nya unwraps her shroud to reveal Ko Skadia's hammer. Even the darkness of this night cannot diminish its splendor, its shimmering handle fiercely elegant in Nya's slender hands. She grips it tight and bends her knees, preparing to lunge at Lex.

I draw Lex's pistol and aim it at Nya. She casts me a challenging glare, and then a sly smirk, not believing I'll shoot her. But I one hundred percent will. Her interference will pit both armies against each other, a costly chaos Anterra cannot afford right now. This duel must play out to its natural end.

Nya bends her knees deeper, about to spring forth with her hammer.

I curl my finger around the trigger. Sweat trickles down my face. This blood feud has carried on since the beginning days of our people, back to when a wolf attacked a shepherd. I'd witnessed the scene with my own eyes, in the memories of the Great Pyramid. Humanity has carried this age-old wound ever since. Be the predator, or become the prey.

I point the pistol at Lex. When my thumb pulls back the hammer, she straightens at the click.

She keeps the spear tip pressed against the back of Regulus's neck and looks up at me with a smirk.

"Oh, Deka, how could you? You've always been such a loyal servant to me. What a devastating surprise. How could I have ever seen this coming?" She nods at the pistol. "Well, go on, do it. Everyone, look! Polaria's next great hero in the making. I bet the boy king will throw you a parade. Here, I'll make it easy for you."

She spreads her arms wide to expose her chest, making an open target of her heart.

Lex's condescending behavior grinds me to my core, but I see there's more to it. She's testing me. She needs to know where I stand. Shoot her or Nya. I don't leave this moment without doing one or the other. It's only a slight shift in aim between them both. So close I could shoot for one and hit the other by accident if I'm not careful.

I size up Lex's army behind me. The shield wall is solid and will withstand every Polarian bullet that hits it. And when the crown soldiers run out of bullets...

Butchery.

I look to Regulus's lines.

"You'll make it," Lex says, "no question." Her tone is almost pleading, her stare borderline imploring, as if she's actually trying to convince me. As if shooting her will make a martyr of her. "What are you waiting for, Deka? Do it."

I pull the trigger—*Bang!*

The pistol kicks back. I jump in fright, as does Nya. Regulus too, who jolts under Lex's foot. The only one unfazed is Lex. She stands tall and unwavering, her foot firmly on Regulus's back. I peer closely for a wound and realize I'd missed, so I pull the trigger again. *Bang!* This time I'm sure of my aim, and yet Lex does not flinch.

Again I pull—*Bang!* And again. *Crack!* And once more. *Bang!*

Not a bullet hits Lex, but something does strike me with each shot fired. The gunfire is fainter than usual.

I hold the smoking barrel to my hand and squeeze the trigger. *Pop*—a blast of hot wind hits my palm. Nothing more.

"Silly boy," Lex says, "you think I'd give you a loaded gun after all you've done?"

I drop the pistol and hold up Little Boy's detonator.

Lex smiles wide with satisfaction. "Oh, you can bet your life that's real. You could blow us all to atomic dust with a single twitch of your finger. Go on, pull the trigger. You won't even feel it hit you."

The metal box shakes in my sweaty hand. I squeeze it tight to keep my grip, and cringe at how close my finger is to the trigger. I grasp the bottom with both hands and hold it to my chest, the trigger facing away from me.

"No?" Lex says. "Didn't think so."

She raises the broken spear over her head with both hands, and then drives it down into Regulus's neck. Well, I don't actually see when the tip pierces his flesh, because a flash of light blinds me.

I drop the detonator and shield my eyes as a wall of hot wind hits me. I'd assume I'd accidentally detonated Little Boy if not for the fact that I'm still able to think, which means I'm not a gust of incinerated ash blowing toward Africa.

I stumble away while swinging my free arm to fend off an attack. My guess is that Nya has recruited her fire diving cousins to thwart Lex's victory. Sekarra would be an easy sway, after what the wolves had put her through.

The heat of their attack blasts my back, steady and unyielding, yet oddly controlled.

I force my eyes open and see the stars of Lex's shield wall gleaming with reflected light.

Nya lands before me, blocking my view. She grabs my

elbows and locks her frazzled eyes with mine. "It's happening," she says.

My blood goes cold.

Nya slides a band over my head and sets two cupped lenses over my eyes. Mali's goggles. I'd know the fit of them anywhere. But how did she come to possess them? I was sure I'd lost them during the Giza battle, when the portal sucked us into the pyramid. But I guess that's a story for another time.

"Ah-hah!" shouts Lex.

She stands behind me with her arms spread wide to welcome a beaming ball of light. Through the green tint of my goggles it looks like a blue sun hovering over the distant horizon.

"Dawn comes early this year!" wails the Wolf. "Look how the gods praise my victory––even the great Apollo himself shows his approval."

"That's an Amplifier, you idiot!" shouts Nya. "The Watchers are attacking!"

Lex lowers her arms and steps back to give the light a better appraisal. When Regulus rolls to a sitting position, she realizes her slip-up and lifts her foot to stomp him, but then restrains herself.

She points toward the silhouetted pyramid standing left of the false sun. Of all the great mountains in its vicinity, it is Mount Tuck that stands darkest and largest of all, like a shadow cast from a hand near firelight. "Go," she tells him. "Defend your kingdom while you still have it."

Regulus scrambles to his feet and races toward his rattled rabble of soldiers. "Back to the balloons! Get to Mount Tuck!"

Nya clings to my arm, and in this light the shadows that have blinded me vanish. There is only one fight that matters, and Lex is walking away from it.

She strides up to me and snatches the detonator from my hand. "I held up my end, Nya. He's all yours now."

I give Nya a curious look. Whatever their arrangement, she doesn't appear pleased by Lex's handling of her side of it.

Standing now between two hostile armies, I feel like Nya must have these past few weeks, a pariah to both Anterran rulers who hold their petty squabbles above all else.

Nya tugs my arm to turn me toward her, away from the light. She lifts my goggles to stare deeply into my one good eye.

"She's gone," I tell her, referring to Jexa. It's just us again.

No matter how fallible Lex thinks I am, I did what she'd never even try. I defeated Jexa in the battle for my mind. With Nya's love, I conquered a spirit darker than any demon from hell, something Lex would not have attempted. She'd have paired with Jexa and used their combined strength to bring mankind to its knees.

Nya sizes up my ruined eye with an anguished stare of her own. I await her pleas for me to run away with her. Convincing me wouldn't be hard. But I see a resolve in her stare I'd not seen in a long time — a date with destiny and no illusions to blind her from it. Besides, she knows the truth of our situation more than anyone: there's nowhere safe on Earth to hide.

"Get to the gate," she tells me. "You'll fare better there than me."

I stare at the black silhouetted pyramid and shudder. I'm not ready to face the Watchers again, especially having seen

Jexa's abilities first-hand. I'm just a foolish boy who lost his eye in a game where he thought he was a knight, but instead was a pawn.

Nya squeezes my wrists to ground me. "Hey, listen to me. You've fought more Watchers than any human alive. Your place is with your people, defending that gate."

Oddly, her wild claim is true. None of these Anterrans have ever even seen a Watcher, let alone fought one. This observation infuses me with a strength greater than any noble title ever could.

I give Nya a good look over, appraising her battered body. "What about you?"

"I'm better off in the sky." She spreads her wings and glances over her shoulder, to a shrinking hole in her upper right flap. Colorful light shimmers through their wilted veins, a rainbow infusion pumping life like the blossom of leaves in spring. As her shriveled wings stretch wide open, her eyes brighten and glow with ecstatic relief. The Watchers have activated the Amplifier for themselves, but it revives Nya as well.

To my right, shields clunk and feet shuffle in unison as Lex's army forms into two columns. Lex then leads them through the arched doorway and into Amyria.

"I'll keep an eye on her," Nya says. "I'll make sure she doesn't do anything crazy."

I wrap my arms around Nya to pull her close. She shoves me away, anger flashing hot in her eyes as she jabs a condemning finger at me. "You don't die today. Hear me?"

I nod.

She steps back, about to spring into flight, then stops

herself and says, "I'll meet you on the mountain when it's all over."

"And if there's no mountain when this is all over?"

Nya's face reddens with anger. How dare I even suggest that?

Tears water her eyes to temper her rage. "Then I'll meet you somewhere else. You decide the place, and I'll find you there."

She launches into flight before I can utter another dreadful prospect, but it's more like an upward dive into water as she disappears through squiggly waves of light.

I turn in time to see Regulus's first balloon lift off. A mob of camouflaged warriors jostles around the others.

My skin crawls under the fabric of my uniform. This violet coat won't blend in well with Regulus's army, but it's an easy fix.

I strip off the garments until I'm as naked as the moment I entered this world. A cold breeze lashes my bare skin, so I pull the padding from behind my shield and throw it over my shoulders. The bear fur is warm and soft, yet damp in spots where it rested against my sweaty arm.

I draw many strange looks as I weave through the throng of Polarian soldiers. Some shout words of disgust at my frontal nudity, but many offer much-needed laughter. A few girls whistle and clap. A few boys do so as well.

I make my way toward the nearest balloon until a brawny lad tackles me to the ground. He pins me down and sticks a knife point to my throat.

"You think shedding your fur will hide the wolf inside? I should've put a bullet in you back there, but it's not too late."

He drags me to my feet. "Firing squad - fall in!"

"Captain," comes a boy's voice from behind. King Regulus shoves through the crowd to join us. "Unhand him."

"Sire, he fought for the Wolf."

I'm about to tell him how I've killed more wolves in one night than he ever will, but Regulus draws first words.

"You really didn't know they were blanks?"

This question draws quizzical stares from our onlookers. Even the captain's grip on my wrist loosens.

"He turned on her," Regulus explains. "For that, the Wolf has cast him out."

The captain points toward Amyria. "He looked pretty cozy with that fairy, the one who convinced you to abandon our capital."

Regulus lifts his chin toward the glaring midnight sun. "And was she wrong, Captain? Amyria won't survive this attack if we give up that mountain, but if you'd prefer to fight over empty buildings, I won't stop you. Me, I'm going to Mount Tuck."

The King's other soldiers need not hear another word. They rush to cram into their balloon baskets. The captain shakes his head and climbs into a balloon with his company, which is about the size of one century and a half.

Regulus throws an arm around my shoulders to usher me along. "Come. You'll fly with me. I'll find you a spare uniform."

CHAPTER 27

NYA

It's a strange thing, this light. After months of darkness, it had come off harsh to the humans and sent them recoiling. Deka's watery eye had displayed severe discomfort and worry, so I'd given him Mali's goggles. The meaning of this offering had been lost on him.

Dozens of balloons drift toward the glaring black sun like inverted teardrops, the tears of a city mourning its defenders.

For me, the light is magnificent. The glittering glow that now washes over my surroundings reveals a bizarre reaction from the vegetation, which struggle to determine how to react. Much like the humans, their initial reaction is to curl away. But as the dazzling light persists, the winter plants not only accept it, they lean toward it. Grass tickles my feet as it reaches for the light with fierce determination. As if lured in a trance, shrubs rustle and trees creak in their stretch toward the black sun and its squiggly rays of blue light. Beneath Amyria's domes, along the tree-lined lanes, royal palms lust for this light so fiercely their trunks crack and break in half.

Shouts of surprise and wails of rage rise from between the buildings.

I zip in through the arch doorway to see a string of slender palms have fallen across the main boulevard, blocking Lex's path. Her warriors stand with their shields and spears at the ready, watching the glass structures around them while Lex throws her arms up in a fit.

"You want a fight? Then come out and look me in the eye."

I crouch on a roof overlooking Lex and chew my fingernails nervously. She knows nothing of the Amplifier's magnetism, and believes the citizens have collapsed the trees to slow her advance.

My heart quivers with worry. What will I do if she has a meltdown and starts slaughtering the innocent in their homes? Considering she'd planned to nuke them, I'd not be surprised if she puts Amyria's children to the sword.

She climbs over the first fallen palm. On the other side, she bends to check under the next for traps. Satisfied, she climbs over the next, and then on to the one after that. Her warriors follow while keeping a close watch on the glass buildings. More than a few study the dome ceiling above in wonder.

As I join them in their upward stare, an idea emerges. All of Regulus's able citizens are at Mount Tuck. Any who remain here are either young, old, sick or frail. They'd all be hiding in their homes, not out hunting wolves. Perhaps they've sheltered underground, or at least under their beds. If Lex goes on a murderous rampage, I can bring down the entire dome on top of her. With any luck, only the warriors caught in the open will get hurt.

I fly up to the dome roof and out through a triangular hole. Intense Amplifier light vibrates through me with physical force, infusing my weary muscles with violent energy, reminding my weakened body of it's explosive power. Cells withered from weeks of endless darkness awaken like plants at the dawn of spring, and this comes from merely a taste. The sensation is surreal.

I land cross-legged on the roof, where I spread my arms wide and lift my chin to invite the restorative light into my festering wounds. Both recent gunshot holes tingle, while my older wounds burn as the rot bubbles and leaks away, infectious cells seared to death by my body's soaring temperature.

I check over my shoulder to monitor Lex's advance through the dome. She now leads her troops down a wide boulevard, unopposed by trees laid by imaginary ambushers, toward the silver spire that marks Amyria's center. It's so tall that, even from atop my dome, I must crane my neck to see its point piercing the sky. The throne below its apex will offer Lex a nice view of her race's final hour.

Her army parades out to the open-air square below the spire, where they form into wide ranks before the flared-out tower base. Here, many warriors lean their heads back to size up the great twisted tower of sleek steel.

It's so quiet when I glide down that the only noise comes from my wings cutting through the air. I bank around to the front of the armed assembly, standing neat in their ranks, and land beside Lex. She stares straight ahead, at an army of wavy soldiers who look back at us from the reflective facade. With their ten-foot spears, dark violet coats and black masks pulled up over their noses, they are the stuff of nightmares.

Lex lowers her head and stares at her squeezed fist. "The crown robbed them of their liberty... Forced good highborn folk into uniform to fight his wars... And here I am, come to restore their freedom, and they hide away from me."

I've seen many of these citizens at Mount Tuck. Nothing about their patriotism felt forced. I'm guessing their mandatory border service has instilled in them a sense of responsibility for their country's security, a burden shared by all, unifying them in ways a stratified society would never understand.

"Your people are not hiding," I say, stepping in front of her. I point over her shoulder, toward the unseen horizon. "They're all at Mount Tuck, fighting for each other."

Lex clutches her heart and winces. A single tear slides down her cheek. "My... *people...*"

She opens her hand to reveal Deka's compass in her palm. The silver eight-point star has been polished from years of wear, its reflection gleaming in Lex's misty eye. She stares at it for a good long time.

Finally, she looks to me with urgency. "Can you deliver a message for me?"

"Depends on the message."

"Get word to Raven. Tell her this is no longer a liberation. Tell her... Tell her..." The words get stuck in Lex's throat. There's a dismay and desperation in her eyes that sits unnaturally with her hardened face.

I nod in understanding. "I'll tell her."

CHAPTER 28

DEKA

The soldiers in my basket throw together a mix-matched uniform that fits me perfectly. They offer me another set for when we disembark, as they assure me the cold mountain air will be brutal after acclimatizing to the heat of the balloon's burner. But I suspect a mountain chill will be of no concern to anyone.

I stand at the forward edge of the basket to confirm my suspicion. The warmth on my face comes not only from the balloon burner, but from the Amplifier as well. But something about its glow has changed in the last few minutes.

I pull down my goggles to find I am able to stare directly at it. It shines like a black sun, with squiggled blue rays escaping randomly, as if covered by a shell with shifting cracks. Or maybe not a shell, but perhaps...

A black mass slides away like a shroud pulled from a crystal ball. Light blinds me once more until I pull up my goggles. Through their tinted lenses I see what makes up the fallen veil: a swarm of butterfly wings swooping toward the base of Mount Tuck.

"How many?" asks an officer.

"Thousands," I say.

A few soldiers around me crouch and hug their knees to their chests. Others sit with their backs to the basket walls, their heads lowered in defeat. Regulus's demeanor fails to inspire confidence. He stares absently at the Watcher attack, his face blanched white in shock.

A young boy shakes his head. "I can't do it. I can't do it. Please don't make me go."

"That's what I said my first time, too," I say. My words earn me the full attention of all.

"This enemy will have you believe they are invincible," I say. "And at first that will appear to be true. But when your bullets fail to stop them, remember that my tribe—a rabble of thirty warriors with spears and rocks and arrows—fought them at the pyramids of Giza not two moons ago, and here I stand before you to speak of it."

My words invite hope into the eyes of a few. A boy raises his head from his knees, his hold on his shins loosening as he perks up for more. So I continue.

"And before that, we fought them in our caves. We fought them in our forests, and we fought them on the open sea. On every continent, all over this great home of ours, your tribe has fought this exact same enemy. Many were not warriors like those I see here today. They were bakers and craftsman, scavengers and spinsters. But when the time came, they did their duty, to buy us time for this very moment, this final hour. The spirit of their resistance beats now in each of our hearts. So long as a single one of us draws breath, their fight shall live on."

Huddled soldiers loosen their holds on each other to watch me with uncertain stares.

I point to Mount Tuck. "Every human death will be paid for there, on the only battlefield that's ever mattered. If this be the last hour of Man, then we shall make it the finest of any that's come before. Many of us will fall, yes, of that there is no doubt. But if you stand tall on that mountain and send just *one* Watcher to its afterlife, then I promise you this: your spirit will endure. It will live on in the nightmares of our enemy."

A few crouched soldiers rise and grip their rifles tightly, a newfound boldness shoving the fear from their eyes. The uncertainty in those around them hardens slightly with a hint of determination.

"This enemy has conquered a thousand races," I tell them. "They have forgotten the names of them all. But they'll not forget us. Live or die, they'll remember our faces until their own dying days.

"So let us all swear an oath, right here and now, to each other, to fight until the last of us. From this moment forward, we never stop fighting. We will fight them in the sky. We will fight them on the seas, in our fields and in the forests. We'll fight them on the mountains, and—"

"And you'll all die!" shouts a blond-haired soldier in the back corner, her golden eyes watching us through a vertical slit in each. "You'll die in the skies. You'll die on the seas and in your fields, and your forests will burn to ash while you cower under rocks with nowhere to hide. You'll retreat to your mountains, and there we'll kill the last of you." Froth seethes through her clenched teeth. "We'll kill you in ways your primate minds can't yet imagine. If you knew what awaits you, you'd throw yourselves from this basket, right here and now."

I reach slowly over my shoulder and grab my sword hilt. It's probably bad manners to kill one of these people so soon after meeting them, but we have a Watcher in our midst, and that's a problem that cannot persist. I just have to be prepared for the backlash, to talk my way out before her mates toss me overboard.

"We'll hang your heads in our dungeons of doom," she says, her mouth foaming, veins bulging in her neck and forehead, "your ridiculous death stares frozen in time, to be forever mocked as the race of fools. Look here! Look upon the faces of those who dared challenge the dragon. Fireflies against the darkness of eternity."

I pull up on my sword, but Regulus beats me on the draw. He unsheathes a dagger and is about to ram it into the blabbering soldier's heart, until an elder woman slips her arm around the possessed girl's neck to choke her out. The gray-haired soldier whispers soothing words in the sufferer's ear as she lowers her to the deck.

The blond girl lies peacefully, unconscious, yet her words hang heavy in the air. The whole outburst has dampened the mood beyond recovery.

Machine gunfire ripples from Mount Tuck, long and steady. Broken streams of red light zip outward from the mountain base.

Regulus shoves his way to the basket edge and leans over the rail for a look at the pyramidal mountain. His soldiers crowd the forward rail around him, everyone jostling for a glimpse of our enemy. A black mass creeps up the mountain base like a rising tide, swallowing streams of machine gun fire much like the sea, pebbles hurled at the floodwaters of an era's end.

The mood around me shifts from fear to anxiety, eagerness swelling in each soldier to rush to the aid of their brothers and sisters. Urgency spreads as half the balloons in our squadron rise while the other half fall in search of more favorable winds. A balloon one thousand feet above catches a strong current and surges forward.

Our pilot cranks open our burner. A blue flame grows, and heat intensifies as we rise with the many other balloons to merge with that air stream. "Brace yourselves."

The balloon lurches forward and throws everyone to the back of the basket, including the pilot. Someone scrambles to haul me off Regulus and kicks those around him to clear away.

Distant gunfire rattles louder by the second. From this height and proximity I see streams of red bullets spray out from the base on the side of the mountain bathed in Amplifier light, where a black mass crawls up from the forest like a creeping shadow.

Shouts of despair echo off the mountain slopes during the rare lulls in gunfire. The attempt of Mount Tuck's sparse defenders to retreat to higher ground leaves them sorely exposed to flying spears. The dark side facing us sees no enemy yet, so the defenders there rush around to reinforce the other three sides.

Regulus's grave expression suggests he sees what I see. The whole backside is open to attack, which will be harder to see coming by his soldiers on the other sides, those assailed by the blinding light.

I bounce with urgency. I need to be on that mountain.

Crazy, I know. But hanging in this basket offers none of us safety. Luckily, our surging air current passes directly over the battle.

Regulus orders his balloons to land in the shadow of the mountain. The first three are descending to a clearing near the base when the Watchers begin their attack up the dark slope. Muzzle flashes reveal where a few shooters have remained to guard this side, but they're soon overrun.

Regulus turns to his pilot. "Drop us off at the top."

The pilot gives his lord a look of caution.

"Do it."

The pilot offers us an apologetic look, then slows our descent and lines our course with the summit.

As we glide over the dark mountainside, movement upslope reveals Watchers weaving through obstacles and leaping over trenches, untroubled by the scattered machine guns peppering them.

An opposing gale prevents our pilot from landing on the summit, and because he can't land on the slope, we're forced to jump from the basket.

Regulus leaps out into a sandbag enclosure that crowns the summit, where four snipers take measured shots down the slopes, the thunderous bangs of their rifles loud and steady. His soldiers jump out behind him without hesitation. They vacate evenly from both sides, two at a time, to keep the basket from swinging, until it's just me and the balloon pilot, and the possessed girl lying unconscious in the corner.

"You getting out?" he asks, as if I have a choice.

I jump before I'm able to reconsider my options.

CHAPTER 29

DEKA

Our balloon rises and drifts away from the mountain. Others are not so lucky. Many unload their soldiers farther downhill, in range of Watcher spears. They whiz up from the forest in silver streaks and punch through the balloons or clink off their baskets.

Wails of terror rise from the balloons as they shrivel and crash onto the mountain, where they burst into flames.

I slide into the nearest trench, where dozens of my balloon-mates have gathered to take measure of the carnage below.

Thousands of Watchers zigzag up the mountain base. They've overrun the Purple and Blue Lines and now use them for cover. Any Blue Line survivors have fallen back to the Green Line, where they're too overwhelmed to retreat any further. Most who try end up with a flying spear to the back. Their only choice is to hold their ground and fight.

In a daring move, one balloon drops directly behind the Green Line and manages to unload half her company before a dozen spears shred her to pieces. But the short fall spares many Polarians who'd not yet made the jump. Survivors climb from the wreckage, with a fair few ready to fight. But they make easy targets for spears and throwing stars.

Regulus leaps over our trench and lands before me. He points his scimitar downslope and yells, "Everyone, to the Green Line. Move!"

He then leads a charge through obstacles down the mountain. Smoke from burning balloons swallows his company and obscures my view, so I climb out to join them.

In the black smoke I slam into a soldier who'd been standing frozen in place, trembling. I'm helping the rattled girl stand when a gray-haired elder slides to a stop beside us, the one who'd choked out the possessed girl in my basket.

"Get moving, Sasha. We have our orders."

When the young girl Sasha looks my way, I'm surprised to see her eyes are far from panic-stricken. In fact, the dainty Polarian is quite calm.

"I know a faster way," she tells us.

The elder's eyes flash wide in remembrance. "The tunnels."

"Show me," I say.

Sasha leads us to a heap of green sandbags piled over a square piece of plywood. "Under there."

The elder, whose name tag spells *Dash*, helps me haul enough bags aside to let us flip up the wood. A dark musty hole greets us underneath.

The smell of grave dirt sends a shiver up my spine. I'm working up the nerve to lead the way when young Sasha slides in without hesitation.

Dash shrugs at me and then follows. I'm not far behind.

The rattle of nearby gunfire fades to distant ripples. The

fresh chill of the night air is replaced by that of the cold dead earth. It has been since time beyond human memory since sunlight touched these walls.

I feel around blindly until a beam of red light cuts through the dark. Sasha aims the scarlet flashlight into the void, lighting a passage that leads deep into the mountain. "This way."

My boots slide over silt-covered stone. The fallen dirt is fresh, recently knocked loose by the havoc above. Cobbled walls are so finely cut that not even a piece of paper could slide between their jigsaw joints. I don't need Sasha's light to see the runes carved into them. The ancient symbols glow with a blue light of their own, old energy awakened by the blood spilled above.

"Come on," hisses Dash from ahead. "Try to keep up."

It would be a nightmare to get lost in this creepy underworld alone, so I hurry along.

Sasha leads us to a rough intersection and continues around a rightward bend. I stop at this junction, where a warm breeze blows up from a sloped passage ahead. Its warm, gentle caress beckons me down to depths unknown. Then a faint green pulse lights up the darkness to further entice me.

"What's down there?"

"Nothing down there," echoes Sasha's distant voice. "The surface is up this way. Come on, stay close."

An image takes shape in the darkness, yet it comes not from before me, but from within—through the window of my mind's eye.

Something soft brushes my ear. Silky black wings flap ahead into darkness.

'Come,' says a raspy voice from the void, 'drink from my well. See what you paid for.'

My dead eye tingles.

Now is not the time to go chasing strange voices through the dark. But I cannot deny my curiosity. It is the very weakness that lured Nya to my door.

And so I wander down into the darkness of depths unknown.

CHAPTER 30
DEKA

A static charge prickles my skin. It's too dark to see, but my echoed breathing suggests I've entered a grand cavern. My breath here is almost deafening. I can think of nothing else. I stand in the cold stillness, listening to my own rhythm for so long I almost forget where I am, or that the noise comes from me. Or who the boy Deka is. Until the other voice speaks again.

'In the beginning there was nothing. And then there was everything.'

A white flash blinds me. The light assails my eye for a long time, sizzling and hissing. And then, from this harsh radiance emerges a most-welcome darkness. Colorful light dances over a cosmic background, only... It is not light.

Gas. Red, blue, green, and colors I've never before seen, all churning in a stunning display. These celestial clouds swirl in colossal circles, condensing smaller and tighter to become dots of light. My eye sees stars, but a deeper part of me recognizes them for sparks, each a Divine Light born of the great fire that gave birth to the universe. Each growing brighter with its own awareness.

Clusters of these stars spiral in galaxies for a billion years before the next miracle graces existence: Organic life. And with it arrives a new opportunity for the stars, which have become infinitely bored in their infinite splendor. They need to go out and feel... something other than being grand and almighty. To feel fear and love, to grow through struggle and strife. To just... experience. And so they did.

I witness the eyes of an alien primate spark with awareness as a stellar sentience possesses its body, taking residence alongside her animal mind. They do this with many species, living many lives through many ages, a universe experiencing itself through the eyes of its creations. And then a terrible tragedy happened.

They forgot who they were.

I see a human huddled in the rain, shaking and afraid, watching the sky with great trepidation.

This was all by design, of course. A clever chaos born of a being so complex no single mind could ever understand its motives on their own. But there was something this celestial designer had failed to predict when weaving its immaculate vision—an element that had slipped into the equation.

Dark Matter.

On its own it was harmless. But when it began to fuel stars, the divine plan fell apart.

These Dark Stars burned ironically bright, powered by a force contrary to its creator's nature, contrary to existence itself. But how that could be?

Some claim it originated with the flicker of an impure

thought, a sliver of corruption hidden deep within the farthest recesses of the Creator's mind. Whatever the cause, the consequential stars grew big, and the gravity of big stars attracts more dark matter to feed them. And so bigger they grew, until they developed their own strain of consciousness. Dark Stars with Dark Hearts. Dark Souls with a design of their own.

I watch a sparkling river spiral into a void, stars pulled from their divine arrangement by an emergent force, a black hole feeding on sparks of the sacred fire, gulping them down by the billions. And yet no matter the effort, it cannot stop the expanding universe. Or *could* not, it should be said, until The Specter Star.

I see a scaled reptilian curled inside a volcano, the moment its golden eye flashes with the consciousness of a black hole, the first dark soul to survive the collapse of its own star. The arrival of this new life-force kicks off a series of mutations... with quantum consequences. A reptilian beast with a stellar core, its innards burning with the power of ten thousand stars, using nuclear fusion to generate power to do the impossible. Feats such as tearing through the fabric of space, opening wormholes to leap across the cosmos. With this gift he ravages planets and their inhabitants, stripping souls from their mortal bodies like a quantum harvester, much like Jexa's spear. But...

Why?

A meteor of golden light hurtles into the black hole— No, not a meteor. A quantum capsule containing sparks of the divine, consciousness captured by the enemies of light. Within the dynamics of a black hole, each weighs more than a million stars.

Fireworks explode far and wide as supernovas leave darkness where, for eons, there glowed stars.

Trying to grasp the concept of stars having souls—that *we* are the consciousness of stars, divine sparks having a human experience, is somehow easy. As if I've always known it. And as with stars, some people shine brighter than others, whether through deed or character, or both.

"So..." I say, "when a soul—or *spark*, I mean—when a *spark* is forced into a black hole, its corresponding star dies?"

'Which leaves less stars to resist the pull...'

The stellar stream feeds faster into the swelling black sphere. Bigger, brighter stars fall into the Dark to further power its pull. The reduction in outside matter, while accelerating the pull, also weakens outer resistance to it. It's a double-edged sword. A catalyst for Omega.

I shiver. Jexa might soon add my spark to that equation.

"This is all very informative," I say, "but there's a battle going on above. I'll come back when it's over. I swear."

The hissing and sizzling intensifies as more light gets sucked into the hole, a stellar vacuum in overdrive. Darkness creeps in around me as the super-charged hole drags the edges of the universe inward. The center shines brighter with swallowed light until the last sparkle swirls into darkness, like a drain into nothingness. It ends with a flash like in the beginning, but no bang.

I stare into a void. I feel cold breath on my lips. But not my own.

A man steps back, and I realize I'd been staring deep into an empty socket, where there'd once been an eye. The man's mangy hair is matched by a long gray beard, and his ragged robe has seen better days.

"Why did you show me that?" I ask.

"To ease your decision."

"What decision?"

He points behind me.

I turn to see a great hall of pillars, each too high to see its top. The base of the nearest boasts a series of suns in an upward spiral around the column, each bigger than the one below it. Carvings underneath display images of vibrant forests that become smaller under each growing sun, while fire and swords rise in their place. My intuition interprets this as the sun's growing negative effects.

Two dozen jellyfish stretch high from the upper sun. Their meaning is less obvious to me, until I examine the section above, where humans shelter in subterranean cities. A second look at the jellyfish reveals they are not jellyfish at all. They are balls of fire rising into mushroom clouds.

The mural above tells of these cities breaking down, of the barbarous deeds my ancestors resorted to in the name of survival. And above that, three pyramids, over which a swarm of murderous fairies arrives to finish them off. It's too high to see beyond this section, but I'm confident I can fill in the rest. Besides, the pillar behind it is of far greater interest to me. The wreath of stars and stripes bulging from its base radiates magnificence. Eagles and steel birds of war soar overhead, rousing a mixed sensation of aggressive peace. For a time, anyway.

The break bordering the next section shows the mingled stars now divided by a jagged line. A few stars themselves are cracked and broken. Others no longer appear at all. Violent scenes escalate upward from there, all the way up to the fiery catastrophes that mar the top.

A brace across the ceiling connects this pillar crown to the next, and then curves onward to the following. At face level the pillars appear randomly placed. The ceiling, however, reveals an inward spiral layout, the outer of which ends with this present era.

Cracks split the stone pillars.

'One gentle push,' says the voice, 'and darkness has lost. Leave the woes of this realm for better days.'

A blue light shines from behind me. I turn to see a glowing doorway in the rock face.

"Where does it go?"

'Wherever you wish. Go to any time, any place. Wherever you end up, they'll call you a god. The time of our people ends tonight. A tragedy like no other, it's true. If you go back far enough, perhaps you can stop whatever has led us to this. You know what brought them here.'

I return to the outermost pillar and look upon the carvings of Watchers above the Giza Pyramids.

Yes, we were poor custodians of this precious gift. We tore each other to pieces for more of what we already had enough of. Knowing what I know now, could I do enough to steer us from this end? How far back must I digress? How many have tried before me? I suspect a lot, given the number of 'gods' who've appeared throughout history. These initiated humans wielded knowledge to influence humanity, using the magic of science to bring civility and light into the hearts of the blind. But at some point they all failed. And when their efforts caused more harm than good... well, there's nothing like a catastrophe to wipe the slate clean.

Would I be responsible for unleashing the floods to undo my mistakes?

A warm breeze blows through the opening. Birds chirp, children laugh. Waves roll gently onto a beach, where surf fizzes. The air is fresh, unlike anything I've ever smelled. A world unspoiled by greed and toxic comforts, in a time ripe with possibilities. A young species destined for greatness under the right guidance.

'Wherever you go, be mindful of your words,' warns the voice. 'Many foul tongues will employ them to their cause. Be wary also of your silence. Some will fill the void with a chorus of their own.'

Blue light shimmers from the hole. I step close to view a sparkling sea. Palms rustle on a clear day. Children laugh. I could enter paradise with fewer steps than those to the hell that awaits me above.

But to doom all those souls above me? Those who answered the call to fight the darkness in the name of light? What would that make me?

'Some saviors must die for their cause. Others are fated to bear a burden far heavier than that.'

A divine cataclysm. Like a mountain collapsing in on itself.

Could I live with that? The only person I actually know up there is Nya, and she is nowhere near this mountain. Of that I am certain.

I press my hand to the cold pillar. I could destroy the gate, but instead of retreating through this portal, I could wait out the storm and then reunite with Nya. Yet doing so would trap the Watchers on Earth. Man's mightiest army would be lost in a pile of rubble. And so Nya and I would spend the rest of our lives in hiding. Always in fear. Ever on watch. Even if we managed to evade the Watchers for decades, age would eventually take me. I'd leave her to suffer a hopeless existence alone for eons to come. That, right there, I cannot live with.

I pull my hand from the pillar.

'So, you choose to doom us all.'

I shake my head. *No.* There is still hope. It lies in the hearts beating above me, hammering and bleeding in a frenzied fight to save what's left of our race. I won't steal this final chance from them.

"You'd have me bloody my hands to fix your mistakes," I tell the stranger. "By the end of this day, my hands *will* be filthy. But not with the blood of my people."

The stranger raises his chin, then offers me a smirk—half-doubtful, part conniving, and yet with a small dash of hope in his one remaining eye.

CHAPTER 31

DEKA

Gunfire lures me back to surface. I emerge from the ground like a worm, wriggling through freshly-collapsed dirt.

"There you are," says Sasha. She kneels behind Dash, who stands on her tiptoes to peek over the rear trench wall. A line of soldiers wearing green armbands jump over the front trench wall behind her in attack.

A flurry of spears strike them down from behind.

I reorient myself and see I've got it wrong. The Polarians are not attacking. They're retreating. Dash is actually looking downslope, the only soldier I see doing so. What remains of the Green Line defenders scramble up the back of the trench to retreat uphill.

Dash steps back from the forward wall, her face white as chalk.

I emerge completely from the hole and peer over the trench to see a few hundred Watchers. They prance nimbly through wire obstacles, their bodies slick with paint of red and black and blades of razor-sharp steel bouncing over their shoulders. Bullets blow through them but fail to slow their advance. Except for the occasional head-shot.

A bullet hits the lead Watcher in the forehead. She stumbles aimlessly in confusion, but the Amplifier's light quickly reorientates her. She sets her sight back upslope, her stare locked on the shooter who'd hit her, and, when she continues her run, she bounces through obstacles faster than before.

A Green Line soldier hustles through the trench toward us.

"Get out of here," he says in a panic. "We gotta blow it."

Squeaking rises from a drum strapped to his back, from which a string of black wire unspools with each clumsy step he makes toward us. "There's ten tons of TNT at the other end of this line." He fumbles a handheld box with a T-shaped handle dangling from the top. "You don't wanna be around when this goes off. Quick, help me up."

I kneel and interlock my fingers. He steps on for me to spring him up over the back trench wall, the drum of wire creaking as he scrambles to his knees on the slope above us. He's not two paces from the trench when a buzzing disk whizzes up and clips off his head.

Sasha shrieks and drops to the trench floor with her eyes closed and hands over her ears.

Dash jumps up and pulls the headless demolition man back down into the trench. She quickly unbuckles his straps and slings the drum over her back, accepting the burden. "Get her up," she tells me. "We gotta move."

Buzzzzzzzzzz.

Whizzzzzzzz.

Buzzzzzzzzzzzzzzzzzzzz.

The head skinners pass higher now, destined for the Yellow Line.

I grab Sasha under her arm and help her up out of the trench. She composes herself remarkably well, still sobbing and trembling yet able to move with little assistance.

A volley of gunfire thunders from the Yellow Line above. Hundreds of muzzle flashes light up the line as they blast the Watcher rush with everything they've got. Everyone from down here has either made it to safety or been struck down, with only us now caught in the open.

Dash surveys the carnage on the downslope side of this trench. Another headless body lies belly down with a drum strapped to its back, from which a blue ribbon waves gently in the breeze.

"Sasha," she says, "be a dear and fetch me that wire."

With true warrior spirit, the young Polarian leaps over the trench to the fallen wireman. She rolls him over in search of the Blue Line detonator.

"He's got both!" she says, her eyes bright with excitement as she holds up a purple detonator with her right hand, and a blue in her left.

"Bring them here," Dash says. "Quickly now, there isn't much—"

Dash stops at the sight of something beyond Sasha. I trace her stare to the tree line, where a new wave of painted Watchers sprint uphill. They number two thousand at least, perhaps even three, all of them with a dozen steel spears slung over their backs. This rush makes the previous assault look like a bump force.

My heart thunders. Yes, those we've faced so far, solo warriors in sporadic runs, were sent to prod our defenses.

Instead, they'd busted clear through our Blue Line and sent the Green in hard retreat. This new force outnumbers them fivefold, and their movements are well coordinated.

"Sasha, get back here! Now!"

Sasha clutches both detonators to her chest and freezes.

I leap down and grab her collar to haul her back. She recovers her wits enough to jump across the trench with me.

Dash pries the detonators from Sasha's grasp and twists a nob on each to release their wires. "Fall back to the Yellow Line. I'll be right behind you."

Sasha can't take her eyes off the horde bounding over the vacant Purple Line. Suddenly fourteen hundred feet doesn't look so far away.

Dash pulls a medallion from around her neck and dangles it before Sasha's face. This does the trick. Sasha's transfixed eyes watch the golden disk sway before her, entranced.

"Fancy a race, Sash?" Dash rises to a knee and hands me the medallion. "Give this to whoever wins. Ready? On your mark, get set, go!"

Oddly, it's the promise of this prize, and not the seething Watchers now seven hundred feet away, that gets Sasha running.

Dash remains on one knee, connecting the three wires into one detonator. "I'll be right behind you," she tells me, her gaze watching the endless flood rise from the treeline. There must be five thousand at least. And there could easily be that many more to come. I don't care to be left behind in Dash's dust, so I accept her invite on the head start.

Sasha smokes me in the race to the Yellow Line. I offer

her the medal as promised, but as she accepts it her glowing stare turns downhill and darkens.

"What's she doing?" asks a nearby soldier.

"She's wiring the bottom three trenches for one big blast." This comes from a soldier who watches Dash through a giant scope on his rifle.

"Keep your heads down. It's gonna be a big one."

Chants rise in unison: *"Lay-Dee Dash. Lay-Dee Dash..."*

"She won't make it to safety if she doesn't get a hustle on," notes the sniper.

He's right. The front wave of Watchers have bounced through the obstacles with ease and are now leaping over the Blue Line, a short seven hundred feet away from Dash. They're light on their feet, invigorated by Amplifier light, ballistic rage driving them like maniacs feening for blood.

Dash rises and sprints toward us. Cheers erupt all down the Yellow Line around me. With a head start like that, even I'd outrun them.

She swiftly gains momentum but then jerks to a stop. A sharp tug on her wires reveals one snagged around a post, and no amount of flicking or whipping frees it.

"Drop it!" shouts Sasha.

"Drop it!" come a hundred voices more.

Rather than ditch the drum, Dash releases the blue wire holding her up. She fumbles the detonator and recovers it, only to drop it again. In a panic she unfastens her shoulder straps and drops the drum. She rises to sprint toward us, free of her burden, but a glance over her shoulder brings her to a stop.

The wave rushing toward us is endless. Watchers surge up from the tree line, bouncing like grasshoppers over the bottom two trenches, with the nearest now only a quick sprint to the recently-abandoned Green Line.

A hail of gunfire tears into them from above. But for every one hundred to fall, only one stays down, the Amplifier hard at work to heal their wounds and keep them moving.

Dash looks back to Sasha. She gives her a sly wink, her eyes glazed with tears. Then she drops to her knees, picks up the detonator, and just as the first dozen Watchers bound over the Green Line to skewer her, she screams, "Fire in the hole!"

KABOOM! A wall of dirt batters my face as the world turns inside out. My arms flail and feet kick freely through the air until hard ground catches me, and from my back I watch a fountain of earth launch skyward, a wall so high and wide I can see nothing else. The ground quakes again from a follow-up blast, and then shudders from another, each farther downslope and yet somehow casting debris higher. The Purple Line goes up like a volcanic eruption, hurling stone up through low-lying clouds.

Pebbles rain down and rocks pelt me as a debris cloud swallows the Yellow Line. As I sit up, something smacks my face and lands on my lap. I wipe the dust from my goggles to see an arm blown off at the elbow.

I jump up and fling it aside. The steel wristbands tell me it belonged to a Watcher, and I'd sooner kiss a venomous snake than touch one of those vile creatures.

More limbs rain down, along with a few Watcher heads in a gruesome shower made worse by Sasha's wails of despair. She sits in the trench behind me, knees hugged to her chest.

We should honor Dash's sacrifice by rallying to brace for the next wave, but everyone in the Yellow Line is a mess.

They cover their ears or eyes, crying and screaming in confusion. My own ears ring with such intensity that their cries sound like distant muffles.

I draw both of my swords from over my shoulders and face the swirling dust cloud. Dash's triple-line obliteration has surely done a number on the Watcher charge, but I've seen how resilient they can be. And with that Amplifier light boosting them up, blazing down on us and burning through the debris cloud like the sun through morning fog... well, I'd say they're far from out of this fight.

The first silhouette bursts through the dust curtain between me and the decimated Green Line. Dust grays her body from head to toe, except for her golden eyes, which holds a determined stare that glows bright in her full-on sprint. And she is not alone.

Two more appear behind her. Then six more to their left.

I test swing both katanas. The nearest Watcher sees this for a challenge and veers straight toward me. When we lock eyes, her dogged stare burns with a rage that builds with each footstep upslope. She doesn't take her eyes off me as her feet bounce through patches of shin-high razor-wire.

The innocent boy in me wants to shrivel up beside Sasha in the trench. Yet, this same fear keeps my feet planted firmly front and center.

Sweat slicks my palms. I grip my sword hilts so tight my knuckles crack. Alone I stand before the Yellow Line, soon to be exposed for the impostor I am. My fall will start with a feeble swing of my blade, or a poorly-timed counter that costs me my head. And yet I shall receive a better death than any of those behind me. At least I'll have faced my demise on my feet.

I grit my teeth and growl.

She picks up speed to close the remaining ground, her legs pumping with a surge of strength, running faster uphill than I ever could move down. With such momentum there won't be much I can do when she barrels into me.

Hundreds more Watchers emerge from the thinning veil behind her.

I hold one sword before me and haul back the other, ready to strike while the other blocks. One good swing. That's all I'll get. If it's good and true, it will be worth it.

At twenty feet she bends her front knee to spring at me. I brace for impact.

Bang!

A hole blows through her shoulder and sends her into a forward stumble. She reaches me in sloppy form, making easy work as I side-step and slice off her head with a swipe of my blade.

A dozen more rush me as her headless body stumbles on by. I try to gage who'll reach me first, and conclude that half of them will at once, in about three seconds. This time no gunshot comes from behind to break their stride.

They're about to slice through me when a Polarian soldier jumps by to my left. He drives a fifteen-foot flagpole into one's chest, and, in a remarkable feat, he manages to skewer two more behind her. Dozens more Polarians accompany the red-haired boy as he releases the pole and draws a sword. They pierce our foe with fixed bayonets, holding them in place while their leader hacks off their heads with wild swings of his scimitar.

For as far as I can see to my left and right, a flood of Polarians washes over the trench to stop the Watcher assault dead at the Yellow Line. They wear armbands of red and orange, green and yellow.

It's a real brawl. Solo Watchers dance their way through the mob while gracefully swinging their blades, slicing and dicing Polarians in their uphill advance, undaunted by the sudden surge against them as thousands of crown troops flood down from the balloons.

The humans blast them point-blank with pistols and rifles. Even at close range their bullets do little, but a head shot will send a Watcher into a daze, which is enough for some sword-wielding officers to hack through their necks.

I charge into the melee with both blades swinging. Enough muscle memory remains from Jexa's tenure to infuse me with a formidable fight. It's an awkward go, though. In such close quarters, my razor-sharp blades nick more Polarians than Watchers. I find myself mostly restraining and searching for open targets.

I look for King Regulus in the crowd, and I spot him just as a Watcher slices clean through his neck.

My heart drops to my feet as his severed head hits the ground.

CHAPTER 32
DEKA

ew Polarians notice the fall of their king in the chaos. Those who do move on with hardly a bother, much to my surprise. Perhaps in their shock they don't realize what's happened. The mind is clever when it must confront trauma, showing us what we need to see to endure, or blocking things out entirely.

I make my way to the fallen King and kneel to pick up his head. In death his cheeks are softer, fuller. And his eyes are brown instead of green. I hold out this head to see the only similarity is in hairstyle alone, and that this is in fact a girl.

I give the headless body a double look-over, to see how I could have been so mistaken, and find a long gray duster decorated with medals, just like the King's. But not the King's.

A decoy.

Another search brings my attention to a cluster of Polarians closer to the trench. Regulus stands at center with a pistol in one hand, his sword in another. He shoots a Watcher in the face to daze her, then chops off her head with a swipe of his sword.

As more soldiers find their footing, they gather instinctively before him, much to his frustration as they block his line of fire. This respite forces him to shift his focus, allowing him to see what I do. We've broken the attack on this side and forced the Watchers around to the sides.

"Gather the wounded!" he orders. "Bring them back to the Orange Line. Red Line, return to your posts. Everyone else, hold the Yellow!"

Soldiers with orange and red armbands pick up their injured comrades and carry them over planks dropped hastily across the Yellow trench. Those with blue and green bands remain with the yellows on their line. Well, most of them do.

A girl kneels beside a dead soldier and checks her surroundings before she slides the red band from his arm. She replaces it with her yellow band and joins the Red Line soldiers retreating to safety above. A boy does the same to my right, hastily shoving a scavenged red band up his arm to buy his way to higher ground.

Regulus sees this but lets them go. There's no use for them down in front. They'll only get in the way.

As the orange and reds clear the wounded away, those who remain shift their attention below, to where a ghastly sight awaits.

Less than a stone's throw downslope, an arm sticks up from the ground, clawing to unbury the rest of its body. The dirt around it rises and falls away to reveal the shoulder and head of a Watcher.

A soldier creeps close and fires a shotgun into her face.

A hand grabs his ankle from behind and jerks his leg to

knock him off balance. As he hits the ground, a Watcher bursts from the debris and plunges a dagger into his heart.

All up the mountainside, between here and the timberline, the ground ripples like a sea of soil. Lumps of dirt bulge and swell. Limbs break free of the loose ground like the dead rising to reclaim the Earth, buried nightmares lured to surface by a hell-sun's light.

Gunfire rattles and crackles from behind. Muffled shouts command those not already shooting to join in. Soldiers kneel and stand before the Yellow Line to shoot at the shifting slope. They fire steadily on automatic with their assault rifles, erratic bursts sweeping side to side, stopping only to reload.

Suddenly my hands feel empty. Apparently I'd lost both swords in the fighting.

I spot one sticking up from the chest of a dead Watcher nearby. It seems more than a hint of Jexa's skill has remained in my muscle memory, residual energy I'll make the most of before I die.

I start toward it until a flash zips by my face. The circular disk buries into a girl's chest behind me with a crunch and a sickening squish. She looks at me with crossed eyes as a string of blood spills from her mouth, then she lumbers forward onto her face.

A flurry of similar disks whiz up from the treeline —*buzzzzz... whizzzzz.*

At least two Polarians in sight of me topple to the ground without their heads.

"Take cover!"

I dive back into the Yellow trench. Many more soldiers pile in on top of me. Together we listen to the passing of head skinners above—*buzzzzzzz... whizzzzzzz... crunch... splat...*

Someone down the line risks a peek over the trench wall. "Incoming, second wave! Stand to!"

Soldiers rise dutifully and fire over the forward trench wall as head skinners continue to streak overhead.

A young boy curls on his side nearby, crying. He reminds me of Sasha.

I gasp. *Sasha!* Where is she?

I scour the trench floor in search of her.

Footsteps pound over planks and stop beside me. I turn to see Regulus offer me a rifle. "Here. We need every finger working a trigger."

I accept the firearm, and he quickly shows me its workings.

"Hopefully you put it to better use than its previous owner. Go ahead, give it a try."

I aim down at the swarm of buried Watchers rising from the dirt and squeeze off a few shots. The weapon kicks back into my shoulder with each bang until it jams, but I clear it like a pro and resume firing.

Satisfied, Regulus moves on down the line. "Stand your ground," he tells his troops through deafening gunfire. "I'm here with you. This is where we hold them. This is where we teach them the meaning of defeat."

I fire my weapon until it clicks empty. Other soldiers remedy this by digging into their vest pouches for spare magazines. I'm lacking such attire, so I step back from the line and scour the trench floor.

Two soldiers swiftly squeeze into my firing position. Polarian troops stand shoulder-to-shoulder against the forward wall, leaving no space to shoulder in between. I pull a half-loaded vest from a dead soldier and scurry down the line in search of a new position to shoot from.

Up ahead, I see Regulus kneel beside Sasha. He hands her a gray envelope and then sends her on her way, then he moves on up the line to pursue other matters.

She flips up a board and dives into a burrow. A soldier reloading on the fire line notices and elbows his partner. They both crawl in behind her, and the desperate look in their eyes raises my alarm.

I kneel at the tunnel entrance to see both men on top of her. One covers her mouth while the other pins her left arm down to slide off her rainbow armband—a ticket for one to the Eagle's Nest. Many would see the summit of this mountain fortress to be the safest place on Earth. They'd be wrong. The isolated locale of Jexa's victory is the last place you want to find yourself.

I shoot one man in the thigh—*bang!* He screams in pain, but it doesn't bother me. I spare no pity for those who prey on the vulnerable.

I aim my rifle at his partner and step back to invite him outside. "Your friend might live if he gets help soon."

He scrambles from the tunnel, giving me a befuddled look as he squeezes by and runs down the line. "Medic!"

Sasha scoots past the wounded soldier to join me in the trench. A fresh wall of dirt blocks the tunnel not far from where her assailants had cornered her. One of Dash's explosions must have collapsed it.

She straightens the King's crushed letter with trembling hands. A scribbled name across the top reads: *Captain Cygnus.*

"He's at the Orange Line?"

Sasha shakes her head, her jaw locked and eyes rattled in fright.

"The Red?"

She nods and whimpers, trying desperately to maintain her composure.

I scan the bodies scattered across the trench floor. All the Red armbands have been looted, but I do find one of the next best.

"I can get you to the Orange Line. We'll have to go over the top though. Stay low and keep your head down."

I boost Sasha over the rear trench wall and climb up behind, and together we crawl across the longest seven hundred feet on Earth. Red tracer rounds zip overhead downslope, while the occasional head skinner buzzes up in the opposite direction. When we reach the trench, I practically shove Sasha over and fall in headfirst behind her.

It's less crowded here at the Orange Line. Everyone seems occupied either tending wounded, refilling empty magazines, or linking bullets into belts to send down to the Yellow. I've landed beside a blond girl linking two machine gun belts, and my unexpected arrival from downhill sends her reaching for her rifle. She aims it at my face, her finger on the trigger, but it's her eyes that light up instead of the weapon. "Deka?"

"Clarian," I say in relief. I haven't seen her since we were captured by the Sea Lord's *Squids*, shortly after I arrived on this continent through the portal. She was deserting from military service, seeking refuge on a distant island. The Sea Lord must have made good on his promise to return his prisoners to Regulus, and he'd kept his word by leaving out the desertion part.

"How's it looking out there?" she asks.

Hardly a soldier in this trench holds a weapon. They have committed themselves to loading for the soldiers in front, their hands shaking and heads down as they whisper prayers of salvation.

"It's—"

A soldier drops between us. Several more spill over the forward trench wall, with a few reaching back over to help down their wounded.

I stand and search for an opening to shoot, but only humans appear over my iron sight. Four soldiers carry a severely wounded companion up from the Yellow Line and lower him into the trench nearby.

"Get a physician!" someone shouts.

"Medic!" wails another.

I step back from my post to see who it is. Judging by the crowd around him, he's either a ghastly sight or someone important.

I stand on my tiptoes to see Regulus slouched against the rear trench wall. He waves help away in a daze, his lips muttering words his tongue cannot deliver. Blood seeps from a bandage on his neck. Someone presses a dressing against a gash on his cheek.

"They took the Yellow Line!" cries a soldier.

"Here they come!"

"Stand to!" orders an officer.

Hundreds of soldiers lean into the forward trench wall and open fire downslope. The acoustics inside my ears feels like a steel drum being whacked by a thousand hammers. It becomes unbearable, until the deafening noise fades to be replaced by a steady ring.

I shoulder my way in between two soldiers and fire into a wave of pursuing Watchers. I hit one in the forehead and send her rolling downhill, but I have no doubt I'll be seeing her wretched face again. All I can do is keep firing.

Clarian crouches behind me and fills my empty magazines with more bullets. I keep my finger pumping the trigger, stopping only to reload or clear the jams that grow more frequent with each shot. I drop my empty magazines onto the ground and, whenever I reach behind, Clarian always has a loaded one ready.

The push from below is relentless. They keep charging at us, lone Watcher heroes and hordes of daring war bands, to keep the pressure ratcheted. Our hail of bullets rips up their forward runners and slows their advance, but the gunfire gradually tapers as machine guns overheat and more soldiers run out of ammo. Enemy numbers remain mostly the same while ours wither away. They'd have overrun us by now if not for one strange compulsion.

The bodies of our fallen soldiers litter the mountain everywhere I look, many killed in retreat and left face down in escape lanes or tangled in razor wire. The Watchers stop and punch holes in their chests with bare hands, dig out their warm dead hearts, and squeeze them to bloody mush for good measure. Exterminators by nature.

They stuff the crimson pulp under their wings, which hug their torsos like pliable armor.

My belly squirms.

A muffled voice defies the racket of gunfire to deliver devastating news: "Green Line - East Side - Folding!"

Then a similar announcement from an observer on the northwest corner: "Green Line - South Face - Folding!"

Sweat slicks my palms. Having so many Polarians in retreat leaves our overall defense vulnerable.

"Green Line - West Side - Folding!"

Gunfire snaps from our left flank. The main Watcher swarm is coming back around to us. Strange how a bulk of them remain in a group like this, working their way around the mountain.

I run to the nearest corner to get a view of both the north and east side. From this vantage I see only half the mountain, but gain the entire picture of what's happening. To avoid trapping themselves between two Polarian fire lines, the enemy have forced us into even retreat. Or... so it would seem.

A survey of the Watcher dead on both slopes reveals a peculiar detail: Not a single one has come within fifty feet of an occupied line. They apply enough pressure to push us back, but are careful not to overrun us. They push a line into retreat, then move on to the next side to do the same, forcing us up the mountain in an even skirt, almost as if...

They're *herding* us.

My heart thunders inside my chest. I look to the summit, below which a growing number of Polarians gather at the Red Line—thousands of warm beating hearts ripe for the harvest.

"South and West Yellow folded!" announces a distant observer.

Panic electrifies the troops sharing my North Orange Line.

"We're blowing the trench!" someone shouts. "Everyone out! Retreat!"

My heart drops like an anchor. This shouldn't be. With a mix of Blue, Green, and Yellow lines, we must number in the thousands at the Orange trench. But by forcing us on the run, the Watchers have driven us into a prey mentality. To counter this we must stand our ground. Fortunately, I'm not the only one who thinks so.

A gruff old officer steps back from the wall and gives the line a good look up and down. "Looks as good a grave as any. Fix bayonets!"

One in ten soldiers fastens a long dagger to the end of their rifle.

A medic jabs a needle into Regulus's leg. It stirs him enough to speak.

"Sit me up where I can shoot."

The gruff officer looks down at me and says, "Get him out of here, son. We'll cover you."

This I do not protest. I have an idea brewing, but it will work better from the Red Line.

I grab Regulus under his arm and lift him. He staggers, but Clarian takes his other arm to steady him. Together we haul the King from the trench by his webbing straps and drag him toward the Red Line.

Red streaks zip down over our heads from upslope. Only the Red Line stands between here and the summit, from which sporadic streams of bullets whiz overhead.

Our approach to the Red Line with the King inspires a disruption in the gunfire. I know as soon as I reach the Red troops that I'll lose access to him, so I set him down a hundred feet from their trench. There is urgent council he must hear from me first.

"We can't let them push us back any farther."

He snorts. "Oh, well, why didn't you say that earlier?"

Blood seeps from his mouth and streams down his chin. We don't have much time.

I dig through his coat pockets and pull out a stack of blank paper with paired envelopes. "Write down this order."

He gives me a critical look. I guess he's not accustomed to anyone telling him what to do, but I don't have time to pander to royal temperaments.

"I hereby order all soldiers to regroup at your respective Red Lines and await my command. On my signal, everyone will conduct a downhill attack in an effort to vacate Mount Tuck. No one shall stop until well clear of its base."

Regulus frowns and sits up on his elbows. "Hand over the gate? Are you mad? Nya said if they set the key they'll doom us all."

I grab his shoulders and give him a shake. "*We are* the key."

His eyes flash wide.

"A coordinated counter-attack from the high ground will break through them," I say. "They've had us on the defensive from the start. A brazen attack at this point will be the last thing they expect."

Regulus nods slowly, contemplating. Then his eyes harden with determination. He takes his pen with a shaky hand and scribbles the order.

"The signal will be three white flares from the summit," he adds.

He signs the dispatch and hands it to me. I slide it into an envelop as he writes out two more.

I spot Sasha helping a wounded soldier limp up from the Orange Line. My shouts to hail her get lost in the racket of gunfire, so I send Clarian to bring her to me at once.

"Take these letters to the commanders of the other three sides."

Sasha gives her wounded King a worried look.

"Are you listening?"

She snaps back and nods.

"Hurry," I tell her. "There isn't much time."

Sasha bolts toward the northwest corner.

A group of soldiers arrives from the Red Line to relieve me of the King. I'm helping load him onto a stretcher when Clarian stands straight and stares downhill with a troubled frown. "The hell is that?"

I follow her gaze down to mid-slope, to where a golden rod burns through the blue haze of sulfur smoke. A lone figure stands with her feet shoulder-width apart, black wings spread and golden eyes staring a hole through me.

My spine shivers and hairs stand on end. *Jexa.*

She points her spear at the summit, and that's when the real attack begins.

From the timberline below rises a flood of painted skin and razor steel, five times what we've so far faced in one coordinated rush. Echoes of gunfire from the other sides tell me it's the same all around. The final squeeze.

Whoever remains at the Orange Line turns in retreat. Soldiers pack into the Red trench, jamming wall to wall, forcing the Red Line defenders to withdraw to the East and West sides to make room. Armbands from every colored trench surround me. By how few Blue there are, and considering how they'd outnumbered every other line by at least double starting out, they've suffered the worst beating of all.

Gunners of Blue, Orange, Red, Yellow and Green blast

the charging ring of Watchers in a steady rattling raucous. Despite the hail of hot lead tearing through their ranks, Jexa's rising ring tightens with each foot of elevation gained. Her Watchers march steadily upward, undaunted, infused by Amplifier light.

"Save your ammo," orders an officer. "We'll blow 'em sky-high at the Orange Line."

We watch the black tide rise in silence. Jexa remains in place, staring me down with a devious smirk and not a single blink.

When they reach the trench seven hundred feet away, someone yells, "Fire in the hole!"

Everyone covers their ears and shields their eyes in anticipation of the blast. Dreadful seconds slip by. Each beat of my heart goes off like an explosion in my ears.

I turn to see an officer yank the detonator from a subordinate's hands. He checks the wiring, then twists the handle with the same result. Silence.

"They cut the wire," says a sniper from behind.

Cold sweat slicks my skin as the waves of Watchers cross the final stretch unchallenged.

I sit cross-legged and lean my elbows into my knees, then pull my rifle into my shoulder. I line my target over the iron sight and squeeze the trigger—*CRACK!*

A Watcher ten feet to Jexa's left takes my bullet in her right eye.

"Nice shot," Clarian says.

Yeah, for whatever it's worth. I'd actually been aiming for the Watcher Marshal. And in the recoil of the shot I've lost sight of her.

My search for her in the chaos is dizzying. The Watchers

sprint in zigzagging patterns, making it hard to line a shot on any single one. It's a miracle they don't crash into each other. I think I spot her glowing spear until I see it's actually a golden broadsword reflecting Amplifier light. This chaos leaves no shortage of targets, with hardly any space between them, so I fire away like there's no tomorrow.

A Polarian girl plops down to my left and fires like me from a seated position. A boy does the same to my right. Many more follow suit, the line of seated shooters growing longer and louder to either side of me. Gunfire rattles also from behind. Hot shells bounce off my head and shoulders from the good many Polarians kneeling or standing behind us. Together we make one last deafening racket.

I rub the sweat from my brow. The heat is enough to blister my skin, and my sweaty hands shake in their struggle to reload. It's that infernal Amplifier. It grinds us down while boosting them up.

I take a deep breath to steady myself. We just need to buy Sasha enough time to deliver the orders to the three other sides. And then a bit more for someone to launch the flares from the summit to signal our downward push.

My finger cramps from steadily pulling the trigger. Then the gun jams. I clear it and fire a few more shots until it stops again. I clear it once more and carry on, but I soon find myself jamming after every shot.

"Here." Clarian offers me a similar weapon. "Should be good."

She's right. I'm able to fire the weapon uninterrupted until the magazine empties. From this position we give the Watchers a real pounding. Our hailstorm of hot lead hammers a good dent in their tightening ring. It's all going so well that it's such a shock when a red flare lights up the sky to my left.

The girl beside me jumps to her feet and watches the sizzling light arch high overhead.

"They broke through!" someone yells from down the line.

The girl at my side steps back and trips over me.

A stream of Watchers scramble uphill to our left toward the summit. The bullets that follow them fail to hinder their mad dash. The hole in the Red Line grows wider, allowing more Watchers through to claim the high ground behind us.

Good. Let them through. This will actually bode better for my plan. More Watchers up there means less down below to resist our retreat. And not only that...

My heart flutters with a realization.

"Clarian, find me the detonator."

"It's right here," says an officer. The crumpled dispatch in his hand tells me he is Captain Cygnus.

Clarian snatches the handheld detonator from him.

"Be careful," he warns. "It's wired to all four sides of the Red. One big *boom* all the way around."

Perfect. Exactly what I was hoping for. When we retreat to a safe distance downslope, I'll pull a Lady Dash and blow the entire summit, obliterating the peak like a volcanic eruption, killing every Watcher who now crosses our Red Line.

A white flare shoots straight up from the summit.

My heart races with excitement. Yes, it's all falling into place. Better than I imagined.

I grab the detonator from Clarian and check to ensure the wire is secure. "Make sure I have a thousand feet of line," I tell her.

Two soldiers haul up a wire drum from the trench. Several more are eager to help strap it to my back. Better me than them is what they're thinking. The original two remain behind to tend the line. Twins—a boy and girl. I've heard of twins but never met any before. I always assumed they'd have to be the same gender to be identical.

An armed escort forms around me. I order most of them away. Can't be drawing too much attention to myself.

"You're all set," Clarian says.

The Watchers downslope follow the path of least resistance, flooding through the puncture in the Red Line.

The second white flare shrieks high into the sky, illuminating the horde scrambling toward the summit but still a good distance away. Still far enough for the signaler to launch the third flare and make his escape down the backside.

I turn the detonator key to check the connections. A green light flashes to tell me all circuits are primed and ready. The Watchers are only halfway between the Red Line and the summit. We got this.

Soldiers all along this Red Line fix bayonets and prop up our wounded. I can only hope it's the same on the other three sides. The Watcher offensive will not withstand this downhill charge if we all attack at once. All we need is that third flare.

Clarian gasps and grabs my shoulder. "Deka, look. The King!"

Regulus's wits have abandoned him. He staggers uphill toward the stream of Watchers, alone, with only a sword in hand. It's a miracle none have cut him down yet. They do strike down any who rush to his aid, however, by spears launched with lethal precision.

Sasha tugs on my sleeve. "Do something. They'll kill him."

Only now do I notice she's made it back to us. I can only hope her valiant venture has not been in vain.

The third and final flare launches from the summit. It's our signal to attack downslope, yet no one moves on this side. Their beloved King's fate demands all of our attention.

Regulus spreads his arms wide and arches backward to behold the flickering white light above. He holds his sword with a steady hand, surprisingly firm for a man succumbing to shock.

The first Watchers reach the Eagle's Nest and capture a dozen Polarians who've taken refuge there. They kill them slowly and in ways that force out wails of agony.

Regulus turns to face us and sticks his sword into the ground with renewed force.

"Bravo!" he says, his face beaming with the smile of a madman. "What a performance. You all really pulled together for this, didn't you. Truly, give yourselves a round of applause. I can't remember the last time I've seen anything like it."

My heart thumps inside my chest. For a wounded madman, his stance is firm and his words well measured.

A swarm of Watchers gather on the slope behind him. Jexa approaches from his left, her spear shaft glowing bright with the souls of her vanquished. A catalyst to end the Universe. The King's soldiers aim their rifles at her, but he raises a hand to keep their weapons silent.

The King has lost his mind. He allows Jexa to within

swinging distance, close enough to rip his soul clean from his body with a stab of her spear. But, oddly, this is not what she does. Instead she drops to her knees, lowers her head, and raises her spear with both hands in... in... offering?

I drop my rifle and rub the sweat from my eye. Surely my vision or my mind play tricks on me. What in the hell am I witnessing right now?

I know. It's the Amplifier. It must have fried my neurons. My brain is short-circuiting as blood vessels cook from the inside out.

Regulus snatches the spear from Jexa and drives it into the ground. He doesn't give it a second look, just growls as he grabs Jexa by the hair and pulls her to her feet. She doesn't resist, even as he pulls her face into his. Her legs spring up and wrap around his waist as their lips lock in an impassioned kiss.

I can't describe what I'm feeling right now. Truly, it's a mix of... of... I don't know how to describe it. I'm sure no human has ever felt this before. Except maybe the confused Polarians around me, but they don't know Jexa like I do.

I have no idea how long the kiss lasts. A minute? An hour? Nothing matters any more, least of all time.

My trance breaks when Regulus cocks his head to look me dead in the eye. Reptilian yellow blooms from inside, and his hardened wounds tell me this is no typical possession. His skin dries to leather and cracks into scales around his injuries.

The dragon cannot hold its flex for long in this body. The scales fade and his eyes return to white, but a wicked grin remains on his face.

All around me, Polarians drop to their knees and cry out

in defeat. It's the worst sound I've ever heard, the wails of a people betrayed by their dear savior.

Sasha sits by my feet, hugging her knees to her chest, sobbing faintly.

I kneel beside her and place a comforting hand on her back.

"Get below," I tell her. "Hide out in the deepest cavern you can find."

"Come with me."

"I'll be right behind you. Go on, now."

She doesn't believe me. It's clear in her puffy red eyes. But she wants to get away from this place, even if it's in the deepest depths of the cold dark earth.

She wipes the sniffles from her nose and nods, then stands to make her way toward the nearest tunnel entrance.

Watchers hiss as they creep closer, a pincer formation squeezing from up high and down low. This Red Line trench will be our grave. Theirs, too, when I have my final say.

I double-check the detonator. A green light tells me all four sides are connected and ready. Jexa and that beast won't get their warm human blood. Nor the summit.

Pity rises in me for Sasha, for what she will endure in the coming days and weeks ahead. Has any child ever faced such a thing?

The Watchers hiss and creep closer.

I grip the T-shaped handle. One twist and it's all over, for us and for them. This whole mountain-top will be but a memory. Our sacrifice here will save the universe from this plague of darkness. Humanity's redemption for all our failures.

"Wait now, Deka," Jexa says. "Do you really want to kill all these good folk in front of their children?"

The Marshal's words stop me. I really don't like the sound of that.

"Look," someone says, as if on cue. "Down there."

At the mountain base sparkles an upside-down pyramidion. The diamond Capstone rocks as dozens of carriers haul it uphill by a rack that suspends its base upward, apex pointing down. I'd order everyone to fire upon the gate key and its bearers, but for the children carrying it. They number in the hundreds, escorted along by men wearing blue uniforms and wedge caps.

Capital Omniguard, whispers say. If they were closer, I'd be able to see their reptilian eyes.

Amplifier light glitters over the Capstone surface, outlining a spiral channel inside. Of course a different gate would have a different lock and key. A flash of Jexa's memories shows me its workings, how the blood of the pure funnels through a series of sacred geometric patterns, producing enough energy to tear through the fabric of space-time.

My belly twists into knots. This is not like the gate of Giza. This generator uses blood magic crafted through dark arts.

"Let's have us a test of hearts," Jexa says. Regulus watches curiously as she walks casually down toward the Red Line, arms wide and a wicked smile on her face. "I'll trade any one of your younglings for five of you."

"Taryn!" shouts the gruff officer.

"Grandpa!" responds a girl from the Capstone.

"Taryn?" This comes from a Polarian woman, and her tone suggests a family relation in line with the gruff officer's.

"Mama!"

The officer and mother drop their rifles and turn to Jexa. "Let her go."

Jexa replies with a sly grin. "You'll have to do better than that."

The old officer pries a rifle from the soldier next to him and tosses it to the ground. Then he smacks a pistol from another. "You call yourselves men? Those are children down there."

A girl drops her rifle in shame. She joins the other four in their march toward Jexa.

Downslope, the young girl named Taryn is released and sent running down to the forest.

Many more weapons hit the dirt. Surrendered soldiers watch the children leave over their shoulders as they shuffle toward the summit.

Jexa, you genius. This Capstone runs better on untainted fuel, the blood of the innocent being the purest energy of all. But they are too few. The next best would be the most good-hearted adults, the type who'd lay down their weapons for the lives of others. And here they surrender in mass.

And so the catastrophe falls into my hands. Is that why no gods live beyond their time? They must accompany their doomed followers into extinction? I suppose it's fitting. And better than hiding away in safety while they meet their end.

I twist the detonator handle to blow up the Red Line. I'd not planned on yelling or giving any indication, for the sake of those around me. Better to not see it coming. But instead my voice bellows loud. It's the only noise in a frightening void. No explosion. No mass extinction by my hand.

I look at the detonator to see the green light has gone dark. A frantic turn of the key back and forth fails to reactivate it.

I trace the wire to the buried boxes of dynamite, where a head skinner sits between two ends of a severed line.

I fall to my knees and hang my head. I'm such a fool. We fought a race that cannot be defeated. And worse, I could have spared these folk all this suffering with the push of a pillar. If we'd have just hid away, they'd have given us a swift death. For our resistance, they'll make us suffer in ways I dare not imagine but soon will endure. We never had a chance. It was all for noth—

*Bar*OOOOOOOOOOOOOOOOOOOOOOOOOOOO*ooM.*

The deep horn blast shakes me to my bones. What new evil does this sound summon to battle? The Watchers must have thrown everything they have at us, but I can't help but feel this heralds the approach of something worse. Come to think of it, I've not seen the Butcher here yet. Perhaps she's coming to make our deaths a long and torturous affair. Yes, she'll skin us alive, one at a time, taking years for the lot of us, savoring every slice of human skin. We're just entertainment for them now.

*Bar*OOOOOOOOOOOOOOOOOOOOOOOOOO*ooM.*

The second horn matches the first in duration and tone. As its call wanes, a third cuts in to continue the signal: *BAROOOOOOOOOOOOOOOOOOOOOM!* As this call dies off, another blasts in—*BAROOOOOOOOOOOOOOOOOOM* —to produce a steady, taunting alarm.

My heart slams against my ribs, desperate to escape this

doomed body of mine. I scan the mountain base in search of the purpose behind the call. I see nothing new below, but... The sound...

It's actually familiar. Like I've heard it before.

I'll thank any god for the words that come next: "Ships in the harbor," says a sharpshooter behind me, "six miles north!"

I'm unsure of his direction, until Clarian jumps to her feet and points. I follow her indication to the grand bay between us and the Amplifier, where its light sparkles on the water, and where three dozen warships now spread out from The Artery and into open sea.

I burst into riotous laughter.

"Squids?" Clarian asks.

All I can do is laugh in response. I laugh like a madman. Mad like a raving hyena.

This gets everyone on their feet. They squint and shield their eyes as they stare down at the raiding fleet that had brought the Wolf to Amyria's door.

The horns persist, blaring long and loud from Lex's war fleet in a constant call to battle. She's aiming to hit the Watchers where it hurts, and she wants them to know it. If she turns out that light, the enemy will lose all their power here.

A landslide of Watchers rumbles down the mountain toward the base to take flight.

The deceiver Regulus barks furious orders at them from the summit. His foreign words fall on deaf ears as every Watcher below the Red Line continues their race to defend their glowing lifeline.

The look on Jexa's face is priceless. She, too, wants to order them back, but their refusal will make her look weak.

And so only those above the Red Line remain, which leaves us in control of the ground between Jexa and the object of her desire, the diamond pyramid that sparkles so brightly below. A rare blunder on part of the Watchers, unaccustomed as they are to surprises on the battlefield.

I cup my hands around my mouth and howl at Jexa. She responds with a clenched fist at her side and a threatening glare. It doesn't stop me from marching forward. The Polarians around me shuffle aside to allow my passage upslope. I howl louder with each step, until I'm only a few feet from the Watcher Warlord.

I bend to pick up Regulus's sword.

Polarian soldiers from the mountain's other three sides spill around to join us. Turns out they hadn't retreated without us after all. And gathered now on this one side, crowded below the narrow apex, we are a formidable sight.

Jexa seems to agree. She orders her remaining Watchers into three wide lines on the slope above.

Polarians with fixed bayonets and scavenged Watcher spears fall into line behind me. Jexa and I stand alone at center, her with her glowing spear and me with her lover's sword. Howls rise from behind me to join the chorus of distant horns.

Jexa raises both arms, palms to the sky, and like a dam gate rising to unleash a terrible flood, her Watchers charge downhill toward us.

I raise my sword in response and shout: "Attack!"

CHAPTER 33
NYA

Horns blast streams of belligerent energy from our ships in every direction. The wind carries our war song toward the slopes of Mount Tuck, where the Watcher army has already claimed the mountain gateway. Half of the assailing Watchers have since abandoned the battle there to accept our invitation to fight.

I cling to the masthead of Lex's flagship to absorb as much Amplifier light as I can. The rhythmic swaying of our boat, along with the bold song of the Wolf's war horns, infuse the Amplifier's regenerative light with dark energy. Serenity and rage swirl inside me, but they do not clash. These opposing forces exist in harmony, each necessary for the other's being. For it's in the deepest dark that our light shines the brightest. And right now, my heart dazzles like a violent supernova.

All these dynamics psych me up, but it's the reaction of my enemy that really gets my blood pumping. Hundreds of diamond formations fly in false daylight from Mount Tuck, each of them desperate to save their precious energy source. Desperate.

An advance party of six diamond formations dives toward us, emboldened by the nearby Amplifier. I stand tall on the masthead and raise my hammer, sporting an eye patch over one eye, and antler crown of my own making atop my head. Let them see me. If I'm destined to die, then I'd rather not waste much time over it.

They veer from the sight of me and carry on. They have orders. My death belongs to their master.

I turn my attention ahead, to the dazzling blue light that glows like a low-hanging sun. A black cable anchors it to a golden cylinder embedded deep into the Earth, siphoning energy from the depths of her core and pumping it into the atmosphere.

A fierce frequency rattles my bones. It shivers down the wooden mast and shakes the longboat hull. The wood groans and begins to splinter from stress.

Lex's attack won't go well if I turn her ship into toothpicks, so I take a deep breath to relax myself.

Our purple square sail bulges below me like a flower in full bloom. The wind is just right. Our rigging moans and creaks from the force of a southerly gale, one that blows our fleet at record speed toward the Amplifier.

And still, grunts grow to growls from the rowers below. Lex's crew must remain at their oars to keep her flagship front and center. Unlike with me, the Amplifier's heat has a diminishing effect on them, but if they strip down their clothes, their skin will blister within seconds.

Lex watches the dark cloud of Watchers surge from Mount Tuck from the back of her boat. She stands with her hands clasped behind her back, nodding in what seems to be either approval or acceptance. She wears reflective goggles similar to her crew. Apparently they just carry these shades around with them everywhere they go. Which I guess makes sense, since it's so hard to track time down here. When the sun finally rises in spring, it doesn't go down for another half year, and would probably blind you after six months of winter darkness, if only temporarily. You'd be easy pickings for the more unsavory Anterrans who'd see you for an easy target. I don't doubt there's some who wait all year for the day, watching for the blind fool who forgot his glasses.

As we near the landing beach, close enough to see the surf's white fizz, half the rowers abandon their oars to take up their shields, while the remaining oarsmen keep the boat on course.

A shadow ripples over our fleet as the storm of wings makes for the Amplifier, a tornado of terror blocking out the light source in one last bid to replenish their energy for this new battle.

"Two minutes," says the man steering our boat.

Lex turns and saunters toward the bow. Her warriors part to allow her passing. She stops at a young male to straighten his collar, then gives his shoulder a friendly squeeze and carries on. She accepts a spear from Karla and her polished shield from Karl, then stands with one foot up on the curved bowsprit, left of the wooden dragon head. The human race's finest fighters line the starboard and port side behind her, each with a foot boldly up on the gunwale.

I bet she can't contain her grin. On that beach ahead lies the greatest stage on Earth, a place where her entire country will watch from the mountain behind. There she'll show them who their true savior is, and I say hats off to her. Whatever works for ya.

The boat bottom crunches over rocks and grinds to a halt. The forward momentum launches Lex over the prow and into knee-deep water. Her warriors spill over the sides behind, with those at midship landing in waist-deep water, while everyone at the back sinks up to their chests.

I swoop down from my perch and splash into the shin-deep surf, careful to land behind Lex, as I've quickly noticed none of her warriors advance ahead of her.

More boats ram the shore to our left and right, spilling warriors over their bows into the rising tide. Hundreds of us slosh onto the rocky beach, where all boat parties fall into an extended line.

A sharp squeal rises from Lex's boat, where a hoist arm swings a shrouded object over the bow. Pulleys wail and lines groan in their struggle to lower their load to the warriors waiting in the water, who form two lines of twenty per side to carry 'Little Boy' up onto shore.

I fall in behind Lex, who walks up the beach like she owns it, marching at center of the expanding forward line. Several more companies fall in beside me and behind, and when all ships arrive to join our advance up the slope, we are seven lines deep.

"Incoming!" warns a boat master from behind. "Six o'clock!"

Gliding low over the water from Mount Tuck, making godly haste toward our ships, are at least a thousand Watchers. They fly in a colossal arrowhead made up of nearly two hundred diamond formations overlapping.

"Shields!" booms Lex.

A cacophony of steel plates rise in synchronized motion. They clatter together with such precision that they swiftly smother me in darkness. Those in front lock their shields at waist height, while the warriors around me hold theirs over the shoulders of the front rank, to overlap and cover them from chest to head. Third rank shields rise to form a sloped covering, which the fourth rank completes with their shields flat overhead, their ornamental stars pointed directly toward the heavens. The back three ranks lock their shields to mirror the forward half, forming a strung-out dome, with the rear rank shuffling sideways uphill.

I shiver under the shadow of the plated shelter, which squeaks and creaks with each unified shuffle. From the sky we must look like a side-stepping millipede inching toward the Amplifier. Well, on second thought, I'd say the lines of silver stars connecting each shield better resembles a diamondback rattlesnake.

Yes, a rattlesnake better suits this menacing bunch.

Beams of light pierce the shade in front. Each flashes for about two seconds, moving in irregular patterns down the line. A warrior beside Lex twists her shield to open a small window. Lex peeks through until it slides shut. Another beam shines through to her right, then closes before the Watchers can identify the opening. And so on.

Sand sizzles and hisses under our feet, and the smell of burning rubber soon invades my nostrils. We're halfway up the hill when the first cries of pain rise from those whose boot soles have melted through. This distress lasts only briefly, though, until the sky comes crashing down on us.

It falls in a sporadic barrage. Deafening strikes drive shield bearers to their knees, sinking the roof enough to allow the assailing objects to the ground—boulders scooped up in haste by our desperate enemy. Others take their knocks better, but this leaves the dropped weight on top. Steel grinds and squeals as the bearers angle their shields to dump the boulders behind our slinking dome.

CRASH—I jump as the shield above me takes an awful hit. It pops out the bearer's shoulder and drops him to a knee, so his companion raises a second shield to fill in the gap. I grab under his elbow to help him along.

Boulders batter our roof but fail to break our stride. We prop up our wounded and help them along. They are far less a burden than the ten-thousand-pound Little Boy, which requires a hundred warriors to drag on its sledge. At first our shield dome had been careful to match their pace to keep them covered, but as the slope's incline increases, so does the burden on the bomb-bearers. They fall behind and out into the open. The shield dome carries on despite their protests.

The Watchers dive in and carve them up in quick passes. They swoop from every direction, slicing with lethal precision. Many *sapiens* fall to the ground without knowing they'd even been hit.

I reach out to grab Lex's coat, to direct her attention to the slaughter behind, but I stop myself when I notice we're already halfway to the Amplifier. If we break our momentum, we may stall into pitched battle here. I can't let that happen.

I turn and weave between the shuffling soldiers, and when I shove through our dome's rear wall, the shields break open easily to allow my passing. They clink back together to seal me outside, leaving me exposed to a swarm of Watchers who buzz like hornets over Little Boy and his transporters.

I raise my hammer and send them scattering like shadows from a torch.

Goosebumps ripple my skin at their reaction. "That's right! You better run!"

I straddle Little Boy and point my hammer at the Amplifier. To the recovering humans, I say, "Onward!"

Only half of them have survived the assault, but they are enough to haul the bomb at a pace similar to before. No doubt the onslaught has inspired their urgency to find shelter under the shields once again. They are rattled and trembling, yet none drops their line to seek shelter sooner.

The warriors under the shield dome stomp ahead in measured steps, undaunted by the efforts to slow them from above.

A pair of Watchers land softly on the roof at center. They pry apart two shields with their spears for a glimpse underneath and are swiftly pulled in by their ankles. Lex's warriors hardly break step as they relieve them of their heads, leaving their decapitated bodies to be trampled upon by the rear rank.

I smile and bite my lip in delight. It seems our foe have met their match...

Until there comes a terrible ripping sound.

The noise draws all eyes leftward to the sky, where Drusilla swoops toward the far edge of our lines. The ground below her explodes in an upward V pattern. This fountain of dirt stretches toward our left flank and plows into the shield dome, hurling warriors in all directions, until a flurry of arrows sends the Ripper twirling away.

Debris and warriors land on the slope before us and

behind. Some don't move. Others roll around in pain, while a fortunate few scramble to rejoin the line.

Little Boy's sled team pulls us under the dome with remarkable speed.

"Ready bows!" Lex says, unwavering in her measured forward pace. "Watch for the next pass, call it out, and send that thing back to hell!"

"*Hoo-ah!*"

The Ripper's next blitz comes from behind but remains beyond range of our crossbows. Instead she blows two of our ships to pieces with a short blast.

Lex looks over her shoulder at me. "Get out there, Nya. Take her down!"

I watch The Ripper carve a trench into the hill ahead of us, blasting dirt and stone that rain down upon our shields long after she's passed. And then she's behind us again, blowing two more ships with an effortless burst. I've never seen such power.

The warriors around me part their shields overhead to allow my exit, but my wings cling tight around my chest. I can't match her in strength. Besides, I'm to fight Jexa. That was the deal. I can't go wasting all my energy on the Ripper.

Seeing her whiz back and forth, wreaking magnificent havoc while wearing that diamond antler crown, makes me feel like a child at play.

I pull my makeshift crown from my head and drop it.

The warriors around me shoot me looks of disbelief. I grab a shield from one of their wounded with my free hand and hold it up into the open space overhead. *There,* I want to tell them. *Do I now do less than you?* I dare any of them to go face the Ripper alone.

They close the gap overhead with their shields and continue on.

Orange light glows from a fireball bouncing down the slope toward us. It crashes into the line left of me and blows through the back with a crunch of bones and screech of twisted steel.

On top of the hill, six more fireballs begin their roll toward us.

I squeeze my shield straps and hold my breath in anticipation as I watch the scorching paths converge on our line. One fateful bounce this way or that, and one of them hell balls will squash me to a pulp.

By some miracle, the only ball on a dead course with me hits a rock and bounces clear overhead. A collective sigh of relief deflates the tension from my neighbors, but we are far from relaxed.

Watchers land on the crest before the Amplifier base— hundreds of them at least. They form a staggered line with an array of jagged weapons pointed down to welcome us. They plant their feet firm and hiss, thirsting to cut loose a river of human blood.

Lex's army marches on without a single misstep. As we near the line of razor steel, a profound realization strikes me: these *sapiens*, for a reasoning race, are incredibly brave. Most think their spark dies with their body, and yet, believing these steps may hold in them their final flicker of life, they face the darkness of eternity with enormous courage. I'd call it madness if not for the calmness on their faces and the determination in their eyes.

More Watchers land to reinforce their line. Metal jewelry of human design rattles from their necks and wrists.

I've seen Polarian soldiers wear these tags for identification, which tells me these reinforcements come from near the top of Mount Tuck. This newly-arrived group bolsters the Watcher numbers to match ours. Only, when a human takes a fatal blow here, the Amplifier will do nothing to save them.

As we close the remaining distance, we keep our ranks neat and our shield wall tight, marching into the Watcher line to plow them back.

The Watchers stab at our shields but find no openings, so they kick and shove our wall with strikes powerful enough to stop our advance dead. The humans struggle to keep the wall tight in close quarters as the Watchers beat and pry open gaps through which to stick their blades.

A warrior to my right takes a spear to her face. She howls in pain as she falls back. When a warrior left of Lex thrusts his spear out through a gap, a Watcher snatches the shaft and heaves it upward. The shields open enough to bury an axe into his chest. He makes no noise as he crumples to the ground.

I step over him and raise my shield to fill the gap.

Lex gives me a harsh and worried look, which I return with a shake of my head. We'll gain no more ground with this plan of attack. The Watchers surge with energy from the Amplifier, impervious to pain or injury. I've seen many take brutal strikes from human blades, but the Watcher wounded need only to stumble back for a few seconds of light to heal them. Then they're right back at us, with not even a scar to show for it.

Lex drives a spear into a Watcher's neck. The Watcher stumbles to safety and stops, then spreads her arms wide to look up at the Amplifier. In a matter of seconds she returns with a double kick that sends a shockwave down our front line.

Lex's troops shoulder their way from behind to replace their fallen comrades in front. This will weaken our rear, which the Watchers are surely waiting for. Only... when I turn around, I see not a single enemy between us and our boats. In fact, aside from the four ships blown up by the Ripper, they've spared the others.

My heart flutters with an inspiring realization. *The Watchers want us to retreat.* And it's not to catch us off guard. It's because they're afraid. The last thing they want is to box us in.

I return my attention to Lex, who has her shoulder shoved into her shield while also taking notice of my observation. The look in her eye suggests she's come to the same conclusion, and I give her a smile and nod of confirmation.

Lex grits her teeth with a wicked grin. She reaches over her shoulder and grabs the hilt of her sword, then shouts, *"HEARTS AND HEADS!"*

She pulls back her shield and swings her sword down into a Watcher's neck. The blade cuts diagonally across her chest and clear through her opposite armpit, severing head, shoulder and arm with a single slice.

The rest all happens so fast. Karl drives his spear into the next Watcher's neck. His sister Karla drops to a knee and stabs the heart of another, driving deep and then twisting for good measure. It's like this all down the line as the shield wall cracks open in a flurry of swinging blades and stabbing iron.

A few Watchers spring into flight, but bolts and spears bring them straight back down. Instead, they leap overhead and land behind us, where our rear rank is quick to face them. And, in doing so, our enemy have thinned their forward resistance to us.

Lex steps over her fallen foe, slamming her shield into a nearby Watcher as she slashes her way through the enemy line.

Blood spatters my face from a nearby strike and stings my eyes. In the time it takes to wipe it away, I've lost sight of Lex in the mayhem.

I squeeze my hammer with one hand and infuse my shield straps with a disruptive frequency, ready to join the fight. But the *sapiens* don't leave me many targets. They hack at the enemy line, using their shields to block and shove while stabbing at Watcher hearts. They stop only to cut off the heads of our fallen enemy, much to my relief.

For a while, all I can hear is cursing and ringing steel from the clash of swinging blades. Human elbows jab me and spear butts whack my shield as I try my best to stay out of their way.

It's too wild here. If I unleash my power, I'm more likely to kill one of my own than a Watcher, so I sling my hammer and pick up a second shield.

A spear slips through the chaos and stabs at my side. I deflect it with my left shield and smack its handler on the nose with my other. As the Watcher stumbles back, I ram my left shield edge into her throat, and it's enough to turn her lights out. As she collapses, I scan my surroundings for anyone else who may take me for an easier target than the blade-wielding *sapiens*.

On the slope above, a half-dozen humans break through

the melee and reach the Amplifier base, but a passing Ripper blast flings them away like ragdolls.

Drusilla wheels around for another pass. This time she blows apart a dome of advancing *sapiens* before rising to avoid a crossbow bolt. Her runs are short and her blasts quick, diving down and swooping straight back up, and to avoid harming any Watchers she targets only clusters of humans outside the melee.

"Get up there, Nya!" shouts Lex. She's broken through the main brawl and stands on the crest between me and the Amplifier, her face smeared with black blood. She points up at the Ripper rising high for an extra big dive.

I shove combatants away with my shields to create space —Watchers and humans alike. At first it's to spread my wings to take flight, but when the Amplifier hits me and I feel its unique surge of strength, I know the power Drusilla must be feeling up there. I'm not ready to face her yet. I need a few more minutes of that light to fix me up.

Lex shakes her head in frustration and sprints toward the cylindrical Amplifier base. A dozen warriors race to join her.

The brawl closes back in around me, blocking my view of that nurturing light. It's impossible to keep them away. Good thing I have another source.

I find 'Little Boy' halfway up the slope and mount him.

"Hey!" shout the nuke's handlers in their struggle to haul it upslope, as if my added weight is anything to its ten thousand pounds.

"Quit your whining," I tell them. "I'll just be a minute."

Before I know it, half of Lex's force have crested the hill and are fighting for control around the Amplifier base.

"Shield ring!" bellows her voice through the clamor.

A curved shield wall clatters together around the cylindrical base of gold, covering Lex's defenders from toes to scalp, with a top row rising overhead to form a roof.

Watchers jab and swing and kick at the shields, but, with nowhere to go, the assembly coils tighter with each strike. The overlap between shields deepens and fortifies the ring. If only the Watchers had come to this fight alone.

A terrible noise rips through the air.

"*NYA!*" This time it's not only Lex calling me to arms. Everyone guarding the base screams pleas for me to take flight, to stop the Ripper from blasting them into oblivion.

I glance back at Mount Tuck, where the *sapien* counterattack has been reversed. I can see by the red tracer lights fired outward that Regulus's army is corralled beneath the apex. If Deka is still alive, he won't be for long. The *sapiens* fighting on that mountain are on their last breath.

The ripping sound jumps in frequency and shakes the earth. I don't even look when I spring into flight toward the noise.

A wall of dirt erupts toward the shield ring. I fly toward the exploding line's forward edge, lining my flight to intercept the Ripper side-on, but I blow by well ahead of her. I credit the Amplifier for my increased speed, and I pray it offers me enough strength to give the strongest of my kind a worthy fight. I do notice now that my hammer feels as light as a tree branch. And my passing did just startle her into breaking her rip channel. So here's to hoping.

I loop around and jet through the falling curtain of debris in the Ripper's wake. When I emerge from the dirt cloud, I notice the blasted trench stops a few feet from the shield ring. A disaster narrowly avoided. For now.

From up here, I witness the greatest show on Earth. The Watchers, to give the Ripper and me the sky, have opted to fight the humans on their level. It's a noble approach. Though, I suspect the risk of them accidentally killing me before their master has the chance is what keeps them far away from me. They are solitary fighters on the ground, easily separated and unable to rally a defensive formation to save their lives. The humans attack them in groups of four. One or two is guaranteed to die in each clash, but often two or three emerge unscathed and join the nearest group, or pick up a straggler — violent grace defeated by desperation and teamwork.

X-Ray bursts from the Amplifier add to the intensity of Man's final chapter. One second I see a gruesome battle, the next it's a field of dancing skeletons swinging their bony arms at each other, with the occasional skull popping off. These bursts come every five seconds and last for a blink. One instant I'm watching a human dueling a Watcher, the next his head is a bare skull spinning from a stumbling skeleton, and a second after that his headless body lumbers to the ground next to his severed head.

It's all so mesmerizing that I must force my attention back to the sky in search of the Ripper. If she was smart she'd target Little Boy's entourage. He's held up on the slope, his haulers engaged in a fierce skirmish. But for now I've lost sight of her.

Lex breaks from the ring and charges to their aid. She slings her shield across her back and draws her second sword over her shoulder, alternating one blade to block while the other hacks off Watcher heads. Some of her kills are cheap shots—blindsided beheadings from behind—but hey, when you're fighting the armies of Hel, best to leave your morals at the gates.

The shield on her back takes a good many hits in the elbow-to-elbow fighting. One Watcher slugs her with a hammer with a backbreaking swing, but Lex spins with the blow and drives a sword into her assailant's heart.

The Watcher grips the hilt and falls, leaving Lex with only one sword.

"Here!" shouts a male warrior. Karl. He kicks an axe from the ground, straight into Lex's free hand.

She blocks a sword swipe with her own and buries the axe into the Watcher's neck. The blade sinks only halfway through, so Lex releases the handle and slaps the back of the axehead to drive it the rest of the way through. As the head falls to the ground, Lex snatches her victim's short sword from the headless body, then continues on with her rampage of singing steel.

I smile. The Watchers certainly have their hands full with this lot.

The air ripples around me like a heat wave, wiping the smile from my face. Then comes that terrible ripping sound. All I can do is hold both shields toward the noise and hope for the best.

An air stream hits me like a shockwave and throws me into a spin. It's like getting caught in a passing tornado, and takes me a few seconds to reorientate myself.

Drusilla hurls another blast from above. I drop to narrowly avoid it and break into a series of evasive maneuvers, zigzagging this way and that, but I quickly realize my erratic swerving isn't necessary.

I slow my flight and watch curiously as the Ripper

attempts to shift her energy stream toward me. Her shoulders flex with tremendous effort, as if with the might to move mountains. I'm able to circle behind her before she cuts her blast short and spins to face me.

She flexes her fingers to produce another shockwave. I dodge this one easily, and her post-blast wrist-rolling tells me she's resetting between shocks. I sometimes do this when dusting, but only after a long session. It usually takes a whole morning of work before I reach that point. So, it seems the Ripper's devastating ability takes too much out of her to keep in constant use.

To test my theory, I hold both shields together like a plow and fly straight at her.

As suspected and much to my relief, Drusilla drops to avoid me.

Cheers erupt from Lex's warriors below.

A wave of goosebumps lifts my skin. Seeing their gleaming weapon tips rise in praise of this minor success sends a flutter of pride through my heart. But... I don't think it's me they are cheering.

Under the Amplifier, their ring has swelled to accommodate the arrival of Little Boy's escort, who have just begun digging a hole at the base. Our mission is almost accomplished. I just need to keep the Ripper off their backs until the bomb is planted. If she were alone this might be a feasible task, seeing how she now flees from me, but alone she is not.

A winged shadow dives at my right side. I spin sideways and deflect the collision with my two-shield wall.

The Aeri attacker tumbles away, along with one of my shields, but her expansive wings stop her dead in a quick recovery. When she resets her sight on me, her face scrunches with animal rage, which forces her right eye to bulge out. She'd look ridiculous if not for the unhinged madness in her stare.

This Aeri clearly has no idea who she's dealing with, so I unsling my hammer and bolt toward her.

She beats her wings and rises, fanning me with gusts that quickly fade until I lose sight of her in the glare above.

A ripping noise draws my attention below, to where Drusilla lines up for another attempt at the shield ring. I dive to intercept her.

Over the ground, two shadows race toward the exploding line of dirt—mine and that of another.

I pull up and bank left. The Aeri stays on my original path, but my brief appearance is enough to break the Ripper's attack.

This time I continue my ascent, all the way up into the ball of Amplifier light. Here I watch as the Aeri flies up past in blind pursuit, unable to see me in the glare. She circles in the sky overhead, watching for my next move.

Again comes the ripping sound from below. I have no choice but to dive.

As soon as I emerge from the glow, I have a tail.

The Ripper this time cuts her blast short. She flies upside down to face me, and I find myself suddenly in a pincer move.

I dart left, hoping the Ripper's blast will hit the Aeri. But she doesn't unleash one. Instead, she falls in with her feather-winged cousin to join the chase. I try to stay where I can see their shadows, which means keeping the Amplifier at my back. When the Aeri shadow grows larger, I know she's rising to get the drop on me. But there's not much I can do about it with the Ripper hot on my tail.

I fly upside down, my back to the ground, to face the Aeri dive attack. We're about to collide when a second Aeri rams her from the side in an explosion of feathers—some grey, others powder blue.

Blue feathers...

Just like those of...

Ko Tora!

The clash sends the two Aeri spinning away from each other. Both are stunned from the impact, but Ko Tora had been expecting it and collects her wits quicker. She smacks her sister across the face with a cudgel and sends her falling to the ground.

"Ko Tora!" I shout in delight. "About time you showed up."

She jabs her silver club at me. "There's no *Ko Tora* here. Only Tora. I won't have my name attached to this disaster as well."

"Okay, *Tora*, how many are you?"

She responds with a disappointed shake of her head. "I am but one."

I sink as I share in her disappointment, but I do not dwell on it. The odds have still shifted from two-to-one in my favor.

The Ripper hovers beneath us, watching her fallen comrade's motionless body for a second too long.

I drop onto her back and drive her to the ground with my remaining shield. We land on a knoll above the fighting, where she thrashes and manages to angle her palm to blast me.

The airwave catches my shield edge and lifts me enough for her to slip her upper body out, but Tora lands across from me and helps pull the shield down. We force Drusilla's arms above her head and pin them with my shield, so the next two blasts hit only dirt. She writhes and kicks, but we manage to keep her pinned. Her muffled swears vibrate under the shield.

Tora nods behind me, to where my hammer sits in the ashy sand a short distance away. It's slightly beyond arm's reach, so I slide my foot back to retrieve it. That's when I notice Lex's army racing downhill toward the shore, to where steel battleships have dispatched black boats for their retrieval.

I gasp in surprise. The Sea Lord has come to join our fight, for which Lex will be mighty pleased. She is no doubt at the head of her retreating army, desperate for the embrace of her lover's arms.

A shiver rattles my nerves. How long did she say the bomb was timed for? Thirteen minutes?

"We need to get far away from here," I tell Tora. "Fast!"

She nods in understanding, but it's cut short when she notices something drop from the Amplifier light.

I turn to see... to see... something that cannot be. The Amplifier has surely fried my brain, or perhaps my eyes, because I swear I see Bercidia the Butcher digging at the Amplifier base. Her four arms fling away dirt to expose Little Boy's tail fins, which she uses to haul the bomb from its burrow.

I watch in horror as she heaves it over her head with a mighty grunt.

Three Watchers land behind her to provide rear guard

for her march down the inland slope, beyond sight of Lex's retreating force.

Tora leaps over me without warning and scoops up a sword from the ground. I sprawl over the shield to mount Drusilla before she notices the loss in downward pressure.

Tora's low glide toward the Butcher is so unexpected that she manages to slice open Bercidia's left calf, dropping her to a knee.

A Watcher skewers Tora with a spear before she can escape. Two more rush to finish the job, hacking her to pieces in a frenzy with their swords.

Drusilla thrusts her hips up under me, and I'm painfully aware that I'm left to face both the Ripper and Butcher all on my own.

Bercidia sticks her leg out to bathe the wound in Amplified light. The wide gash shrinks and seals shut, and leaves not a scar to remind of Tora's heroic sacrifice. Then she stands and heaves the bomb overhead, with not so much as a wobble in her stance.

A jet of air whistles past my ear. When I return my attention to Drusilla, I see she's slid her right arm down enough to bend her elbow.

I rattle the shield with a vibration to jar the Ripper good, but it's not enough to incapacitate her. She's still well in this fight. And the Butcher... she marches on as if Tora's attack had been little more than a fly bite.

My jaw clenches and teeth grind in frustration. What do I do? I've never been so torn!

"Hey!" barks an unseen girl. "That's my baby you've got there!"

I look to my right to see Lex staggering upslope toward

the Butcher. She carries her standard with its purple banner in one hand, a shield in the other. A clump of ash sticks to a blood blotch on her cheek, and bootprints on her back suggests she'd been knocked unconscious and then stampeded over by her frenzied army.

Lex wobbles and catches herself on her banner pole.

Bercidia sneers and turns to continue her march.

"Troll! I'm talking to you! Where do you think you're going with my bomb?"

The Butcher's three rear guards prance toward the wobbling Wolf, giddy at the prospect of the fun they're about to have with this lone target.

Lex drives her banner pole like a spear at the first. The Watcher bats it away with her sword, but Lex uses the momentum to swing the pole around her back and sends it crashing into her target's backside.

The Watcher stumbles aside, clearing the way for when Lex winds back and launches the pole into her second opponent's chest. The force lifts that Watcher from her feet and slams her onto her back.

Lex flings her shield aside and pulls both crossed swords over her shoulders. Her stance is firm and her gaze sharp.

The first Watcher recovers from her stumble and lunges at Lex with a thrust of her sword. Lex deflects the blade with one sword and cleaves through the Watcher's neck with the other.

I watch in wonder as Lex turns to face the third Watcher charging from behind. She hurls her katana and buries it into her opponent's chest, right down to the hilt! It's a bad move though, because as the Watcher falls, Lex cannot wrench the blade from her victim's sternum. Only the

Butcher remains, but she is not one to go lightly armed against.

Lex shrugs off her long coat and uncoils a whip. She snaps it at the Butcher's leg, catching her ankle mid-step, and the bomb's tremendous weight overhead sends her toppling forward. They both hit the ground with a boom.

Bercidia just lies there for a moment, watching Lex over her shoulder, nostrils flaring, fuming. Then she springs to her feet in a twisting backflip and stomps toward Lex.

Lex kicks up a broken spear and overhand flings it at the Butcher. The tip punches through her shoulder and out her back.

The Butcher doesn't even flinch. Instead she quickens her pace to a trot, closing the distance between her and her human challenger.

Lex skips forward to pick up a platinum spear, then launches it straight into Bercidia's chest. The Butcher breaks step, but only briefly. Her nostrils flare and her jaundice skin reddens as she barrels onward toward the Wolf.

Lex rolls sideways and scoops up two axes. One she flings into Bercidia's neck; the other buries into her chest, next to the spear. The Butcher roars and pulls all three weapons out. As she tosses the spear aside, another pierces her gut. And then another.

Lex is going all in, bringing the glory of the Old Way back to life, dueling with a beast that even the bravest of heroes would shamelessly cower from. For a performance like this, she'll receive a god's welcome to her afterlife. Supposing she's actually capable of dying. The way she dances around the Butcher... could she really be the one-eyed champion of mankind returned?

There is no shortage of weapons for the Anterran samurai. In half a minute she has the Butcher looking like a steel porcupine with razor-sharp quills. Lex hurls anything she can get her hands on—spear and axe, sword and dagger—along with a few devices I've never heard named.

The Butcher yanks out the weapons as she stumbles toward their source. Lex makes her way in a circle, making a real show of it, giving the performance of a lifetime. She works faster than the Amplifier, reopening The Butcher's wounds before the miracle light can seal them shut. It's a shame no one will be around to remember it.

Bercidia keeps her pace while Lex slows down. Blisters swell from her face and neck as radiation cooks her inside out. So, Lex does the unexpected by charging straight at the Butcher, not a weapon in either hand. At first I think she's going to pull a spear from Bercidia's belly, which is what the Butcher sees as well. But at the last second she dives aside into a forward roll. When she rises, it's with a whip handle in hand, the end of which is still lashed to The Butcher's ankle.

Lex strings her whip around a planted pole and hauls with all her might. The Butcher falls onto her belly, driving the spiked weapons deeper.

Lex pounces on top of her, grabbing an impaled spear and cranking it this way and that to bore a wider hole into the Butcher's back.

Bercidia reaches behind and grabs Lex's leg. The Wolf yelps in surprise at the Butcher's flexibility as she's plucked from her back and flung aside. Lex lands a hundred feet away, where her head smacks a shield that knocks her into a daze. Her attempts to stand end in stumbles to the ground.

Bercidia rises, firm in her footing as she stomps toward

Lex. She pulls a dozen blades from her torso, and, thanks to the Amplifier light, there's hardly a scar to show for Lex's battery when The Butcher reaches her. In fact, she's better than new. And Lex...

Sensing The Butcher near, she scrambles toward a short sword. Bercidia grabs Lex's ankle with her bottom set of arms. Lex rolls onto her back with an upward swing of the sword, cutting off the Butcher's lower right arm with a single slice. A swift downward swing then lops off the Butcher's lower left arm. Lex sits up and then drives the blade deep into her chest, right down to the hilt.

The Butcher clamps her upper left hand around Lex's throat. Lex kicks and struggles as she's lifted from her feet, but Bercidia's flexed muscles remain hard as steel. X-ray bursts from the Amplifier intensify, one every three seconds as Bercidia pulls Lex's face close to her own, where one eye stares into one eye.

Lex's legs fall still as she accepts the futility of her resistance. Instead, she shifts her focus to Little Boy with a side-long look.

A lump swells in my throat. How much time has passed since her warriors planted it?

It doesn't matter. When I return my attention to Lex, I see the detonator in her hand by her side. She convulses in the Butcher's tightening hold, and it was only a matter of time before Lex squeezed the device that shall forever change this planet.

My end starts with a flash of blinding light and a wall of hot air. There's no time to panic. No time to process it. And just like that, my fight is over.

I am sparks.

CHAPTER 34

DEKA

I witness history repeat itself in the worst of ways. The fireball balloons high into the sky with a steady rumble, a growling song of annihilation. As the black mushroom cloud pushes up into the atmosphere, a heavy burden drives me to my knees, for I am the only human to have witnessed both days of reckoning.

I return my attention to the Capstone. It sits between the Red Line and the summit, just a short push from the Eagle's Nest.

Our fight hasn't gone so well, I know. Half of the Watchers had kept us contained while the others went to retrieve the gate key. Fortunately for the capital children, Sasha had been watching from a nearby tunnel. She'd waited until the Omniguard wardens shifted their focus to the battle and then whisked them to safety below. So at least there's that. But Jexa had stationed a backup crew on standby, Ori and wingless Fori brought down from the north, among them Mora. She'd struggled in a harness at the head of the tugline during their labored ascent.

Watcher weapons clink to the ground as their mesmerized eyes water at the sight from which they cannot look away, this weapon of mass destruction a messiah to their genocidal hearts. Their jaws gape and quiver with ecstasy as dark energy whirls deep into their blackened souls.

Jexa stands on the slope below me, shaking her head with her back to the blast.

The Capstone's hauling team slip from their harnesses and sneak past their distracted captors. Mora leads the way. They take their pick of the many weapons lying about, then scramble up to join us. We forgo the reunion hugs and instead huddle together in a defensive position.

The mushroom cloud pushes into space like an enormous jellyfish of fire, stretching thin at the bottom and swelling wide at the top. The continuous rumble jiggles my heart and lungs.

I myself must have fallen captive to its radiance, because before I know it I'm staring at a colossal column of smoke where there had once shined a brilliant Amplifier.

Dark silence falls over Mount Tuck.

The Watchers turn slowly to face us, though they lack the hostility they had when their precious Amplifier promised them immortality. We hold the high ground, they the low, with the Capstone in between us. We've lost a good many fighters, but dug into the mountain peak, we survivors promise a brutal fight yet.

A few Watchers crouch and feel around aimlessly. Harsh whispers reveal panic growing among their ranks. Their attempts to recover their weapons result in a few accidentally cutting their fingers or tripping over each other.

It takes everything in me to not laugh at the blind fools.

And even more restraint to not taunt them with what now approaches.

A river of bobbing fireballs traces the Artery toward us. I've seen a similar display not long ago, in the valleys of Ortaria. Raven's army is still a day's ride away, but the threat of their proximity is good enough.

I pull my goggles down around my neck. "Your fight here is over."

Jexa spreads her arms in resignation. "Of course it is. Can't you see what this is about? We just want to go home." She gives us a pleading look, but I see it's all mockery. "Just let us pass, and we'll be on our way."

"Drop your weapons," I say. "Then we'll discuss terms."

All surviving humans aim their firearms at the Watchers downslope. Without their regenerative light, and with endless darkness in every direction, a few of the unblinded flinch and step back.

Jexa whistles for her warriors to drop their weapons. This leaves me wary, until she tosses me hers.

I catch the glowing spear and hold it in amazement. All those souls, once doomed to a darkness designed to kick-start the collapse of the universe, firmly in my grasp. I'll not get a better sign of her compliance than this. And what else are we to do with all these Watcher captives? Hold onto them long enough and they'll devise a way to reclaim the upper hand.

"Fall back to mid-slope," I command. "Then we'll open the gate."

"I don't doubt your intentions," Jexa says. "But I can't help but wonder how you plan to power the portal."

"You harvested the blood of our dead," I remind her. I'll never forget the images of her Watchers carving out their hearts. But even in death, our noble fallen still serve our cause. "Hand it over."

"I'd say it's gone a bit stale by now. We were counting on a quick run to the top. You put up a better fight than expected. But... I suppose we could spice it up with some fresh stuff in the mix. Fifty of your finest should do."

I size up the diamond capstone, the spiral channel inside, then the number of surviving Polarians. No need to sacrifice a single one of us. A pint from each should suffice.

We haul up the Capstone and set it onto its seat, slightly off center. I climb a ladder against its rack to the wide flat top, where a drain spirals down to the apex and then up the middle. Holding my hand over it, I slice my palm with a knife to send the first spurt of fuel down into the gate key. It swirls down the funnel and spatters into the apex.

My blood goes cold. My offering is a mere drop in a bucket bigger than I'd guessed. I am asking more from my kin than I should.

A Polarian officer shoves me aside and slices her hand to spill her blood. Then two troops climb up the opposite side to pay their pints. Two more wait eagerly behind them to do the same, and more still take to the sides so that there's at least eight contributing at one time.

The Capstone rumbles in its rack as blood pools and begins to circulate upward. The shudder intensifies with each new group to offer from their life-spring.

I keep my eyes on Jexa and her tight group the entire time. "If any so much as flinch," I tell our guards, "kill them all."

The Watchers stand perfectly still, watching with hardly a breath between them.

The Capstone rack rattles fiercely. A steel pin shakes in a corner joint between two braced sides. I pull it loose and hold my breath, but quickly see my worry is for naught. The supports fall away to leave the upside-down pyramidion balancing firmly on its point, the base above standing steady, unwavering. It needs only a slight push into place to unlock the gate. And, of course, a destination.

I size up our subdued enemy waiting patiently downhill. Some wave their hands before their faces, their blinded eyes slowly tracking, their vision coming back to life.

We don't have much time. But where to send them? The Dark would be a fitting place, but sending them there might further service their cause. How much does a dark soul weigh in the depths of a black hole? Perhaps I can send them somewhere where they can do no harm. A desolate planet. Or...

Judgment. Yes, that's it. I'll send them to their overseer, the Protector of Light and Life. The Magister will know best what to do with them.

"Halt!" shouts a soldier.

I look downhill to see Jexa marching up toward me. She proceeds alone, undeterred by the thousand firearms aimed her way.

"My dear Deka," she says. Her lips move to match her words, but at this distance they should be inaudible. "You disappoint me. I opened my heart to you, yet you dared not look. If you did, you'd have seen that I am no stranger to the weapon you call 'love'."

My heart flutters, but it is with an excitement not of my own.

"You thought you locked me out when you closed that

door. Instead..." Her lip curls with a mischievous grin, and inside my head I hear her wicked voice: *"You locked me in."*

A fierce gale knocks me off balance. Only... This wind comes not from without, but from within, a force that blows my arms this way and that in a storm of violence. It ravages me so fiercely I can do nothing but watch in horror as my hands twirl my spear, the end of which cuts down everyone around me. Humans, my own people, slain by my own hands.

They're so taken off guard they do nothing to stop me, and before I know it I've dropped them all.

I turn toward the Capstone, though not by my own volition. My arms rise in front and press against the shuddering diamond. I can do nothing to stop it when I push it forward and onto its seat with unnatural strength. It's the worst feeling ever. But I am simply a conductor. What awaits beyond the portal of Jexa's alignment draws the Capstone to its seat with a power beyond any of us.

And in my mind Jexa introduces me to feelings unknown to any man. It is affection but not love. It is heat but not warmth. Blackness that is white. It is the lust of a wicked heart. The light desperate to escape the depths of a black hole. And as soon as the Capstone locks into place, I know we have lost.

CHAPTER 35

NYA

Death by atomic blast is a surprisingly slow affair.

Heat sears my feet and head as I shrivel behind my shield, which takes the brunt of the firewall engulfing me. Time has once again become my enemy, crawling slowly along to ensure I suffer through every nanosecond of this horrendous end, a death bathed in flame that swirls around me like a tornado. Fiery death that swirls *around* me, but not...

I look down to see my knees resting in soil.

Impossible. An atomic blast should have incinerated everything in sight by now, regardless of Time's laziness, soil and bones included. Although the blast has succeeded in ripping the skin from my bones, even my shaking skeleton should now be dust.

I risk a peek around my shield to see another skeleton kneeling before me, arms extended forward to defy the firestorm. The wall of flame breaks five feet from its bone hands, where an invisible energy field deflects the blast to either side of us. The skeleton digs its rear foot deeper to slow its backward sliding.

Hot wind blows my face and whips my hair, which I'm surprised to still have, and this assures me I can lower my shield.

The sphere of fire begins to glaze around me and take on a shiny appearance. This phenomenon starts before the bone statue and spreads past it. When it reaches me, I find myself staring at the reflection of my own skeleton.

The white atomic light flickers, and, in this dark blink, the bone statue before me reclaims its natural form, revealing to me my savior.

The Ripper's skin glows red from energy overload. Her shoulders shiver and her legs quiver against the pressure coming from without as well as surging from within, but it doesn't dull her radiance. Nothing could. Resisting the might of an atomic blast, she is magnificent.

The brightness of detonation flares back to reveal her inner workings once more, and the sight sucks the breath from my lungs. An emerald organ pulsates inside her chest, pumping lime-green energy through her arms to her hands. A strange process converts it into blue pulses in her fingertips, which in turn skip into a reactive frequency pattern relayed down from her brain.

What happens from her fingertips outward I am all too familiar with. It is the projected force I use when dusting. It leaves her hands in geometric patterns, visuals I'm seeing for the first time. Usually I sense them in my chest and heart, cosmic vibrations matched beautifully by what I now bear witness to.

I look down to see a similar green light inside my chest,

and the sight of my hands almost makes me faint. I'd think the skeleton fingers were not my own if they didn't move when commanded. But they do, which means the green glow from inside me is really—

"You's different than the rest of us," echoes Sheffa's voice inside my head. She'd told me that back in Africa, when referring to the time I'd almost come undone trying to blow up the Capstone.

I need only to study the Ripper's inner workings to understand my own. The power of her destructive ability comes from a nuclear reactor, her hands converting the atomic energy into electric pulses.

I gasp with a realization. *I'm a machine!*

I look at my chest to further compare my own interior, but find my skin has returned to deny my view.

The glass wall to either side of us curves inward to meet behind me, sealing shut to form a bubble.

Crushing darkness befalls me. Only a faint orange glow radiates from the soil, which is enough to illuminate Drusilla's surprised expression as she surveys our glass enclosure. She cranes her neck back unnaturally to study the protective bubble until coming around to me.

She jolts and throws up both hands. I instinctively do the same.

She frowns at my reaction and blinks to focus her eyes, eyes blackened by mad, senseless rage. Eyes intent on seeing the demise of all those who scorned her. Upon recognizing me, her arms tense and fingers flex. I imagine the nuclear reactor in her chest spinning out energy to her fingertips, where electrical pulses crackle, eager to smash my atoms.

Within this bubble I cannot dodge her attack, so I turn to

face Mount Tuck and make my peace. All I see there is darkness. Good. I'd sooner that than a portal lighting up the polar sky. Hopefully King Regulus has subdued Jexa's force. Even if he hasn't, without the regenerative Amplifier light, any surviving humans will make the Watchers suffer dearly for another foot up that mountain.

I suddenly find myself breathing deeply to catch my breath, so I sit cross-legged and close my eyes to welcome my death. It's the perfect place to cleanse the darkness from me before I reunite with my maker. It couldn't be better, really. Drusilla will have exacted her revenge by killing me inside a device of her own making, and I'll have removed her threat from this world. There'll be justice and balance. All will be right and well.

"What are you doing?" she says. "Can't you see I'm about to destroy you?"

"Go ahead. One of us has to die alone. May as well be you."

"Die? Hah! This tiny bubble cannot contain my power! See..."

THUNK!

I don't need to open my eyes to witness the Ripper's surprise. She'd punched the wall with all her might and didn't even dent it. I'd watched the bonds of that atomic glass form, layers woven into layers within layers. She may have even hurt her hand if she wasn't careful.

I breathe deeply to savor my last taste of Earth's sweet air. There's truly nothing like it, of this I am sure, for in this moment of my death I see all my lives flash before my eyes. Scenes long forgotten flood back to me as my spark slips loose from its seat way down deep. I accept each inhale with a smile, knowing it is the richest breath of air I shall ever take again.

"Stop doing that," Drusilla says, panic rising in her voice.

"*Stop doing that!*" I mimic, my voice laced with scorn. "You should hear yourself. Pathetic. Is that how you want to go out? Screaming like a fool?"

Drusilla notices a golden handle protruding from the ground at the base of the bubble. She hauls on it with both hands, but Ko Skadia's hammer won't budge.

"The hell is wrong with you?" she says. "Haven't you been listening to me? You're going to die. *We're* going to die."

I shouldn't discourage Drusilla from speaking. Every word that leaves her mouth fortifies the conclusion my oxygen-deprived mind has been crafting—that even a wretch so lost to darkness as the Ripper has enough light in her to still fear the dark. Me, on the other hand, I've kept my light bright, and so the dark can do nothing to dim my spark wherever I may end up.

Loud wheezing reveals she's right in front of me. She shakes my shoulders. "Nya, *please*. Help... me... break... this... wall."

"Why? So you can kill more of your own kind? You should be grateful. Your sacrifice here might undo some of your wicked deeds."

"Wicked deeds? I fought for our people and they betrayed me."

"My mother betrayed you. Your own daughter, remember? The others had nothing to do with it."

"Their inaction could not go unpunished."

"Oh, it didn't. But I guess you missed that part."

"What are you talking about?" Her wheezes grow louder. Faster.

"The *Scorch*. Jexa's dragon. The flames. The burn that... The burn that never... never goes... away. And then... comes... you. A terror... almost... as... bad. No... *worse*. Because you... you should... know... better."

Drusilla drops to her knees. "Oh, Great Maker... what have I.... I'm... I'm a... monster."

I don't need to open my eyes to witness the miracle. My words have invoked the impossible—a spell broken with neither death nor destruction. Just words and words only, turning the Ripper's eyes from the cursed black to whatever color they'd been back when her heart pumped with light instead of darkness.

Peace warms me. I've done well here. I can finally relax now. I don't think I've ever had a proper rest.

My wheezing rises, and draws to it the demons of my afterlife.

"What do you think you're doing?" Jinny says, her fists balled tight and teeth clenched. "You don't get to die like this."

"Yeah," says Kassini from behind me. "This isn't how a star goes out."

"That's right," says Sheffa as she shoves her way into view. A stitched ring around her neck holds her head in place. "When a star dies it's the most brilliantest thing ever. And she takes everythin' around her with it."

"They'd never just fade away in silence," Jinny says, and the raw pain in her voice is rife with disappointment in me. "Especially not an Evening Star."

My heart burns as boiling tears slide down my cheeks.

Even in martyrdom I cannot escape the torments of my past. It's too bad, because even if I wanted to leave, I can't. If the Ripper can't bust open this bubble, what chance do I have?

I keep my eyes closed and take one last shuddering breath.

The ground shakes with a rumble. I'd attribute this to a flurry of desperate punches from the Ripper trying to break free, except for the caress of blue light over my eyelids. I've felt this cold glow before, and here it's enough to pry open my half-dead eyes. It's the only time I've ever known full-blown, instant regret.

My heart slides up into my throat and near chokes me, for through the warped glass wall I see a silver bulb throb over Mount Tuck. And it brings with it a familiar noise.

The screech would subdue me here as it had at the Battle of Giza if not for my protective bubble. But back then we'd been lucky, for we were able to close the gate before the beast could cross. But I see here we'll have no such luck.

A shadow darkens the shimmering portal. So big. And from this colossal darkness explodes a stream of fire that engulfs the mountain peak, spraying nuclear death with each breath. Swaths of timber explode like solar flares around the base.

My heart squeezes as I watch the ring of fire ravage the mountain. Such range and power.

Tears sizzle in my eyes. My death here will be for nothing. I can sacrifice myself in this bubble and it won't mean a damn thing. Sure, I'd drag the Ripper and her sobered rage with me from this world, but Earth still hosts evils far worse than her. Darkness will grow and become stronger in my absence. And so it becomes clear.

My job here is not yet done.

I'm suddenly aware of how desperate my wheezing sounds. It seems the blissful acceptance of my fate had spared my mind from panic and my physical body from unconsciousness.

The Ripper slouches against the wall across from me as if in sleep. In a bubble devoid of moisture or air, the two of us shall lie here for eternity, a living memorial of our folly. It's clear I've inherited my stupidity. Perhaps survivors will erect a plaque to explain it to visitors: 'Here lies two generations of the same bloodline so desperate to exterminate each other that they'd sooner kill themselves just to see the other perish.'

Rage burns inside my chest. I imagine the nuclear reactor there spinning in overdrive, glowing bright green as it pumps emerald liquid to my hands. My fingers tingle with electricity, my heart flutters with purpose. I will not die here. Not like this. And certainly not until I'm sure my dear Deka is safe.

I spring to my feet and press a hand against the elongated bubble wall. The frequency that resists me is the strangest thing I've ever felt. It's a mix of atomic blast and a touch of supersonic energy, two catastrophic forces clashing to forge nuclear unions found nowhere else in the Universe. Its violent majesty sings to my very soul. I revel in this gift, a harmonious tune sung just for the unnatural freaks like myself.

This divine harmony would soothe me into a trance if not for oxygen deprivation squeezing my lungs, which gets my heart racing full throttle in panic.

I remove Drusilla's crown from her head. My mother's energy courses through my hands and up my arms, infusing me with the strength of a thousand ancestors. I pull the diamond antlers back to my chest with both hands, each arm tensing like a spring, and aim the dozen points at the wall. One hand alone won't stand a chance at breaking the bonds of these woven layers of atomic glass, which means I only get one shot. The wrong frequency will shatter every bone in my body. And that's if I'm lucky. So, yes, I have only this one try. And so I'll need some inspiration.

I think of myself, of all the stupid things I've done since arriving on this planet—from telling Ko Mirah about Deka instead of waiting for the Magister's arrival, to falling for Lex's trickery when she lopped off Sheffa's head—and in the reflection of the glass bubble I see my bright green eyes darken to emerald.

For good measure, I summon forth the memory of Jexa stealing my mother's spark. This gets my hands vibrating so fiercely that, when I spring into a double punch and drive the antler crown into the bubble wall, shards of the glass hit the back of my neck at the same time as my face.

I suck in deeply for air but find none. Instead, my wheezes echo like thunder off my solid confinement. My swirling vision steadies to focus on an angel staring down at me from the smooth glass ceiling. Only... she blinks when I do.

A glittery spiral decorates my face in the pattern of infinity. I prod under my eye and wince at the pain of my touch, but a poke is all I need to know what happened. I destroyed mother's crown. Imagine that, *diamond*, blown to pieces without leaving so much as a scratch on the glass!

"It's okay, Nya," says Jinny. "You did your best. Go to sleep now."

My echoed wheezing turns to sobs. As tears blur my eyes, I see in the reflection that I am not alone. Deka lies at my side. My starving mind plays tricks on me, but I welcome these delusions. I could do worse for a last memory.

I lie here and accept the fantasy. My open mind allows it to flourish, and suddenly I find myself staring into a timeline that will never be. One where Deka and I have found peace long enough to truly know each other. Where our children roam freely, each descended from the outcasts of their people, yet each of them the best of their kind.

My throat collapses in on itself. I savor the image of her face, the daughter I'll never have and the son I'll never know, their sweet faces bright and smiling to usher me from existence.

A shriek sends a cold quiver through my heart. That infernal beast.

The sweet image dissolves. I've lost them.

My heart weeps. Then burns, then bangs loud upon my spine. My whole body shakes as my heart swells. With every beat it reveals its secrets to me. The key to its power. Its message becomes clearer with each thunderous thud: *Fight not for your hatred of Jexa.* If anything, she deserves my pity. I am to fight for Deka, and my love for him gives strength to my heart that no hate ever could. It is my heart that powers this body, after all, and a heart runs best on only one kind of fuel.

I crawl to my feet, knees wobbling and head spinning. I place both hands over my heart and bow to Drusilla, giving thanks for her role in gifting me this life. I cast love to everyone I can think of, including Jexa, for it is she who needs it most. And this time when my fist hits the glass, a crack forms where my knuckles had connected. It's hardly wider than a strand of hair, but it's enough to let in some air.

I lean close to suck in as much of that sweet radioactive fallout as I can. Wheezing becomes lighter. Thoughts become clearer. The outside air introduces me to the other half of the equation. With both hands pressed to the glass on the inside, and the final elements seeping into my lungs from outside, I can finally piece together the whole picture, so that when my fist hits the glass this time, it crumbles like a wall of sand.

I grab my hammer and launch into flight without sparing the Ripper even a glance. She doesn't matter. Not when a two-hundred-thousand-ton soul-sucking lizard is wreaking havoc upon my friends.

I set my course on the stream of fire circling Mount Tuck and prepare to redo what my mother had done once before. But back then, Klora had an advantage that I do not, for when she'd stuck a spear through that dragon's eye, the great beast had been asleep.

CHAPTER 36

DEKA

Back in Africa, at the entrance to the caves of my home, there stands a grand archway of stone. No one knows who carved the strange guardians that wrap its columns — they'd been there since times before ours — but I could never force myself to look upon those dragons for more than a second. Here, however, on the slopes of Mount Tuck, I have no choice.

A violet fireball smashes the southern slope like a meteor. The whole mountain shakes and throws me off balance as the timber ring around the base explodes under a stream of purple flame.

High-pitched wails rise loud in the night.

"Deka," hisses Mora from the trench beside me. "Get down!"

Wind thrashes me as the dragon beats its colossal wings to circle the mountain, spraying fiery death now into the trench lines. Pockets of Polarian soldiers evaporate in sporadic flashes.

Mora's pleas fade into the background. All I can do is

stare at the beautiful carnage. *Angel fire.* If there exists a greater magnificence, I've yet to see it.

A fire patch burns nearby, yet the night remains too dark for its light to reveal much around it. In fact, the flames offer no light at all. They cast only shadows.

An earthquake rocks me as the wails fade and then grow louder again.

The southern slope glows bright with purple light. A spread of black wings rises over the summit to block out half the sky. I squint and see the beast's form only through the absence of background starlight.

Violet flame explodes from his mouth with a violent boom. It sweeps the ground like atomic fog, but damages not rocks nor fallen weapons. Only living things like bones and bark, Polarians and trees turned to sizzling mist with each nuclear breath. And somehow those who meet this end appear to be the lucky ones.

The cosmic terror lands before a crater, where a group of Polarian wounded have gathered. Light from a burning ammunition cache gives his smooth form an inky sheen. He blasts the group with a jet of fire. They burst on contact, leaving only colorful sparks in place of their incinerated bodies.

Flash ionization. I'm not sure if this term comes from Jexa, or if I'd stumbled across the word in my studies, but it doesn't matter.

He draws in a breath, producing a swirling vortex. The sparks vibrate fiercely, resisting the pull toward his mouth in a futile effort. They disappear into the black void beyond the gates of obsidian teeth.

I can't imagine a worse fate. Eons trapped deep inside

that beast with no way out. Another dimension between life and death, their suffering the fuel that sustains him through dark ages of hibernation.

A stone smacks my shoulder. I turn to see Mora cowering in a trench, her desperate eyes pleading for me to join her.

Purple fire bathes the east slope. I hadn't even noticed him take flight again.

How long can he go on like that? There must be some limit to his power.

I get my answer when he reaches our side of the mountain. He heaves back for another breath, and when he blows he unleashes only black smoke. He sputters and coughs, then lands on the summit.

Mora tugs on my sleeve. When I turn to face her, she points to a soldier behind us. He sets a shield face down in the ash and slides down on his belly. The shield carries him straight down to the base within seconds.

I scan the mountain and spot another shield. Odd. I'd not seen the Watchers carry these, and Regulus's army rely solely on sandbags and firearms for defense.

Having seen the success of the first slider, another scrambles to a shield and pulls it from the ash. Blue firelight from a burning plasma pool outlines a design on the mangled shield. Though dented and twisted, I manage to make out a star with eight points.

I look to the column of black smoke where the Amplifier had recently stood. Lex must have detonated the bomb with some of her warriors in close range. Or perhaps the shield belonged to a slain warrior, whipped up by the shockwave and flung like a frisbee all the way here.

Mora grabs my wrist and points excitedly. I follow her

direction to a shield embedded in the slope only a short scramble below us. All we need to do is wait until he passes to the other side of the mountain.

On the summit, the hunched shadow perks up and looks around. He stares down the south side, away from us, and his flexing legs reveal he sees something of interest. He's about to jump, to give Mora and me our opening, when a rocket streaks up from a crater to my right. A trail of smoke follows the orange fireball until it pounds into the dragon's hind leg to knock him off balance.

To my right, a machine gun unleashes a hail of bullets into the beast's flank. I trace the stream of zipping red lights to a group of humans, perhaps twenty, hiding in a trench a good distance from me. They fire away with all they have.

The dragon pounces from the summit and lands on the slope within swiping distance of them. Light catches the edge of his scales, only visible from the rear, giving him a fluid-like appearance. To view him from the front or side, where no edge is visible, he appears as a matte-black shadow, a hulking mass that absorbs light. A black hole.

A hard edge presses into me. A shield. Mora must have scampered down and retrieved it while I wasn't looking. Her wide, desperate eyes implore me to take her for a ride.

I climb from our hole and sit on the shield's concave backside. Mora nestles between my legs, which I'm about to lift to send us downward, when something stops me.

I jump up and shove Mora downhill. Her frantic mutters fade as she swishes down the mountainside, spinning slightly on the shield toward the mountain base. I turn my attention toward the towering beast.

"Raxor!"

I don't know why I say that name. When telling the story of the Giza Battle, Nya and her folk had called the dragon who tried to cross the portal *Blaze.*

Wherever it had come from, it works. The dragon whirls around and, before I can flinch, I find myself staring at two steaming nostrils. Heat blasts me from both snarling holes. His golden eyes, each with its vertical slit, each itself a portal into the crushing depths of darkness, remind me so much of Jexa's, and I realize that's where the name had come from.

Part of me wants to run away or shrivel into the ground at my feet, but a greater, *fiercer* part, has a different idea.

My hand reaches forward. This not only disturbs the loud frightened part of me, but the dragon as well. He frowns and leans back, clearly thrown off by my presumption. And yet he cannot resist. He leans forward to allow my touch.

His golden eyes gaze deep into mine, and he sees something there, something that seizes his breath. When my hand rubs his onyx scales, I see it too, memories of carnal love between two beasts of different natures yet of the same mind. A fiery romance in the steamy depths of a volcano, isolated from the world in a place into which only a fool would dare trespass. A place where two dark souls become one.

My heart flutters. "Raxor..."

His eyes soften, hard lids sliding down in euphoric bliss. I sense the joints between his scales relax. His eyelids seal shut and rest heavy. Harsh breathing becomes gentle, faint wind in his nostrils that could be a sea-breeze through a cave. And from that darkness comes a frightened whisper.

"*Save us.*"

A shiver rattles my spine. When I pull my hand away, Raxor remains still with both eyes closed.

I search the ground for a Watcher spear, one long enough to drive deep into his eye, and find a six-footer just a short tiptoe away. I'm careful with my footsteps as they crunch over loose shale. When I take the spear in my hands, it extends with a slight twist of the shaft, granting me another six feet to a total of twelve. Perfect.

As I creep back, I size up the best scales over which to climb up onto the bridge of his nose. I can't see any of the seams from the front, so I make my way to his neck, to get a better angle from behind.

"Kill him!" shrieks Jexa from downslope. "Kill them all!"

Raxor's head shoots up. He locks his eyes on me, his golden stare now chill and hard and lacking any of the warmth he'd just held for me. A sudden surge of panic tells me Jexa has left me to face him alone.

He snatches me in his hand and squeezes so tight my eyes feel near-about to pop from my head. He holds me high and grips me tighter, savoring my agony as he crushes the life from me. My ribs crack and sternum compresses. Terror floods every part of me as my body recognizes my imminent death. I'm about to die.

I'm about to die! My jaw pops open to cry out, but no sound escapes. The pressure is so immense it keeps even my eyelids wide open.

Thud-thud... thud-thud-thud-thud-thud... thud-thud... thud... Bullets pelt off Raxor's side.

He snorts in irritation. I follow his stare downslope, to where Mora wields a machine gun. Goddess of the Ori bless her for each burst that sends her spinning into a stumble, posing a bigger risk to us humans than the beast she calls 'Blaze'.

Raxor snatches her up and holds her alongside me, squeezing the life from her as well.

I'm fading from consciousness when Raxor's death grip loosens. He perks up, his eyes scanning the sky for the source of something more pressing than our deaths.

I hear it too, a great gong bellowing an ominous tune from a distance. Though it's faint to my ears, I can tell it's a great annoyance to my captor, so great he actually releases me.

I hit the ground and first suck in two lungfuls of ash. My thirst for air overcomes me. I can think of nothing else, not least trying to escape in the distraction. It's the same for Mora, who takes no notice of me in her struggle for air. And then, by the grandest of miracles, the great destroyer of civilizations springs from the mountain into flight, two miles in a single leap, a god of death and terror rippling through the night sky like a silk ribbon in the wind.

This I *do* take notice of, for Jexa races down the mountain while whistling for him to return. Her distress hints at a trap, and his haste tells me it's a fine trap indeed. But unlike her eternal companion, she cannot take flight from Mount Tuck's slopes, so she must race beyond the borders of the gateway's Anomaly.

Pain stabs my chest like a spiked vice as a few broken ribs make themselves known, yet they don't stop me from laughing. Whoever is making that noise, whatever their plan, it's working.

I pick up my extended spear and lock eyes with a nearby Watcher. When Mora falls in beside me with a short sword, which in her hand looks more like a long sword, the Watcher turns to run uphill. Mora gives chase despite my protests, so I run to back her up.

I'm not on her for long when she slides to a stop, which happens at the instant she sees our prey is not so much running away from us as she is responding to a summons at the summit. A summons to rejoin her unit.

She joins a ring of Watchers around the Capstone. Regulus stands on the upside-down pyramidion above, sharpening his scimitar as a pair of Watchers drag his next victim up to the diamond gate key.

My breath catches. *Sasha.* Of course. She is pure enough to open the gate on her own, if only briefly, and only the Dark Star knows what will come through this time.

A swift survey around reveals a rabble of dusty humans emerging from half-collapsed trenches. They quickly see what I see: That there's no safe place to run. May as well make a fight of it.

They draw bayonets and fix them to their rifles. Metal rattles from the bayonet rings sliding down their rifle barrels until they click into place.

"At least we won't spend eternity in the belly of that beast," says Mora from my side.

"And we won't die alone." I give her a good look over. "But it seems you still have a ways to go. You don't have near enough Watcher blood on you."

She gives her short sword a swift appraisal, then tosses it aside. She takes up her machine gun in its place.

I give her a nod of approval, and together we begin our uphill stomp to give the Watcher ring one last rattle.

CHAPTER 37
NYA

My plan works faster and better than expected.

The swarm of Watchers fleeing Mount Tuck like bats out of hell are so transfixed by the carnage behind them that most don't see me coming. The ones that do just give me this befuddled look, like they can't believe what I'm doing until it's been done. Having the Ripper on their side has inspired most to ditch their armor. I leave them alone. Instead I go for armor-clad cowards. There's something supremely satisfying about the smack of my hammer on their titanium chest plates.

I hammer my way through the frenzied swarm, having such a marvelous time with my ring-ding swings, that I forget what they're fleeing from and what my purpose for coming this way was — *Blaze*, the flying furnace trying to scorch all my allies on Mount Tuck. And, speak of the devil, here he comes now, beckoned by the racket of my clamorous amusement, all two hundred thousand tons of him, his nebulous wings taking up half the sky.

To confirm my assumption, I whiz far to my left, toward a

retreating Watcher, who nearly jumps from her armor when she sees my approach. Her attempt to outfly me brings us far off Blaze's heading. When I'm about to catch her she whirls around with her spear raised, ready to skewer me until she gets a good look at me. Her polished breastplate offers me a good look at myself.

I must admit I'm quite the sight. Swirling bands of diamonds embed my arms, shards impaled into me from when I'd blown apart the bubble of atomic glass. And my face... My cheeks should sting from the circular patterns of diamond encrusting them. But my eyes reveal to me the reason for this. All-black pools, consumed by riotous darkness, tell me I have gone Berserk. And I love it.

I smack her chest plate—*DING!*

She tumbles across the sky, and her fading scream brings a smile to my face. But it doesn't last long. The two hundred ton fire-breathing sack of soot alters course toward me, confirming my theory.

I've never seen a dragon in flight before, so when he closes half the distance between us without a single beat of his wings, instead rippling through the air in an undulating motion, as if swimming through the fabric of space, it takes me completely by surprise.

I freeze my wings and drop a hundred feet, then whiz toward Mount Tuck as he glides overhead. The breeze of his passing almost drags me back along with him, and it takes tremendous effort for me to maintain my forward flight. He wheels around to follow, and half a beat of his wings brings him to within chomping distance.

I drop again and turn sharply to fly in the opposite direction. He wheels hard and faster this time in pursuit. For a beast his size, his agility is as impressive as it is alarming. But even anticipating my drops and dodges, he cannot match my speed. My four wings allow me to turn on a blink. It's part of the reason why the Watchers had failed to slaughter us in the sky around the pyramids. And right now, I'm so amped up that it's only a matter of time before I wear him out. It might take until polar sunrise, but I'll have him napping on the ground sooner or later.

I continue this dropping and dodging until something smacks my arm. A swift look reveals a streak of blood ooze from a gash in my shoulder.

Blaze takes a snap at me, coming dangerously close, but I manage to narrowly fall from his bite.

Another jab to my shoulder sends me veering left. Then a whack to my right forces me rightward. Neither of these somehow leaves a mark.

I roll to fly upside down, and that's when I spot them — Watchers. A dozen have formed a loose a circle around me, ready to poke me with their spears when I stray, coercing me into straight flight for Blaze to catch up.

A dozen more arrive to tighten the snare. They hang back, just beyond my peripheral, but I feel them there, their stares keeping the hairs on my neck stiff as sprigs.

I swing my hammer backward and send them scattering, but their formation snaps back like an elastic.

Humans must have this idea about flight, that it offers a bird's-eye view of everything around me. Sure, of the ground it does. But in the sky I have so many blind spots. And the Watchers know exactly where they are.

I look over my shoulder and catch sight of one as she rolls out of view.

Hot wind blows me into a tumble. The stink of cosmic dust and ionized aether, and the snort that comes with it, tell me it's no squall though.

My heart slams against my navel. *He's so close!* And as if facing the devourer of civilizations wasn't enough on its own, I'm now forced to fend off a swarm of Watchers too.

I glance over my shoulder to see Blaze open his mouth. The wails of cursed sparks cry out from the opaque blackness of his throat.

Wait...

Blackness?

Blaze could easily incinerate me at this range, yet no fire glows in his gullet. And with so many Watchers circling me, Jexa could have swooped in to skewer me by now. Which means...

A force tugs on my legs and hauls back on my wings, dragging me toward the beast's mouth. I swing and flail to no avail. The gravity of the black hole inside him has claimed my spark to torment for eternity.

My heart hammers a million beats a second. It seems I was fated to the Dark all along. My refusal to go to it has not dimmed its thirst for me. Instead, it has sent its agents to come usher me into its crushing depths.

And so backwards I fly, screaming and flailing until I'm drawn so close that the stench of cold bitter smoke gags me.

A burst of energy infuses my wings, my body's one last attempt to escape the eternal suffering inside a crushing vortex, so that when his teeth chomp down, they barely miss my feet. I'm able to spring off them and launch forward in the brief pause in suction.

I don't get far before the vacuum resumes, and no burst of

energy comes this time to save me. I slip between rows of obsidian teeth, then come to a sudden stop as my hammerhead wedges between barbs in his tongue. It's my last salvation as the sharp gates of hell snap shut to seal my fate.

I unleash a shameless cry. It echoes down into a vortex of eternal darkness and then back again, amplified so fiercely it rattles my eyes. It continues to grow louder and louder until a familiar noise rips through the air, and then...

CRACK!

My whole world spins upside down. I hit the roof of Blaze's mouth and then bounce off his inner cheek, and then I'm tumbling freely through open air. Streaks of white pervade the darkness around me. I flail my arms and kick my legs to steady myself, and I see the streaks shrink to silver dots.

I laugh in relief. *Stars.*

Below me, Blaze's wings splay wide and curl to stop his downward spiral. A Watcher whistles and points to his right, drawing his attention to... to...

The Ripper!

She must have sent a shockwave into his belly and sent him spinning, and the unexpected blow had forced him to spit me out.

Blaze blasts her with orange fire. *Orange.* No swift end through quark-cracking mist for her. He wants her to feel every second of this.

She flies sideways to escape, but he follows with his stream of flame, enveloping her good. The inferno swirls around her like a tornado, long and steady. Relentless.

My heart weeps for her. Yes, she tried to kill me and my cause, but it's still her blood that surges through me. The one who gave my mother her dear life. Without her I'd be nothing, or worse — suffering inside the belly of that beast from now until time's end.

The scorch persists for a whole half minute. When it finally wanes and dies, what's left of The Ripper is a glass bullet suspended in mid-air, much like the atomic bubble that had saved both of our lives.

When Blaze opens wide to draw in breath for another blast, he gets more than air. The glass bullet shoots into his mouth, lodging deep to wedge his jaw wide open.

The Ripper flies out through a hole in the back of the glass, for it had not sealed shut behind like our atomic bubble had.

The Watchers scatter at the sight of my grandmother.

Blaze bites down on the glass gag. A shard snaps out and knocks Drusilla on the head, which sends her into a daze. He swipes at her with his onyx claws, his jaw bulging and throat huffing as he tries to shatter or spit out the glass plug. She flies backward with both hands raised over her lowered head, which tells me she's hurt bad.

"Hey!" I shout to the dragon.

He cocks his head back my way, but quickly loses interest. Drusilla has become the source of his annoyance, and she must die.

The fresh memory of Lex calling the Butcher a troll inspires me to come up with an insult of my own.

"Hey, lizard breath!"

Lame, I know, but it works. This time he cranes his neck all the way around and, when he does, I swing wide and hard with my hammer. The golden head cracks the side of his face with the sound of thunder, shattering the glass between his jaws.

Black gobs of blood and yellow snot fling from his nostrils. His eyes spin around inside his head, which then falls back as if he's about to lose consciousness. And then he actually does.

I watch in amazement as he falls limp toward the ground. I savor the sight. How often does one land such a shot upon such a beast? And then the gravity of it hits me.

I did that.

The triumphant feeling is short-lived, however, for suddenly my hands feel empty.

I gasp in fright. The hammer must've slipped from my grip upon impact. I scan the debris falling below and see plenty of shattered glass, but no spinning hammer.

The Ripper hovers before me, and her proximity is enough to divert my frantic search. She stares at me with wide-open eyes, her mouth agape, and it's now that I notice a golden cloud glittering around us. And it's in this cloud where Drusilla, the great shaker of mountains, takes both of my hands into her own.

"Light of my light," she says in awe, her black eyes admiring my palms. The sight of Blaze attacking me must have driven her Berserk again.

A shiver rocks my spine and brings with it a wild realization. Not only did I knock Blaze senseless, but I actually dusted gold!

Drusilla presses my palms to her cheeks. The blackness in her eyes dissolves to reveal emerald pearls and a softness that spreads down to her jaw, where tension loosens her neck and the bulged-out veins retreat under her skin.

She opens her mouth to say more but then stops. Darkness floods her eyes once more. She grits her teeth and hooks her hands under my armpits, then flings me aside with a growl.

I recover swiftly and throw up both arms to defend myself. But The Ripper isn't looking at me.

I turn in time to see Jexa crash into Drusilla. The Marshal's spear lances through my grandmother's chest, and if I'd remained where I was we'd have been skewered together.

They both tumble toward the ground. Swings and blasts from Drusilla force Jexa to release her spear. The glowing bar impaled in my grandmother's chest allows me to track her as she flies off. In the dark sky, the shining rod makes an easy target for the swarm of black dots that join Jexa's pursuit.

I'm about to dive down to help when Blaze sneaks up from behind and snaps his mouth shut around my chest.

Cosmic gas blasts from his nostrils, blinding me as pressure squeezes the air from my lungs. It's odd that I'm even feeling this. His jagged teeth should have cut me in half instantly, but I feel my legs kicking freely inside his mouth. And when I push on the enclosure around my waist, instead of diamond-hard teeth, my hands encounter a soft, fleshy wall.

I push against his upper gums with one hand and his lower gums with the other. Add to that a jarring frequency, and I'm able to wiggle free.

I hover back and can't help but burst into laughter as Blaze smacks his lips and slides his tongue in search of his missing teeth. The sight is absolutely priceless.

His surprised stare lasts only until he locks eyes on me — the one prey who's ever dared mock him.

He blows orange fire at my face to remind me it's not his bite that I need fear. *Orange* fire, instead of the purple ionizing inferno. He wants me to feel this burn.

I drop to avoid the scorch, but when my wings halt my descent, I find a long stream of fire rip across my path. I drop again and swerve back to pass under his belly. The stream breaks and reappears before me, forcing me leftward. His neck cranes to follow wherever I go, ever ready to greet me with fire in whichever direction I seek.

I sweat fiercely as a tornado of fire follows me from above, though it's not the flames that have me so rattled. Blaze's breath carries the anguished cries of the countless souls imprisoned inside him, all the way from the crushing depths of The Dark, sparks desperate to escape their eternal torment. Their wails grow louder with each flare.

I cover my ears as blinding orange light consumes me, swerving this way and that. The shrieking tornado is so incredibly disorienting that I can't tell which way is up! The only direction that matters is where the flames are not. At one point I fly right under him, close enough for him to swipe me with his hand.

I tumble through a whirlwind of flame. In my spin it appears as if I'm caught amongst a flock of dragons shooting criss-crossing streams of fire.

I search for an opening through which to escape and spot a black figure wielding a spear of golden light.

A lump balloons in my throat. Jexa has returned to herd me into the fiery vortex!

She cuts diagonally across my path from left to right

before disappearing into a wall of fire. Somehow she maintains her incredible speed when, a moment later, she reverses course and whizzes down in a blur from right to left. And then she whizzes across a fire stream again from my left, moving impossibly fast for even an atomically-charged Jexa. And she seems to have lost her spear in this brief time.

No, she'd never. It's the only thing more precious to her than her beloved Blaze.

More Watchers arrive to assist her in my demise. This is confirmed when two dive in perfect unison across my path in an X-pattern. With fire and Watchers all around, suddenly the Dark doesn't sound so bad. I can do nothing but fly on and hope the heat is too much for them to get too close to me.

The fiery blasts shorten, and soon I'm graced by a cool breeze. It actually seems like forever since I've felt fresh air.

Somehow Jexa and her Watchers have lost sight of me, because they continue to whiz crossways through the fire stream, this way and that, and it's clear Blaze has mistaken them for me as well. He unleashes puffs of flame at the four figures buzzing around his head, and snaps his jaws whenever one ventures near. It's an odd sight, seeing them turn on each other like this. Strangest of all is when Jexa dives at her lover's face. And I do know it's her by the streak of golden light from her spear.

Blaze snaps at her to fend off the attack. With his head turned, a Watcher swoops in from behind and hurls something at the back of his skull. He responds with a sweeping jet of fire that sends all four of the harassing party diving away.

I watch the display with intense puzzlement. My confusion flares into bewilderment when Jexa dives at Blaze's attackers and crashes into the one holding her spear, who I now see is actually not the Watcher Marshal at all. Obviously.

The golden staff flies wide and spins freely toward the ground. One of Blaze's antagonizers catches it, and its golden light reveals to me her four dragonfly-like wings. This, along with her glazed rippled skin, suggest Blaze's pests can be no other than...

Fire Divers!

The sight of my Fori cousins unleashes a flood of tears down my cheeks. Just like Leeta and Kassini's gang at the outset of our rebellion, the fire-diving Fori could not resist the chaos indefinitely. Especially a fiery carnage such as this.

"Hey, freak!" calls a nearby voice.

I turn to see a fire diver hovering nearby. She's remained behind while her three sisters lead the dragon away. I recognize her dark skin and rainbow hair from the Battle of Giza, where she'd risen to become a squadron leader. *Sekarra*, they'd called her. *Black Rainbow*.

We race to meet each other, and I'm about to slap her for calling me a freak when she winds back her arm and throws something at me.

A cold splat on my chest takes my breath away.

"Rub it in everywhere you can," Sekarra says as she reaches me. She smacks another slime-ball between my wings and smears it with both hands. Already it soothes my blistered skin. I've heard of fire divers using this protective salve, but it's so rare it's considered distasteful to waste on yourself. A real fire diver saves all means of preservation for the trees. It's the ultimate sacrifice.

Selfishness or vanity, I don't care. I'm just glad Sekarra has spared some for me.

I get to work, lathering my arms and hands, then start working down my legs until Sekarra gasps in fright.

"Stay close," she says.

I follow her stricken stare to her three sisters speeding toward us, with Blaze hot on their trail. When I turn back, I see Sekarra already making haste toward the mountains of Ortaria, so I hurry to join her.

Her three sisters have enough speed to soon catch up to us. They form a diamond around me — one in front, one behind, and one to either side. I'd try to take the lead if not for Sekarra's clear direction. She seems to have a specific destination in mind.

We dive under the green canopy of an unnatural winter forest. Our diamond formation stays tight, breaking only to weave around trunks and under branches.

An orange flash from behind pushes shadows from the trees up ahead. Then a fireball hits like a meteor and incinerates every timber in sight. Wood explodes in spectacular fashion. If Sekarra's sisters have laid a trap in these woods, then they are fools.

Sekarra wheels hard left and up through the firestorm. Black smoke blinds and chokes me. A hand clamps my left wrist and pulls me to follow, and I feel as if I'm flying straight until I bump into the fire diver to my right. She loops her arm over my elbow to guide me until we plow free of the caustic veil.

A sheer mountain face immediately greets us. Sekarra darts into a narrow canyon that splits the face as the rest of us race to catch up. Normally I'd never fly into such a dark place at this speed, but I trust my leader. The others around me do as well. If one goes splat, we all do.

Sheer rock walls funnel us through the narrow chasm. Rumbling cliffs and tumbling rocks reveal the mad pursuit of our predator. I applaud my cousins for this plan until the chasm widens into a canyon. A look over my shoulder reveals Blaze slithering his way through, his sleek arms providing him incredible speed where his wings cannot.

His head shoots forward and chomps the rear fire diver in half. Sekarra shrieks from up front.

Inside I scream like a frightened little spawn. This is hopeless. He's far more evolved than us in every way. The ultimate predator who always gets his prey. Today is no exception, despite our valiant defiance. This is all just fun to him. Our terror is his amusement. Our fear ripens our bodies, seasoning us for his big payoff.

"Heads up!" shouts a voice from up front.

I turn to see a web spread across my view. Its woven strands are spaced wide enough to allow us to slip through, but definitely not for the shadowy beast on our tail, whose viscous form spills through the canyon like a flood.

I turn in time to see him plow into the net. The end anchors explode from the walls, releasing stone chunks that are too small to do any damage to him.

My fire-diving cousins fly straight upward to exit the crevice, where a long line of Fori kneel along the ledge. I recognize one of the seniors as Vera, Ko Mirah's understudy. I haven't seen her since after our Hive elder's murder, when I promised not to fight Jexa. When I assured her that we'd only cause a ruckus to distract the Watchers. Now look at us. She better not be here to scold me.

I land behind her as she turns and raises her hand. She swings down in a chopping motion, almost striking me, but she spares me hardly a glance. Her focus is on a line of Ori standing two hundred feet back from us. A dozen of them respond by swinging their hammers down upon wooden stakes. Cracks in the rock spread out from the wedges to a series of other stakes planted between them and us. These stakes fall through the widening cracks as the ground beneath me shifts and crumbles.

Myself and the Fori leap into flight as the canyon-side collapses onto the dragon. Across the crevice, another team of Ori send the opposite wall crashing down onto our enemy as well. A plume of dust rises from the gap, so we hover away and land next to the Ori standing at the widened chasm edge. No one says a word, and I find myself holding my breath while listening for movement.

"You think that did it?" asks a young Fori.

"No way he coulda survived that," replies an Ori senior.

"I need volunteers," says Ko Vera, "to go down and check."

Most of us lining the ledge shrink back and huddle, myself included. Unacceptable. I force myself forward. "I'll go. The rest of you stay here and cover me."

An Ori offers me a spear of iron ore. "Stick that in his eye, just like your mother did."

A second Ori offers me another spear of similar making. "For his other eye."

I accept both weapons and flutter high above the ground for a better look below. The debris settles and thickens at the bottom, obscuring my view, and I'm about to descend blindly when—

A fountain of dirt erupts from the chasm and whips me back. The dragon's head rises with it, his mighty claws digging like razors into the fresh cliff face as he scrambles up to face us.

The Fori scatter in every direction, including the fire divers, leaving myself and the wingless Ori to confront the unstoppable beast alone.

Anger burns my neck and face. *Cowards!* I'm about to go round them up when the Ori start yelling and hurling rocks at Blaze's face.

My fury fizzles to sympathy and despair. *Fools!* They need to get out of here!

I watch in bewilderment as the Ori continue flinging rocks at Blaze. It's a brave yet pitiful sight. Each hit is a mere flick to his scaled armor. Each poke a stoke to his rage. They've all lost their minds. They must have, I'm sure of it, until I see the display for what it is. A distraction.

Eight Fori dive down from up high and drop a noose over Blaze's head as they swoop overhead. The vine rope pulls taut and cinches tight around his neck, and their momentum is enough to jerk his head back.

Blaze springs from the canyon and blows back the Ori with startled beats of his wings. Dozens more Fori fly in and grab hold of the vine leash, and together they manage to haul him back. Blaze beats his expansive wings harder and jerks his head forward with enough force to rip Fori shoulders from their sockets.

"Hold him steady!" I shout, my hands itching to drive both spears into his eyes.

More Fori rush to grab hold of the leash. They've run out

of room on the main line, yet many have brought scraps of vine to lash onto the tether for extra hand-holds.

Blaze thrashes his head side to side, flinging a good few of them away. But more arrive yet still, breathless from their frenzied flights. I drop my spears and squeeze in to join the effort.

It takes nearly a hundred of us to steady his thrashing. Blaze writhes and beats his wings furiously with renewed force. The sudden movement rips the shoulder of a Fori next to me from its socket. Not even with my destructive nature do I find the pop satisfying.

With tremendous effort we steady the line. But what do we do now? If that double landslide failed to keep him down, what will? We're like pestering flies to him, and his erratic thrashing will ramp up again soon to further whittle our numbers. We have to make a move before he takes out too many of us.

Thunder rumbles in the distance. No, not thunder. Not in this clear sky.

A stream of red fireballs streaks up from the sea and pelts Blaze's back. I trace their origins to the bay between Mount Tuck and Alexandra's Crater, to a fleet of the Sea Lord's battleships.

Blaze's wings beat harder in response to each strike. Those bullets are only aggravating him, fueling his rage. After a few dozen he's back to flinging us around. But he's had enough of this messing about.

He stares straight down our line and opens his mouth. Hot wind blows back my hair as an orange glow lights up the back of his throat.

My arms tremble uncontrollably. It takes everything in

me to hold onto the leash as everyone's panic shoots down the line like electricity. It's a miracle none have abandoned us yet. Though, I'd say a good many are frozen in fear.

The light changes color and shines brighter, like a magenta sunset, almost blinding. The line shudders furiously, threatening to break my grip as the Fori heads up forward darken to silhouettes before the glow.

I spot Ko Vera a few heads in front. She looks over her shoulder, at the sea, her eyes hard with determination.

"No!" I scream, but it's too late. The hive mind has already spoken. Their united shouts drown out my protests: "One... Two... Three... *HEAVE!*"

We haul on the line to pull the dragon toward us and down. The sudden, coordinated effort gives us a downward momentum that cannot be reversed, by neither us nor our dragon captive. We are committed to our course, hundreds of us forest folk pulling darkness incarnate toward the ever-shifting abyss. And as a steaming ball of fire we plummet toward the sea that shall soon become our graves.

CHAPTER 38

DEKA

W hat a time to be alive. The things my eyes have witnessed...

The dragon streaks down from the night sky like a meteor, capturing the gazes of both humans and Watchers alike. Orange light fizzles like fiery froth from his mouth, blown back over his tail by the wind of his downward trajectory. A billow of black smoke trails behind him as his wings flare wide to slow his plummet. Well, they try.

They fail.

I squint to see a string of small winged figures ahead of him, towing on a tether.

A shiver rocks me as I watch those Fori drag the beast toward the sea.

"Deka!"

Mora shouts to me from uphill. She stands with a group of Ori and humans below the Capstone, preparing to clash with Regulus's fifty guards. The Watcher-possessed Omniguards stand in a ring around the upside-down gate key, on top of which their possessed king looms in all his glory, a sword to Sasha's throat.

Cold sweat slicks my skin. The essence of that poor innocent girl might be enough to revitalize the vat of blood, fueling the gate for another opening. I can't even imagine what other terrors he's trying to bring here. I'd rather not even try.

I look back to the sky.

A young girl screams.

I turn back to see the blade dig into Sasha's throat. Blood streaks down her neck.

It's happening. The Dread. The moment my entire race has feared since our earliest days. An angst we have all carried for this moment, a terror shared by those who somehow knew they carried the genes of a cursed species.

Urgent murmurs rustle our line. It's time to attack. Regulus's guards are not watching us. Their eyes remain fixated on the sky behind us. A group of Watchers observe from the slope to our left, ready to pounce should we overrun the Omniguard, yet even they cannot resist the sight to our rear.

I follow their stares northward in time to witness the reptilian meteor crash into the sea. A fountain of water explodes high and wide with such force that I swear I feel a drop spatter onto my cheek.

My heart grows so heavy the weight of it buckles my knees. I scan the sky for Nya, desperate for her approach.

A howl overcomes the thunder of Raxor's impact upon the water. This nearby wail fluctuates between growl and screech, and it sends such a fright through my heart that I collapse to my knees.

I dare not look. What is happening on that summit I need not see.

"Deka!"

Don't look. It is the greatest mercy I can give myself.

Footsteps skitter toward me. Mora grabs my arm to turn me toward the howl that somehow persists, clawing its way up from Regulus's throat. It is not the sight I'd been expecting.

Sasha sits on her behind atop the upside down Capstone, scooting backward from Regulus. Her possessed King leans back, howling at the sky while shielding his eyes from some unseen light. His Omniguards on the ground drop their weapons and cover their eyes, but their reaction is far less dramatic than that of their leader above. He steals every bit of the show.

He screams loud and long, until he can scream no more. Until all he can do is collapse onto his hands and knees atop the upside-down Capstone. His guards follow suit, leaving themselves open to attack, but all we do is watch with great suspicion.

When Regulus finally lifts his head, I see in his human eyes what has happened. The beast is gone. The Fori had sought to avenge their perished kin, and their thirst for revenge had empowered them enough to defeat the nemesis of their kind — the great nemesis to us all, dragged from his reign in the sky to a watery grave.

I shift my focus to the cluster of Watchers on the slope to our left. They all stare at Regulus in disbelief as he surveys the ravaged mountainside, his eyes watering and lips quivering with despair.

When his gaze falls upon the Watcher company a short

distance downslope, his eyes harden and jaw clenches. He kneels and picks up his sword from the diamond Capstone at his feet. His guards recover their weapons from the dirt, and so we ready ours, and suddenly the Watchers are evenly matched. Only, they have just lost their champion, who founders now in the sea. But we just regained ours. And he is furious.

He clenches his teeth, foaming at the mouth, desperate to own every one of those Watcher heads. And when he raises his sword and shouts, *"Kill them all!"* Well... no human who hears it dare disobey.

I sprint across the slope, shoulder to shoulder with my Polarian tribe, eager to send our enemy to whatever life awaits them after our blades hacks off their heads.

CHAPTER 39

NYA

Hitting seawater from three thousand feet feels a lot like splattering onto concrete. Add to that the impact of a colossal leather sack of lava landing on top of you, and it's a damn near meteor strike.

A boom and sizzle welcome us to our end. Water vaporizes as heat from Blaze burns a hole into the sea. We fall some distance through steam, well below the surface, before I actually hit water.

The next few minutes are a nightmare. Walls of seawater smash us from all sides, swirling me in a whirlpool of flailing limbs. At one point Blaze's vine leash hooks my leg and almost rips my body in half, instead tearing the ligaments in my ankle.

In my flailing, I manage to snag the vine in another pass. I grapple with the leash for dear life as colliding currents ravage me. Limbs from my Fori cousins assail me in the swirling chaos, yet through the calamity I manage to hang on as Blaze rises from the depths.

When he breaks into open air and bobs on the surface, I

scramble onto his neck and flop onto my back to siphon a breath. But instead of air coming in, a geyser of hot water explodes out from my mouth.

Splashing and gasping nearby reveals that I am thankfully not the only survivor. Fori swim desperately to safety, the situation so dire that our only refuge is a soul-sucking lizard. His outstretched wings offer a few of my cousins sanctuary, but I see dozens more who'd never had a chance. They float now face down, looking like dead mosquitoes next to the dragon's enormous body.

Those before his face splash outward in fear of getting sucked in, but I know what they do not. I felt Blaze's neck snap the second we all yanked on the line. It's possible the beast still lives, but only in mind. His body shall soon adorn the seabed.

Bubbles rise from his nostrils as his face goes back under. Then his whole body starts to sink. When the water reaches my knees, I know for sure he's done.

I'm about to cheer out in victory when screams of despair stop me. A quick scan of my surroundings reveals several Fori clinging to Blaze's sinking wings, all gasping and breathless.

No. These muffled screams come not from them, but from within the depths of darkness — the sparks of those whose deaths had lit the fire of my mother's rebellion.

My heart plummets like a meteor. Will they be trapped in the belly of this beast forever? Have I damned them all to an eternal smoldering hell? I need to release them. But how? The dragon's scale armor cannot be breached.

"You did it, Nya!" yells a fire diver as she flies overhead.

Another swoops past in a yellow streak, light cast from Jexa's spear.

I gasp. *Jexa's spear!*

I bounce and wave my hands. "Hey, give it here!"

Sekarra circles back and tosses the spear to me. I catch it and immediately check the sky for Jexa. She'd not let her coveted weapon of terror go easily to another, least of all me, yet she's nowhere in sight.

"Where is she?"

Sekarra points north, up the peninsula. "Heard she tucked tail and ran."

With her precious weapon and lover both here, I find that hard to believe. "Keep watch," I say.

A few Fori arrive with vines to evacuate their waterlogged sisters. If only they were all who needed saving.

I grasp Jexa's spear with both hands and drive it down between Blaze's wings. The tip slides through scale easy as mud and stops a third of the way in.

The shaft rattles and heats in my grip. The warmth moves up my arms and tingles down my spine.

Panic throbs through the polished black diamond in my hold, but this fear is not my own. It comes from the numerous sparks who now embrace the suction of this gateway to escape the vortex inside the dragon's innards.

After a few moments, the panicked frequency abates. A few moments more, and the fear shifts to relief, telling me I've freed at least half. But I sense the terror of many more still trying to escape the pull of Blaze's inner vortex and beyond — from the depths of The Dark itself.

"Nya, hey! Up here!"

The voice comes from a fire diver hovering overhead. She must be concerned about the rising water level, which has just reached my neck.

"Just a bit longer," I say. I have time.

"Jexa has your... She has..." The fire diver frowns as she struggles to find the right word, but I don't need to hear it to catch her meaning.

"Jexa is lying," I say. "Deka is on Mount Tuck." Whether he is dead or alive, I may never know.

The diver flutters close and opens a cloth to show me a brown ear.

It takes everything in me to not short circuit.

"She wants to make a trade," the fire diver says. "Your lover for hers."

I drive Jexa's spear deeper into Blaze's back. Hopefully her deep connection to him somehow allows her to feel it, too.

Bubbles rise from his submerged head, the head that has been under for nearly five minutes now. How long will it take for his brain to die?

Salt water sloshes into my mouth and up my nostrils. I seal my lips and tilt my head back to buy myself a few seconds more, but it's no use. Even if I thought Jexa wasn't luring me into a trap, there's no way we could ever recover this beast from the sea. This watery grave has already claimed him. And he's not going down alone.

Water reaches my chin and splashes over my head. It's time to let go.

I pull up, but the spear doesn't budge. A second and third try yield no better results. *Stuck.* That's fine. I can let the spear sink with Blaze, then return for it after the battle. It'll be safer down there anyway.

I try to let go, but my grip remains firm.

A dark, heavy energy laces up my arms and weaves into

my spine. It locks my hands around the shaft, tightening fingers that would break before they'd ever let go.

My whole body trembles. I'd reached too far, dug too deep. With the souls of the damned comes now the spark of the Dark Star. His primordial essence tries with all its might to join us. And so enormous and dense is his spark that it clogs up the spear's intake, locking us all in place.

The sea pulls my head under and swallows me. My mind begs my hands to unlock and rise to surface, but my grasp remains tight around the golden shaft of diamond, my nuclear core providing all the energy needed to keep this escapeway open. I can't let go no matter how hard I try. And so together we sink into the cold dark abyss.

I'm sorry, Deka. I've failed you.

I failed us all.

CHAPTER 40
NYA

Thunder welcomes me to the watery underworld. It rumbles from distant clouds, distorted by bubbling water. The lord of this realm casts his net up from the depths to ensnare me, to haul me down as if I actually have somewhere else to go.

The net flares around me like a perforated jellyfish, then shrinks shut to seal me in. It drags me gently toward the thunderous abyss, where squiggles of silver light dance before me.

Shadowy figures take shape in my peripheral vision. One wields Jexa's spear, which I hadn't realized I'd released until now. Whoever they are, they'd somehow done what I could not by pulling it from Blaze's back. Their fins suggest they are my Nixy cousins, but their featureless faces tell me they are actually the aquatic angels of death. And in true angel-of-death fashion, they pull the net to usher me deep into their underworld.

The squiggles of silver light shrink to become dots. *Dots?* Yes, but not just any dots.

Stars.

It seems I had it all wrong. The starry sky I see beyond the wavy surface is the same from which we'd wrestled our nemesis to his death. And those angels of the netherworld? None other than human divers dressed in all-black gear — tanks, flippers and goggles used to trespass into the hostile depths.

My full weight sags into the net as I rise from the waterline.

"That's her!" someone says.

I squirm in the net to shift for a better look behind me. The gray hull of a large ship rocks within arm's reach, from which a steel arm extends to support my swaying net. At the other end of the lifting arm stands the Lord of the Sea. The decks of his battleship are crammed with Lex's salvaged wolf pack, hundreds of them.

"She lives!" shouts one, and the others erupt into cheers and applause.

They shuffle away as the steel arm swings inboard and dumps me at their feet. Strands of net fall around me and open up like a blooming flower to release me. Lex's warriors watch me in awe. I hear their whispers loud and clear.

"That nuke should've killed her."

"It did. Nothing could've survived that."

"Well, she *survived. Obviously."*

"Must be immortal..."

"A god..."

"Can't be. I heard she flew away at the last second."

"Yeah, that's what I heard too. She must have."

"Almost lost you there," says the Sea Lord as he shoulders his way through the crowd. He kneels to take my arm and helps me up. "I hope this makes up for shooting you."

I try to stand upright, but dizziness sways me. My belly stirs and pumps up a gush of water through my mouth and onto the Sea Lord's coat. Vomit comes close behind and splats onto his boots.

I wipe my mouth and say, "Now I think we're even."

The Sea Lord manages what seems to be a genuine smile.

Muttering rises amongst the throng of Lex's warriors. An argument of harsh whispers and sharp elbows escalates until finally a man relents with a shake of his head. He pulls something from a bag and makes his way to the front to offer it to me.

My makeshift antler crown has seen better days. I'd dropped it under the shuffling shield dome, to conceal my location from the Ripper. He must have picked it up in their retreat, seeing it for a nice trophy or keepsake.

I accept it with shaking hands. Then I narrow my eyes on Mount Tuck. "You Squids ready to get your hands dirty?"

Lex's warriors whack their weapons on their shields. The Polarian sailors among them cradle their harpoon guns and raise their chins. Some can't hide the fear in their eyes, but a fair few seem eager.

The Sea Lord casts his gaze across the crowd of chanting *wolves*. They grunt in unison, banging louder. The Sea Lord named *Toris* looks up to the ship's control deck, where an elderly man stands behind the wooden wheel.

"Set course for Mount Tuck."

CHAPTER 41

DEKA

The dragon is dead, but I am far from saved.

I stare down the barrels of two dozen rifles, and yet they are nowhere near as unnerving as the vile creature that clings to my back. Jexa's arms coil around my neck like a snake, squeezing just enough to choke my words but not my breath. She uses a pressure point that not only paralyzes me, but makes my head want to explode. Her pale legs wrap around my waist for good measure, her feet hooking inside my knees to force my legs apart. She reeks of sulfur and blood, and though her skin is smooth and warm, her touch sends a squirm deep to my soul.

"What do we do?" asks a crown soldier. Every other Watcher has been slain, hacked to pieces in a frenzy of revenge. Only their leader now stands before absolute victory.

"*Shoot me,*" I say, but the words sound only in my head.

Two soldiers advance with their weapons aimed at Jexa's face.

"I'll break his neck," she warns. "Then you can explain to his lover why you killed him."

They both stop dead.

Jexa bites my ear, taunting. Warm blood still flows from where my other ear used to be.

"Look at their weakness," she says in my mind. *"So strong, yet so soft. Pathetic creatures ruled by emotion. Your race is an abomination — a mixture of love and hate that will never know peace. It's little wonder the Magister wanted you gone."*

The Magister would never condone this, I say in my head.

"Of course not. The almighty Protector of Light and Life would never do such a thing. Why else would he assign a murderous race to watch over the weak and helpless? He must wield such a big heart, beaming with forgiveness and trust. But what choice did you give him? His grand design requires harmony between all races. You can't even get along with your own. And for that he must don a different cloak. Your absent protector goes by many names. The forest folk call him Magister, yes, but to his soldiers, he is our Magister *Militum.*"

I urge my body to move. Jexa bites harder on my ear, and the pain paralyzes even my mind.

"You hear the truth in my words," she says. "You've seen what I've seen — the danger of your people. Look around. Look at what you've done here. Us Light Ones have never tasted defeat until we met your kind. Each and every one of you is a menace. Your victory here has sealed your fate. You'll meet your end by my hand or your own."

"Jexa!" The girl's voice comes from somewhere downslope. "Where is she?"

The crowd parts before us to reveal Nya leading a force

of Lex's Wolves and Toris's Squids uphill. With an antler crown on her head and swirling diamond studs embedded into her face, she is the definition of divine.

My heart spins like a pulsar.

Jexa's arms tighten around my neck, but my heart is one thing she cannot control. My one remaining eye, though... It rolls back in my head.

"Harm him," Nya says, "and you'll taste a fate that not even *you* deserve."

Jexa's hold loosens enough for me to refocus on Nya. She holds Jexa's glowing spear over her head.

"You wanted to make a trade," Nya says.

Jexa's heart thumps against my back. It's the first time I've actually felt its beat.

"I have his spark," Nya says as she stares lustfully at the glowing spear. It rattles beyond her control, shaking her whole arm. "Almost killed me to catch it, but it's here."

Jexa straightens up behind me.

"You could be together. I'll maroon you both on a deserted planet where neither of you can harm another soul. But you'll be together. But that's only if you let Deka go."

"A generous trade," Jexa says. "But you're as likely to kill me than keep your word."

Nya shifts uneasily. It's clear to me that is indeed her plan. Jexa must see it too.

She has no authority to judge the Marshal of Watchers, I say to Jexa in my mind. *Let alone execute one. Only a Magister* Militum *can do that.*

"Deka, you clever boy." Jexa's hold loosens enough for me to speak. *"Go ahead and tell them that."*

I share with Nya the same words I told Jexa, how it is not

her place to kill the Marshal if she surrenders. Nya gives me a confused look, but does not protest.

"If you truly believe your cause to be just," I tell the Watcher Marshal, loud enough for most to hear, "then allow me to open a gate to your judgment. If what you say is true, he'll welcome you home with open arms. Then you may return with a new army to reclaim what you've lost."

Jexa's legs uncoil from around me. She plants her feet to either side of my hips and stands with me wrapped in her arms.

"I want you to know, Deka, that what we shared was truly special. I've never known a host like you before. So strong and caring. So steadfast until the bitter end. They'd have never stood a chance without you. There's a saying among my people: One drop of a champion's blood is worth a thousand from an innocent. *Let us see if that's true."*

A sharp squeeze seizes my shoulder below the neck. I open my mouth to scream, but nothing comes out. I can do nothing as Jexa bites harder to suck the lifeblood from me. It's a new low for her, to allow the blood of a lesser species into her body. I can feel her revulsion. It is the most vile thing to her. But my blood is her ticket home.

Nya flings the sizzling spear aside. Jexa releases me and springs to catch it, most unexpectedly. When she lands below the Capstone, she doesn't miss a beat. She leaps up onto the flat base of the upside down pyramid, and into the spiral vat she spews my blood.

A flash of blue light blinds me. Footsteps swish through ash around me, and then comes a *BOOM*, followed swiftly by a blackout. When my eyes adjust to the renewed darkness, I see Nya standing on the summit next to the diamond

Capstone, which now lies on its side. She casts a sweeping gaze over all four slopes in search of Jexa.

"She's gone," Mora says.

Silence follows for a few seconds. Then cheers and applause rise loud into the night. I'd not be surprised if they could hear the celebration in Amyria.

I bristle. It seems too bold. As if Jexa may hear this for a taunt and come back. I'm not sure how I should react until Nya's concerned expression brightens with elation. Her relief comforts me in a way nothing else ever could.

A unified chant rises from Ortarians and Polarians alike. It starts off scattered but quickly falls into sync, one word that makes my heart flutter. *"Ny-ah! Ny-ah! Ny-ah!"* The most beautiful word in the whole universe.

They all look to her, but she's got eyes only for me. She kneels at my feet, and with both hands she offers me her crown.

My breath catches. With this single act she has made me the last king of man, and the first without enemies. Everyone knows her hands are mine to command. Her heart beats for mine, and mine for hers.

I accept her crown with one hand and help her rise with the other. When she looks into my eyes I see our future staring back at me. Our children shall reign long after I'm gone, first of their kind, protectors of all that is good and light.

I pull her close and squeeze her tight. She locks her hands behind my back and presses her hot cheek to my chest. I rest my chin on the top of her head and smell a mixture of sulfur and seawater, fresh air and scorched timber. Coming from her they are the most intoxicating combination. Watching her take on the dragon in the polar sky, him with his streams of fire and her with her streaking hammer, was the bravest thing this universe has ever known. My girl. How could anyone not love her?

"All hail the king!" shouts a girl.

My heart slams against my ribs. Though her words are no different than those of the nearby chanters, her tone drags an ice dagger up my spine.

I open my eyes to see one of Lex's warriors standing a stone's throw downslope. Karla stands with her feet shoulder-width apart, a spear butt planted in the ash by her right foot. But it's her bulging eyes, those yellow reptilian orbs, that send a chill through me.

She winds back her spear and launches it at my belly. I feel the pressure of the impact before I can even flinch. But there's no pain from the razor-sharp steel cutting me in half. No weight of a platinum shaft lever drawing me forward onto my face. All I feel is Nya's body stiffen and press harder against me.

My right hand slides instinctively down her back until I feel warm blood spilling over cold steel. I meet her stricken stare as she sags to her knees.

I lower her gently onto her side. Mora hisses directions to a few wingless Fori to stabilize the spear.

Stabilize. They don't intend to remove it.

My heart squeezes tight like a fist. I lay on my side next to Nya so our noses nearly touch.

She wheezes and gasps, her terrified eyes desperate to tell me what her quivering lips cannot. I glance over her shoulder, to where Mora examines the wound. She senses my stare and gives me a grave look.

Nya's wheezing grows louder. My heart squeezes tighter. I stroke her hair and say, "*Shhh,* it's okay."

Nya, bless her wonderful spark, takes my word for it. She forces a smile and closes her eyes, falling quickly toward her death-sleep. Her breathing becomes lighter, each breath a whisper, every exhale blowing out the last of her life.

Her end is near.

CHAPTER 42
DEKA

"Do something," I tell Mora. *Anything.*

My voice is tight, my face grimaced with agony. I can't lose another so dear to me. Without her, I'll have nothing. I'll *be* nothing.

Mora wrings her hands, unsure how to respond.

"Mora!"

She jumps in fright and raises her hands. "Easy. If we remove the spear, she'll die within a minute. Two at most."

Why does that matter? One minute... two minutes... five... she's leaving us either way.

As if sensing my question, Mora adds: "Without all of her body's systems functioning, she'll have a meltdown. We're not ready for that."

I'm not sure what Mora is talking about. How can a dead body harm anyone?

"I don't know how it works," she says, "but we'll all be poisoned. We need to evacuate the wounded and get everyone as far from her and this mountain as possible. That spear is the only thing buying us enough time."

Memories of inside the Great Pyramid return to me. Ko Skadia's body had remained deep within its dark recesses while the Ori searched swiftly for a way out. A way to distance themselves from some sort of fallout. Only the Watchers know how to properly handle a dust maiden's remains, and they are all vanquished.

Mora and her Ori whisper commands to the surviving humans. *Gather the wounded and leave. Fast.* Some of these words may be directed at me — pleas to vacate at once — I'm not really sure. I don't care for anything other than to cherish these final moments with Nya's warmth. Soon her soft skin will rot in the ground. Her silky hair will dry to dust, and the earth of my home will claim her.

A tear falls from my cheek and onto hers.

No. She deserves better than that. And in my heart I feel for the first time the desire that drove hers.

"Get the gate key in place," I say.

My Ori onlookers back away, fixing me with stares of caution. They look to Mora for direction, and she responds with a cautious nod to proceed.

It happens in a blur around me: the rising of the Capstone, the offering of blood to revitalize the gate key, the gentle removal of the spear from Nya's back. The one-minute timer counting down in my head, one second for every three beats of my own dying heart.

Mora gives my shoulder a squeeze. "It's ready when you are."

I'll never be ready to let her go, so I won't deny her heart's deepest desire any longer. I stand with her cradled in my arms and carry her to the gate. Looking at her fluttering eyelids, I press my hand to the slanted diamond wall and push.

A flash of blue-green light blasts me, but does not blind. Wind thrashes my coat as I give Nya one last look over. It's the hardest thing I'll ever do, but also the most important.

I extend both hands and offer her to the skyward stream. It accepts her without pause, and faster than I can blink she is gone.

The whole world falls in on itself. It's the quietest end ever, divine silence like that which follows the last flake of a thousand-year snowfall. There is no doubt she is gone, I feel the loss in the air I breathe.

Mora hugs my leg. When I look down, she meets my stare with watery eyes and a quivering lip.

The stream pulsates, dims and then surges as its power wanes.

I give Mora's shoulder a friendly squeeze and then step back to allow the crowd of Fori and Ori access to the gate. Mora leads the way, and that's all the others need.

When the last of Nya's folk jump through the gate, I tip the key from its seat. I'd love nothing more than to wander the fields of her home and prepare her final resting place, but my future lies here.

"They're gone," Regulus says. He leans on a pair of makeshift crutches, one eye swollen shut and blood seeping from several wounds.

A southerly breeze hardens the tears on my cheeks.

Gone?

"No," I say.

This draws many confused looks to me. A few no doubt think I'm in denial.

I turn and survey the vast dark lands of Anterra. Though I have just witnessed their departure, I feel no loss of them from this life.

"They are the earth beneath our feet," I say, "the air that fills our lungs, and the water that gives us life."

EPILOGUE
NYA

Sizzling light whirls around me like a tornado. It crackles and hisses like cosmic gas, heating me. Burning me. Burning!

I open my mouth to scream, but the light stuffs my throat and chokes me. Only... *choke* isn't the right word, because I can still breathe. Only... breathe isn't the right word either.

I feel weightless, like I'm flying through a windless sky with no up or down.

This strange experience goes on for some time, so long that I become bored and start to fall asleep. Then shadows darken the light and give shape to objects.

I start to focus on them, trying to figure out what realm I'm crossing over to. These structures hold my attention only briefly though. Straight ahead of me shifts a black blob. It has more substance than the other shadows. Its presence commands my attention.

As I draw closer, its round edges sharpen into four limbs and a head, and I soon find myself looking at a man.

A *man.*

The sight of him sucks the breath right out of me, but it's not from fear. It's a feeling I cannot describe. It's the feeling of seeing someone you don't know how you should feel about because they gave you life while at the same time condemning you to unspeakable suffering. It's a feeling of love and hate all woven together in a tight braid that can never be unraveled.

All I can manage is one word, and it sounds breathless in its echo into eternity.

"Father..."

BOOKS BY JR DEVOE

Onero's Hunt

The Dark Monarch Series
Prequel: The Light Ones
Book 1: Dust
Book 2: Ashes
Book 3: Sparks
Book 4: Stardust (Forthcoming)

AFTERWORD

Interested in exploring more of Anterra?

Curious about Lex and the Sea Lord's history?

Discover their world 15 years before *Sparks* in

Onero's Hunt

ACKNOWLEDGMENTS

I'd originally intended to launch this now-long-overdue book in Autumn 2020, but my path took an unexpected turn, as it did for many. With the state of the world creating uncertainties that required reflection and redirection, I took a leap and went to college to study marine navigation. The four years that followed brought thrills, challenges, and moments of despair I wouldn't trade for anything. Thank you to everyone who shared those moments and helped shape me into who I am today—from the classroom to the high seas and everywhere in between.

Reaching this point in the series has been a marathon, one where a balance of hard lessons and encouragement kept me moving toward the light at the end of the tunnel. Unlike in previous books, I'm not going to mention specific names here, because doing so would surely exclude someone who played a crucial role in my journey. Suffice it to say, those I mentioned in previous acknowledgments—from *Onero's Hunt* to *Ashes*—have been with me throughout this journey. Those who began this journey with me back then are on every page of this book.

But most of all, I would like to thank you, the reader, in whose hands this story has found a home. Writing is a labor of love and, at times, a solitary endeavor, and knowing these stories have found a place in your library makes all the effort worth it. If you ever feel inclined to reach out, even to simply say hi, I would love to hear from you. Until then, fair winds and happy reading.

ABOUT THE AUTHOR

J. R. Devoe grew up on Cape Breton Island, Nova Scotia, in the town of Sydney Mines. He has since traveled to six continents, including Antarctica in 2013 to research elements of his debut novel, *Onero's Hunt*.

In 2014, he pedaled a bicycle across Canada to raise money for WaterAid Canada, a charity that provides clean drinking water and sanitation services to developing countries. In 2016, he pedaled a bicycle across New Zealand for the sheer joy of it.

J. R. Devoe currently works as a professional seafarer, where his voyages continue to inspire his writing and fuel his passion for exploration.